THE PAINTER

THE PAINTER

BY

TOM LOWE

K

Kingsbridge Entertainment

ALSO BY TOM LOWE

Library of Congress Cataloging in—Publication Data - Lowe, Tom.

ISBN: 9798655210936

THE PAINTER by Tom Lowe – First edition, September 2020

THE PAINTER is distributed in ebook, paperback print, and audiobook editions. Tantor Media is the publisher of the audiobook.

Cover design by Damonza.

Formatting and conversion services by Ebook Launch.

Acknowledgments

This is my favorite part of writing a novel – thanking those who helped me get it to you, the reader. My sincere thanks and deep appreciation for the talented people that had a hand in sending this book out and into the world. To my wife, Keri. Her imagination and enthusiasm are boundless. She's my brilliant editor and first reader. A special thanks to my beta readers who are the best of the best: Helen Ristuccia-Christensen, Darcy Yarosh, and John Buonpane. Way to go team! Thanks to the talented people at Ebook Launch. To the graphic designers with Damonza. And finally, to you, the reader. Thank you for reading and being part of the journey.

Writing *THE PAINTER* was quite a departure to me. And it was a challenge, as most novels tend to be. This one was different. Not because it wasn't my usual genre—crime, mystery and thriller, but rather because I wanted very much for the story to resonate with every adult reader on a personal level. Yes, it's fiction, but some of life's best stories can be told in a fictional form so the average reader can relate and identify to the plight or the struggle of the characters. Life's about living to its fullest. Searching for meaning and a deeper personal experience. It's about succeeding. Failing. Learning. Loving. Redemption. Preserving, through bruises and coming out better for having gone through the experience. I hope that this story will entertain you and maybe in some way inspire you to always paint yourself into this wonderful canvas called life.

Enjoy!

-Tom

"Art washes away the dust of everyday life from the soul."

- Pablo Picasso

.

For my wife, Keri.

I'm enthralled by your brilliant mind
and inspired by your compassionate heart.

ONE

Michael Vargas had no idea that he was being watched. It was his third and final day painting the outdoor mural, and he thought he was alone. He wanted it to be his secret. At least for now. At age seventeen, Michael was tall, six feet. His hair was black as a raven's feather, and his sky-blue eyes revealed an instinctive curiosity with the depth of someone far beyond his age. He stepped back from the exterior wall of the old building, gaining a wider visual perspective, his hands covered in paint, specks of red, blue and yellow on his cheeks and forearms. Face shiny and beaded in sweat.

"Yes!" he shouted, his eyes roaming the large mural. "Almost done!"

It was a former shipping warehouse, long since abandoned, with a sagging and rundown chain-link fence around the perimeter. The aged brick wall he painted faced a portion of Charleston Harbor. It was mid-summer in the Deep South, the humidity oppressive, nature exhaling her sultry breath across his young face. The air smelled of salt, drizzled with the scent of blooming lilacs that seduced the honeybees.

He wiped his brow with a red rag he had stuffed in the back pocket of his faded jeans and blew out a breath. The first people to see his mural, he figured, would probably be the shrimpers when they returned from the sea in a few days, maybe some of the commercial fishermen, too.

He was wrong.

Michael had eight half-gallon-sized cans of paint opened and set on the parking lot near the wall. The asphalt was cracked and laced with the pockmarks of time and neglect. He used eight brushes, some the size that house painters used. He could apply paint faster and cover more with the wide brushes. The detail on the mural was done with one- and two-inch brushes.

He stood about thirty feet from the wall, studying the images, deciding what needed to be done to finish it. He was painting a scene of Charleston Harbor back when South Carolina was one of the thirteen colonies. The mural depicted large, three-masted schooners tied to the docks, sailors loading bales of cotton onto the decks. The sailors, for the most part, were muscular, some carrying a bale of cotton on one shoulder, faces filled with grit and strength.

Michael painted from memory, and his keen imagination. The memory was from some of the images he'd seen in his high school history books. He walked fast back to the wall, moving a stained, wooden ladder to the left. He dipped two brushes into the paint and climbed the ladder close to the top, fifteen feet above the parking lot. He worked quickly, the brushes moving with bold, assertive strokes, the paint flowing into the thirsty cracks of the worn, brick-like, liquid nourishment, giving the wall a new makeover, illustrating old Charleston. The colorful mural was that of a spring day in Charleston, blooming dogwoods in one corner, the deep blue sky dotted with cumulus clouds, so realistic it looked like they were floating above the harbor.

Sweat beaded on Michael's forehead, some drops rolling into his eyes. He blinked out the perspiration, his eyes burning, his right arm moving like a frenetic orchestra leader with a baton conducting a symphony. But in Michael's case, the baton was a paintbrush, and the music he heard was the birdsong in the oak and jacaranda trees along the waterfront, the trees filled with lavender blooms. Two mocking-birds warbled, each trying to outdo the other. He could smell the paint, turpentine, and the briny scent of the harbor following him up and down the ladder like a shadow you couldn't see.

A man on a thirty-five-foot, wooden sailboat that was moored to the docks watched as Michael painted, the brushstrokes never hesitant, daring, quick, moving with intent and precision. He smiled, watching the kid on the ladder painting with the speed and finesse of an Old-World impressionist trying to finish before the sunlight faded and shadows became ghosts.

The man observed from the deck of his boat, less than one hundred yards beyond the building and mural. Even from that span, he knew a rare and artistic talent was painting the wall. He had to meet the young artist. The man stepped from his boat, walked down the dock and across the back street toward the property. He approached the fence, empty liquor bottles and flattened beer cans littered the enclosure, weeds sprouting, the painter's back to him. He paused to watch the finishing touches, then cleared his throat and asked, "Are you going to sign it when you're finished?"

Michael looked over his shoulder. He quickly descended the ladder, almost losing his balance on the last few rungs. He started to run, but there was nowhere to go, the man standing next to a gap in the fence, a hole that vandals had cut last summer. Michael scanned the perimeter, his eyes scared and furtive. He licked his dry lips, sweat trickling down his rib cage. He didn't answer the man, quickly picking up his brushes, pitching them in a paint-stained, yellowed pillowcase, tossing it over his right shoulder, looking for another exit.

"Whoa!" the man said, holding his right hand up like a crossing guard. "What's the hurry? You haven't finished."

Michael stopped and stared through the fence at him. He wasn't a police officer. Maybe he wasn't even the owner of the building. And maybe he wasn't there to stop him from painting. "Your work is excellent," the man said. "What's your name?"

"Michael Vargas."

"How old are you, Michael?"

"Seventeen."

The man nodded, looking from Michael's face to the painting and then cutting his eyes back to Michael. "For a seventeen-year-old lad, you paint well. Where'd you learn how to do something like that?"

"I don't know ... I just do it."

"A natural talent. It's something you're born with, you'll struggle with, and eventually, either let it carry you like a surfer's wave, or you'll get out of the water. In cases like yours, there's no in between, no compromise."

Michael said nothing, not sure what to say.

The man smiled, made a chuckle. "My name's Derek Mack."

Michael studied him for a few seconds. He looked to be in his fifties. Wavy dark hair turning gray. Tumbleweed eyebrows, and soft brown eyes that trapped the morning light and seemed to smile. He said, "I've been watching you off and on the last couple of days. Are you going to finish it today?"

"I want to."

"Then you'd better get your brushes back out and finish."

Michael smiled, looking down at the tainted pillowcase in his right hand. "Okay."

"Good," Derek nodded. "Are you out of high school for the summer?"

"Yes. This fall I start my last year. I work a part-time job baggin' groceries and paint when I can get time."

"Do you want to study art in college?"

"That'd be great, but my father isn't too keen on me doin' that. He thinks every artist is a starving artist, and if they're really good, they'll only make money after they're dead."

Derek chuckled, watching a brown sparrow alight on the top section of the sagging fence less than ten feet from them. "What do you want to do?"

"I'd like to go to art school and see if I could make a living doing what I love."

"Then do it."

"It's not that easy, you don't know my father."

"No, but I know real talent when I see it … and I see it in you. The raw talent, the stuff of genius is rare." He motioned to the sparrow as the bird flew away, lost in the shadows of the oaks and dogwood trees. "And it's something you should never take for granted or boast about, because it can go like a bird in the wind."

"Yeah, but my dad …."

"I'm a painter, too. And I've made a living doing it. Mostly land-scapes. South Carolina, the Lowcountry, the Deep South—it all provides magnificent and endless backdrops." Derek leaned down and maneuvered through the cut hole in the fence. He reached in his shirt pocket and handed a card to Michael. "Take this. Next to my house, I have a studio. On Saturday mornings, I offer free art classes to folks who want to improve. I've been doing it for the last ten years or so. Students come and go. There's usually a pot of chili on the stove and lively conversation, as well as art lessons. My sweet wife, Jewell, puts up with it all." He glanced at the mural and shifted his eyes back to Michael. "Are you going to sign it when you're done?"

Michael looked sheepish, pursing his lips, blowing out a long breath. "I'm kinda afraid to. What if the owner sees it and gets mad, maybe calls the cops? You know, like he found graffiti on his building."

"What if it's the opposite? What if he sees it and loves your work? It's as easy to think positive as it is to consider the negative."

"Yeah, but …"

"But what? What you're leaving behind is a vast improvement to an abandoned building that's probably going to be leveled by the wrecking ball and become a condo. This whole area is slated for development. Condos. Shops. Restaurants. But right now, that old wall is a stone canvas for a magnificent piece of artwork."

"You really like it?"

"Yes. If I didn't, I wouldn't say that I liked it. Another reason you should sign it, even if you only use your first or last name, is because it's a creative extension of you. Look at yourself. Your knuckles are bruised, scratched and bleeding from scraping against the wall. You're drenched in paint and sweat. Not only is your paint on that wall, your blood is there, too. Literally and figuratively. Take pride and ownership of your work. Something like this could lead to commissioned art— either more murals on other buildings or something that can be framed."

"That sounds great. My job in the grocery store doesn't pay much."

"But, as good as your art is … there's something missing that will make it better. It's missing the unique and magical, mysterious special sauce."

Michael tilted his head, a bead of sunlight coming through the limbs of a tall oak and falling on half of his face. "Magical, mysterious special sauce. What's that?"

"I can tell you, and you might accomplish it, or I can show you … teach you, and I feel certain that you'll learn it."

"What is it?"

"Come by the studio Saturday morning, and I'll show you. Catch the surfer's wave while you're young, Michael Vargas. If not maybe you should get out of the water. Class starts at nine a.m." Derek pulled a small camera out of his pocket and snapped a picture of the mural. "I'll have this developed before Saturday. We'll need it as a reference. If you pay attention during your first day in class, come back here and make the changes, then you can sign your name in the lower right or left corner, but not until then."

Michael said nothing.

Derek smiled, turned and slipped back though the fence, walking across the one-way street, over a short embankment toward the marina. Michael watched him stroll down one of the long docks, gulls shrieking above his head, boats tugging at their mooring lines, the chortles from the gulls now sounding like laughter in the muggy air.

TWO

There were only forty-five seats in the entire restaurant. No one was admitted or seated without a reservation, and reservations were so sought after, the tables were booked weeks, sometimes months, in advance. Michael Vargas and his wife, Kelsey, arrived at the *Epicure Restaurant*, forty stories above Manhattan, a few minutes before 7:00 p.m., and were escorted to a table overlooking the city as dusk arrived with them.

Kelsey, a natural blonde, tall with classic good looks, wore a black dress, and a strand of white pearls around her long neck. Michael was in the same dark suit he'd left their home in ten hours earlier. At age forty, his temples were showing a touch gray.

The restaurant featured an opulent, yet cozy bar with low, twinkling lights embedded in polished wood. Two of the bartenders on duty had worked there for decades. Crisp uniforms. Black bowties. Candles flickering on the tables set with white linen, silver utensils, and flowers. Lots of wood, subtle leather and plants. Expensive fine art, lit by low wattage, clear glass bulbs, hung from dark green walls. Soft piano jazz played from hidden speakers.

Kelsey looked through the large windows at a picturesque view of the city and said, "We have the sitter until eleven. I hope Adison and Judith aren't late."

Michael glanced at his Rolex. "They'll probably be here in ten minutes. His secretary had called for his driver before I left."

Kelsey made a half smile. "I know how big this account is for the firm. If you get it, I just hope that Adison will let some others work on the design. You're not the only architect in the company. There are more than two dozen architects working there, and they're all very good, or they wouldn't be employed by one of the top architectural firms in the nation. Adison relies on you way too much. I just wish he'd spread the work around more."

"I've had some of the largest projects in the last few years because I worked hard to prove myself. In the meantime, I'm building my own brand. People around the world know my work. Many can recognize it in cities like London, Dubai, Buenos Aires, Atlanta and here in New York."

"Yes, but at what price? Michael, you're rarely home, jetting across the world in meeting after meeting. When you are home, you're often working until late in the night designing buildings. All I ask is that—"

A waiter in dark pants, black jacket and white shirt with a bowtie approached. "May I bring you folks something to drink as you wait for your party?"

"That would be great," Kelsey said. "A glass of chardonnay … no, make that cranberry juice with no ice, in a wine glass, please."

"Yes, ma'am. And you, sir?"

"Belvedere over ice, thanks."

"My pleasure." The waiter left, vanishing around the plants and dark woods. In one of the four booths, the laughter of a woman mixed with the soft jazz. The restaurant had the slight scent of fresh cut flowers, butter and candles.

Kelsey said, "I am so very proud of you, Michael. But, somehow, you need to balance a work life with a home life. I left my career in law to take time off to make sure Mandy could know her mom. I didn't want a stranger raising her. She needs to know her dad, too."

"I'm aware that it's a sacrifice … and it's not easy. Your decision to take a leave from your career came after we were both working sixty-hour weeks. You were burned out and wanted to start a family. I'm appreciative that you can be a stay-at-home mom. You're good at it, and Mandy's better off for it. I'm glad my income can allow you to do that. I just have to work extra hard to sustain and grow it. We both know it's not forever."

"I don't take that for granted, and I don't want you to take Mandy and I for granted either. She needs to see you more. I need to see you more. You're great at designing buildings. Please try to be a tenth as great at building a family life with us." She bit her lower lip and took a deep breath, her eyes hurt and misting. "And, with the new baby on the way, family has to be a top priority." She used a tissue to pat her lower eyelids. "I have to run to the restroom. My hormones are feeling a little challenged right now."

"Okay, I'm sorry. I don't mean to come across as uncaring or indifferent. I love you, and all I want to do is build the kind of life that we both wanted. The financial security we both never had growing up."

"There's so much more to life than that. Mandy reinforces it in me each day she puts her little arms around me." Kelsey looked at her wedding ring, the diamond catching the yellow candlelight. She licked her lips and glanced around the restaurant, the rebuilt Twin Towers gleaming as darker twilight rolled over the city. She left the table, walking to find the ladies' room.

Michael stared at an oil painting on the wall, less than ten feet from their table. The painting was of a small harbor, two docks extending from an old wooden shack, a fish house, near the shore. The words *Fresh Fish* were partially faded on the side of the shanty. A half-dozen small boats were tied to the docks. One shrimp boat, the outriggers like vertical butterfly wings, was moored to the end of a pier.

Michael sipped his drink, the vodka burning as the alcohol entered his empty stomach. He stared at the painting and thought back years earlier to Charleston Harbor with its shrimp boats and fishing fleet. He remembered the mural he'd painted as a teenager on the side of the old building near the docks. And he remembered the first Saturday morning he'd spent in Derek Mack's studio.

The studio was really an extension of Derek's home—a rambling house built in the 1950s, whitewashed wood—oak and pine, two stories, large front porch that wrapped around half of the house, and a mermaid weathervane on the top of a gabled roof. Purple and white bougainvillea grew on yellow pine terraces aligned near a deck, which overlooked a dock that wove through the South Carolina Lowcountry marshes to the shimmering waters of the Intercoastal Waterway.

The studio itself was less than a thousand square feet, filled with artwork, most unframed. Until Michael entered the studio, he had no idea how good and prolific Derek Mack was in his many years as a painter. In addition to being self-taught, Derek had studied in two of the best art schools. Frederic Holtz, one of the most renowned impressionist painters at the time, had mentored him. And, thirty years later, Derek was most happy when he could return the favor to new students. Much of his art was landscapes, seascapes, harbors, docks, boats and people—people experiencing the moment in that period of time.

There were four students already in the studio that first Saturday morning. One rode his bike to get there. Another, a black man in his early twenties, drove his car. A young mother left her six-year-old with a sitter. And the only teenage girl in the class had her mother drop her off. Michael remembered the smell of fresh-ground coffee in the studio, blues and jazz playing from vinyl records—a holdover from Derek's younger years, and a warm summer breeze blowing through wide, screened-in windows.

But, mostly, he remembered the attention Derek gave to each of his students. Spending plenty of time at their individual easels, studying the work in progress, encouraging and thoughtful comments—challenging, suggesting ways to improve, often showing examples in his own work, and that of the master impressionist painters.

He recalled how Derek would hand out five-by-seven photographs of a landscape or maritime scene he'd taken with his camera, telling each student to set the picture next to his or her canvas and use it for reference only as they began the painting. And then he'd begin his own painting of the scene, moving quickly with fast brushstrokes and a palette knife, commenting and teaching as he painted and hummed or sang to the music.

"Never try to imitate a photograph," he'd say. "They are two different forms of art. A painting should leave something to the viewers' imagination. It's something that should be felt and interpreted, connecting with the human emotion." He'd laugh and say, "Find the story in the scene and paint more with your heart than your hand."

It was toward the end of that first two-hour lesson when Derek pulled up a stool next to Michael's easel, offering suggestions to improve the painting. After a few minutes, Derek opened a manila file folder and took out an eight-by-ten color picture of the mural Michael was painting on the building. He sipped black coffee and asked, "Based on the first two hours of today's session, can you see something missing in your mural?"

Michael felt slightly embarrassed. He looked at the picture. "Maybe I painted it more with my hands than my heart."

Derek smiled. "You did a combination of both … but you relied *more* on your hands than your heart. I think, for most paintings, those on an average-sized canvas, the viewer doesn't need to step up real close to see and feel something. Nor should they. Even from ten feet away, the painting needs to make that sensory connection from the viewer's brain to his or her heart. And that connection begins in the heart and soul of the painter."

"I'm not sure I know exactly what you mean."

"The artist paints a paradox, blurring and then painting over the lines between fiction and real emotion."

"How?"

"You must believe in the reality of your painting, the sense of place, to make an emotional connection with the viewer. It's not unlike literature, and I'm talking about fiction, Michael. Although the reader knows the story is fiction, they'll suspend disbelief to allow their hearts to follow the story with care and curiosity. The writer must create both. If we care about the story, we want to see what's going to happen to the characters. Art is very similar. The visceral reaction to the painting, although completely made up by the artist or at least his or her interpretation of a scene, should immediately transport the viewer to that location. You do this through composition, color, light and substance. It's as if the viewer is swept through time and place. They should see and *feel* the scene as if they were standing right there, too. This, Michael, is the mystery and the magic of great art. We see it, but most vital is that we *feel* it on an emotional level. It's like great music. Good movies. Theater. Art needs to be experienced—to be felt in the soul. It's the connection you, the artist, makes or doesn't make with your audience."

"I guess I didn't make that connection very well in the mural."

"You're not finished with it. You haven't signed it. Before you spell the word, painter, you have to spell the word pain. You earn the letters t—e—r. Go back tomorrow and add life to it."

"How?"

"It's your world that you're creating. You must decide. All I'm suggesting is that the hand of the artist must reach out from the paint, draw us in by touching our collective souls. You have a true gift. Your greatest, personal offense to yourself, a felony of the heart perhaps, would be to not follow your talents. It may not be immoral but, in the long run, in those lonely times of self-reflection, you'll feel you cheated yourself."

Michael was quiet for a few seconds, considering what Derek had said. "I understand. For my immediate future, I can easily paint a few people in the picture, maybe have them walking down that old cobblestone street near the harbor. They can be enjoying the day and watching the schooners being loaded."

Derek smiled, leaned back in his stool next to Michael's easel. "That's a spectacular idea. Let the people—the characters in your painting, feel the sunlight on their faces, and let us feel that same warmth."

Michael remembered returning to the mural the next day, standing back and staring at it for a full minute, seeing it in a different light. And then he opened the paint cans, picked up his brushes, and spent the next five hours adding people on the waterfront meandering along a cobblestone street bordering the harbor. Men strolling with women in long dresses, some holding colorful parasols, children on bicycles. One boy chasing a dog, another flying a kite where the sea gulls played.

When he was done, paint splatter went from his hands to his elbows. He stepped back and assessed what he'd just accomplished. He smiled and walked over to the bottom right corner, Derek's words following him, *"It's as if the viewer is swept through time and place. They should see and feel the scene as if they were standing right there, too. This, Michael, is the mystery and the magic of great art. We see it, but most importantly, we must feel it on an emotional level."*

He dipped a brush in a can of red paint and added one final thing to his work—his name: *Vargas*

THREE

"It looks like you're one cocktail ahead of us."

Michael cut his eyes from the painting on the wall to his boss, Adison Manning, and his wife, Judith, standing next the table. Manning, early sixties, square jaws ruddy from a close shave, silver hair neatly parted, said, "I know that before architecture, you studied art. You seemed mesmerized by that painting."

"I was just admiring the composition—the way the painter used light off the water and the boats. It's an excellent painting."

"Is it an artist we might know?" Judith asked. She was near her husband's age, five months into her second facelift. Prominent cheekbones, full lips, and platinum hair swept up fashionably and held by a diamond-studded clip.

Michael said, "The name in the lower corner is Nathan Dubois."

"That doesn't ring a bell," Judith said, taking a seat at the table. "However, I'm sure Charles wouldn't have it in his restaurant if the artist's work wasn't highly sought after."

Manning sat next to his wife and glanced down at the table, noticing the slight trace of lipstick on the wine glass at a place setting next to Michael. Manning shook out a white linen napkin, setting it on his lap. "Where's your bride?"

"Kelsey went to the ladies' room." He looked across the restaurant. "And here she comes now."

Kelsey approached the table carrying her purse. Manning stood, kissing her left cheek. "So glad you could make it," he said.

"It's good to see you, Adison." She smiled and leaned down to embrace Judith. "You look beautiful. I love that dress."

Judith beamed. "And you look like a runway model. That figure is to die for. Michael, you need to feed your wife."

"I do my best." He smiled. "She gave up sugar."

"But not pizza," Kelsey said, sitting down. "Although, in the last month, since I found out I'm pregnant again, pizza seems to be having a waning appeal. That didn't happen when I was carrying Mandy."

"Then maybe the next one will be a little boy," said Judith. "I know with my two, I craved some foods with the first, Jonathon, and detested them when I was pregnant with Heather."

"Speaking of food," Manning said, "this place is listed in the top five restaurants in the city. But, before I even look at the menu, I could use a cocktail." The waiter approached, took drink orders, and left. Manning cleared his throat and looked over at Kelsey. "Your husband is making quite a name for himself in architectural circles. Our PR agency says *People Magazine* will do a story on Michael. And, if that's not enough, he's supposed to be on the cover of next month's *Architectural Digest.* An architect with movie star good looks and the design talents of Leonardo da Vinci."

Michael said, "Hardly." He sipped his drink.

Kelsey managed a smile. "I'm very proud of Michael."

"Where'd they shoot the cover photo?" asked Judith.

"In London. They wanted the Infinity Tower in the background," Michael said.

The waiter served drinks to the new arrivals and said, "Some of tonight's specials include Chef Vinson's version of Dover Sole, red snapper livornese, Copper River cedar-plank salmon, crab-stuffed filet mignon—"

Manning held up one hand. "We'll make some choices after we finish our drinks."

"Certainly, sir. I'll check back." He turned and left.

Manning lifted his glass of Macallan scotch, the whisky older than Michael. "Let's toast our recent success and our future success, hopefully with the design of the tallest building in Hong Kong."

They raised their glasses, Kelsey trying to show excitement when very little was there. But what was there was a headache in her temples and a sharp pain in her stomach. They all clinked glasses and sipped. Manning said, "Now that you are becoming a world-renowned architect, undoubtedly through early tutelage and excellent management of the firm, tonight we want to offer you a partnership. Manning, Edelman, and Vargas." He grinned. "How does that sound?"

Michael looked at his wife and then at Manning. "I'm speechless. This is unexpected. I'm not quite sure what to say. I'm flattered."

"Say you'll accept," Manning said, leaning back in his chair.

"I'm honored. I'm deeply appreciative that you, Edelman, and the board of directors have that kind of faith in me."

Manning swirled the scotch in his heavy crystal glass. He grinned. "We'll talk executive compensation this week. I must admit, though, I knew the day would come. And I feel prouder than a Super Bowl coach with a win. The offer keeps you with us, we hope, for many years. And gives you the opportunity to travel the world, leaving your signature buildings on seven continents."

* * *

After the babysitter left, Kelsey checked on Mandy. She was sleeping in her bed, sprawled like a starfish, her right arm around the neck of a stuffed bear. Michael loosened his tie and entered his daughter's room. He watched Kelsey adjust the blanket around Mandy. He bent down and kissed his daughter on her forehead, the corner of the little girl's mouth moving in to a smile, eyes closed, sleeping. "Daddy loves you, Mandy." He stood and stared at his daughter for a long moment, moonlight coming through the window.

Michael and Kelsey left the bedroom and walked into the family room, the sound on the TV muted, a romantic comedy streaming from Netflix. The view of the city from the tenth floor of their Tribeca condo was stunning. Kelsey picked up the remote control and turned off the television. She looked at Michael. "Why did you have to accept the offer before we could discuss it at home?"

"Because it'll have an excellent compensation package, and I hope less time away from you and Mandy."

"But you don't know that. You're assuming. What if it's not what you want? You've already told Adison you'd be a third partner."

"After the offer is officially made—in writing, if it's not what you and I want, I'll change my mind and not accept."

Kelsey said nothing, inhaling through flared nostrils. She reached for the back of the couch and slowly sat down. "You always told me that you didn't want to work all your life for a large architectural company. You said that you wanted to build your signature brand and be your own boss—to own the company. That's not going to happen if you take their offer."

"Stop! Okay? What do you want me to do, Kelsey? At this point, I'd probably work more hours striking out on my own, building and staffing an architectural firm, renting office space, borrowing money and pouring capital into a start-up. That's extremely labor intensive."

"But you're not starting up. You're well known. You have clients. Some would follow you wherever you go. Others will too. Maybe you could operate a small boutique firm, just you and a couple of other architects. You could delegate more of the work, select the projects that you really want to do, and be here to watch your children grow up."

Michael said nothing. He let her vent, Kelsey's face looking paler. She said, "The last thing in the world I want to sound like is a nagging wife. I love you, and I know the depth of your talent. I recognized that when I first saw your paintings. Sometimes, I wish you'd stayed with it—your art was beautiful. I think you would have been happier. But, in college you chose to major in architecture, and that's fine. Deep in my heart, I don't believe it's what you really enjoy doing. You're just very good at it because you have the talent, a great imagination and the drawing and composition skills to wrap stories around buildings and give them an identity. It's the cornerstone, the foundation of your work."

"Sure, I miss the art. But I can't count what ifs or dwell in the past. Architecture, at least the way I try to design, is sort of a hybrid between art and adhering to building codes, sometimes trying to change the codes to fit designs and materials that didn't exist when the codes were standardized. I create beauty in lifestyle choices … often combining work, living and play."

She paused, looking down at her fingernails, the red polish catching the overhead light from the ceiling. "But somehow, Michael, I think you're a conflicted hero. You persevered to carve out this highly visible career, primarily for your family, but I believe your real happiness—the emotional connection—has been hijacked. And that's uncomfortable for me as your wife. I don't feel well."

"I shouldn't have jumped the gun, giving Adison my initial okay with the offer without coming home to discuss it with you." He walked over to the couch, leaned down and kissed his wife on her forehead. He let his lips remain there for a few seconds. "Are you okay? You feel hot, almost feverish."

"I've been feeling strange, off and on for the last three days."

"Why didn't you tell me?"

"Because you haven't been here." She stood. "I'm just going to spend a few minutes in the bathroom, maybe splash some cool water on my face. After a good night's sleep, I'll be fine." She managed a half smile and left the room.

Michael took off his suit coat, setting it on the back of a chair in the room. He walked into the kitchen, opened a bottle of water and took a long drink. He placed the cap back on, standing at the kitchen sink, staring at his reflection off the dark window, a sprinkling of city lights in the distance. He thought about his conversation with Kelsey. In his heart, he knew she was right, but the life they'd built together demanded the income and the hours needed to generate that kind of salary and bonus, especially if they wanted to maintain their lifestyle in retirement. *Maybe in two or three years,* he thought.

"Michael!" Kelsey screamed, her voice frightened and primal. "I need help!"

He ran through the condo, almost slipping on the tile floor, into the master bedroom and the bathroom. His wife was standing near the toilet, dress off, blood streaming down her left leg, her eyes welling with tears.

FOUR

During the next three weeks, some of Kelsey's convictions began to suffer hairline cracks. She stepped outside onto her terrace for a moment, Mandy playing with two small dolls on the living room rug behind her. Kelsey could sense a trace of rain in the air, the clouds over the city leaden. The moisture in the air seemed to rub shoulders with the concrete buildings creating the musty scent of an early Spring approaching. The gray sky paralleled her mood.

She always considered herself to be a strong woman—physically and emotionally. When she practiced law, that resilience made her very good at her job. And it would open doors and rebuild her career when she decided to go back to work. She also had believed that would happen after both kids started school. *Both*. But now there was only one child, and Kelsey wasn't sure if there would ever be a second. Between Michael's work schedule and her sporadic monthly cycle, maybe the stars wouldn't align again.

But the self-imposed guilt was the worse as it chipped away at her soul.

Why did the miscarriage happen?

* * *

"Spontaneous abortion," the obstetrician had said. "For whatever reason, your body rejected the pregnancy. Unfortunately, it happens to one in four couples." The doctor was in her early fifties, chestnut brown hair with a scattering of gray, intelligent eyes filled with compassion. She had two grown children of her own. After Kelsey's miscarriage, the doctor spent plenty of time with her when she came in for the first and second checkups, explaining the possible reasons for the miscarriage. "Often we never know. Perhaps there was a defect with the embryo, and your body simply discarded it."

"Then why do I feel so guilty, as if one child is all my body can ever handle?"

"Because sometimes there's psychological trauma in this. It's built on hopes and dreams, a new life building within you … and you and your husband discussing building a life for the child—a future. When that living thing—that tiny infant is gone, within the mother, there's often a sense of hollowness. A feeling of loss, anxiety and depression can come seemingly out of nowhere. And, should you have another crisis, perhaps the death of a loved one, the layered stress can rub salt into the wound, compounding the issues. People don't like to talk about miscarriages as if the end of a pregnancy is somehow taboo. That's why many couples don't tell anyone about the pregnancy until after twelve weeks."

"I was just at twelve weeks. After the birth of Mandy, I assumed the next one would be even easier. Easier to get pregnant and easier to deliver. I was wrong on both accounts."

"You didn't have the opportunity to deliver." She paused and looked down at Kelsey's chart. "My prescription for you is to spend some time doing fun things with your family. Go to the park. Maybe on a beach vacation. Walk in the fresh air. Get your mind involved and focused on the present. Should you become pregnant again, my prescription is the same."

* * *

The cell phone vibrating on the outdoor coffee table got Kelsey's attention. She picked it up and looked at the screen. It was her mother calling. Kelsey answered and stepped back inside, out of the cold, closing the sliding glass door. She glanced over at Mandy who was quietly playing. "Hi, Mom."

"Hi, sweetheart. Are you doing a little better?"

"Yes. It's been a rough road, but I'll be okay. How are you and Dad?"

"Your father's fine, but I wish I could say the same for me."

"Mom, what's wrong?"

"The cancer's returned. I just thought it was severe arthritis in my bones, but the oncologist told me I have the fourth stage of breast cancer. It's moved into my bones and spreading to some organs. But you know me. Like you, I'm a fighter."

Kelsey could hear her mother's voice crack, a soft weeping.

FIVE

Michael looked at what he hoped would be the future—at least part of the future skyline in Hong Kong. He was in his large, corner office seventy stories above Madison Avenue, a Styrofoam and plastic miniature model of the Elysian Tower on a large table in the center of the office. The tower didn't resemble any other skyscraper in the world. There was nothing boxy or square about it. There was a colossal, four-sided pyramid structure that, if built, would rise more than two-thousand feet above the city center of Hong Kong.

The model was a mix of glass, concrete, and steel with a sapphire and smoky gray appearance. The four sides had undulated ridges not unlike small waves or the gentle roll of mountains at a distance. The purpose was to reflect the look and feel of the mountainous terrain around Hong Kong and to capture the culture and history of the area.

Michael walked from the model to a podium-like bench with a ninety-six-inch, flat-screen monitor on a stand in front of it. The monitor was connected to one of the most powerful computers in the world, easily able to build and render 3D images and simulated video at near lightning speed. His fingers flew across the keyboard, an aerial image mockup of the Elysian Tower appearing near the center of Hong Kong. The image was stunning, gleaming as sunlight beaded off the exterior, like the golden reflection of a sunrise over the ocean.

There were two versions on split screens. The one on the left was a rendering of the tower in the day, taking its cornerstone heritage from iconic buildings in the Old World—the Egyptian pyramids, arched entrances inspired by Roman and Greek architecture, and yet creating a soaring monolith with a modern, interstellar look. The tower had a sense of place and motion, even standing still above the edge of the world. It projected the feel of water in movement over the rolling, structural curves, similar to a fall of soft rapids, defying gravity, climbing from the ground to near the top where the building became a black pinnacle at the summit.

The rendering of the Elysian Tower at night was breathtaking. Thousands of LED lights were inset in winding, strategic patterns from street-level to the single glowing light at the top of the peak. It resembled a guiding star in the night sky—the brightest, Sirius, giving the model a cosmic feel as if it had a lighted path from earth to the heavens. Michael used the computer's design tools to make a slight tweak to the suspended glass bridge leading from the tower to the adjacent convention center.

Adison Manning entered the office through the two open glass doors and said, "The clients will be here soon. How are the last-minute nips and tucks coming?"

"Almost done."

"Good. I don't have to tell you that this is, by far, the most significant presentation the company has ever done. What you're designing is being called the building concept of the century. I'm glad our PR team offered some initial teases to the media."

"Build a fire, right?"

"In this case, it has to be a bonfire. You're the lead dog in the presentation."

"I suppose the view is better from that perspective." Michael smiled. "To exceed their expectations, we have to wow them, and I believe these renderings, the virtual fly-through the building, and the model on the table have the wow factor. I want to show them how the Elysian Tower will be the most spectacular, most green, energy-efficient building on the planet. It combines the aesthetics and art of design with the lean form of simple function."

Michael's phone vibrated in his pocket. He slipped it out and looked at the screen. Kelsey calling. He let it go to voicemail, inhaled deeply, and looked at Manning. "There are a lot of great skyscrapers out there. But this isn't designed to scrape the sky, its conceived to caress it and offer a meaningful connection between the earth and the universe. That's the impression I'd hope for people to have, whether they're standing at ground level looking up, or they're standing on one of the highest observation decks looking down or up … or toward the curvature of earth."

* * *

Kelsey stood back from her terrace window, a cold rain falling over New York City. She held the phone to her ear. "Michael … it's my mom. She's … she's not well … she's dying … please call me." She lowered her phone, letting it fall onto the couch. She wiped back tears, her crying overridden by the burst of lightning and massive clap of thunder so powerful she could feel the building tremble.

* * *

Manning nodded. "Michael, you sound like Frank Lloyd Wright in some kind of restored form." He grinned. "I don't believe in reincarnation, but I do believe in the genius of raw talent. Wright coined the phrase *organic architecture*. But you figured out how to use it with today's building tools. I've worked with a lot of designers in my career; however, what you bring to the table is very different. It's some kind of hybrid between fantasy art and functional design that creates a unified whole. You don't get that by earning a master's degree in architecture from any university. Where did you learn it?"

Michael thought about the first time he heard that question. It was when he met Derek Mack, when they initially spoke through the fence around the old building. *"For a seventeen-year-old lad, you paint well. Where'd you learn how to do something like that?"*

"I don't know … I just do it."

Michael's phone buzzed on his desk. He didn't answer it, cutting his eyes from the computer screen to Manning. "I don't know … I just do it. I'm lucky I suppose."

"Luck has nothing to do with it. Talent has everything to do with it. I'll have a couple of the interns wheel the table model into the conference room." He looked at his Patek Philippe watch. "It's almost time. The clients love the name you coined for the building, the Elysian Tower. I like the reference to the word Elysian in Greek mythology … a place set aside for the souls of heroes. If you nail this final contract down, you'll be a superhero."

"The last thing I want is to be a hero. The name, Elysian, at least the way I perceive it, has more to do with a special place, like Mount Olympus, for everyone—a marvelous destination for all people to experience, not reserved for heroes only. You don't have to show your Justice League membership card to enter." He smiled.

There was a light knock on the glass panel of the door. Michael's secretary, late forties, dark hair worn short, stepped inside his office. "Excuse me, sorry to interrupt. Mr. Vargas has an urgent call on line—"

"Unless it's the president of the United States calling," Manning said, his eyes narrowing, "there's no time for a phone call."

"It's Mr. Vargas's wife. She said it was very important."

"I'll take it, Tina," Michael said, his eyes moving from the phone on his desk to a framed picture of Kelsey and Mandy. He'd taken the picture during a day trip last summer to the beach in the Hamptons, blue ocean behind them, wide smiles. Both wore different colored sun dresses—Kelsey in soft yellow, Mandy in blue, Kelsey wearing a wide-brimmed straw hat.

As Michael walked around his desk, Manning said, "See you in the conference room in three minutes. Michael ignored the comment meant to draw a line in the sand. He answered the phone, "Hi, Baby … you okay?"

"Michael, it's Mom. She's very sick. The cancer, the one we thought she'd beaten, has metastasized. It's in her bones and organs. She's trying to act fearless, but she's very scared."

"I'm so sorry to hear the cancer's returned."

Kelsey stood in their bedroom, folding clothes and placing them in two suitcases, Mandy holding a doll and standing in the threshold of the doorway. "I need to go be with her, Michael. My sister, Ashley, can't get time off for a couple of weeks. Mom needs me. I want Mandy to spend as much time with her grandmother as we have left. I know how busy you are … but can you find time to take us to the airport? We'd both like to say goodbye in person with long hugs. Maybe you can come to Mom's house when you get a break."

"Have you booked a flight yet?"

"There are three more good flights remaining today. The last one—a nonstop to Dallas, leaves at five."

Two graduate student interns, a man and woman, politely knocked at the open door, uneasy expressions on their faces. Michael used one hand to wave them into his office. They entered quietly and walked over to the table with the miniature scale model on it. They bent down to release the locked wheels on all four wooden legs, carefully pushing the table across the carpeted floor toward the door.

"How about the flight schedule tomorrow?" he asked.

"I don't know how many more tomorrows Mom has. Every day counts. If you can't take us, I'll go with Uber."

"The presentation with DSB Holdings starts in a couple of minutes. If all goes well, it'll probably wrap—at least my part, in an hour, maybe two. I'll call you after that. Love you."

"Love you, too."

Michael disconnected, staring down at the photograph of Kelsey and Mandy. He touched the glass over the picture with the tips of two fingers. He looked up as the interns left with the model of the Elysian Tower, the conversation with Adison Manning echoing in his thoughts. *"If you nail this final contract down, you'll be a superhero."*

"That last thing I want is to be a hero."

He thought about the night he and Kelsey had their last argument, because right after it, she had a miscarriage, her words ricocheting in his thoughts. *But somehow, Michael, I think you're a conflicted hero. You persevered to carve out this highly visible career, primarily for your family, but I believe your real happiness—the emotional connection— was hijacked.*

SIX

Michael thought about the times Kelsey, as an attorney, had faced a jury. Sometimes the faces unreadable, the awkwardness because the communication was one way—the attorney speaking and the jury only listening. "It was a double-edge sword," she'd often said. Kelsey shared how the approach of truly persuasive conversation is usually more effective in a casual, two-way-street exchange of dialogue. The presenter using facts and terms that stroke chords of sensibility, steering the discussion. When the communication was coming from only one person, the speaker had to be more than eloquent. He or she had to be definitive and convincing with whatever tools were available. And, sometimes, in a court case, the tools were in gray areas.

Michael looked into the faces of the senior representatives of DSB Holding. Twelve people. Eight men and four women. All Asian. All politely listening and watching his presentation. But, like good poker players, they held their cards close. Very few physical tells as to what they were thinking or how they were feeling about certain points he was making. Some of them scribbled on legal pads in front of them. Others tapped notes into tablets.

Adison Manning sat at the head of the conference table. He smiled and nodded at all the appropriate places, commenting twice to reinforce a point Michael made about how the design of the tower would reinforce the history and culture of Hong Kong. Three of the clients, one woman and two men, looked pleased at the references to their country.

Michael spoke for thirty-five minutes, pausing to make points by motioning to the scale model on the table, or to show visuals of the proposed tower on a large screen. He smiled, made all the emotive pitching points and then said, "I wanted to share a short, three-minute, virtual reality video we produced to show you what the visitor will see and feel approaching the Elysian Tower, entering it, and experiencing it from multiple points of view. The video incorporates the components of the building occupancy with restaurants and the mixed use of the tenants, as well as the adjacent conference center. All part of the new world the Elysian Tower will offer."

Michael scanned the faces, one of the women smiling and leaning back in her chair. She said, "We've looked forward to this moment."

"All right, without further ado, let's dim the lights and focus on the eight-by-ten-foot screen at the far end of the conference room."

One of the interns hit a series of buttons on a remote-control device, the lights in the room fading and images emerging on the screen with music and voice-over narration. The first scene was a shot of earth from a high-resolution camera on a satellite, the blue planet almost surreal orbiting the sun. The tempo of the music building as the video moved with quick shots of earth, and the universe. The narrative began: *"Since the dawn of mankind on earth, we've always looked to the heavens for everything from inspiration to solace. There's a sense of wonder, of quiet revelation gazing at the universe. And, when the Elysian Tower is built, the distance from earth to the moon and stars just became closer."*

The video cut to breathtaking scenes using time-lapse photography of the night sky, stars so close you can feel their light on your face, meteors streaking across the inky sky. The narrative continued: *"The Elysian Tower captures the intrigue of the galaxies with its cornerstone formed on earth and deeply embedded into the history and culture that is uniquely Hong Kong. Twenty centuries ago, it was often said that all roads led to Rome. Today, when the Elysian Tower becomes a reality, many human journeys will lead to Hong Kong to see and experience something that has never been accomplished in the history of the world."*

Michael watched the faces of his clients. Now, the cards were being revealed. Lots of smiles. Heads nodding. One younger man, the CFO of DSB Holdings, tapping his finger on the table to the beat of the music. The images, a mix of real places and animation, were powerful, all produced in 8K resolution, the music was an original score and edited to the exact frame of video. The scenes were from a life-like image of the Elysian Tower at night, the aerial perspective circling it, Hong Kong and the lights of the harbor twinkling.

The narration concluded: *"For centuries, Hong Kong has been a port-of-call for the world. When the Elysian Tower is built, its light—like the world's tallest lighthouse, will shine its beacon across the harbor—a sentinel of the sea, a guiding star offering safe passage into the heart of Hong Kong."* The video pushed into the twinkling light at the top of the tower, high above Hong Kong, and then morphed into the Sirius star in the night sky, earth below, as the video and music faded out.

The clients burst into applause. Smiles and quick conversations in Cantonese and then English.

Michael smiled as Adison Manning stood and said, "No doubt, when built, the Elysian Tower will be one of the wonders of the world and one of the places people feel they must see before they die." At that point, the questions began, dozens of them. Most were directed to Michael. Manning, Alex Edelman, as well as the senior vice president of legal, making comments.

Almost four hours later, Michael looked at his watch.

It was approaching five in the afternoon. *Kelsey ... Mandy,* his thoughts raced as the clients continued asking questions, all now appeared to be completely on board with the proposed project and ready to sign a contract worth over a billion dollars, making the firm the architect of record. The oldest man in the group of clients, Cyd Woo—the CEO, white hair, kind eyes, impeccably dressed in a dark suit said, "We really enjoyed the presentation. Your company has done everything we asked and more, from early concept renderings to what we see here today. If you would give us a few minutes to further discuss the project, we will have a decision for you shortly."

"Absolutely," Manning said, standing. "Take all the time you need. There's still plenty of refreshments—chilled water, sodas, juices, teas and fresh coffee—at the rear of the room. Please discuss it and let us know if you have any questions that may add further clarification."

"Thank you," he said, sitting back down.

The partners, two members of the board, and two members of the in-house legal team exited the room. The PR director and interns left, too. Michael looked in his briefcase and found his phone. One missed call. It was from Kelsey. He walked out into the hallway with his team, the conference room doors closing behind him.

Manning said, "Excellent presentation everyone. Michael, it looks like you nailed it. But rather than count our proverbial chickens before they hatch, let's all stay on this floor, ready to answer any questions, and hopefully ready to celebrate a new business chapter with our clients. If we land this, we'll take them to dinner at the Rainbow Room at the top of Rockefeller Plaza."

"I can't wait until the restaurant is built at the top of the Elysian Tower," Edelman said. He was a dark-haired man with a pronounced Adam's apple and a five o'clock shadow on his face. Michael looked at his watch.

His heart sank.

He cut his eyes over to Manning. "Excuse me for a minute. I'll be right back." He walked down the carpeted hallway under soft lights, framed art on the walls, opening a glass door and stepping out onto an enclosed, wrought iron balcony with a spectacular view of the city, Madison Avenue seventy floors below him. The breeze was cold, the washed scent of the buildings after an afternoon, late winter rain.

He played Kelsey's message on his phone. "It's me …" there was a pause, as if she was taking a deep breath or hesitant for some reason. "Mandy and I are at the airport—LaGuardia. We're boarding our flight in a few minutes. I know how busy your day was, and probably still is … we just wanted to see you before we left. I don't know how long we'll be at Mom's house. I spoke with Dad a little while ago. He said Hospice nurses will come to the house during the day. That's what Mom wants … it's where she wants to be when she takes her last breath." She sniffled. "He said the only things she's regretting are the things she didn't do that she really wanted to do. I knew this day would come sometime … just not now … not so soon. She's still young, was always healthy until recently." Michael could hear his wife softly crying. He pinched the bridge of his nose, his eyes welling.

"Mandy wants to say hi." There was a brief pause, the sound of the phone changing hands. "Hi, Daddy … we're going to Grandma's house. She's real sick. Mommy's going to buy flowers for Grandma. I miss you. Are you coming to see Grandma?" Michael could hear the airport's PA announcements in the background and then, "I love you, Daddy."

The phone exchanged hands. Kelsey said, "I hope your presentation went well … like you said, maybe it'll give us more time together as a family. Life's too short … we're strong people, but our hearts are too fragile for the things that don't matter. For the things that do matter, let's do them … time is running out for Mom. We can slow it down for us, okay? No regrets in the end. I love you, Michael. Call me when you can. Oh, our plane is supposed to arrive in Dallas around nine. We're flying Southern Airlines to Dallas, flight 197. Bye."

Michael hit the redial button, the call going to Kelsey's voicemail. He glanced through the glass doors, down the hallway, Adison Manning grinning, motioning for him to return. He turned his back, looking from Madison Avenue to the cityscape directly east. "Kelsey, I got your message. I'll call you tonight when you get to your mom's. The presentation went well. I think it's ours." He stopped, a movement from the eastern horizon catching his eye. A large black plume of smoke rose, twisting in an abhorrent sinister vortex, like a dark funnel cloud drifting into the afternoon sky. But he knew it wasn't caused by the weather. It was cold, but the sky had cleared. "I agree … let's put the brakes on time. No regrets … I love you very much."

Michael looked at the smoke in the distance. He knew it was very near LaGuardia Airport. He simply stared at the curling black smoke, snaking from the ground, turning low-hanging clouds an ashen gray. *Maybe a building was on fire.* His thoughts raced, his rational mind telling him it was probably nothing. But his heart telling him another story.

SEVEN

As Michael approached his colleagues at the end of the hall, he knew they'd landed the contract. Lots of handshakes. Back slapping. Wide smiles. Adison Manning looked up and said, "It's a whole new chapter for the firm. DSB loved the presentation. Their legal guys are in the room dotting the i's and crossing the t's. Not only are they completely on board, they've decided to spend another several million to acquire the adjacent six acres for the development of the theater and art district that you proposed. Congratulations, partner!"

"It wasn't just me," Michael said, looking at his colleagues. "It was all of us. Everyone contributed." There was a soft round of applause. More handshakes. Neckties loosening. Some people milling about the hallway and adjacent lobby area, white Italian marble on the floor, a chandelier above a series of public elevators. A few of the associates made quick phone calls, telling family members the good news. "It'll be the largest and sexiest building in the history of the world," one colleague said into his phone.

Manning looked around at a few of the employees, finding and signaling for a woman in a soft red business suit to join him. She was a statuesque brunette. Late thirties. Flawless, tanned skin, the look of coffee with cream. Maria Merino was the director of communications for the company. Manning said, "Maria, I know you and your team have developed some preliminary PR strategies, assuming that we would lock this contract. Now, you can turn it on full bore. Michael and I will be available to do the morning talk and news shows here in New York. For the other cable networks and those on the west coast, we can do Q&As live from the cameras set up in one of our conference rooms."

She nodded and smiled. "Knowing how talented you all are, we've done more than preliminary strategies and media releases, and they already include quotes from you two. And we have designated areas where we'll insert quotes from whomever DSB wants us to include. We'll be on the phones as soon as the contract is final. The PR includes traditional news media, as well as key bloggers, influencers, and podcasters. We'll also be streaming video to cable, industry, and other appropriate social news media. This will be an international release. What a story! It reaches far beyond a piece about architecture. This will be an historical achievement—up there with the other seven wonders of the world."

"I love the comparison," Manning said.

"It should be looked at in those terms." She smiled at Michael. "Your presentation really brought the Elysian Tower together in one comprehensive package. As lead architect, and now a partner in the company, I'm sure most of the media will want some one-on-one time with you. I'll start with my friend at the *Today Show* and go from there."

"Just let me know when and where to be," Michael said.

Manning laughed. "I know where you'll be in a couple of hours. DSB will join us at seven o'clock at the Rainbow Room. Reservations are secured. We'll have a private dining area with a great view of the city and the East River, even Roosevelt Island. Why don't you call Kelsey, see if she can join us?"

"She's flying to Dallas with Mandy. Kelsey's mother is sick … the breast cancer returned. It's not good."

Manning nodded, his face concerned. "I'm sorry to hear that."

Maria reached out and touched Michael on his arm. "Please tell Kelsey we're thinking about her. Our thoughts and prayers will be with her and her mom."

"Thank you."

Maria smiled as the doors to the conference room opened and four members of DSB came out, one man had removed his suit jacket, both sleeves of his white shirt rolled up to his forearms. The CEO, Cyd Woo, exited with a wide smile on his face, removing bifocals from the tip of his nose. Maria said, "Looks like a perfect time to get a quote from him." She glanced at Manning. "Just give me the high sign that the contract is ready, and I'll take the PR from there."

"Will do," Manning said, signaling for the firm's senior counsel to follow, Manning making his way through the people over to greet and speak with CEO, Cyd Woo.

Maria smiled at Michael and said, "This will be good. It's going to be our Taj Mahal moment—all the way from the announcement to the groundbreaking, and over the next four years leading up to the ribbon cutting and grand ceremonies to officially open the Elysian Tower." She watched Manning shake hands with Woo. "It's photo op time," she said, motioning to a member of her staff, a tall man with a Nikon camera hanging from straps around his neck.

Michael watched them converge, people walking back into the conference room for pictures and champagne, a half-dozen bottles of Dom Perignon rolling in on a caterer's table from an adjoining room. The mutual congratulations continued, the sound of champagne corks popping. Michael noticed a graduate student intern, a young woman, blonde hair pulled back in a ponytail, standing in an alcove, watching something on her phone. The expression on her face was of shock, holding the tips of her fingers to her mouth.

Michael walked over to her. "You look like you're watching a horror movie on your phone."

She looked up, her eyes filled with fright. "Oh ... Mr. Vargas. It's worse than a horror movie. It's real. I'm watching a live newscast. A plane crashed taking off from LaGuardia. They don't believe there are any survivors."

Michael felt a jolt in his heart. "Are they saying what plane—what airline? Where was it going?"

"No, at least I haven't heard yet. I just got the news alert, and I've only been watching it for a minute. Look." She angled the phone screen so Michael could see. The live video was streaming from a horrific scene of flames and black smoke. The carnage was surrounded by fire trucks and emergency vehicles, the pulse of blue, red and white lights barely seen in the drifting smoke.

Firefighters, most in hazmat suits, shot white fire-retardant foam from high velocity hoses, the foam cascading across the broken and shattered fuselage, the jet's wings clipped like a downed bird hit by a bolt of lightning. Through the phone's speaker, Michael could hear sirens and the crackling sound of flames fueled by hundreds of gallons of jet fuel devouring the plane.

And then the reporter's voice could be heard.

A woman off camera said, "At this point, it's not known exactly why Southern Airlines flight 197, bound for Dallas, fell from the sky within one minute of take-off. We don't know if a flock of birds hit the engines, whether it was due to mechanical failure or, perhaps, an act of terrorism. What we do know is that 213 people and five crew members were on board when the plane crashed and burst into an explosion of huge flames, some reaching more than one hundred feet in the air. The plane crashed on the west side of the airport. One witness said it appeared as if the pilot was turning the jetliner back around, maybe for a landing, when he apparently lost control, and it fell from the sky. There are dozens and dozens of firefighters on the scene trying to extinguish this horrific fire. We also don't know if anyone was able to survive the horrendous crash and fire. But it's highly doubtful. Reporting live from LaGuardia Airport, Penny Jacobs … now back to you in the studio."

Michael's heart pounded. He could barely catch his breath, the color draining from his face. The intern looked at him, biting her lower lip. "Mr. Vargas, are you okay?"

He said nothing, bracing himself against the wall. The hallway, lobby area, and entrance to the conference room began blurring, sweat popping out on his face. The intern dropped her phone into her purse and grabbed him by the arms. "You don't look well. Your face is completely white. Can you walk? I think you need to sit down. Did you know someone on the plane?"

Michael caught his breath, his hands trembling. He looked at her. "My wife and daughter were on that plane."

"Oh, dear God … I'm so sorry."

Michael broke from the intern's grasp, staggering down the hall-way, legs weak, the walls distorting. He needed fresh air. He stumbled once on the carpet, barely stood back up and continued toward the end of the hall where the balcony was located. He got to the glass door, opened it and walked out onto the balcony, the cold air hitting him in the face. He could see the plume of smoke drifting in the east. He stared at Madison Avenue more than seventy stories below him. The traffic looked like it moved in slow motion, almost animated.

Michael lifted his eyes from the street to the horror in the vista, staring at the ominous smoke, trying to find answers to the inexplicable. He gripped the railing, the wrought iron cold in his hands. He wanted to jump, sail through the sky for the three seconds he'd have from the balcony to the street. Maybe, in those three seconds, he could find some kind of clarity—some insight—some answer perhaps achievable when the world stops turning during the freefall of flight. But he knew he couldn't defy gravity any more than flight 197 did.

Why? Why was this allowed?

There was no answer. Things happen. Bad things with no discrimination for its victims. An airplane doesn't have a conscience any more than a bullet does. But a bullet doesn't fire itself. *Did someone sabotage the plane, killing Kelsey, Mandy, and the other innocent passengers?* He stared at the streets, the people walking, going home to loved ones. A few looking to the east at the black smoke, probably oblivious as to what happened and the loss of human life.

Michael felt faint—the street below going in and out of focus, his hands shaking so much he could barely grip the railing. He dropped to his knees, holding his face in his hands, sobbing, tears flowing onto his shirt, his stomach churning. He looked up at the late afternoon sky, a sliver of moon appearing to the far east above the ocean on the other side of Long Island. Michael thought of the Elysian Tower overlooking the Hong Kong harbor. He leaned to one side and vomited on the wrought iron balcony, the outlying sound of traffic and frustrated cab drivers blowing their horns far below him.

EIGHT

A week after the plane crash, Michael, sleep deprived and slightly hung over, stood at the master bathroom sink and stared at Kelsey's toothbrush in the plastic holder. It was the little things that hit him the hardest. The simple reminders of her presence that he often didn't take the time to notice when she was alive.

Now that she was gone, the objects broke their silence and almost shouted at him. The book she was reading atop the nightstand on her side of the bed. Her favorite coffee cup with a long-eared beagle's face on it. The houseplants she watered faithfully. Her clothes, a trace of her favorite perfume, like a ghost in her closet. And the shoes, all organized. He could remember when she'd slip on a pair and ask him if he thought the shoes went with her dress before they'd go out for an evening. It was her smile, her touch in the house that made it a home.

The same for Mandy. Every morning and night, Michael opened the door to her bedroom and stood at the threshold. Not going inside, but rather taking in what remained and missing what didn't. The sweet smell of his daughter after her bath. A plush animal on the floor. Her lavender princess dress sometimes discarded when she decided to change clothes for the third time that day. But she wasn't there. And never would be again.

He brushed his teeth and stared in the mirror, almost not recognizing the vacant face that looked back at him. An alter ego without an ego—robbed of his spirit. He hadn't shaved since Kelsey and Mandy died. His eyes were puffy, red, and seemed to have lost some of their blue color in the irises. It was as if part of his own life had gone down the drain into a dark sewer. Although he didn't physically die that day, something spiritually died inside. He could feel it like a cancer with small, dull teeth gnawing at the outer wall of his heart.

He walked down the hallway from the master bedroom toward the kitchen, stopping to look at some of the family pictures framed and hanging on the wall. He tried to remember the last time he stopped and looked—really looked and thought about the moment the picture was taken and what he was thinking or feeling when that slice of his life was frozen in time.

For almost a week, Michael didn't want to get off the couch.

He walked into his kitchen and put on a pot of coffee. He wore gray sweatpants and a black, wrinkled, long-sleeved T-shirt. He looked at one of Mandy's drawings attached by a magnet to the refrigerator door. Although she was only four-years-old, he could tell she had composition and drawing skills. Her latest sketch, done with green, blue, and red crayons, was of a park scene. Trees in the background, fluffy blue clouds, birds in flight, and two people—a mother and child walking a dog on a leash. Michael remembered the last time she asked him if she could get a puppy. "Please, Daddy. I promise to take care of her."

"Her? You want a female dog?"

"No, I want a girl dog. Just like the kind Mommy has on her cup. She said it's a beagle." Mandy grinned, her dimples popping.

The coffee pot made a final hiss and stopped dripping. He opened the cupboard for a cup. He looked at Kelsey's cup with the face of a beagle on the side of it. The dog had large eyes and almost seemed to be smiling. Michael blinked back tears, lifted out a blue cup, poured black coffee into it and walked from the kitchen through the family room. He glanced at his blanket on the couch, pillow flat, the pillowcase in need of washing. A half-empty bottle of scotch sat on the coffee table next to a home decorating magazine. He looked at Kelsey's plants, a fern, two orchids, and two peace lilies, trying to remember if he'd watered them.

He took a deep breath, opened the sliding glass door and stepped out onto the terrace. It was Sunday morning, the city more quiet than usual, the air brisk, the sound of church bells in the distance.

He sat down and stared at the New York skyline. The view, one that they'd paid a premium to have, seemed bland, as if the city had changed—turned into a sepia tone the tint of desert sand. "Maybe it's just me," he mumbled. "If I were a photograph, maybe I'd only be the negative … not a lot of positive stuff around anymore."

His phone buzzed. He looked at the caller ID. It was Adison Manning's private number. He'd call twice in the last couple of days. Michael didn't feel like talking. It was hard enough to talk with Kelsey's parents, her mother weak from cancer, trying to make sense of the deaths of her daughter and granddaughter. Kelsey's father devastated, his voice raspy, exhausted, attempting to sound brave when his personal breaking point had its cold hands around his throat.

Michael looked at the phone screen and pressed the button, answering. "Hello."

"I'm not even going to ask you how you are. There probably are no words." Adison paused, taking a deep breath, standing in the driveway leading to his sprawling house in the Hamptons, a waterfront French-Normandy mansion. "I just want you to know everyone in the firm feels so bad for your loss, Michael. If there is anything we can do, anything at all that you need, please let us know."

"Thank you. I need some time Adison …"

"Of course."

"I have to take a leave of absence. My head's in a pretty bad place."

"Take all the time you need. The Elysian Tower project will be four years in the making. "It's not going anywhere, Michael … at least not without you at the helm. The clients understand. Your office will be exactly as you left it when you get back."

Michael said nothing. Feeling cold, he stepped back inside and stared at a toy female troll, a smile frozen on her cherub face, large eyes, long pink hair straight up, a flowered headband, blue dress. The little troll stood at the corner of the table right where Mandy had left it.

"Did you get the flowers the office sent?" Manning asked.

"Yes, thank you."

"We were going to send them to the funeral home, but … I'm sorry."

"But there are no bodies to bury. The plane became a massive crematorium. Jet fuel can burn at two-thousand degrees. It disintegrated the plane and everyone aboard. I can't get the images of that twisting, black smoke out of my head." He paused, closing his bloodshot eyes. "I have to go, Adison."

"If you feel up to it, maybe you can join Judith and I for dinner Friday night."

"Right now, I don't feel up to it. But thanks for the offer."

"Take all the time you need, Michael. I don't want you to take this the wrong way, however, during periods of grief, after a while, it's good to focus back on what you love doing. To throw yourself back in your work because it'll be a form of therapy for you. When you're ready."

"At this point, I'm not sure it's what I love doing. Not anymore."

"Sure, it is. You were born for this work. But right now, you need time to mourn. Take it. Do what you need to do. We'll see you when you're ready to come back. If you change your mind for dinner on Friday, just let me know. Take care of yourself. See you soon." Manning disconnected.

Michael set his phone down on the coffee table and picked up his daughter's toy. He held the little troll in the palm of his hand. He remembered sitting on the couch with Mandy as she introduced the troll to him. *Her name's Poppy.*

"Really. Where did she get the name, Poppy?"

"I don't know, Daddy. Maybe her grandmother named her."

"What is it about Poppy that made you want to bring her into our family?"

"I just wanted to. She's nice. And she loves to sing."

"Really?"

"Yes. And she hugs her friends lots of times every day. Guess what?"

"What?"

"She loves to hear a cowbell ring." Mandy grinned.

"A cowbell … why?"

"Because it plays beautiful music for her."

At that moment, Michael could hear the church bells from a block away. Odd, he'd never noticed them before today. He tried to think of the last Sunday morning he was home. He couldn't. But now, the tolling of church bells were floating up to his terrace with the breeze, the distant ringing, was the sweetest music he'd heard in a long time. He stared at Mandy's toy in his hand, a tear dropping from his chin and falling onto the smiling pink face of Poppy.

"She hugs her friends lots of times every day."

Michael thought about his wife's voice message left on his phone, the last thing she ever said to him. *"Maybe it'll give us more time together as a family. Life's too short ... we're strong people, but our hearts are too fragile for the things that don't matter. For the things that do matter, let's do them ... okay?"*

He closed his eyes and wept.

NINE

Two months later, Michael still felt numb. He'd gone back to showering a few weeks earlier and no longer falling asleep in his clothes, but he still hadn't returned to work. He took long walks each day near the East River. He had the appearance of a homeless man, scruffy whiskers, longer hair, but he was a walking dead man—at least inside. He kept trying to find some perspective, some kind of solace. There was no closure. Maybe there never would be. Not in the sense of turning the page from the tragedy and moving on with his life.

He had no direction to move, no motivation. Whomever said, 'time is the great healer,' Michael thought as he walked along a greenway path adjacent to the East River, hadn't lost a family when he or she said it.

In a way, he thought maybe he'd betrayed Kelsey and Mandy. Not in terms of lying or deception, but more aligned with a form of abandonment as he spent less and less time with them while spending more time designing buildings, creating his own brand as an architect, inflating his ego while marginalizing the two people he loved the most in the world. Broken trust shoots an arrow into the heart first. When the heart dies, it takes a prisoner—the soul.

The trauma of their deaths hijacked his spirit and moved it to a form of self-prescribed purgatory. His life no longer had the meaning and purpose it once had. He walked around in a shroud of guilt and blame, seeing their faces and hearing their voices in a psychosis of post-traumatic stress disorder that thrust guilt into his conscience with the force of a sledgehammer.

The day was unusually warm for that time of the year. It was late-afternoon with a deep-blue sky reflecting from the river, the view of

Roosevelt Island and its lighthouse close to the center of the East River. Michael stopped walking near a park bench where an older man sat looking at the waterfront. The man was under a leafy elm tree, dappled sunlight breaking through the branches. A blonde woman, her hair in a ponytail, jogged by, earbuds on the sides of her head.

The old man's face was carved by time with deeply etched wrinkles. His bone-white eyebrows looked windswept, like twisted weeds sprouting. He sat alone with his thoughts, windbreaker unzipped, flannel shirt, khaki pants, and a gold wedding band on a finger bent from arthritis. His shoulders were stooped. A breeze moving across the water blew the slivers of his white hair, which hung from under a gray fedora like silk strands of a spider's web.

Michael nodded and said nothing. He leaned up against the railing adjacent to the path and watched a freighter churn the water as it moved down the river. It was passing Roosevelt Island and the lighthouse at the northern tip of the island. The air carried the whiff of diesel fumes and fresh cut grass in Carl Schurz Park behind him. From the distance, the lighthouse appeared to be no more than fifty feet high. Michael had seen the lighthouse once before and wondered about its history.

"Are you a tourist?" asked the old man, looking up from the park bench, closing one eye in the mottled sunlight.

"No, why? Do I look like a tourist?"

"You look like you might need directions. Sort of lost, if you don't mind me saying."

"I live in the city. I just recently started walking and jogging this path by the East River."

"It's a special place here. I walk to this bench almost every day, weather permitting. The park behind us, Carl Schurz Park, is lovely. Lots of rhododendrons and azaleas are blooming early. The daffodils and hellebore flowers are awake, and the tulips are peeking through the ground. In the center of the park is a bronze statue of Peter Pan. He's sitting on a stump looking at a fawn, a rabbit, and a toad." He pointed to the waterfront. "In the middle of the river, where you see the lighthouse, is Roosevelt Island. You ever go over there?"

Michael stared at the lighthouse. "No, I haven't. I've always wanted to, but I just never made the time."

The old man chuckled. "What's your name?"

"Michael Vargas."

"I'm Jacob Isenberg. It's a pleasure to meet you. Time is what Roosevelt Island was all about. For many years, it was known as Blackwell's Island. It was where they built a prison. There was also a hospital with a horrible past."

"How's that?"

"Well, for one, more than thirteen thousand people died in 1856 from small pox at the hospital. There were so many bodies that they stacked them up like cord wood in the yard behind the hospital, burned them, and dumped the ashes and bones right into the river."

"I had no idea that happened. That's a sad story. You seem to know the area history well."

"I taught history at Columbia for more than forty years."

"What's the history behind that lighthouse at the tip of the island."

Jacob smiled, looked up, and rested one gnarled hand on the handle of a polished, wooden cane propped up next to the bench. "It's believed to have been built by a mad man."

"What do you mean?"

"Are you sure you want to hear the story?"

"Yes, why do you ask?"

"I make this walk from my apartment through Carl Schurz Park every day, greeting the Peter Pan statue, and then walk the greenway to this park bench. I've seen you a few times, sort of strolling by without so much as looking at the river. Forgive me, but, as a university professor, I've been a lifelong student of the humanities. You appear to me as a man in search of something he lost. Sort of like the look I get when I've misplaced my cane. Like an elder Oedipus, I need three legs to get around." He chuckled. "If you really want me to tell you the story of the sins of Blackwell Island … and the mad man who built the lighthouse, I will. But I don't want to give you useless information."

A young couple, a man and a woman, walked with a dog on a leash down the path. The dog was a beagle, its ears flopping, tail wagging, black nose to the ground intrigued by the many smells. Michael glanced at the lighthouse and then at Jacob. "No, it wouldn't be useless. I'd like to hear the story."

TEN

Jacob Isenberg waited for the horn blast from a freighter to end. He looked up at Michael, who remained next to the railing, the East River and Roosevelt Island behind him. "There used to be an insane asylum over there," Jacob began. "This was when it was called Blackwell's Island, all through the eighteen-hundreds. It was an awful place. Nellie Bly, the first female investigative journalist in America, wanted to write a newspaper story about the alleged horror stories inside the asylum. So, in 1887 she faked insanity to get admitted into the facility. She almost didn't get out. The publication she was working for had to vouch for her. After Nellie wrote her story, which offered graphic details of the inhumane way many patients—including her, were treated, the story was picked up all over the nation. Lots of sadistic torture of the patients by staff and one psychiatrist in particular, a truly evil man. That article caused wide-scale changes in the way the mentally ill were treated. Especially on Blackwell Island where the city's first lunatic asylum was located. Anyway, one of the mental patients, a creative genius, built the lighthouse. A man who'd apparently lost his mind but retained his design and building skills."

"Who was that?"

"John McCarthy, a fella who wanted to build a fort over there because he thought the British were coming to invade New York a century after the Revolutionary War. I remember his name because, at one time, there was a historical plaque near the entrance to the lighthouse." Jacob closed his eyes for a moment, thinking. "The inscription read … *'This work was done by John McCarthy, who built the lighthouse from bottom to top, and all who pass by may pray for his soul when he dies.'* I'd read that the director at the asylum, and others, recognized McCarthy's natural born talents, and let him out during the daylight hours, long enough to work on the project."

"Did he do all the work himself?"

"Much of it. They used prison labor for the heavier stuff. In my research, I learned that he took to the task like a man possessed, rarely speaking for hours at a time as he busied himself with every detail, much done by hand. It was really an amazing feat, considering the year and the tools or lack of them he had at his disposal. Before the lighthouse was built, some ships ran aground on the area of the river they called Hell's Gate, the dangerous waterway between Queens and the Bronx."

Michael gazed at the lighthouse, thinking about the story Jacob had just shared with him. He was intrigued. "Even from here, I can tell the construction of that lighthouse was quite a feat for its day. John McCarthy must have been a remarkable man."

"More than remarkable. He was driven to accomplish a hard task. And that lighthouse has withstood the tests of time and the elements." The old man studied Michael for a moment, eyes roaming his face and then his hands. "May I ask … what is it you do for a living, and what do you do for pleasure?"

"In a way, you could say I design and build lighthouses."

"Oh, perhaps it brings you joy as well. With today's technology, I wouldn't think there'd be much demand for lighthouses and those who design them." He smiled.

"I'm an architect. I recently finished design plans for the world's tallest building. And, at the top of the building's pinnacle, there will be a powerful light."

"That kind of design and construction takes a lot of skill." He paused, observing as Michael turned his head to look across the river. "Excuse me for being forward, however, at my age—eighty-nine, I allow myself that option if I feel it's worthwhile. I don't sense a lot of enthusiasm from you about the project."

"I've had a lot on my mind. Two months ago, my wife and daughter died in a plane crash. I haven't been able to return to work yet."

"I'm deeply sorry for the loss of your wife and daughter. A tragedy like that can certainly sharpen or change one's perspective on life, the fragility and finality of it. My wife of fifty years, Deloris, died nine months ago. Our only child, Isaac, was killed by a drunken driver when he turned twenty-two. It was the day of his birthday, and he was graduating from Columbia ready to make his mark on the world. That wound never healed. You will grieve for the deaths of your wife and daughter for the rest of your life … but what you can't allow is to give tragedy permission to dig a third grave."

Michael said nothing, looking at the old man's compassionate face and then glancing across the river at Roosevelt Island and the lighthouse. Looking back at Jacob, he said, "I'm sorry for your loss, too."

Jacob nodded and asked, "What will be the name of this grand building when it's finished?"

"The Elysian Tower. It'll be built in Hong Kong, and it will take four years to complete."

"Elysian … interesting. The Elysian Fields … known as the final resting place the Greek gods offered their tireless heroes. I'd imagine that John McCarthy was a tireless hero to have built that lighthouse from the ground up. After all that work, I wonder if there was a resting spot for him in the Elysian Fields." Jacob paused and took a deep breath. "McCarthy was trapped physically on an island, and mentally he was entombed and locked away in an asylum for the insane. I guess they couldn't lock away his talent. But was he really crazy or just miscast in life, perhaps by his own doing? Playing a lifelong part that he never auditioned for, just accepting the role because he feared the risks of failure, and he succumb to mediocrity. That might drive a creative person mad."

"I suppose we'll never know."

"Indeed. Although I've been retired for years, I still enjoy a lively discussion and the chance to pontificate. You, Michael, are a good listener. An old colleague of mine at the university, a professor of psychology, mentioned a parallel sometimes seen between highly creative people and some forms of mental illness. She had examples. One, I remember, was that of Michelangelo. When he did commissioned work, he was believed to have suffered from what we know today as bipolar disease. The illness was said to have subsided when he did his own projects."

Michael was silent, watching a tour boat—a yellow water taxi, churn down the river, heading toward Riker's Island. Jacob said, "A good way to get reacquainted with the city is to see it by boat. I used to sail out there years ago. There's magic light off the water and the cityscape during sunset. You won't find that on the subway."

"As a kid, I grew up around boats in a town with a harbor. Not like New York City, but it had its own special charm."

"Where was that?"

"Charleston, South Carolina."

"You ever get back down there?"

"Not in a long time."

The old man nodded. "Do you like what you do? The design of giant buildings?"

"I thought I did. Now, not so much."

"May I offer you some advice?"

"Sure."

"I'll be ninety in September. I doubt I'll live long enough to see your building, the world's tallest lighthouse, completed. But that's okay. I have the one in the center of the river to view. It's not extraordinary. It's ordinary, but it wasn't built by an ordinary man. Nothing worthwhile truly is. A century ago, boat captains never took that lighthouse for granted. As I come to the end of my time, one thing I've learned is that a life lived without risks … with fear of failure, is not worth living. Taking risks, putting your heart and soul on the line for who you are and what you believe in, is hard stuff and very daunting. But it's not as frightening as coming to the end of your life and asking yourself this … what if I'd taken the risks? What if I'd done what I really wanted to do, not afraid to expose my vulnerable side, the side that's closest to my heart?"

He paused and slowly stood, both hands gripping the wooden cane. "What is it you really want to do, Michael?"

"I don't know. I thought I did … but being known for designing recognizable or iconic buildings doesn't have the appeal anymore. Maybe it never really did."

Jacob nodded. He stepped around the bench, his right hand gripping the handle of the cane. "I'm going to walk back to my apartment. It's close by here. I'll stroll through the park and spend a moment with the statue of Peter Pan. There's an irony molded and cast in that bronze boy. Peter didn't want to grow up or grow old to follow his dreams. The fact is we all have to grow up. If we're lucky, we grow old. If we're honest, we knock the dried paint off and open the window of chance and vulnerability to allow such things as joy into our lives. If you put yourself out there, take risks, for what your soul really longs for, when you get to my age, you won't have to harvest the seeds of regret. I wish you the best on your journey. I enjoyed our little chat."

"Me, too. Thank you … what'd you say your name is? I'm sorry."

"Don't be. It's Jacob Isenberg." The old man nodded and shuffled down the concrete path, the tip of the cane making a thumping sound, the distant blast of a boat horn on the river. Michael watched the banana yellow ferry boat as it passed by Roosevelt Island, dozens of tourists snapping pictures of the island and its iconic lighthouse. Probably no one knowing anything about the man who'd built it.

Was he really crazy or just miscast in life, perhaps by his own doing?

Michael thought about that as he turned and walked away. He had no real destination. He wasn't sure he was even on any kind of journey as Jacob had implied. He just knew he had to walk, to clear his head. He didn't want to go back home. The ordinary things that Kelsey and Mandy did, were now the extraordinary personal landmarks in his life. He wanted to think about them as he walked. To relive family scenes with them that seemed like bit parts at the time, but now, when combined, they were the parts of the story that really mattered—that ended before its time.

ELEVEN

Michael ignored the gnawing in his stomach. He kept walking. He hadn't eaten since yesterday, and now it was getting close to seven p.m. He had followed the pedestrian path along the East River from the area of Carl Schurz Park all the way to the United Nations building, the sky darkening as rain clouds moved in overhead. He turned onto 42nd Street, thinking about his conversation with Jacob Isenberg. He could smell the stench of garbage from cans set out on the curb. Michael headed toward the New York Public Library, a soft rain beginning to fall, the scent of wet cardboard from the alleyway.

He turned the collar up on his coat in the misty rain, his hands now cold. The main library was in the distance, across Fifth Avenue, a buttery light coming from the three stone arches at the library's entrance. A cab zipped by, its red taillights reflecting off the wet street. He stepped around a puddle near a curb, crimson neon light shimmering off the water.

Michael walked up the library's concrete steps, past the twin marble lions on either side of the entrance, the gurgling sound of water splashing in a fountain behind one of the lions. He stood out of the rain under the center arch and watched the traffic and a few pedestrians in silhouette gripping umbrellas. He sat down on the top steps sheltered from the drizzle, thinking more about his conversation with Jacob Isenberg, the evening turning cooler from the rain.

"Why? Do I look like a tourist?"

"You look like you might need directions. Sort of lost, if you don't mind me saying."

Michael's feet and legs were tired, his head pounded. He knew he should eat, but he didn't have an appetite. He tried to think of the last time he sat down for a meal of real food. He couldn't. Maybe he'd microwave a frozen dinner when he got back to his condo.

After less than twenty minutes, the rain stopped, a mist arriving. Michael stood, starting to walk back down the steps. A black man slowly pushed a bicycle with two flat tires at the base of the steps. The man wore a white sweatshirt, smudged in dirt and grime. Jeans, torn and soiled. Brown penny loafers scuffed, soaked, and almost paper thin. The man's hollow face scruffy, with half-inch whiskers the color of ash. He sang, *"It's a rainy night in Georgia … oh Lord I feel like it's rainin' all over the wooorld … neon signs flashin' … taxi cabs and buses passin' through the night …"* He grinned, looked up at Michael. "I see Fortitude's got your back."

"Excuse me?"

"Fortitude, that's the name of the lion behind your back. The lion on the other side of these steps is Patience. Fortitude and Patience. The king of beasts on guard."

"Is that what you named them?"

"Naw, man. The mayor of the city gave 'em those names, Fortitude and Patience, way back when the library was opened in 1895."

"Is that right?"

"Absolutely. Accordin' to the historical plaque on the side of the library. I wonder how many people ever stop to read it. Kinda odd since most folks are goin' inside to find somethin' to read. That's the first thing I read when I got up here from South Carolina, ten years ago." He smiled. "I'd bet you gotta be from somewhere in the South. I got a good ear for dialects. I can sense a lil' accent … more than not, South Carolina."

"I'm from Charleston."

He grinned. "Charleston's a fine city. My man, Brook Benton, I was singing his song, a *Rainy Night in Georgia*, was from South Carolina, too. He came up here to make records. He cut a few records and then died young … way 'fore his time … but his music lives on, least in my heart."

"You have a good voice. Were you a singer?"

"Man, I still am a singer. I suppose I'll go to my grave singin'. I sing for my supper. You name the song, I'll sing it. I memorized a thousand of 'em. If you like it, you can put some bread in my can. If you don't, that's cool, man." He lifted a Maxwell House blue coffee can out from the wet knapsack on the bike's handle bars, setting the can on the third step in front of him. "Call out the song."

"I don't have any."

"C'mon, man. You gotta know at least one song. Whatcha like? Blues? Country? Put me to the test, just for fun, okay?"

Michael folded his arms across his chest, licked his lips, and smiled, his whiskers still damp from walking in the rain. "All right. How about *Dock of the Bay* by Otis Redding?"

The man grinned, his dark eyes reflecting the golden light from the library arches. "That's too easy, but it's cool. Great singer. Like Brook Benton, Otis died way too young 'fore he should have." He cleared his voice, closed his eyes for a second and began, *"Sittin' in the mornin' sun ... I'll be sittin' when the eveeenin' comes ... watchin' the ships roll in ... then I'll watch 'em roll awaaay again ... I'm sittin on the dock of the baaay ... watchin' the tide, roll awaaay ..."* He continued singing, passersby ignoring his perfect pitch echoing off the front of the library.

After a minute, Michael walked down the steps, clapping his hands and then pulling three twenty-dollar bills from his wallet. "Hope this helps—you might be able to get your bicycle tires fixed." He leaned over, dropping the money into the singer's coffee can. The man nodded and kept singing, now going into the second verses of the song. Michael listened a little while longer, smiled, and walked across the pedestrian footpath in front of the library. The man continued singing.

When Michael crossed Fifth Avenue, he turned around and watched the singer under the moonlight for a few seconds longer. The man was now standing next to one of marble lions, singing to the lion he'd called Fortitude. *"I left my home in Georgia ... and I headed for the Frisco Baaay ... cause I got nothin' to live for ... looks like nothin's gonna come my waaaay. So I'm just sittin' on the dock of the bay ... wastin' time ..."*

Michael turned, lifted his collar back up and walked through the city streets, to the East River and the meandering concrete path that would take him in the general direction of his condo. He headed north, walking at a brisk pace, his thoughts jumbled due to hunger and exhaustion. The sky had cleared, the moonlight reflecting off the surface of the dark river. He seemed to be the only person walking tonight, pockets of light spilling from lampposts onto the pathway.

Soon he was approaching the southern tip of Roosevelt Island to his right. He stopped along the seawall railing, the sound of a boat motor somewhere on the river. There was a slight burning pain in his stomach. It was the second time today he'd felt it. The first was when Jacob Isenberg had talked about the plight and irony of the man locked up in an insane asylum at sunset and given permission to build a lighthouse during the day. The sole purpose of his creative efforts was to give ships safe passage at night.

Michael walked northward, ambling under the aerial tramway cars at least one hundred feet above the ground, the cable cars moving like a slow-motion carnival ride from Manhattan to Roosevelt Island. He couldn't see if anyone was aboard the tram cars, each one painted the color of a used firetruck. He watched the tram's lights skidding across the East River, the colors vibrating over the surface of the swift current.

He walked on, lost in thought, ignoring the pain in his stomach. He was coming back up to where he began earlier today, the park bench under the leafy elm tree. As he got closer, he looked toward the lighthouse on the north end of Roosevelt Island, a light fog lifting off the river. Something near the bench caught his eye.

A couple sitting alone, talking, watching the harbor lights. Their focus was on a tugboat moving through the mist.

Not the person moving up from behind them.

Michael stopped, the man holding either a gun or knife, the couple not seeing him. Michael had a decision to make. And he had only seconds to make it.

TWELVE

Michael was still at least one hundred feet away from a crime scene that was about to happen. He saw the intruder slip up behind the couple, say something to them, both the man and woman quickly standing, the woman holding one hand to her mouth. She screamed. The mugger shouted, "Shut up!" Under the soft light from a streetlamp, Michael could see the glint of a gun barrel.

He pulled his phone from his pocket and dialed 9-1-1. The operator answered, "9-1-1- ... what's your emergency?"

Michael whispered. "I'm at the East River right across from Carl Schurz Park. A guy with a gun is mugging a couple—a young man and a woman. They look like teenagers. Please send the police."

"Is the incident happening right by the river or in the park?"

"By the river. At a park bench. It overlooks the lighthouse on Roosevelt Island."

"I'll dispatch officers."

"What is your name, sir."

Michael disconnected, fearful that he was about to witness a double murder. The mugger brandishing the pistol, slightly rocking back and forth, staring at the couple. Jeering. He waved the gun in the night air. Michael could hear the threats. "You wanna die tonight? Huh! Give me your wallet and your purse. Now!"

The girl said nothing, hugging her arms. Her companion said, "Okay! Take it! Just no violence, okay dude?"

"I'm not your dude!"

"Not a problem," the young man said, reaching for his wallet, tossing it toward the mugger. The girl took her purse off her shoulder, holding the strap in one hand and extending her arm. "Take it!"

The robber stepped forward and snatched the purse from the girl's grip. For a second, it looked like he was going to run away. Michael watched as the robber aimed the pistol. "Into the park!"

"Why?" the girl blurted out. "We gave you our money."

"Move!"

The couple left the bench, visibly stunned, walking down an ancillary path leading into the wooded park. The man followed right behind them, his gun extended, fog drifting through a cone of diffused light from a streetlamp near the park entrance. Michael wasn't sure what to do. *How long will it take for police to get here? Will the guy kill the couple?* He decided to do whatever he could. He couldn't hear police sirens, only the long blast from a tugboat whistle, the vessel now blanketed in the white mist over the surface of the river.

Michael jogged toward the park entrance, running on grass to muffle his approach. At the entrance, he stopped, breathing through his nose. Heart racing. Listening. He could hear muffled conversation. Direct orders and threats from the attacker. He heard the girl utter a bloodcurdling scream. Michael headed toward the sounds, staying in the dark shadows cast by the oaks and dogwood trees.

Within seconds he came to what appeared to be the center of the park lit by two lampposts. It was a wide cul-de-sac of stone and old brick, a half-dozen benches along one wall less than three feet in height. High trees were on the other side of the wall. In the center of the area was another circle, quarry stones about ten feet in diameter, surrounding the colorful array of blooming hellebore flowers. In the very center was a bronze statue of Peter Pan wearing a feathered cap, looking at a fawn, toad, and turtle.

But no one was there.

"Get down! On your knees!" The command came from the east side of the area. Michael could see a secondary path leading into the pine trees. He followed it, not having to go far. The path opened into a secluded, wooded area, the light from the two lampposts coming through tree branches. The attacker was pointing the pistol at the girl on her knees, her body shaking, tears streaming down her cheeks. She looked to be no more than seventeen. Her young boyfriend, eyes like a deer in the headlights, was forced to sit on a bench that was surrounded by blooming pink azaleas.

Michael stepped into the flecked light. "Leave her alone!"

The attacker turned, his eyes wide, mouth twisted in a sneer. Under the shadow of the hoodie, his dark eyes had the look of a feral dog hiding beneath the steps of a front porch. He had the wild stare of a drug user in bad need of a fix. The man grinned, two of his lower teeth missing. "You wanna be a hero tonight, bro?"

Michael held the palms of his hands up. "Just leave. You have their money. You can go, and you'll get away. Police are coming. I called them when I spotted you pulling a gun on these kids."

There was now the sound of a siren in the distance. The man panicked. The hand holding the gun, shaking. He snorted, turning the gun away from the girl and aiming it at Michael's chest. "You made a bad mistake calling the cops. It'll be your last mistake." He pulled the trigger.

Michael saw a white burst come from the barrel at the same instant the bullet tore into his shoulder, the girl screaming, the pop sound of the gun surreal. It was as if he'd been hit by the full swing of a baseball bat. Through the puff of smoke, he saw the man's hot eyes gleaming, filled with delight. Filled with evil. His nostrils quivering like a wolf on the hunt. He mouthed something with his thin lips and fired a second shot. This one hit Michael in his chest. He stumbled back, almost losing his balance.

The man ran by him, smelling of cigarettes, urine and dried sweat—the odor of rotting cabbage. In seconds the shooter was gone. Michael held his bleeding chest with his left hand, the blood oozing through his fingers and over his wedding ring. He stumbled along the path back into the scattered light of the central area. The sirens coming closer. He could hear the couple following him, the girl sobbing. The teenage boy was on his phone with a 9-1-1 operator. "A man's been shot! Carl Schurz Park! We need an ambulance! Please hurry, okay?"

The sounds began to swirl in Michael's ears. He stumbled to his knees near the statue of Peter Pan encircled by flowers. Michael lay on his side, staring up at the night sky. The stars were some of the brightest he'd ever seen. He felt someone touching his shoulder, hearing the soft sobs of the girl. "Please don't die … help's coming."

Michael closed his eyes, the flat stones cool against his right cheek. He could feel his blood seeping out from beneath his hand. He thought of Kelsey and Mandy, the last time they'd talked and laughed together. His wife's voice, a gentle but distant whisper in his ears. *"We're strong people, but our hearts are too fragile for the things that don't matter. For the things that do matter, let's do them, okay?"*

"Okay, baby," Michael whispered, his eyes welling with tears.

He heard Mandy say, *"Her name's Poppy … she loves to sing?"*

"Really?"

"Yes, and she hugs her friends every day … I love you, Daddy."

"I love you, too, sweetheart." Michael coughed, the coppery taste of blood in his mouth. His chest felt on fire. He looked up at the statue of Peter Pan sitting on a stump, glancing down and smiling at a fawn, the bronze face reflecting a pure and youthful radiance in the moonlight. Michael blinked back tears, his body cold, going into shock. He heard the voice of Jacob Isenberg, the old man's words like a whisper in the night air, *"Peter didn't want to grow up or grow old to follow his dreams. The fact is we all have to grow up. If we're lucky, we grow old. If we're honest, we knock the dried paint off and open the window of chance and vulnerability to allow such things as joy into our lives."*

Michael closed his eyes, the sound of sirens growing closer, the face of the statue blurring and fading, the stars gone, darkness descending all around him.

THIRTEEN

It was ninety-three seconds of time that Michael would never forget and, yet, never be certain he remembered. He was rushed to the nearest hospital with a trauma center. In the ambulance, the paramedics managed to stop the exterior bleeding. That wasn't the case inside Michael's badly wounded body. The bullet that had entered his chest, narrowly missing his heart, traveled through shattering a rib bone, destroying arteries and collapsing his left lung. The bleeding was internal and profuse.

He was wheeled on a stretcher into the emergency room and immediately underwent surgery. A team of doctors and nurses fought hard to save his life, the lead surgeon clamping and sewing up arteries while Michael underwent blood transfusions. Into the second hour of surgery, all of a sudden, Michael's blood pressure dropped causing his heart to become erratic, the electrical pulses misfiring.

"He's in ventricular fib," said the lead surgeon, his voice calm, intense eyes, tiny specks of blood on his glasses and surgical mask. He glanced at one of the monitors, reading the undulating lines and then looking inside Michael's open chest, his heart quivering. "Give me a hundred cc's of Epinephrine."

It took a nurse just seconds to hand the prepared hypodermic needle to the doctor. He administered the medicine, looking up at the monitor. After a few more seconds, he said, "Paddles … let's see if we can get this heart under control."

Another nurse handed him two rubber-insolated defibrillator paddles, each with a coiled wire attached to them. The heartbeats were barely registering on the monitor, the beeps almost inaudible. The doctor placed the metal plates on both sides of the chest. "Clear!" he said, pressing the button and sending a jolt of electricity through Michael's body. The heart rhythm became even more obscure, as if the heart muscle itself had given up. Tired. Dying on the table under the bright lights.

"Another defib," said the doctor. "Clear …" The surge of electricity caused Michael's body to jerk slightly. But his heart only quivered and then stopped. The doctor looked at the monitor. No signs of electrical energy. No impulses. Nothing. Michael's heart had flatlined.

During the first ten seconds, the doctors moved methodically, checking clamps, sutures, looking for bleeding, tracing the immediate circulatory system.

During the next ten seconds, they administered another heart-starting drug. The surgeon gently massaging the heart muscle, looking up to the monitors. Nothing.

The doctors continued their procedures, their voices in calm monotones. No one panicking. Two nurses exchanging anxious glances, their true concern partially covered by the surgical masks they wore.

"Suction!" said the lead surgeon, using his fingers to probe inside the chest cavity. A nurse turned on a machine and then used a rubber tube with a tiny nozzle on the tip to suck out pooling blood in Michael's chest. The doctor looked through two small magnifying lenses attached to the front of his glasses, working to repair hidden damage to a coronary artery.

Suddenly, Michael's face drained of color, a bluish cast appearing on his lips and cheeks. He was no longer breathing. No sign of a heartbeat. The lead surgeon's forehead glistening with perspiration.

Michael wondered if he was having the strangest dream of his life. He was somehow above his body in the operating room, looking down as the surgical team fought to restore his heartbeat. *Had I died?* he thought. *It's okay. Everything will be fine.* There was no sense of time or space. For that matter, he was not experiencing a sense of place anymore because he was no longer in the operating room.

He felt as if he was traveling down a long corridor at a fast speed, through a mist, toward a smoldering light in the distance. He thought of the lighthouse on Roosevelt Island, a white light penetrating the fog. It drew him closer, the fog swirling, the light guiding him. Then he flew past it, moving at an accelerated speed into the dark toward a brighter light. It was the one at the top of Elysian Tower—the tallest light in the world.

The voice from the video seemed to boom from all round him. *Since the dawn of mankind on earth, we've always looked to the heavens for everything from inspiration to solace. There's a sense of wonder, of quiet revelation gazing at the universe. And, when the Elysian Tower is built, the distance from earth to the moon and stars just became closer.*

The image from the top of the Elysian Tower looked out at the ocean. Michael could see another light, this one at the crest of earth, like something radiating on the sphere of the world. In seconds he was there—the entire universe seemed drenched in light. He felt naked. Unclothed and unashamed. Every pore on his body exposed. His entire being—his entire life revealed. But to whom? There didn't seem to be anyone judging him, only accepting and loving him. He felt lost but somehow found. Unafraid.

"I wish you the best on your journey ... I enjoyed our little chat."

"Jacob ... is that you?" Michael heard himself ask. Yet, he hadn't moved his lips. He wasn't sure if he still had lips or a mouth. But he had his mind ... his thoughts clearer than at any other time in his life.

The old man's voice seemed to come from nowhere yet everywhere. Maybe it was toward the warm light in the distance across the vista. Michael felt as if he was freefalling in slow-motion, not toward the ground, wherever it was ... but above. Somewhere in a dimension that defied the laws of gravity. He was soaring like a bird toward the sun, the light warm, filling his face and the pores of his body with love and acceptance.

"Michael," he heard Kelsey say. *"Everything will be fine. Mandy and I are well. It's not your time yet, my love."*

He couldn't see his wife. Only hear her voice. But he felt her presence all around him. In the distance, somewhere in the glimmers of light, he could see Mandy's face. Smiling. Angelic. *"Daddy ... I love you ... "* her voice like a prayer on the wind. But there was no sense of wind in his face. He was moving, somehow. Not walking. Not running. Not in any type of vehicle or plane. But he was soaring to heights, to places, far beyond all human calculation. Traveling toward a light flowing with tenderness and saturating him in unconditional love.

He wanted to reach out his hands, open his palms to feel every molecule of the radiance. As he held his arms up, embracing the light … he was no longer there. The dimension turned black, as if a blanket was tossed over the universe. There was nothing but absolute darkness.

Then, Michael could hear the doctors and nurses around him.

"We have a pulse."

"Well done, Doctor Lavin."

"Let's close him up. Good job everyone. We had luck on our side today."

* * *

In the recovery room, Michael didn't even try to open his eyes. His body ached, lying on a portable bed with wheels. He was cold. His thoughts blurring. Groggy. Trying hard to concentrate. *Think.* He wanted to catch the bits and pieces of his trek, which were illusive, like grabbing at slices of a dream as they were fading into shards of a broken mirror, never reflecting the complete image. He wanted the graphic pixels to coalesce into a whole picture, to somehow hit the *save* button forever.

But that wasn't happening. There was no digital link to where he'd been … to what he'd experienced and felt. He'd crossed some kind of mysterious threshold and returned. Maybe the visual mileposts weren't precise, but the sense of place he had while … *while what?* he thought. *How long? Where?* From beneath the sheets, he could smell the coppery scent of dried blood, cauterized flesh, singed hair on his chest, antiseptic and bleach.

His mouth was dry, his throat burning even an hour after the anesthesiologist had removed the endotracheal tube from his mouth and throat.

The lead surgeon entered the recovery room, approaching Michael's bed and gently touching him on the shoulder. "Good to have you back."

Michael tried to speak, his voice gravelly. "Thank you, doctor, and your team." He coughed. "I saw how hard you worked to save my life."

"You saw?" The doctor smiled, removing his glasses and cleaning them with a tissue. "Not only were your eyes closed, you were under anesthesia. Sort of hard to see much, I'd imagine."

"Maybe I heard you ... I'm not sure of much right now."

"You need to get some rest. Your heart had stopped for ninety-three seconds. Considering the damage from that bullet, you're a fortunate man. You'll be with us in the hospital for at least two weeks, providing you don't develop any secondary infections. Sleep is the best healing prescription I can suggest. I look forward to seeing you on my morning rounds. The bullets did some nasty stuff. I'll go over all of it with you later. For now, just get some sleep. The police will want to talk with you. That's fine, but not until tomorrow. I'll leave orders to that effect. You had a very close call, Mr. Vargas." He nodded, touched Michael's shoulder one more time, and left.

* * *

Three hours later, back in his private room, after the nurses had left and the sun had gone down, Michael lay in semi-darkness. He stared at the red roses sent by the staff in his office. He thought about the flowers, the multi-colored hellebore, surrounding the statue of Peter Pan. He could see the face more clearly now. The playful animation in the eyes, the same thing reflected in the bronze statues of the fawn, turtle and toad. *Mr. Toad's wild ride*, he thought, touching the hospital gown with two fingers, feeling the stiches from the top of his chest to his stomach.

Was it a dream? Or had I really gone someplace? He thought about what the doctor had said: *Your heart had stopped for ninety-three seconds. Considering the damage from that bullet, you're a fortunate man ... not only were your eyes closed, you were under anesthesia.*

In ninety-three seconds, Michael felt he had the most visionary passage of his life. He no longer feared death. What he feared was a life not well lived. He had no idea where he'd gone during that time, but he knew where he was going. And he would begin that journey the day he could walk out of the hospital.

FOURTEEN

The following day, at 3:10 in the afternoon, two detectives from the New York City Police Department knocked on the door to Michael's hospital room and entered. The senior detective was a man in his early fifties. He wore a tan sports coat and tie. Average height, short cropped, dark hair, graying at the temples. His poker face unreadable.

The other detective, a pretty woman in her mid-thirties, had straight brown hair cut blunt at her shoulders and eyes that revealed a sense of compassion and curiosity. Very little make-up. "Hi, Mr. Vargas. Doctor Lavin said we could spend a few minutes with you. I'm Detective Rita Brenner. My partner is Detective Paul Welch. We're with NYPD, and we're investigating what happened to you in the park—the shooting and attempted murder. How are you feeling?"

"Like I've been run over by a city bus."

They came closer to Michael's bed. Detective Welch cleared his throat. "We won't take much of your time, but we need to hear what you saw and heard. The man who shot you is still at large. The two teenagers gave us a detailed description the best they could. They're very grateful you came to their aid." He nodded, tilting his head, glancing out the window to the city skyline. "Mr. Vargas, what you did was noble but very dangerous. We listened to the recording of the 9-1-1 call that came from your cell phone. Did you make that call?"

"Yes."

"You knew the man had a gun, you saw it. And, yet, you entered that park to face him unarmed. Mind if I ask you why you did that?"

"Because those kids needed help."

"You literally took a bullet for them. You took two bullets as a matter of fact."

Michael said nothing.

Detective Brenner looked at the IV tubes hooked to Michael's hand and at the heart monitor. "The media are calling you a vigilante hero. Somehow, they found out that you're a world-renowned architect, and they're riding that notoriety wave. You designed the Pan Star building in Midtown, right?"

"Yes."

Detective Welch said, "When my wife comes into the city, she always comments on how much she likes that building. I'm sure, as soon as you're up to it, the news media will be knocking on your door to do interviews. They love hero stories."

"No thanks. I'm not a hero. I just did what I felt was the right thing to do at the moment."

Detective Brenner nodded. "Can you walk us through what happened? You had no weapon, but yet he shot you twice. Were you coming toward him, threatening the shooter?"

"No. I just asked him to leave. When I told him that I had called the police, he shot me."

"Did you get a good look at his face? Good enough so you might identify him in a line-up?"

"He wore a black hoodie jacket. It was dark. Not a lot of light in the park. I didn't get a clear look at his face, at least not enough to make a positive ID."

"All right," said Detective Brenner, folding her arms. "Let's take it from the beginning and try to remember everything the shooter said, okay?"

"Okay." Michael told them all that he could recall, stopping to sort out details. When finished, he asked, "Are the teenagers okay? After I was shot, I didn't know if the guy came back out of the bushes and hurt them."

"They're fine," Detective Welch said. "The parents of the girl want to give you a financial reward for what you did."

"Tell them to put it toward their daughter's college fund ... if she wants to go to college."

"We'll pass it on. In the meantime, if you can think of any further details ... something that might connect us with the perp, please call us." They both pulled out business cards and put them on the bedside table. "We do have two physical items that will link us to the shooter if we find him and his gun. We have one of the two bullets he fired and are searching the park for the other. The second item we'll not disclose at this time. Luckily, the two teens you saved were able to give us enough of a description for a composite drawing. Now, we'd like to catch the man who tried his best to kill you."

* * *

For almost a month, Michael had managed to dodge the news media, refusing to do TV or newspaper interviews. The reporters, producers and camera operators found his home address, some waiting in their TV news trucks in front of his apartment building. When he had to leave, mostly for follow-up doctor's appointments, he'd quickly walk around the reporters, ignoring their questions with a "no comment."

The headlines, blogs, podcasts, and cable news pundits were labeling him as the star architect turned superhero. High above Manhattan, a satellite radio host opened his microphone and said, "Heroes are people of action, not simply good intentions. This guy, Michael Vargas, may be well known for designing some of the coolest buildings in the world, buildings that have an impact on people … but what is even cooler is the impact he had on the lives of those two teenagers, Cindy Bergman and David Zeff. Bergman's dad is movie producer Seth Bergman. Maybe Bergman should do a movie about Michael Vargas. Seems like he's had a charming and interesting life with some tragedy dropped into it. Keep in mind that this is the same Michael Vargas who recently lost his wife and daughter in that Southern Airline plane crash at LaGuardia. Maybe he feels he's got nothing to live for, doesn't fear death, and now he's a vigilante. Remember, this guy took two bullets for two kids—teenagers he didn't even know. All that said, Michael Vargas is keeping an extremely low profile. I'd like to ask our listeners which actor they'd want to see in that movie role. I'd suggest Chris Hemsworth. Let's go to Chet on the line from the Bronx."

The caller said, "I don't have a pick for an actor, but I wanted to say that we should be putting up a statue of Mr. Vargas in Central Park. This guy's a real hero."

"Yes, he is," said the radio host. "Funny you should mention a statue. My producer, in doing her research, said, there's a statue of Peter Pan in the park where Vargas was shot. Go figure. We understand Michael Vargas hasn't reported back to work at his Manhattan office since he was released from the hospital. Moving on, I have a call from New Jersey. If this gets made into a movie, who would you like to see in the lead role? I understand Vargas is a good lookin' guy, not a pretty boy. That's why I'd like to see Chris Hemsworth in the part. What do you think?"

"My money would be on Brad Pitt. He's got the chops."

"Interesting choice. Now back to a caller from N-Y-C—who'd you like to see in the role?"

"Definitely, Chris Pine. I've seen Vargas on magazine covers, and he looks like Pine, especially with those gorgeous eyes."

* * *

It was mid-morning, almost sixty days to the day after Michael was shot that he caught a cab to take him to his office. The doctors had given him a relatively clean bill of health. The stitches were removed, the two wounds healing well. The pain from the snapped rib was still there, especially when he coughed or sneezed. He wore a dark suit, white shirt with no tie. He entered the Manhattan office building and rode the elevator up seventy floors to the offices of *Manning, Edelman, and Vargas.*

He stood outside the glass doors and looked at his name above the main entrance. It had taken him more than twenty years to reach this point, and he had mixed emotions. Glad he survived and did it. Sad that it had cost him so much. He walked into the office, first greeted by the middle-aged receptionist with a wide smile, "Mr. Vargas! It's so good to see you. How are you feeling?"

"Much better, Robin. Thanks."

"Good. It's been all over the news. Reporters called every hour that first day. I'm so sorry for the loss of your wife and daughter … I just … everyone here was devastated. And then what happened to you in that park … horrific."

Michael nodded and proceeded down the long, carpeted hallway toward his corner office. Employees, many in wide-glass offices, some in cubicles, some getting coffee or water, looked like they were seeing a ghost walk among them.

"Welcome back, Mr. Vargas," said a smiling junior architect as he came out from behind a computer monitor.

"Thanks, Hal." Michael kept walking, greeting people with a smile and handshake. To avoid causing physical stress, the employees were especially mindful not to hug or pat him on the back, but everyone was sure to extend their sincere greetings and well wishing. "So good to see you. Hope things are better. How are you holding up? Glad you're back. We missed you."

Michael gave quick, courteous answers, a dull ache and throbbing near his heart where the bullet had pulverized a bone, turning it into splinters. When he finally made it all the way back to his office, he quickly found the key, opened the door and turned on the lights. There were sealed greeting cards on his desk, at least a dozen from staff, some from clients, and others from names and addresses unfamiliar to him. He looked at the New York skyline as his secretary tapped on his glass door and entered. She tried to smile, her mouth not obeying, her eyes welling. "Oh, Mr. Vargas …" She walked across the office toward him.

Michael extended his hands and took hers in his. She said, "I've thought about you every day … prayed for you. The tragedy that happened to your family … there are not adequate words to express my sorrow."

"Thank you, Tina."

She stepped back, clasping her hands together, motioning to his desk. "As you can see, there are a lot of cards—from clients, members of our staff here and from our other offices, and from postmarks all over the world. You've also received tons of well-wishing emails. I know you'll be so involved in the Elysian Tower project, but there are some ancillary things I can run by you after you settle back in your office." She bit her lower lip. "I'm so glad you're back. Please let me know if there's anything I can do for you."

"Nothing pressing at the moment. Thanks, Tina."

She smiled, starting to leave and turned back around to him. "Oh, Mr. Manning and Mr. Edelman want to take you to lunch. I've booked reservations at the Bistro Club." She nodded and left his office, going less than fifteen feet outside to her cubicle.

Michael stood by the computer screen next to the vertical podium where he kept his computer keyboard. He preferred to stand when he designed. It was something that had followed him like a shadow since he painted murals on the sides of buildings, always standing in front of a wall, board, or canvas. He felt more spontaneous, more creative, when he was on his feet, often without shoes.

He slipped off his leather, Italian-made loafers and stood in front of the screen. Touching the keyboard, the monitor quickly faded up from black to a screensaver image. It was the architectural rendering he'd drawn of the Elysian Tower, the finished concept as it would appear during the day. Michael tapped his keyboard and the image changed to a night scene from the same perspective. He stared at the light at the top of the tower spire, the light radiating out in all directions. He thought about what he'd experienced when his heart had stopped for ninety-three seconds. He remembered holding his hands up to the light, as if he could catch its energy—reaching to feel the source of its power, core, and inspiration.

Looking at his screen, he stood mesmerized by the light at the top of the tower. He slowly reached out to touch it, his fingers trembling.

The instance he touched the light, the screen cold to his fingertips, Adison Manning walked in his office and said, "Great! You're already back at it. In the office less than twenty minutes, and the urge to design has you up and running. I love it! We've kept abreast of your physical progress the best we could. Although I wish you'd checked in more often. The entire staff was worried. You had a splendid team of doctors at your side that awful night. How are you feeling?"

Michael withdrew his hand from the image, looked over the screen to Manning. "Physically I'm fine. Emotionally, not so much. We need to talk. There's something I have to tell you."

FIFTEEN

Michael stepped around his computer screen, glanced at the New York skyline out the window, and turned to face Adison Manning. "I've had a lot of time to think."

Manning held up the palm of one hand and grinned. He licked his dry lips, eyes worried. "Before you tell me what it is you've been thinking about, can I ask you to wait until lunch? I'd like for Edelman and myself to officially welcome you back and hear whatever it is that's on your mind. This morning in the office will give you time to settle in, maybe speak with a few of your clients, get back in the saddle, okay?"

"Adison, I won't be here for lunch."

"What do you mean? You're a full partner."

"Not after today. I'm very appreciative of everyone here. I'm glad that I had the chance to work with you. It was you who gave me the opportunity to rise to where I am today. And I will always be grateful. But it's not where I want to be."

"What do you mean? You've spent the last twenty years of your life climbing the ladder. Now you're at the very top."

"I don't want to spend the next twenty years trying to figure out how to get off it. I'm through climbing corporate ladders. I'd rather be climbing mountains, painting landscapes. All I want to chase anymore is the elusive daylight, trying to capture in paint what nature reveals between the shadows as the sun plays hide and seek with its light. I've always loved impressionist art. It's in my roots. I want to go back … to return to that one thing I can do that offers something far beyond money. It's personal joy. And, if other people like what I do, maybe it can be shared."

Manning was at a loss for words. "What you do here is shared all over the world."

"But I don't want to do it anymore. I need to return to my art. No mechanical pencils. No computer graphics. No 3D animation or virtual reality. Just goin' back to the basics of oil paint, a brush, and a canvas."

"You're known as a great architect, Michael. You want to slip into obscurity as … as a painter?"

"At this time, nothing could be more appealing or rewarding."

Manning took a deep breath and looked at the image of the Elysian Tower on the screen. "You've undergone two horrible life experiences. You lost your wife and daughter, and two months later, you nearly lost your own life when some deranged druggie shot you. You're not thinking clearly. No one could be under those awful circumstances. Michael, you've reached your breaking point. And it's not your fault. You just need time."

"I can't create time … but I can create within the remaining time I've been given. I need to prioritize, to do what I'd buried in my heart. If I don't make time for myself, who will? Time is so finite, so precious, the most priceless resource we have, and that's what makes it so valuable. Time doesn't wind up in the lost and found bin like car keys, cell phones and dust bunnies. You can't put it in a canning jar, punch holes in the lid and capture time like fireflies. Both have a short shelf life. Adison, what I'm trying to say is, since our time is so limited, I won't waste it. To do so, is to waste life itself. And the gift of life is irreplaceable."

"Before you walk away from everything you worked toward, think hard about it. Think about the consequences of quitting." He motioned to the computer screen. "Look at that. It's a masterpiece of architectural design—your design and creation. You are, not only in my opinion, but in that of many other people in and out the industry … you are the greatest architect of our time. Hell, maybe even of all time. You owe it to your profession, your colleagues, even the world, to finish the Elysian Tower. You can't walk away from something you put your blood, sweat and tears into for so long. This tower, when built, will truly be one of the greatest wonders of the world. You can't turn your back on it."

"I'm not turning my back on it. I'm giving you the opportunity to move it forward. I'm handing it off to you, the other architects here, the clients and the construction company. The design and the construction plans are done. I finished them. You know that. The blueprint is here. You and your team can take the torch and light the top of the tower with it. You don't need me to do that. And I don't need to do it anymore." Michael walked by Manning, heading for the door.

Manning said, "If you change your mind … the job will still be here for you. Just don't wait too long."

"I won't change my mind, and I've already waited too long. Goodbye, Adison. Build Elysian … I look forward to visiting it one day." Michael stopped by his secretary's desk and briefly hugged her. He walked down the long hallway to the elevator, never looking back.

* * *

Michael spent the next two weeks going through every room in his apartment, packing boxes, trying to decide what to keep, what to put in storage, and what to leave behind. When he slid open the door to Kelsey's closet, he reached out and touched one of her winter coats, his hand simply resting on the shoulder of the coat. He remembered the first time she'd worn it. They were going out to a Christmas party the third year of their marriage. *"How does it look?"* She smiled and turned around like a model.

"On you, it looks great."

Michael withdrew his hand from the coat, eyes moist. He closed the closet door and walked across the master bedroom to the large, sliding glass door, which overlooked another portion of the city different from the living room view. He stepped onto the terrace and paused, recalling the number of times he saw Kelsey out there in her favorite chair reading a book or magazine. He lowered himself into her chair, and then pulled his phone from a back pocket to call Kelsey's sister. "Ashley … it's Michael. I—"

"I don't want to even ask how you're doing. It seems like such an asinine question." Ashley, late forties, light brown hair parted in the center, stood in her kitchen, pouring coffee. "Since the funeral or rather the memorial for Kelsey and Mandy ... after you were shot ... it's still been like some kind of horror movie ... attending Mom's funeral and worrying about you in the hospital. Are you back at work?"

"No, I'm not going back."

"Ever?"

"Ever."

"Oh, then what are you going to do?"

"I'm putting the condo on the market and moving out of New York. I listed it yesterday with a friend—she's a top real estate agent in town."

"Michael, where on earth will you go? How can you walk away from the career as one of the best architects in the—"

"Ashley, just listen, okay? I don't know where I'm going, but I know I can't stay here. Not any longer. Too many memories. You and Kelsey were about the same size. I'm leaving her clothes in the closets. Maybe you can come over and take what you want. Same thing with Mandy's things ... if you know someone with children. If not, I'll give them to charity. The items that Kelsey and I bought together ... the stuff with shared memories, I'm boxing and putting in storage. I'm leaving most of my suits. They should fit your husband, Simon. If not, I'll have them boxed and given to charity."

"What about the furniture?

"I'm selling the condo furnished."

"Michael, what's going on? You're leaving New York as the best-known architect in the city, maybe the world. You're giving away all your clothes and stuff. I know you've been through hell, through the worst trauma. But you can't just walk away from all you've accomplished."

"Sure, I can. Should have done it sooner. Maybe Kelsey and Mandy would still be with us."

"The plane crash was not your fault. More than two hundred other people died in the disaster. Maybe getting shot by a mugger is your fault because you went in there, into a dimly-lit park, knowing that creep had a gun. But that's a whole different story. When are you leaving?"

"Late today."

"I can't get there before Friday. Maybe Saturday if I can get Simon to come help me."

"That's fine. I'll give you the realtor's contact information. She knows to unlock the doors for you. Please let me know when you're done. Thanks."

"The realtor, her name, is it Teresa Darnell? If it is, remember that she's one of the star agents on that Bravo TV show. Last thing you want is somebody like her parading gawkers through your apartment. You're famous. People are weird. It's not enough to—"

"Her name's Margie Wallace. She's not on any TV show. When it comes to her clients, she uses the upmost discretion, and for the potential buyers, too." He glanced at his watch. "I have to go. Take care of yourself." He disconnected, walked back into the room, and tossed his phone on the bed.

Michael folded jeans, T-shirts, a pair of boat shoes, packing everything neatly and putting it all in a black suitcase. He picked up the suitcase and phone, turned off the light and walked out of the room. In the living room, he headed for the sliding glass door to the outdoor terrace. He started to lock the door, glancing at the cityscape and then down to the little troll he had left on the table.

He opened the door, stepped onto the terrace and picked up the toy. *"What is it about Poppy that made you want to bring her into our family?"*

"I just wanted to. She's nice. And she loves to sing."

Michael stared at the toy's wide eyes. "Poppy, are you a little tired of this view? What do you say we go on a road trip, just the two of us, okay?" He stepped back in the apartment, locked the door, unzipped his suitcase and placed the toy inside. "Take a nap. When you wake up, you will be in a land far, far away."

SIXTEEN

Michael looked out the window as the big jet touched down on the airport runway in Charleston and wondered if he was making the wrong decision. Because it was here, as a boy, where he was told his decisions didn't matter—because he didn't matter. At least not when it came time to choose his life's goals. He was too inexperienced, too naïve, too ignorant to understand the complexities of the world, or so his father thought. That line of thinking became harsher when the old man was deep into a bottle of whiskey and his own insecurities. Michael wasn't sure if he was arriving home again or passing through a place that he once believed was his home.

Charleston was his birthplace, where the cornerstone of childhood imagination was set, where youthful dreams were nurtured or extinguished. His parents were both dead. He had no remaining family here. But he had roots, an ancestry that was planted in the South Carolina Lowcountry's sandy soil, where he roamed the tidal flats fishing and playing as a boy. He could never forget the musty scent of the life blooming in the marshes—the shrimp and crabs scurrying around the flats like shadows crawling on sand and mud just beneath the water. Oyster bars baking in the sun at low tide. The sunrises that turned the marsh grasses into stems of gold.

All these years later, there was still a tidal pull on his heart. He could feel it as he remembered watching and listening to the surf breaking under the light of a full moon. Tasting it in the salt marshes and smelling it when a soft rain soaked the long gray beards of Spanish moss as it hung from the old oaks along the dirt roads of Edisto Island. He couldn't deny the impact this place, this culture, had on his soul any more than he could deny his birthright.

But Michael carried old scars from a southern culture that, in those days, sometimes turned a blind eye to physical abuse when it happened behind closed doors and within the family. He was in the fifth grade the first time his father hit him with a closed fist. It took two weeks for the black eye to heal. No one in his school, teachers or administrators, asked him why his eye was partially swollen shut. Maybe, today, he had returned home to lick and cauterize old wounds that never fully healed and then to walk on, pushing straight through the ghosts of the past as he sought a new future.

While Michael waited for his suitcase to tumble onto the baggage carousel, he thought about the irony—the juxtaposition of emotions. Charleston, with its history, harbors, and threshold to the Atlantic, was now his port-of-call. He returned to his place of birth like the sea turtles did years after darting across the sand into the relative safety of the ocean. More than two decades ago, he'd cut through the anchor chain, pushed off and swore never to return.

But there truly was a song of the South that strummed his heartstrings with a harmony of sights, sounds, smells, and traditions. It was music to his soul. The cryptic melody called him back like some mythical Siren in the mist. The source of the composition, like the wellspring of his creative spirit that bubbled up from this region, had always been the invisible wind in his sails. The nurturing bosom of the South summoned Michael to it with a magnetic pull he didn't fully understand. He felt like a migratory bird compelled to fly south in search of sustenance found nowhere else.

But where to begin?

He picked up a rental car, tossed his bag in the backseat and had no idea where he was going. Beyond booking the one-way plane ticket and reserving the rental car, he'd done nothing else. No hotel room reservation. No phone calls to a few remaining friends. Nothing except an exit from New York. Michael sat in the car inside the rental car pavilion not far from the airport terminal's baggage claim area. He looked at the car key, the ignition start button, but didn't press it. He stared at the second hand on his watch. Time moving. *Tick … tick … tick …*

He gripped the steering wheel and closed his eyes, trying not to think about his conversation with Adison Manning and then with his sister-in-law, Ashley.

You're known as a great architect. You want to slip into obscurity as … as a painter?

Michael, what's going on? You're leaving New York as the best-known architect in the city, maybe the world.

He wasn't running away because he had nothing to run toward except a silent calling, a veiled itch, like a button missing from the fabric of his identity. Maybe there was some unfinished, personal business he needed to accomplish, something buried in his southern past that could help chart a path for the future. All he knew was that he had to leave the frenetic hustle of New York and discover some kind of stillness. He longed for moments to breathe deeply, to sit in the crook of an old oak tree limb and watch the moon rising above the marshes on a summer's eve, to linger over a bowl of shrimp, rice and tomatoes served on the back porch of a home on Daufuskie Island.

He started the car, put it in gear and headed toward town. He wouldn't use the GPS on his phone because he no longer wanted to follow the lead of technology. He wanted to trace roots that led back to the crossroads of his past, to a place where he compromised his heart so long ago. He'd go back there, if possible, back to the intersection of defining moments in his life. And with luck and perseverance, he might find the junction he'd missed.

And, for the first time in a long time, he knew where to start.

SEVENTEEN

Michael drove straight to the Charleston Harbor. Although he hadn't been to the specific area in years, he followed the road by instinct and the few landmarks that remained. Crossing the Ravenel Bridge, he could see the tall steeple of St. Michael's Church in the historic waterfront district. In the distance, he spotted Shutes Folly Island, the remains of the Castle Pinckney, and a large freighter churning the waters where the Cooper River joined the Atlantic Ocean. From the old seawall monument, called The Battery, to the iconic and colorful Georgian houses of Rainbow Row to Liberty Square, he knew the area.

It was where he'd first painted in public. He remembered the newspaper stories written about the mural he'd painted on the side of the abandoned building that, twenty-three years earlier, had been the headquarters for Cooper River Marine and Boatworks. Michael recalled the time he was interviewed by a newspaper reporter, going back to the location with the reporter and a photographer to take pictures of the mural. They wanted him to stand in front of his painting and to face the direction of the harbor and docks. *"Look as if you're watching an eighteenth-century schooner arrive in the port,"* suggested the photographer with tousled, dark hair.

Michael's mother had clipped the story from the Sunday paper and saved it. He was amazed at the interest from the public, people making special trips down to the waterfront to see and take pictures of the mural. One food truck vendor had set up near it and sold out of food the first day, and many weekends thereafter.

Michael remembered what the mayor had said during a follow-up TV news interview sometime in the spring of Michael's senior year. "It is historically accurate and reflects the early history of the area. I only wish the building didn't have to be razed or there was a way we could preserve the one wall that Michael Vargas painted. I'm glad residents and tourists alike will be able to enjoy it for a few more months."

But Michael didn't stay for all of the remaining months. Before he left for college in the fall, he'd spent as much time as possible taking art lessons from Derek Mack. He'd thought about those lessons and the man who so freely gave them. Derek never charged money, only insisting that his students practice and spend the time needed to master the challenges of painting—especially on-location, impressionist painting.

"Strive for a sense of awe in your work," he recalled Derek saying the first time they'd painted on location, walking up to a mammoth old oak tree on St. Johns Island. "It's called the Angel Oak," he said, his eyes roaming the tree from top to bottom. "The Angel is more than five hundred years old. Imagine the history it has witnessed."

The tree was the largest Michael had ever seen, its girth near the ground was as wide as a pickup truck is long. Seven of its massive limbs touched the ground, like the old tree was bracing itself or preparing to walk away. He remembered Derek saying, "Nature delivers a sense of awe in everything she does. Whether it's a summer storm building over the marshes, or light pouring through the limbs and fingers of the ancient oaks, the artist must capture the energy of life in that brief time. And that moment will be fleeting. That's why you must learn to paint with quick, bold strokes. Make it instinctual from your eye, through your heart and to your hand. Once you give yourself permission to do so, you'll paint freer, and the honesty of your work will complement the awe that first attracted you to your subject. Never try to copy nature. Be influenced by it and seize the scene in front of you—the light, the life … if there are flowers, strive to paint the fragrance that you're experiencing at the time. If you want your audience to see that … to feel that, then you must feel it first and even deeper."

Michael drove by Marion Square, then down Calhoun Street toward the docks and waterfront. When he approached the block where the Cooper River Boatworks once stood, he pulled over to the side of the road, parking near crepe myrtles filled with pink blooms and the sound of bees. He got out of his car, the old warehouse long since gone, and in its place was a high-rise condo complex with a six-foot-high, wrought iron fence around the property. Through the fence, he could see a swimming pool on the ground level, the sun reflecting off parked cars, and residents lounging by the pool. The Tom Petty song, *Free Fallin,'* drifted from the outdoor speakers.

Michael looked up more than twenty stories toward the penthouse suites, some residents sitting on balconies. One shirtless man in sweatpants was opening the cover to a grill and fanning the billow of white smoke from his face. Michael got back in his car and drove down to the harbor. He parked, got out, and walked toward the docks, a marine horn blasting as a sightseeing boat pulled away, tourists snapping pictures.

Michael walked the docks, boats creaking as they bobbled, tugging against the lines, the wind across the harbor warm in his face, the smell of salt and marine paint in the air. Gulls dipped and soared, beating their wings and chortling above the masts of sailboats. He watched a ferryboat pull away from the docks, heading to Fort Sumter, two dolphins following the boat's wake, as if they were playing a water sport.

He remembered the slip where Derek Mack had docked his wooden sloop, *Simplicity.* With its sleek lines, teak wood, brass fittings, the classic sailboat made a statement even while tied in its slip, like a thoroughbred horse in a locked paddock before a race. Michael strolled down the docks, past the sign that read: *Boat owners and guests only.* He came to slip H-29. The old boat, of course, was no longer there. In its place was a glistening white powerboat, more than forty feet long, a for sale sign hanging from the safety line near the cockpit.

Three tall masts at the very end of the pier caught his eye. He walked down the long dock toward what appeared to be a floating nautical mirage. However, the illusion was real and looked as if it had sailed off a page of history into the mouth of Charleston Harbor. And for Michael, it hit even closer to home. It was an Old World, three mast-schooner—a sailing ship from the land of the ancient mariner.

And it was a dead ringer to the schooner he'd painted in the mural years ago.

EIGHTEEN

Michael paced the end of the pier from the schooner's bow to its stern and thought about the mural he'd painted on the warehouse just a block away from where the sailing vessel was now moored. In his mural, the clipper ship he painted and the one docked at the city marina were uncannily similar—almost as if they were or had been the same. Probably close to a hundred feet in length, lots of polished wood, most of it appeared to be mahogany. On the transom was the name of the yacht—*Sea Wolf.*

There was a sign on a chain near the schooner that read:

Be part of the golden age of sailing aboard the schooner – Sea Wolf.
Sunset sails nightly: Tues – Sun.

Michael heard the planks of the dock creak as someone walked up behind him. "We set sail in four hours. Come join us."

He turned around, and a man in a captain's cap, mid-fifties, short gray beard, crinkles around his playful eyes smiled, gesturing toward the boat. "*Sea Wolf* is a replica of many of the schooners that sailed into this harbor from a trans-Atlantic voyage. The period, in its heyday, was from about 1850 through 1900. She's got the same classic lines of the American schooner that sailed to England, beat the British and won what was forever known after that as the America's Cup, sailed back and never looked back."

"She's a beautiful boat."

"Are you a sailor?"

"No, at least not in the sense of something this grand. Although, it's always been one of my fantasies, on the bucket list. When I was a kid, I used to sail a small Sunfish off Edisto Beach."

"You're a native, eh? I thought for a second you were a tourist. Most of the customers are tourists. We get the locals, too. Depends on the time of year. More often for special occasions—charters for weddings, big family reunions and whatnot."

Michael smiled. "I might as well be a tourist. I've been gone from here for most of my life."

The captain fished a pipe from a deep pocket in his khaki shorts and tapped the bowl of unlit tobacco with a stubby index finger. "Where'd you go when you left here?" He used a vintage Zippo lighter to heat the tobacco, blowing smoke out the left side of his mouth. The tobacco had the scent of cherries and apples.

Michael said, "New York. That's been my home for a long time. I just listed my condo there."

The captain studied Michael's face for a moment. "You sound like a man who's grown tired of the cold winters. Are you moving back to Charleston?"

"Maybe. At least for a while." He motioned to the transom of the schooner. "*Sea Wolf*, where did you get that name?"

The captain drew smoke though the pipe, blowing it into the breeze. "She was already named. I'm thinking the original name came from Jack London's novel, *Sea Wolf*. Although, in that book, the sailing ship was called *Ghost*."

"I sort of feel like I'm seeing a ghost ship."

"Why is that?"

"Because, years ago, as a teenager, I painted a large mural on the outside of an old warehouse that long since was torn down. It's a condo now a block up the street. But back then, I painted a schooner coming into Charleston Harbor, before the Civil War … around 1855. It looked a lot like your yacht. And the name, *Sea Wolf*, is the same. I'd painted it on the boat in my mural. I used to bury myself in art and books. *Sea Wolf* was one of my favorites."

The captain's blue eyes opened wider. He clenched the pipe stem between his teeth. "You're the one! Finally!"

"The one … what do you mean?"

"The painter. For years I've wondered who the prodigy was—the painter. And I don't use that term, prodigy, lightly. Come aboard, please. I want to show you something."

Michael followed the captain up the gangplank onto the deck of the sailboat. He led him into the wheelhouse. The polished wooden wheel, with its ornate spokes and intricate carving, was the diameter of a car tire. The captain pointed to a pecky cypress wall. Among the framed maritime certificates and two pictures of him posing with the former governor of South Carolina and one with a well-known Lowcountry author, was a framed picture of the mural Michael had painted.

The captain said, "I took that picture the day the construction cranes and the wrecking ball arrived. I was so moved by your art, what you'd left behind on that wall, that it inspired me to do what I always wanted to do."

"What was that?"

"To own and operate a charter boat like this one. After I took the picture, I was fortunate enough to inherit some money from an estate years later. I found the picture I took, hired some of the best marine architects, and they designed this schooner you're standing in today. Your work was so stellar, so inspiring, when I first saw it, I stared at the mural for a half-hour, standing in the same spot. I came back a dozen times before the building was destroyed. I've always wanted to meet the artist. And now I have."

He took the photo off the wall and used a pipe stem to point to the signature in the lower right corner. "Vargas! What a name. What a painting. It drew me to it like a moth to a flame. I felt like I was on the docks, in the shadow of this yacht two hundred years ago."

Michael held the framed picture, Derek Mack's words haunting, like a prophecy that took decades to fulfill. *It's as if the viewer is swept through time and place. They should see and feel the scene as if they were standing right there, too. This, Michael, is the mystery and the magic of great art. We see it, but most vital is that we feel it on an emotional level.*

The captain said, "Anytime you or your family want to sail, it's free. You gave me something, the least I can do is return it in some small way."

"Thank you."

"Can you join us this evening? The crew will be here in a couple of hours. We have a dozen guests. Please, join us."

"Thanks, but I can't. There is someone I must see."

NINETEEN

Michael drove a little faster than the speed limit. He wanted to get there before dark, but he didn't want to risk a speeding ticket, especially driving a rental car. The last time he was on the property, he was eighteen. But he remembered the way. Three acres on the Intercoastal, a Lowcountry home with wrap-around porches, lots of open-screen windows, and the jazz and blues music Derek Mack always played from vinyl albums in the adjacent art studio.

He remembered Derek's wife, Jewell, too. She'd been a warm person with a wide smile and a great sense of humor, and she was an artist as well. She hand-drew scenes and captions for greeting card companies. Funny cards for birthdays, especially children's birthdays, were her specialty.

When Michael pulled off the road and onto the gravel driveway, he drove beneath century-old oaks, acorns popping under his tires. The house was exactly as he remembered it. The low-slung feel of a 1950s fish camp, a half-dozen blue crab traps stacked beneath a lean-to shed. The weathervane was still on top of one of the gables, the mermaid figure facing the wind. A canoe was turned upside down and positioned between two railroad crossties, pine needles on top of the canoe. A small boat on a trailer was parked near a weeping willow tree between the home and the art studio.

There was a late model pickup truck in the driveway, near the front porch. Michael parked and got out, walking up the four steps to the wooden front porch. He stood there for a moment, two blue jays squawking in one of the oaks, a dog barking in the distance, the briny smell of the marshes on the eastward breeze. He rang the doorbell and waited. He could hear someone stirring inside the home. Michael hoped he wasn't disturbing their dinner.

There was the sound of two locks moving, a chain and then a deadbolt. Although times had changed in all these years, Michael remembered that Derek and Jewell had rarely locked their doors during the day. The studio was always open, mostly in the event one of his students needed a hot meal and a place to stay for a night or two. "The artists," he once said, sipping his black coffee, steam fogging his glasses, "sometimes are like lost sheep. All they need is kindness, a cot, and maybe a good shepherd to help point the way."

The door opened a few inches, and in the dappled light, two suspicious eyes stared out at Michael. "Hi, I'm Michael Vargas. I was wondering ... does Derek Mack still live here?"

"Who?" The woman's voice was raspy, as if he'd awakened her.

"Derek Mack. He taught art in the studio out back. I was one of his many students. He's probably long since retired. I'm trying to find him."

The woman opened the door a little more. She looked to be in her late forties, tousled hair in need of a brush, ripped jeans and a black hoodie. "There's no one here by that name. My husband and I bought the place about three years ago. As I understand it, the property had gone through a few owners. It was in need of renovation. Septic system was not very good. High water out here, you know."

"With the Intercoastal almost in your backyard, I guess that's why it's called the Lowcountry." He smiled. "Well, thank you for your time. I hope I didn't disturb your dinner."

"No bother." She paused as if she was trying to remember someone's face. "What'd you say the man's name was?"

"Derek Mack."

She nodded. "We purchased this house furnished. A man, his wife and two kids lived here for five years before we bought the place. We didn't keep all the furniture, but we did keep a painting on the living room wall. It's a beautiful painting of a sunrise over the marshes. It's got a little cottage in it and a mother and small child walking next to the water. The expression on the mother's face reminds me a lot of my mother. The signature on the painting is one word, Mack. We didn't know if it was someone's first or last name. Maybe it's the same fella."

"Yes, I remember when he finished that painting."

A tabby cat appeared between the woman's legs, next to her bare feet, chipped pink polish on her toenails. Michael smiled. "I appreciate your time."

"No worries. If you see the artist, tell him how much we like his painting."

"I'll do that."

* * *

It was after nine p.m. when Michael checked in a hotel near the center of Charleston's historic warehouse district by the harbor. Some of the old structures were originally built in the later part of the 1700s. The renovated hotel had the charm of the period—French tapestry rugs over polished hardwood floors, brass lighting fixtures, and overstuffed chairs in alcoves with bookshelves lined against the walls. Many of the books were about the history of Charleston and South Carolina. Framed oil paintings, lit with low wattage bulbs, were on walls in the lobby and the hallways.

Michael took the elevator to the third floor, unlocking the door to his room. He set his suitcase on the corner of the bed, stepped to the sliding glass doors and opened them, the view overlooking Charleston Harbor. He could see Fort Sumter and Sullivan's Island across the bay, lights like stars twinkling off the surface of the dark water. He thought about what the woman in the house had said, *The signature on the painting is one word … Mack. We didn't know if it was someone's first or last name.*

Michael pulled his laptop computer from his suitcase, sat at the desk and went online. He searched the local obituaries, looking for death notices. It didn't take him long to find what he was looking for—at least part of what he was searching to find. He read the obituary written for Jewell Mack. She had died twelve years earlier after a long fight with cancer. *Mrs. Mack was a greeting card illustrator whose work helped to brighten the lives of untold numbers of people through her thirty-year career. But it was her giving and warm personality that would shine on everyone she met. She is survived by her loving husband of forty-five years, Derek Mack. Mr. Mack is a well-known painter whose work is appreciated by collectors around the world.*

Michael searched further and couldn't find any reference to the death of Derek. *Maybe he was still alive. But where? Did he move from the area?* He closed his eyes, took a deep breath and slowly exhaled, thinking about one of the times Derek's wife had delivered a pot of chili to the students in the art studio. Derek would look up from working with a student and say, *"Jewell, God bless her, she remembers that we should not be starving artists while in her home."* He'd laugh and shuffle across the room to give his wife a hug. *"She's my precious Jewell. No diamond can come close to her beauty."*

The students, including Michael, would grin, and Jewell would playfully say, *"That doesn't mean that diamonds aren't a girl's best friend."*

Michael took a deep breath, the sound of a freighter's horn somewhere in the harbor. He looked at the sheer drapes in front of the open sliding glass door, the curtains curling in the night breeze. He closed his laptop, pushed away from the desk and mumbled, "Where are you, Derek? Still in Charleston … still alive? I met a lady who told me that a woman in one of your paintings reminded her of her mother. So, you're living on through your art. I'm going downstairs to the bar where I will raise a glass to you."

TWENTY

It was a step back in time for Michael. The bar evoked a Charleston of yesteryear. There was a replica of a 1733 map of Charleston Harbor framed and under glass on one wall. Dark woods, ambient lighting embedded in cherry wood, plush leather club chairs, a fireplace and fine art paintings. The bar itself made a near circle, a dozen high-top chairs aligned in front, the bartender pouring a martini into a chilled glass.

Three people sat at the bar. A half-dozen customers sat in club chairs, flickering candlelight bouncing off their faces, cocktail and wine glasses on the tables. Laughter mixed with the soft music through hidden speakers, the soulful voice of Norah Jones singing, *Come Away With Me.*

Michael took a seat at the bar. He nodded at a man and a woman a few seats away, the man in a steel gray suit, maroon tie loosened. The woman, a blonde dressed in a black business suit with white trim, smiling, red lipstick on the edge of her empty wine glass.

The bartender, late thirties, trimmed moustache, quick hands and eyes, used a white towel to polish a glass. He approached Michael. "Yes sir … what can I get for you this evening?"

"Stella Artois, if you have it."

"Absolutely." The bartender opened a cooler, removed a bottle of beer, popped the top and set it on a napkin with a tall glass in front of Michael. "Enjoy, sir."

"Thank you." Michael poured the beer into the glass, watching the foam rise. Out of the corner of his eye, he noticed a woman sitting alone looking in his direction. He finished his pour and shifted his eyes over to the woman who sat directly opposite him on the other side of the bar. He assumed that she was near his age. Dark brown hair, worn just below her shoulders. High cheekbones. Full lips. And, even from a distance of ten feet, her hazel eyes were absorbing, as if she knew a secret about you. Michael nodded, the woman returning a warm smile, and then glanced at her half-empty martini glass. She touched the rim of the glass with one finger, staring at the red polish, maybe thinking it was time to book her next manicure.

Michael sipped his beer. He thought about the obituary he'd read in his room. He recalled that Derek and Jewell Mack had no children of their own. Instead, they fostered young artists, always trying to give them encouragement along with lessons in art and life. He had been one of them, and many of those lessons had stuck. All except one—the one that, now in retrospect, was the most important. It was one of the last things Derek had said to him. *"Your greatest, personal offense to yourself, a felony of the heart perhaps, would be to not follow your talents. It may not be immoral but, in the long run, in those lonely times of self-reflection, you'll feel you've cheated yourself. I don't believe you can ever atone for that. In your heart, Michael, is where your true talent lives."*

Michael sat back in his chair and looked at some of the artwork on the walls. The genres ranged from still life, abstract, portraits, cubism and surrealism. There was one landscape painting. It was on the wall behind the woman nursing her martini. Even from the distance, Michael knew the artist because he recognized the style of the painting. And, even from across the bar, he was drawn to its composition and color. He'd found a painting by Derek Mack. Maybe he could find the man, too.

He got up from his chair and walked around the bar, the woman sipping the remains of her martini, smiling, her lips wet and sensuous, perfume faint. Michael moved by her and stood a few feet from the art. The painting was of a black family dressed in their Sunday best, the mother with a yellow sunhat and a flowing dark green dress, the father in a brown suit carrying an old Bible, a little girl wearing a blue-ruffled dress, the family entering a small brick church in the Gullah Lowcountry. Michael recognized the area, marshes in the background, an oak tree dripping with hanging moss in the foreground, the old church had been on the same spot since before the Civil War.

TOM LOWE

He'd never seen this particular painting, but the style, with its quick brush and knife strokes, was there. The colors and composition, the feel of Sunday morning dawning over the Lowcountry, the reverence the family has for what church means to them. It was all there. And at the lower right corner was the simple signature, *Mack.*

Michael stepped closer, reaching out with one finger to touch the signature. "That's a really beautiful painting," the woman at the bar said. She'd turned in her barstool, facing Michael, wide smile. "I love landscapes. I wonder if that was painted around here."

Michael nodded. "Yes, it was. It's from Daufuskie Island."

"It's lovely. Makes me try to remember the last time I went to church."

Michael said nothing, taking two steps back from the painting.

The woman on the barstool crossed her shapely legs, one black high heel shoe dangling from her foot. "I'm not from here, Atlanta's my home. Do you live in Charleston?"

"I grew up here. Moved away. And now I'm back ... at least for a while."

"It's a really great city ... so much history." She looked at the painting and then cut her eye back to Michael. "That place you mentioned, Daufuskie. Is it near here?"

"Not too far. It's one of the southernmost islands in the Lowcountry, south of Hilton Head. Lots of history and Gullah country charm on Daufuskie."

"Gullah, I've heard that term. Not exactly sure what it means."

Michael smiled. "The painting tells the story better than I can. Gullah is really a way of life for many people in the Lowcountry. It originally had more to do with the language, an English, Creole and African combination sometimes called Geechee. Daufuskie was short for the first key. Through the years, after slavery was abolished, the folks on some of the islands developed a culture of their own. The language, the food—seafood with soul, the sense of family, traditions and old-time religion ... is distinctive and has its own Lowcountry magic."

"I'd like to visit the area. I'm such a foodie, too. I love trying new dishes. You sure seem to know your Charleston history well."

"It's hard to grow up here and not be exposed to the history. The first shots of the Civil War were fired less than a mile from where you're sitting. Charleston was originally called Charles Town, as a tribute to the British King Charles. But some of the bloodiest fights for independence were fought in this harbor."

"Sounds like lots of fighting. Charleston today seems like such a romantic city." She glanced down at Michael's wedding ring. "Does your wife like Charleston?"

"She used to. She passed away."

"I'm sorry, really. I don't mean to pry." The woman crossed her legs again, her hands draped over the chair's armrests. "My name's Sharon Tatum … and you are?"

"Michael Vargas."

Sharon extended her hand. "Nice to meet you Michael Vargas. That's an interesting name, Vargas. Is it from German heritage?"

"No, it was exported from Spain."

"I don't want to appear nosey, but if you're from here, why are you in a hotel? Don't you have family in the area?"

"Not anymore. I'm sort of transitioning back."

"Well, let me be the first to buy you a welcome home drink." She signaled for the bartender. "Please bring my friend, Michael, another round. And while you're at it, I'd love another martini. You make them so good … they just slip down my throat."

"Glad you like them, ma'am. Comin' right up." He turned and began mixing the cocktail. Sharon looked at Michael. "There are seats on either side of me. You don't have to go to the other section of the bar, unless you like drinking alone. Also, with an easy stool spin, you can see that painting a lot better from here."

Michael smiled and took a seat on a barstool to her left, glancing back over his shoulder at the painting. She smiled. "You really seem to like that artwork. There are dozens of pictures hanging on the walls in this cozy bar. Can I ask what it is about that particular landscape that has such a strong attraction for you?"

"It's the composition, mostly. The painter knew what to paint. Sort of how Hemingway knew what to write, how to find the heart of a character-driven story. In art the viewer can only see what's in the frame. It's up to the painter to capture a scene that's worth framing. Beyond the composition, it's the use of color and light. But the most important thing in the mix is the way you feel when stepping up to the painting—the emotional connection you get."

"Sort of like love at first sight."

"That's one emotion. There are others, too. It's the artist's responsibility to create something that moves people."

The bartender brought the drinks. "Enjoy."

"We will," Sharon said, sipping her martini.

The bartender nodded and started to walk away when Michael said, "I like the art here in the hotel. It looks like management has made quite an effort to build this collection."

"Yes, sir. We've sort of become a destination for art lovers. During the day, the hotel offers two guided tours with our curator. One tour is in the morning at ten and the other is in the afternoon at three with tea. She walks guests through the hotel and its gallery, giving folks a brief history about the pieces in the collection and the artists. The artwork changes occasionally when the owner acquires new pieces. He takes some on loan, too."

"Are any of the paintings for sale?" Sharon asked.

"Yes, ma'am. Some are listed for sale. There's more about that on the hotel's website and in the gallery store. The proceeds go toward saving South Carolina's wildlife."

She smiled, her lips wet. "That's nice. How about the painting right behind us?" She motioned to the landscape. "Do you know if that one's for sale?"

"No, ma'am. I doubt it."

"Why?" she asked.

"Because the hotel owner is a good friend of the artist. The artist used to come in here a couple of times a month up until about a year or so ago. He'd have lunch with the owner. I've worked here seven years, but it's been awhile since I last saw the guy."

Michael said, "You mentioned that the hotel owner is a good friend of the artist, not was a good friend. Is the painter still alive?"

"Far as I know he's still with us. Man's name is Derek Mack. He does really good work. I don't know about the rest of the paintings in the hotel, but as far as the ones in this bar are concerned, that painting behind you seems to attract the most people lookin' at it. And, if people in a bar are lookin' at art, that's a good thing." He chuckled.

Michael smiled and sipped his beer. "What's the hotel owner's name?"

"Robert Wellborn."

"Do you know if he's in tomorrow?"

"Unless he's traveling, he's in every day. Usually in the morning for a few hours. He has this hotel and one more on Hilton Head."

"Thanks."

The bartender nodded and took a drink order from another customer. Sharon sipped her martini. "Are you going to try to buy that painting from the hotel owner."

"No."

"What if I bought it for you? Had room service deliver it to your room."

"Thanks, but no thanks. I don't want the painting."

"What do you want?"

"I don't want the painting because I have a good idea it was a gift for the owner. Most people don't sell something that was gifted to them." Michael stood next to the bar. "What I do want, though, is a good night's sleep. Thank you for the beer."

TWENTY-ONE

Michael could tell the man was the owner of the hotel just by the way he walked into the restaurant. Michael drank black coffee at his table. He watched the man as he moved through the hotel restaurant. He was impeccably dressed in a three-piece, powder blue suit. Late fifties, silver hair parted on the right side. He strolled in with a sense of proprietorship, his eyes taking in the entire dining room in fast glances—quickly inventorying the number of diners, the fresh-cut roses on the center of each table, the servers on duty and their appearance. He stopped near the middle of the room, seemed to nod to himself as if all met his morning inspection.

Michael stood as the man approached. He said, "Good morning, are you Mr. Vargas?"

"Yes, Michael will do fine, thanks."

He extended his hand. "Robert Wellborn. It's good to meet you. Thank you so much for staying with us. The concierge said you had some questions about a particular painting in the hotel."

"Yes, please have a seat." Wellborn sat at the table. Michael smiled. "It's not so much that I have questions about the painting … it's about the man who painted it."

"Oh, whom might that person be?"

"Derek Mack."

Wellborn's eyebrows arched. He leaned closer to the table, cleared his throat. "Yes, a remarkable artist. No doubt one of the greatest painters in South Carolina. In my opinion, Derek Mack has done more to capture the Lowcounty history and ambience than anyone else. I assume you saw his landscape in our Yacht Club Bar?"

"Yes. It's beautiful."

"He painted it a few years back, before he got sick. The scene is from Daufuskie Island. After Derek's wife died, he'd go down there a few days, set up his easel and paint, often leaving with at least two or three paintings. However, his work wasn't confined to Daufuskie, he painted scenes all over the South Carolina coast. But I think he had a special bond with the folks who call Daufuskie home."

"You said he did that painting before he got sick. Is he not well today?"

"Not so much in the physical sense. If you don't mind, may I ask you why the interest in Derek Mack?"

"He was my mentor at one time. That was a long time ago. I was one of many kids who took art lessons from him. He encouraged me to follow my passion, my love for art. But I took a different path and spent a lot of years doing what I really didn't want to be doing."

"That happens. Are you a painter now?"

"I want to return to it. I'm a little rusty. That's one of the reasons I wanted to touch base with Derek. Maybe do a couple of paintings and get his feedback. He was always a great teacher and mentor. It'd be good to revisit with him."

"When was the last time you saw Derek?"

"When I was a teenager. The first time I ever met him was on top of a wooden ladder painting a mural on the side of an abandoned building near Charleston Harbor. When Derek shouted to get my attention, I almost fell from the ladder. I thought he was going to call the police. But he did the exact opposite. He encouraged me to finish it. He offered suggestions on how to make it …" Michael paused, looking at the rose on the table. "He wanted the viewers to smell the flowers along the waterfront, which I didn't understand at the time how a painting could evoke a sense of smell. He was patient. I soon got the metaphor, finished it, and signed my name."

Wellborn smiled, nodding. "Did the mural have a sailing schooner unloading on the waterfront?"

"Yes, it did."

"I've lived here all my life. Always been very interested in fine art. I remember seeing the mural in the local paper. By the time I got around to going down there to view it, the building was in the midst of being demolished. I wonder if you are or were the prodigy that I heard Derek mention."

"I doubt it. He taught a lot of students over the years."

"Yes, but over a bottle of wine and dinner here at the hotel, he once mentioned the young painter who '*got away*' as he called it. He wasn't making a refence to some kind of catch-and-release education in art. He was referring to someone who had an instinctive, commanding, innate talent who chose to go another direction and did so because of negative influences."

Michael said nothing, looking across the room at a painting illustrating a Civil War battle scene in Charleston, cannons and rifles firing, ships in the harbor ablaze. Young men dying.

Wellborn said, "I don't think he was bothered so much that one of his art students had taken a different direction in life, that happens. Probably the norm. But what I believe he referred to had more to do with his own personal failure because he wasn't able, as a teacher, to override the negative forces in the student that had been planted by seeds of doubt and insecurity. I think he was like a coach who recognized the progress in a natural athlete who refused to join the sport, walking away from college scholarships, maybe a shot at the pros or even in the Olympics."

"If Derek is here in Charleston, I'd like to go see him."

Wellborn looked away, his gaze following a family that the restaurant hostess was seating at a table in the center of the room. He eyed Michael. "That might be difficult to do."

"Why? Please don't tell me he has cancer and is in Hospice."

"He's not, at least not yet. He's suffering from another kind of slow death. He has the first stages of Alzheimer's disease. He knows it, and he's doing his best to deal with the prognosis. He hasn't painted in a while now. I doubt he ever will again." He took a deep breath and released it. "I'm sorry to have to tell you that."

Michael started to sip his coffee but put the cup back in the saucer, his mouth dry. "Can you tell me where I can find him? Is he in some kind of elder care?"

"No, not yet. He's living in a small home … a cottage, really. It's on the Isle of Palm overlooking the bay. He's been there since his wife died, which is when he sold the house they lived in for forty years."

"When was the last time you saw him?"

"A couple of weeks ago. My wife and I visited with him. His progression appears to be slow, but it's definitely there, and the doctors tell him it'll only become much worse over time."

"Do you have the address?"

"Yes, I can get it for you. When do you want to go there?"

"Right now."

"All right. Please keep in mind that he may not remember you. May never remember you as one of his students. And, if you are or were the young man who was the sensation he talked about, even that might not jar his memory if he's slipped further into the grasp of the disease."

TWENTY-TWO

Michael wasn't sure what he'd say when he knocked on the door. He drove under old canopies of longstanding oaks with moss dangling from their knotty shoulders, mottled sunlight streaming through limbs thicker than many trees. He followed the GPS directions, turning onto a gravel road. The hamlet of riverfront cottages had the look and feel of bungalows built in the 1970s, single-story and small, many originally used as weekend getaways.

The cottage was exactly the way Robert Wellborn had described it—one-story, pine wood exterior painted olive green, front porch for sitting, a brick fireplace poking through the back of the aged shingle roof. Michael parked his car near a crepe myrtle tree filled with lavender flowers and the whirr of bees. He sat behind the wheel for a moment, window down, watching the cottage, hoping he'd see a curtain move or a lift in a blind. Nothing moved except a squirrel scampering up a tall pine to the left of the house.

There was a hopeful sight. Baskets of petunias and ferns hung from the eaves of the front porch. Michael could tell that the flowers had been watered and looked in full bloom, the ferns appeared verdant, deep green and thriving. He got out of his car and walked up the wooden steps to the front porch. A breeze from the river delivered the musty scent of rotting leaves and honeysuckles. There were two white rocking chairs on the porch, a small wicker table between them.

He knocked on the door. There were no sounds from someone stirring. He waited, his throat dry, a windchime on the porch softly jingling in the breeze. He heard the hammering drone of a woodpecker at the top of a dead cypress tree. Michael waited a few more seconds and knocked again, this time louder.

There was a sound from inside.

Someone moving slow, shuffling across the wooden floor.

The door opened and a man that Michael barely recognized stood in the shadows. Derek Mack seemed smaller. Shoulders slumped. Silver hair disheveled. His face narrower, hollowed, dark circles under puffy eyes. Heavy creases on the sides of his downturned mouth. Short patches of bristly white whiskers like weeds sprouting through cracks in the sidewalk. His eyes, once playful, were suspicious. The odor of old clothes lingering in the shadows. "Can I help you?" he said, his voice raspy.

"Robert Wellborn gave me directions to your home. I'm staying in his hotel. Last night I saw one of your paintings of Daufuskie. I was drawn to it. I could feel Sunday morning coming down, almost hear the sounds of a choir singing inside the church."

The old man nodded and smiled. "Well, that's good."

"I don't know if you remember me, but I was one of your students a long time ago. You found me at the top of a ladder painting a mural down by the Charleston waterfront."

Derek angled his head. He stepped out onto the front porch, his eyes roaming over Michael's face. "I do remember you."

"You helped me put life into the mural, and when I finally signed my last name, Vargas, it was one of my proudest moments."

The old man's eyes welled. "Vargas … Michael Vargas. You've returned." He lifted his arms, and they embraced, Michael's eyes misting. Derek's body seemed small and frail in his arms. After a moment, they stepped back, and Derek said, "I've thought about you often. For years I never saw hide nor hair of you. Then, almost outa the blue, I'd see your face on the covers of magazines. I read all about your career as the best architect in New York City."

"I don't know about the best. I just worked very hard at it. Too hard, frankly."

Derek stared at Michael, as if the dull edge of memory was suddenly sharpened. "Even in the pictures of the buildings you drew, I could see your style. For the most part, it was confined to straight lines, but it was there." He chuckled. "Let's sit on the porch. I want to hear all about your life."

They took seats in the rocking chairs, and Michael asked, "How are you doing?"

"Not too bad for a man in his seventies. We can talk about me later. I want to hear about you, if that's okay?"

"Sure, that's fine." Michael told his former mentor about his success as an architect and the events of late that changed his priorities and everything else in his life. Derek listened without interruption as Michael concluded. "And, so now I'm back. Not sure which direction life will lead me, but I want to do it with a paint brush in my hands."

Derek nodded. "I'm so very sorry to hear about your wife and daughter. And, despite what some people say, even some therapists, there's no moving on because your wife and child will always be part of your life. You can move forward, but you do it with those memories always in tow. He lowered his eyes, staring at the back of his right hand, his painting hand, now bent and checkered with brown age spots. "Grief is a pickpocket of the soul. Just when you gain a sense of poise, something reminds you of the person you lost. You reach for that keepsake of them, but its stolen from your breast pocket, the pocket closest to your heart. Time doesn't heal that kind of suffering. After I lost Jewell, I didn't have the passion for life I had with her. But, in those long, quiet moments of grief, of self-induced misery, I'd hear her voice reminding me I must still live the gift of life. I had to get off my chair of sorrow and move."

"What'd you do?"

"That painting you saw in the hotel, the one that you said you could almost hear the choir singing inside the old church … that was the first one I did after Jewell died. I stood there the whole Sunday morning, watching families come and go to church services. It was cathartic for me to be wearing my old straw hat and working outside again."

"It's a great painting." Michael paused, looked at the wind chimes, then shifted his gaze back to Derek. "Robert Wellborn told me about your battle with Alzheimer's disease. Is there anything I can do to help you? Anything … no matter how large or small."

"I'm told there's little that can be done. The doctors call it a slow deterioration of the cognitive ability—the organization, of my brain. They've given me some pills they say may slow it down a bit, put a bridle in the mouth of an insidious disease. But there's no cure."

He rocked in his chair for a moment, stopped, his eyes lingering on Michael's face. "I'm taking it in stride. I know what's happening to me. I don't know why, but I'm aware of my changing condition. I suppose what should frighten me is when I'm no longer aware of that … I'm just whatever's left of me at that point. No reason to be afraid, I suppose. Because I won't know the difference … but that's the frightening part. I don't want to be a whisper of the man I once was. It's as if the candlelight is snuffed out, but the curl of dark smoke still drifts above you without much form. I don't want to be a ghost of myself. No one does."

"I remember that you and Jewell didn't have children. Do you have any other family to help you?"

"I had a sister, older. She died a few years ago. Can't remember how many now. But, Jewell and I did have a son. He died as a baby—docs called it crib death. Broke our hearts. Our art students became our children. Jewell was an only child. So, it's just me. But I've made arrangements. They'll come here first. They call that type of care in-home assisted living. Sort of like an adult day care in your house. When things progress to the third stage, I'll go to a lovely facility called the Memory Care Center of Charleston. It's a decorative name for what will amount to a nursing home. I hope they have some fine artwork on the walls and in the rooms."

"I do, too."

"Enough about my condition. If you live long enough, the upholstery frays. Stuff just falls apart." He grinned. "You said you want to take up painting again."

"Yes."

"You've never left it, or it's never left you. It's in your DNA. However, as I used to teach you and the other students … you get better by doing. There's no substitute. I'd suggest you start doing. You asked me earlier if you could help me. The answer is yes. You can help me by helping yourself, by painting … by creating. Your creator, God, gave you that gift. Never take it for granted. But your license will expire, like all things in life."

"I'm not sure where to begin."

"Begin right here. I have hundreds of tubes of paint. I finished my last painting a year ago. I don't have the stamina to stand at the easel in the field. And, in the field, is where the sweet spot in life is found to paint. I have plenty of canvases and brushes. Take them and put them to good use."

"I can't take your easel, paints and brushes."

"Why not? Sure, you can. I'm handing the torch to you. What will you do with it?"

Michael smiled. "I'll paint the best I can. I'll take you up on your offer with one condition."

"What's that?"

"You coach me for as long as you feel up to it. And, when and if you do go to that lovely care facility, you let me hang one of my paintings in your room."

"That's a deal. What will you paint first?"

"I'm not sure. Something here in the Lowcountry."

"May I offer you a suggestion?"

"Of course."

"Don't confine your work to just here. You're from the South. I challenge you to travel the Deep South, paint its magnificent landscapes and its people. You need time, Michael. Time not to move on … but to move forward. Begin by traveling around the South. Find those things that you want to paint and paint them with all your heart. It'll be the best journey of your life."

"I think I'm ready."

Derek looked at a hummingbird darting between the petunia blossoms in one of the hanging baskets. "Oh look! I've always loved hummingbirds. They seem to pop up out of nowhere. Like a little character from a fairytale. When many birds seek insects, nuts and seeds, the hummingbird works hard to find the sweet spot in flowers—it's sometimes hard to find nectar in the heart of the blossom. There's something about the way they fly, no bird can even come close. With their colors, the buzzing of their wings, their brief visits, the hummingbirds remind us to seek the magic in life. Look at our little winged visitor today as a sign of good luck and joy. Now, come inside. Let's get you set to go outside where I have no doubt you will seize the days ahead in paint."

TWENTY-THREE

Michael got out of bed at 4:30 in the morning to go there. He wanted to be set up and ready to paint when the morning light arrived. He didn't know if the place would be like what he'd experienced as a boy. Change happens even in the most Edenic of spots on earth. But he wanted to see if it still existed as he remembered it, to stand on the side of the old dirt road and paint images he'd never seen anywhere else in the world.

This magical land was unique to the South Carolina Lowcountry and a place he walked in his dreams long after leaving Charleston. A week after visiting with Derek, Michael bought a used van. Built a rack for the easels, paints and canvases. Tossed a mattress and pillow on the floorboard and set off to paint, choosing this location as his first. He was anxious and yet calm. Although he hadn't picked up oil paints and brushes in decades, he thought he might find his form again, his rhythm. It always began as he mixed paints on his palette. He never used oil paints directly from the tube. Instead, he chose mixing and experimenting with them to create distinctive blends of color.

He drove toward Botany Bay on Edisto Island, a place where he'd spent a lot of time as a boy fishing and doing charcoal sketches of birds and wildlife. The dawn was breaking when he parked the van in a spot off the little used backcountry road and got out. The view was exactly as he remembered it. Maybe even more spectacular. The sun was just coming up over the ocean, which was less than a few hundred yards to the east. It would be a challenge to paint what he had in mind, but if he was going to do this, he wanted to jump in the deep end.

Michael stared down the long dirt road. For almost a mile, it was as if the live oaks on both sides of the road had agreed to form an arch and wrap their limbs together, creating a natural tree tunnel as far as the eye could see. The image had deep visual perspective in addition to the substantial amounts of variegated sunlight that would be pouring through the gaps in the branches. He remembered how, in many places, it looked as if the shafts of light flowed like celestial waterfalls, striking the leaves and branches and dusting the Spanish moss with highlights of gold flecks in the early morning light.

He walked up to one of the mature oaks and put his hand on the gnarled, damp trunk. Michael closed his eyes, his fingers caressing the tree bark, feeling between the rough furrows. Along with the scent of rotting wood and moss, he could just smell the salt in the air from the ocean beyond the canebrake and marshes. A praying mantis, green as a new leaf and as long as his hand, crawled on a branch just above him. The insect tilted its heart-shaped head, staring down at Michael. "Good morning" he said, smiling. "I don't mind an audience."

He opened the door to the back of the van and removed the gifted paints, brushes and painting knives. He positioned his easel a few feet off the dirt road, secured a 24-by-36-inch canvas to it, and then waited.

Michael knew it was just a matter of time, maybe a half-hour before the sun rose in the sky high enough to begin creating the stunning visuals of diffused light, which would be so pronounced in shafts, you almost might see particles of energy flowing. He poured black coffee from a thermos and sipped, thinking about his conversation last week with Derek and his brave struggle to face a cruel disease with humor and a positive resiliency. *You're from the South. I challenge you to travel the Deep South, paint its magnificent landscapes and its people. You need time, Michael. Time not to move on ... but to move forward.*

A barred owl flew from a perch in a tree near him and sailed down the long canopy of limbs, the bird silent in its flight, beating its wings and flying toward the end of the tunnel, soon absorbed in a sea of green. *Maybe the owl is a harbinger*, he thought. Because, as soon as it disappeared, the morning sunlight arrived. It began creeping through the nooks in limbs that were interlocked like fingers.

Michael stared down the long tunnel of trees for a moment, deciding which paints to use. He looked at the many different colors of the forest greens, the thick ferns beneath trees, palmetto bushes the shade of jade, the subtle hues of the tree bark, and the yellow and blue wildflowers growing in patches along the road. Then there was the road itself, wet from last night's rain. No sign of tire tracks. He unscrewed caps and squeezed ten different colors of paints on the palette.

He stood in front of his easel and watched, anticipating the perfect moment to start the painting. He remembered something Derek always used to say to students. It was a quote from Claude Monet: *'When you go out to paint, try to forget what objects you have before you, a tree, a house, a field or whatever. Merely think here is a little square of blue, here an oblong of pink, here a streak of yellow, and paint it just as it looks to you, the color and shape.'*

Within seconds, he picked up a two-inch-wide brush and began painting a sky, trees and limbs on the canvas. Michael painted quickly, watching the light through the branches spill onto the morning dew on the dirt road. He mixed colors like a man beating scrambled eggs, using his palette knife to create tree trunks and twisting limbs. He worked with speed and precision, the light his task master, commanding him to capture it or lose the dance at daybreak.

Within an hour, he'd roughed out the painting, filling the entire canvas with paint. And then he began the details, adding shadow and light, creating only with a series of palette knives, giving the scene color on color, paint applied in generous spreads, the magic of his talents and the pigments working in harmony with nature. He worked for three hours straight, only stopping for brief seconds, long enough to watch the scene change, the shafts of light pouring at slanted angles as the sun crept up in the morning sky.

Michael knew that when the sun was in the mid-day position, the light would pour straight down through the crevices in the limbs. It was as if he was a tracker, a bounty hunter with a paint brush, tracking the sun through the sky as it cascaded down with a presence but leaving no visible tracks. His only bounty, his reward, was a gift from nature, fleeting but tangible in the moment. He watched the sunlight caress the Spanish moss, changing the gray whiskers into spun gold—creating a forest of the golden fleece.

Michael painted without stopping to eat or drink water, sweat dripping down his face. His hands were covered in paint. He alternated between five different palette knifes he used with the skill of a surgeon. He'd mix the paints, spread out a two-inch blend on the palette, and then use the edge of the knife to cut through it, producing a thin roll of paint on the side of the blade. From there he'd add the subtle colors, creating the impression of light and shadows among the trees and the long dirt road. As he painted, birds sang in the treetops. A dark blue butterfly alighted on the easel just above the painting. The butterfly stayed for a few minutes before flying down the long tunnel of trees.

It was close to four in the afternoon when Michael heard a sound that didn't come from the natural surroundings. He noticed it when the birds suddenly became silent. It was the sound of an approaching pickup truck. The truck was coming from behind Michael, heading down the dirt road. He continued painting as the driver pulled up and stopped near him. Michael stopped painting for a moment and drank from his water bottle. The driver lowered his window. "That's a fine lookin' picture." He was middle-aged, lean brown face, white T-shirt, and a tattoo on his upper arm of a woman's face behind a veil.

Michael smiled. "Thank you."

The man nodded. "I hate to drive down the road and mess up your picture. It'll most likely leave tire tracks in the road."

"No problem. I'm almost done."

"I always wanted to be an artist, to do what you're doin'."

"Why don't you?"

"Just never took the time to learn, I suppose. Maybe when I retire, I'll take it up. Mind if I watch you for a minute?"

"No, I don't mind."

The man turned off the truck's motor. Michael looked down the road, staring for a few seconds. Then he picked up a small, tapered brush and began painting an image of a woman riding a bicycle in the center of the road. As he painted in the details, he switched to a palette knife and finished. He looked down the road again. This time he used a smaller, tapered brush to paint the image of a young girl on a bike, riding next to her mother. Again, Michael used a small knife to add the texture to create the impression that he wanted. When finished he glanced down the road again.

The man in the truck said, "That's amazing. There's nobody on that road. Yet you picked up 'em brushes and painted it just like that woman and little girl were there on those bikes. How'd you do that?"

"Because they are there."

"Excuse me. Whadda you mean?"

"I see them as clear as I see you, just in a different way. They're my wife and daughter."

The man nodded. "You have a beautiful family. I best be on my way. That's one really good paintin'. I've driven this old road most of my life, rode my bike on it when I was a boy. You captured it like I've seen it only a few times in my life. I don't know much about art, but that picture sort of takes your breath away. Makes me feel like I'm on that road with my bike as a kid."

TWENTY-FOUR

Michael finished all but one part of the painting—the signature. He secured the wet canvas in the van and drove from Edisto Island to Derek Mack's cottage. In the gravel driveway, he took the painting and the easel out of the van, put the painting back up on the easel and set it in the shade of a live oak in Derek's yard. He stood there for a moment and looked at it before walking up the front porch and knocking on the door.

"Thought I heard a car engine in my drive," Derek said, opening the door. He looked at Michael and grinned. "I can see and smell that you've been painting."

Michael looked down at his hands. "I used turpentine and water to remove most of the paint from my hands. I was somewhat successful."

"Wear it as a badge of honor. Where were you painting?"

"Edisto Island. I went into Botany Bay before daybreak. I wanted to paint the tunnel of trees as the morning sunlight arrived."

"And did you?"

"I'm a little rusty, but I gave it my best."

"Where's the painting?"

"On the other side of my van, on an easel in the shade of that big oak."

"May I see it?"

"Of course. That's why I'm here. Remember our deal, you're going to give me feedback."

"Well, let's have a look." Derek held the handrail as he slowly walked down the steps from his porch to the front yard. Michael walked with him. "You picked a good day to paint. Great weather and light."

"I watched the weather forecast and headed out before five this morning."

They walked around the van and Derek saw the painting. He stopped and stared. He said nothing, just simply looked at the painting. Then, he took a few steps and came within ten feet, stopping again. Silence. A dog barked somewhere down the road. Derek stepped closer. His eyes moving across the painting, looking at the detail, the colors, the way the light poured through the steepled branches, the shadows. The vast attention to detail that gave it the impression of organic simplicity, as if the imagery almost grew out of the canvas.

Derek looked up at Michael through misty eyes. "It is magnificent. The layers of paint, light and shadow, the use of color and composition, it's all off the charts. I know you want feedback, but there's nothing more I can teach you. That year with me, all those Saturday mornings, you worked so hard, you bloomed into what I see today. Although you haven't painted in years, you didn't lose what you'd attained. It lied dormant inside you, Michael, waiting for the water of desire to seep back into the cracks of your soul. And now it's blossoming."

"I'm glad you like it."

"Like it … I love it." He moved one step closer. "And what I love the most is what I see coming down the old road straight at me. The woman and child on their bicycles. You took a natural wonder of a long tunnel of trees—ancient oaks, and captured the majesty of light, shadow and composition … but then you added the sweetness of the mother and child enjoying their time together. It's the kind of moment that the little girl will grow up and relive in those special memories of her life. She'll tell her family about the time she and her mother rode bikes through a tunnel of trees, and how unique it was to her."

Michael said nothing. Looking at the painting and taking a deep breath. "The girl is my daughter, Mandy. The woman is my wife. Mandy will never tell her family about that experience because she can't."

"But you can and did. People, folks you'll never know, will see that painting and vicariously experience the scene. And who knows, maybe they'll go for a bike ride and strive for something similar. Your imagination will spur theirs. Your art becomes shared beyond only viewing it. The painter dips his or her brush into their soul and bleeds on the canvas. In the work, Michael, not only can people lose themselves … but they can find themselves, too."

"Thank you. I have one more thing to add. Just like that mural so long ago … I didn't sign it until you gave me your advice. Same thing today. I waited to sign it. I wanted to wait until you saw it."

"That part is done. Now it's time for the artist to sign his work."

Michael smiled and opened the back doors to his van. He removed three tubes of paint, dark red, black and white. He quickly mixed a little paint from each tube on his palette and used a small brush, swirling it through the paint. He stepped over to the canvas and wrote his name in the lower right corner. After a few seconds, he stood and looked at the painting, his signature now there: *Vargas*

Derek nodded, his eyes filled with affection.

Over the next week, Michael did two more paintings, one of the marina and the other of the historic district. He and Derek discussed artistic expression and personal styles, including choosing angles for perspective and the use of lighting, brush sizes and color—the things artists would think about for their own creations and admire in the works of others. Sometimes Derek repeated himself without realizing it, but Michael was okay with hearing a story a second time.

"I've really been enjoying our time together, Derek."

"I have, too. But you have something you need to do. Go, Michael. Travel the South and capture its culture."

"I'll call you. I want to stay in touch on a regular basis. Just answer your phone."

"I still have my hearing." He grinned. "Before you leave, may I ask a favor?"

"Of course. What is it?"

"May I borrow the painting you did on Edisto Island? It was the first one you did since you left my studio. I'm not sure where I'm going will have art on the walls. This will ensure that I see great art every morning that God allows me to awake."

"It's yours."

TWENTY-FIVE

Michael was a gypsy. A vagabond with paints and canvases traveling the South. Driving the van with no particular destination in mind. Only the desire to be on the road. He left the Lowcountry and headed across the backroads, staying off the interstate highways and main roads, in search of people and places to paint. Everything he captured was spontaneous, candid. Nothing posed. Nothing orchestrated like a Hollywood director with a film crew and actors. He searched for realism to paint and shift into impressionism, to give his art the truth of the moment.

The van was his home. He often slept in it when he was too tired to drive, pulling into a campground, or some remote area of beach or woodland. He bathed in the clear running rivers, jumping from rock to rock in white water rapids, standing under a water fall at Table Rock Falls near the border between South and North Carolina. Sometimes he'd stop and spend a night at a roadside motel for a shower. He hadn't cut his hair in a month, face unshaven, but his body and spirit felt rejuvenated as he finally took the time to take the time, painting whatever he wanted, whenever he wanted.

On the Outer Banks of North Carolina, he set up his easel to capture the wild horses of the islands. Michael got gas for his van at a bait 'n tackle shop on Nag's Head. A ranger with the National Park Service, a woman in her mid-twenties, auburn hair in a ponytail, was pumping gas into her government-issued Jeep. Michael asked if she knew the best places to possibly see the wild horses. She had smiling eyes, eager to offer information. "Many of the locals call the horses 'Bankers.' The breed first arrived on the Outer Banks about 500 years ago. It's believed some of them managed to swim from Spanish shipwrecks offshore to the Outer Banks. What you may see today are the descendants of the Spanish mustangs. The Bankers are small in stature, but they are very much survivors … pound-for-pound, probably the toughest breed of horse in the world."

"How have they managed to survive on barrier islands? What can they find for food? Is there any fresh water for them to drink?"

She smiled, finished pumping her gas. "When they have to, they use their front hooves to dig shallow wells for fresh water. The horses are excellent swimmers. They'll swim across channels to other islands in the Outer Banks looking for greener pastures. They graze mostly on spartina grasses. These mustangs are nomads, living off the land, roaming the islands, surviving hurricanes, disease and man since the Spanish galleons ran aground in shallow water known as the graveyard of the Atlantic."

"Where's the best places to see the horses?"

"Mostly the Cuttirick Banks, Shackleford Banks, and down at Ocracoke." She looked at his van. "Do you want to take pictures of them? Are you a photographer?"

"No, I'm a painter. I'd like to paint them."

She laughed. "Well, I hope you're a fast painter. Remember, they're mustangs, which means they can run fast. You may see some grazing around the dunes or marshes. Occasionally, you'll see them at the beach cooling off and staying away from biting insects further inland. In the next instant, they're off and running like the wind. If you're lucky, you might see a few. I can't imagine you'd have the time to actually paint them. Good luck."

Michael thought about his conversation as he walked the northern section of the Outer Banks, looking for horses. He found a surfer. The man appeared to be in his early twenties, tanned face, long hair, wearing a wet suit vest, a pair of shorts, and cut-off jeans. He straddled a surfboard and paddled out to the breakers, the late afternoon sun golden over the Atlantic, the trade winds laced with salt and floral scents.

Michael sat down near a sand dune peppered with sea oats and watched a hermit crab lugging a portable shell across the sand. A gull shrieked overhead, the wind changing directions. It didn't take Michael long to find horses. Or maybe they found him. He heard the neighing and snorting. He stood, slowly turning around. At the crest of the dunes, where the white sand met the hard-blue sky, he saw their impassive faces. Wild horses that didn't appear so wild, but rather more curious. They trotted about forty yards away from Michael and ran toward the surf.

Although untamed, the horses showed no fear as Michael stood in front of his easel and canvas. The herd sauntered along the edge of the waves, seven horses. One stallion, three mares, and the rest were young foals, staying close to their mothers, a steady breeze across the Atlantic keeping insects away. He painted quickly as they stood in the surf, the gentle waves rolling over their hooves, tails swooshing, the horses frolicking in the water and afternoon light.

Michael watched the surfer catch a wave one hundred yards out in the Atlantic and ride it toward the shore and the small herd. The horses romped, as if they were playing a game of tag, the stallion nuzzling and courting one of the mares, the foals running through the surf like kids splashing, gulls in the sky cheering them.

As the surfer rode the crest of a wave, the stallion and one mare rose up on their hind legs, touching front hooves in a frisky dance, with the foals playing in the surf. That was the image Michael painted. In his mind's eye—a solo surfer riding a wave as wild horses romped in the foreground. He'd freeze-frame the scenes into drawings in his mind that he could pull from as the action moved faster than he could paint. He looked up from the canvas every four or five seconds, painting in a flurry of palette knives and brushes.

The action continued for another twenty minutes and then the horses, as if they heard some unseen command, ran northward. Soon the herd was only small moving dots in the distance, trotting between the surf flotsam and golden sea mist.

Michael left the Outer Banks, left the wind-swept world of wild horses cavorting through rolling breakers as a surfer rode a wave in the background. It was one of those rare scenes as isolated and desolate as the land itself and the horses that roamed the long slivers of islands for centuries. But, for just a moment in time, no longer than the sun breaking through moving clouds, the horses played in the same surf as did a man on a board. It gave Michael the chance to paint—to capture the contrast and union of wild horses, rolling surf, and a man riding a wave all in the same moment.

He drove his van southeast, refusing to use his phone for GPS navigation. He preferred using an old road map that came with the van when he bought it. The map had been kept in the van's console, the front of it was stained from use, the folds a little tattered. And that was just fine. It was easy to follow the squiggly lines that were most often backroads. That's where he knew he'd, most likely, find the people, places, and stories he would want to paint.

Before he traveled farther, he wanted to check in with Derek. He called once a week, it usually taking at least ten rings before Derek could get to the landline phone to answer. When Michael called today, he counted the rings. After fifteen he disconnected. He'd wait a little while longer and try again. He didn't want to think what options he might seek if Derek didn't answer.

TWENTY-SIX

A few hours later, as Michael was entering Belhaven, North Carolina, he called Derek again. On the ninth ring he answered. "Good afternoon."

"Derek, it's Michael … are you okay?"

"No complaints."

"I've been trying to reach you. I was worried."

"I took a little walk and became a tad disoriented. But I'm fine now. Where are you?"

"North Carolina. I've done three paintings. The last was on the Outer Banks. I spent some time watching the wild horses of the islands romp in the surf while a lone surfer rode waves in the background. It was a great scene to get in paint."

"I look forward to seeing it. You sound better. But how are you doing?"

"I'm still sorting through the grief. It's hard. Each new interaction I paint, each family I observe, is awakening special memories I had with Kelsey and Mandy … but it's also a reminder that we didn't have enough of them. I robbed them, Derek, of a sweeter, simpler life."

"Life is an ongoing journey, Michael. We learn, and we grow. Life, like painting, can be an awakening and a reawakening, a birth and a rebirth. You can spend all of your time beating yourself up, or you can get out there, do something different, and make a difference. If you're only an observer, you'll never really live—you have to be present. And, just so you know, in this I'm also speaking from experience. We're not perfect. There was a Danish philosopher and theologian from the early 1800s … his name was Soren Kierkegaard, who said it this way: *Life can only be understood backwards; but it must be lived forward.*"

"Thank you. I needed to hear that. Not only are you a wonderful mentor in the arts, but you're also full of interesting quotes and human wisdom … like the dad I never had."

"Thanks for the compliment. Where are you going next?"

"I have no idea. North Carolina has a lot of lake areas. I'm just driving the backroads looking for inspiration. It's all around."

Derek sat on the couch in his living room. He looked at a framed picture of his wife on the end table, and then shifted his glance up to a painting on the wall. It was the one Michael had given him before he left. "The backroads are excellent passageways. But, remember, flowers don't grow on a road."

"I understand. I'm doing a lot of walking." Michael pulled his van off the road, stopping at a gas pump. "How's it going with the people from the Alzheimer's facility? Are they coming on a regular basis?"

"I can't remember." Derek chuckled. "Yes, there is a sweet nurse who's coming here three days a week. I'm just never sure what days. Which is okay. That way I have a pleasant surprise. Here's another quote for you. Van Gogh used to say … *I've put my heart and soul into my work and lost my mind along the way.* Maybe that's what I did." He smiled, staring at the painting. "Don't worry about me, Michael. You need to be taking care of yourself."

Michael pinched the bridge of his nose. "I'll call you in a few days."

TWENTY-SEVEN

From a distance, he could see Grandfather Mountain. As he came closer, Michael could hear the sound of Scottish bagpipes. He was somehow drawn to the Appalachian Mountains. Something about the antiquity of land, more than 500-million years old, the mist that often drifted near their peaks, giving them the folk name—Smokies. It was the folklore of the region that drew him to the area of Western North Carolina. And, it was in the area of Mt. Mitchell and Grandfather Mountain that he remembered feeling the most pull on his internal compass, a place where he had vacationed with his grandparents as a young boy.

Could it be here where he might find a piece of his childhood innocence, back when dreams and hopes still mattered? He felt that he had let Kelsey and Mandy down. And it hurt, deeply. He also felt that he had let himself down by losing who he was over time and by robbing himself and others because of his failure to not prioritize what should have been the most important. And, somewhere in that process, something diminished inside him. Kelsey tried to tell him, but he was afraid to step back to move forward. Could he actually paint himself back to life, he wondered?

Part of the southern folklore of the mountains include stories of the mountain people, the descendants of Scottish clans that came here more than 250 years ago. For almost seven decades, they've gathered at the base of Grandfather Mountain at a place known as MacRae Meadows for the annual Scottish Highland Games. Michael wanted to watch some of the events, to see the athletes participate in games that had origins back to medieval times, and how those Scottish traditions had evolved in the American South. He wanted to hear the stories of the people who have lived in the southern Appalachians longer than America has been a nation. And he wanted to paint the color—the pageantry, the fields of folklore traced from Scotland to the American South. Maybe he could discover how the roots of Scottish clans, long ago planted in fertile mountain soil through North and South Carolina, grew new traditions as the people played old games in the shadow of an even older mountain.

Michael parked his van under a tall fir tree near the base of Grandfather Mountain at the perimeter of MacRae Meadows. He sat behind the wheel, rolled the window down and watched people descend on a land that has become an annual rite of passage for many of the mountain people and their extended family, people who live far from the mountains. Hundreds of folks were dressed in traditional Scottish clothes popular centuries ago—men wearing kilts, beret-style hats, women in tartan skirts, sashes and capes, plaid colors ablaze. He could hear Celtic music coming from the meadows, the scent of wild heather in the air.

Michael got out of his van with paints he kept in a fishing tackle box. He secured a canvas to the easel and carried it over his shoulder. And then he followed the crowds and the music. Hundreds of RVs, posh motorhomes, Airstream trailers, and tents were on the fringes of the area where the games were held. Campfire smoke drifted over the campers, the smell of bangers or Scottish sausages in silky air mixed with laughter and music.

MacRae Meadows resembled an Olympic track and field. There was a large oval track where a parade marched with drums, flutes and bagpipes, all the participants in Scottish regalia, hundreds of people on the sidelines watching, cheering and clapping. As the parade wound down, the Highland Games began. It was a show of strength and endurance. Husky men in kilts tossing heavy hammers. "Swing it, Jason!" shouted a woman as a young man turned in a circle and released a twenty-two-pound hammer, people cheering as if Thor was among the competitors.

Michael set his easel down, simply watching the athletes and the reactions of the crowd, with Grandfather Mountain serving as the backdrop of the scene. He studied the way the light hit the trees, the

116

deep shadows, the veins of narrow, white clouds near the summit, how time had carved the rocky profile of an old man on one side of the mountain. He watched as men in plaid kilts lined up to toss what resembled a telephone pole. Each took turns lifting the pole from its base, running no more than a dozen steps, tossing the pole in a herculean effort to send it end over end.

"It's called tossing the caber," said a man walking up to Michael. The man wore a tam beret, a green-plaid kilt to mid-knee, high socks, and an Argyle jacket over a white shirt. He looked to be in his sixties, reddish-gray beard tapered, waxed moustache, roguish eyes the color of a deep swimming pool.

Michael said, "I'm amazed that they could lift it, let alone toss it."

"Takes strength and practice. The caber pole weights 175 pounds. It's about twenty feet long. The idea is to lift and toss it as straight as possible for it to move into the twelve o'clock position when it lands. And, to do it so it looks like it's standing upright for a split second, before falling, takes a lot of precision. Look at that!" He pointed to one tall, broad-shouldered contestant who launched the caber into the air like he was tossing a fencepost. The pole stood upright for just a moment before yielding to gravity and falling over opposite the man who'd thrown it. The crowd exploded in cheers and applause.

"So that's how it's done," Michael said.

"That was a perfect example. Unless one of the next seven gents can master it as well, that fella will be the champion of today's caber games. After this it'll be a tug-of-war like you've never seen. Sometimes it can last for an hour, hands bloody, like hamburger. The winning team secures bragging rights until next summer. It's something that's shared over whiskey and warm fires the following winter. It gets cold way up in these mountains. I've lived here all my life, third generation." He grinned, his beard parting. "Are you an artist?"

Michael smiled. "I don't know about that … I'm a painter, maybe a guy who's striving to one day becoming an artist."

"My name's Hugh McCallister." He extended his hand.

"Michael Vargas." They shook hands as a woman joined McCallister. She was about his age, silver hair, striking face, and a wide smile. She wore a red plaid dress down to her laced-up boots.

"This is my wife, Alana. In Gaelic it means beautiful, and she has always been beautiful to me. Alana, meet Michael the reluctant artist."

She glanced at the easel on the ground and looked up at Michael. "It's nice to meet you. Are you going to paint something today?"

"Maybe. I never know. I sort of check out a place and see if there's something that would be good to capture on canvas. And, if I feel the inspiration, I try to follow the muse."

She laughed. "Of course. The muses—the female influence that leads the artist to creativity."

Michael smiled, "Or, as an old friend of mine says, leads him to insanity."

McCallister chuckled. "With my creative friends, I'd say there is a fine line in there somewhere between sanity and real creativity."

"Did you descend from Scottish ancestors?" Alana asked.

Michael shook his head. "No. But I think I have a touch of the DNA. I love Scottish salmon."

McCallister grinned, adjusting his beret. "Coincidently, we're putting some on the grill this evening. If you're around, perhaps you can join us for salmon and a taste of fine Scotch whiskey. We're in our RV—it's called *Dunrobin*. The name was taken from one of the most beautiful castles in Scotland. We're camped with dozens of likeminded transplants over in an area called the grove."

"Thanks. I don't know if I'll be here that long, but I appreciate the invitation."

"Indeed. If nothing else, should you find something here that's worthy of your canvas, maybe we can have a look and raise a glass to your work."

"You haven't seen it yet. It might not be worth toasting a glass of fine Scotch to something undeserving."

Alana smiled. "I think the meaning of art is in its interpretation. Some of our friends love modern art that is more or less without any form. I guess that's the art of the art … to like something that you can't define. But, for me, the traditionalist, art has to move me. And I'm not talking about in a negative way. Our oldest son and his wife are art collectors. They like western artists. I'm a southern gal with deep roots."

118

"I grew up in South Carolina … Charleston." Michael glanced at the next contestant lifting a caber pole, teams of other men lining up to participate in a tug-of-war, the long rope more than three inches wide. He looked up at the sky and then at the shadows falling over Grandfather Mountain, the profile of an old man's face now more visible on one side of the mountain. He nodded at the McCallisters. "I think I'll stick around to paint. So, if you'll excuse me, I'm going to walk about fifty yards to the left and set up my easel facing Grandfather mountain. The light's good."

Alana folded her arms. "Will you promise to show us your painting? My intuition is telling me the muses, something or somebody is really driving you. I'd like to see what you choose to paint in the games of Scots. Promise us, okay?"

"Okay."

TWENTY-EIGHT

Michael set up his easel, out of the way of the direct action, but close enough to see the faces of the participants, to hear the grunts and groans of the athletes. On his wide canvas, he first painted the sky, clouds, and Grandfather Mountain in the background. He watched the last contestant toss a caber pole, the big man's bellowing grunt traveling across the crowd. As the winners were crowned, Michael painted.

Musicians began playing flutes, fiddles, drums and harps on a wooden stage near the concessions stands, the music seeming to echo from the hollows and valleys of the mountain. Michael paused, listening to the music, watching the faces of the revelers, many people dancing traditional Scottish folk dances, kilts and skirts twirling in a sea of plaid colors.

A half-dozen people stood at a respectable distance behind Michael, watching him paint. The tug-of-war teams walked out onto the field in the warm sunlight of late afternoon. This was to be the final game of the day. There were ten men on each team, all in shorts. One team in red T-shirts, the other in green. One man, tall and broad-shouldered, in one of the red T-shirts, had painted his face with war paint—blue, like a character from the movie Braveheart.

As the contest began, Michael paused and watched. The men dug in, growls and defiant shouts coming from both teams. Muscles knotted in thick calves, thighs and arms. Each man leaning back, feet in front, hands gripped around the rope. The crowd cheered for their favorite clans and jeered for the opposing team.

Michael painted with the same sort of physical and emotional fury he observed in the meadow, painting with a powerful force—the brushes moving and colors flowing from a pain deep inside him.

Broken shards of his life coalescing into innovative shapes and forms on canvas, the loss of his family, the subtle illustration of the internal kid he was trying to find, and the new man he was struggling to become. He used brushes and palette knives in a passionate style that caught the eye of the crowd. They whispered and pointed, no one coming too close. In less than five minutes, there were more than a dozen people watching. "That guy's fast," said one man to his wife. "Look at Grandfather Mountain in the background."

The tug-of-war resembled a battle of titans, a show of strength and intimidation. Each time one team pulled the rope a foot or two, the opposing team somehow found the muscle and psychological resilience to regain their traction and the rope. Back and forth it went, the crowd growing louder every time there appeared to be a gain or loss. Suddenly, it was like dominos falling as the team in the green T-shirts managed a surge, a staggering pull. One member of the opposing team tripped and fell. His falling triggered a chain reaction, and out of the ten members of the red team, only three remained standing.

The crowd erupted into a loud cheering, members of the winning team thumping their chests and lifting clenched fists into the air. As the players on both teams slapped open-palm high-fives and congratulated each other, Michael continued with the painting. He finished adding the details of contorted faces, knotted muscle and brawn, young warriors in the foreground while a sleeping grandfather dozed like Rip Van Winkle on the mountain.

"What a cool painting!" a teenage girl shouted as the crowd continued to grow behind Michael, watching him finish with the details. After a minute, he used a small tapered brush to sign the lower right-side corner: *Vargas*

"Is it for sale?" asked a man in a dark red kilt and wearing a plaid tam cap. "I'd like to be the first to make you an offer."

Michael turned around, wiping his hands on the cloth rag he carried. The man said, "I've been comin' to the Highland Games here at Grandfather mountain for thirty-five years, and I've never seen anyone capture majesty and human power of the games quite like that … even with a camera. What will you take for the painting?"

"I don't sell them. I'm just painting the places I go to sort of document what I see and do … mostly what I see in others and watch them do." Michael smiled.

"Where are you going?" asked a red-haired woman in a tartan dress with a sash over one shoulder.

"I never know until I get there."

"Where have you been?"

"All around the world."

She laughed. "Wish I was you."

"Maybe … maybe not."

The man reached in his pocket and pulled out a card. "If you change your mind and decide to sell the painting, here's my card. I'm Liam Murry. I'll be staying and camping here for three more days."

Michael took the man's card. "I appreciate your kind words about my work."

"It's all true." He motioned to the painting. "I don't know much about art, but what you did out here … what you painted on that canvas just smacks of action and raw power. The dirt flying, the sweat on their faces. It's man against man in a beautiful meadow with mountains, trees, wildflowers, and even birds in the air. Sort of like young gladiators battling in a pasture with the profile of Grandfather Mountain behind them. Good stuff."

"Thank you."

The man looked at the paint on Michael's hands, arms, and forehead—the sweat stains on his denim shirt. "You want some water? I have an unopened bottle. Looks like you could use some hydration."

"No thanks. I have some in my van."

* * *

By the time Michael had cleaned up and stored his paints and easel back in his van, the sun was beginning to set behind Grandfather Mountain. He was tired, thought about resting on the mattress in the van, leaving the doors and windows open to limit the odor from the oil paints on the canvas. Then he remembered the promise he'd made to Alana and Hugh McCallister. *Will you promise to show us your painting? My intuition is telling me the muses, something or somebody is really driving you.*

Michael took the painting out of the van and headed toward the place Hugh had referred to as the grove and an RV named for a Scottish castle … *Dunrobin.*

TWENTY-NINE

The grove wasn't a hard place to find. It was the area where a lot of the Highland Game veterans came year after year to set up campsites, renew old acquaintances and meet new people. Michael only had to ask one person in what part of MacRae Meadows he could find the grove. One of the game judges, an older man with a whistle around his neck and a nametag that read, Ian McNair, pointed to the northeast. "It's God's little acre out here. Closest spot to the valleys and has a great view of Grandfather Mountain. Head toward the far corner. You'll see all of the RVs amongst the hickory trees and the old spruce."

There were more than a dozen RVs, including one silver Airstream trailer parked at the grove. In the twilight, he could read the names on the RVs, most linked to some place or something in Scotland: *Nessie, Skye, Shetland Pony* and many others. He spotted *Dunrobin.* It was toward the end of the RVs, which were all parked in a semicircle like a wagon train of yesteryear, near the Tiki torches where yellow flames barely moved in the still air.

The McCallisters had strung clear outdoor lights, vintage Edison bulbs, on four poles around the front of their RV. There was a picnic table and two foldable Adirondack chairs under the lights, the smell of salmon and sausage cooking on a grill, and laughter coming from pockets of deep twilight shadow. Michael set his painting on the grass, propped it up against one of the poles under the lights.

Hugh McCallister came out of the front door, a drink in one hand, a can of bug-spray in the other. He looked over at Michael. "You're here! Excellent. Did you start and finish your painting?"

Michael gestured to the canvas. McCallister set his drink down on the picnic table and walked in front of the painting. He said nothing, simply staring, his mouth slightly parting. After a half minute, he looked over to Michael. "This takes my breath away. It's powerful. How'd you manage to capture the essence of the Highland Games, the extreme faces of the contestants, the faces of the crowds, the dancers and the mountain like that?" He turned toward the open door to the RV. "Alana, come out here. You gotta see this."

Alana came down the two metal steps, wiping her hands on a dish towel and standing next to her husband. She looked at the painting, and then at Michael, staring back at the painting and taking slow steps toward it as if she was being summoned. "This is so beautiful. How in the world did you stand out there and manage to find the best of the best, the core of the games and the people? I'm amazed. It's beyond striking. It looks like the kind of rare art you'd see in places like the Louvre in Paris … maybe better."

Michael said, "I wouldn't compare what I just did to the works of the great masters. This painting can't hold a candle to those."

"I'd beg to differ with you," she said. "Your art, the colors, the people … it comes alive. Not only can I see it, but I can feel the energy."

"Me, too," Hugh said. "I feel it deep down in my old southern bones. Please have dinner with us."

"I don't want to impose."

"No imposition whatsoever," Alana said. "I'll fix the plates. We have salmon, bangers and mash, a garden salad, sweet tea, beer and wine. Sit with Hugh. I'll be right back."

"Thank you," Michael said, taking a seat at the picnic table, opposite from Hugh. They talked about art for a few minutes, and then Michael turned the conversation toward one of the reasons he'd come to the place. "I know you have roots that go back to Scotland, but I'd like to hear more about your southern roots in these mountains, if you don't mind."

"Mind, you're asking a Scot to talk about himself. That's easy."

"I'm also asking a man raised in the South to talk about his heritage here."

Over dinner and drinks, with Alana offering comments, Hugh explained how his family had come to the Southern Appalachian region. "There's a lot of Scot-Irish heritage all over these mountains," he said, sipping a glass of Glenfiddich. "My family fought in the Battle of Kings Mountain in South Carolina, helped beat the British, and got land grants to settle in the mountains of the Carolinas. The region wasn't a whole lot different from where they'd come from in the Scottish Highlands. It began as a search for freedom of religion for a lot of those early Scots and some of the Irish, too. Quakers didn't care for us too much. Here, in these mountains, after the Revolutionary War, we could be left alone to build churches, raise families, and create music with whatever instruments we could build. A lot of today's country and bluegrass music have strong connections to this land and to the Scots that became Americans. I was baptized in the muddy waters of the French Broad River, the same river my great grandfather was trying to cross on horseback when he ran up on a bevy of Cherokee scouts. They made peace and learned to live together. Our language is unique. Same thing with our southern accents. It's a little more nasal, closer to the inflections of the old country. We sort of highjacked the Queen's English and put the spin of Scot-Americans into the cauldron, and the pot liquor is what you hear today. Even sayings like jack-leg preacher … if you know what that means?"

"I'm not sure," Michael said. "Although I've heard the term."

"A jack-leg preacher is a fella who's self-taught to be a man of the cloth. But that term isn't unique to preachers. It applies to anyone who learned on his or her own. A jack-leg mechanic is a good example. I've hired a bunch of 'em in my days. Our kinfolk constructed log cabins, pretty much invented moonshine and perfected barbeque. Before we could raise hogs, we'd kill possums, deer, squirrels, whatever. The old folks would make a sauce from the garden—tomatoes, onions and whatnot, slow cook the meat to mask some of the wild taste and slap it with plenty of that sauce to make it easier on the palate." He cut off a piece of salmon and lifted it up with his fork. "As you can see, we've come a long way. However, I'm not sure many would think to pair the salmon with bangers, but it sure is good." He laughed.

"What are you going to do with your new painting?" asked Alana.

"After it dries, I'll put it in the rack area inside my van with some others I've done."

"Will you eventually sell your work?" asked Hugh.

"I'd rather give them away. But right now, I'm saving them to share with an old friend of mine when I get back to Charleston. He was my art teacher many years ago. He's in the early stages of Alzheimer's. I'm hoping the paintings might resonate with him when other means of communication become harder."

"That's so noble of you. He must have been a great teacher because you do great work."

"I owe him a lot."

Alana glanced at the paint flecks on Michael's wedding ring. "I see you have paint on your wedding band. Is your wife traveling with you, maybe back at the motel?

"I lost my wife and daughter in a plane crash."

Alana touched her lips with two fingers. "I'm so sorry."

"How long has it been?" asked Hugh.

"Six months—last winter."

The sound of a bagpipe started. Michael looked toward the music. The lone bagpipe player stood in his kilt, vest, and tam beret in near silhouette on an outcropping of rock with Grandfather Mountain in the background. A light breeze blew his sash. The man began playing a haunting rendition of *Amazing Grace*, the setting sun below the mountain, an orange tinge outlining the grandfather profile shape in the rock, the trace of light bordering the bagpipe player. Michael stared at the man on the rocky ledge, listening to the music.

"Let me fix you a drink," Hugh said, using tongs to lift one ice cube from a bucket near the table, dropping the ice into a glass and pouring from a bottle of scotch. "To your art and your journey, Michael." The three of them lifted glasses in a toast, the lonesome sound of the bagpipe touching Michael as the music of *Amazing Grace* carried over the mountain and down into the dark valleys.

He sipped his scotch, leaning back on the picnic bench. Michael cleared his throat. "That song, *Amazing Grace*, was one of my wife's favorite. She'd sing it often."

"Like your art, it's powerful … goes right to your heart and squeezes it."

"Look over there," Alana said, pointing to some trees. "I see a couple of fireflies in the pines. It's that time of the year for them. In some areas on the mountains between here and Gatlinburg, you sometimes can get lucky and see the fireflies rise up from the ground and begin blinking their lights in a near perfect synchronization. It's one of the most magnificent things in nature. A symphony of light. Hugh and I have only seen it once, about fifteen years ago in a remote place in the woods near Maggie Valley."

"It was spectacular," Hugh said, finishing his second drink.

* * *

Michael wasn't exactly sure how he got there. After dinner and drinks, he left Hugh and Alana and walked around MacRae Meadows, listening to pockets of laughter, people telling folktales, and both Scottish and mountain music in harmony. The scotch whiskey dulled his sense of direction. He held the painting in one hand and drifted around the forest like wood smoke, the campfire lights casting shadows against the old spruce trees, the starlight as his guide.

Unexpectedly, he was in a small valley, darker than the meadow, the night sky clearer than he'd seen since leaving New York. As if by some unheard command, twinkling lights rose up from the earth, crawling out from under wet leaves and pine straw. Within minutes, hundreds, if not thousands, of fireflies ascended from the ground, their tiny lights somehow coming into sync, all the lights blinking on and off at the exact same time.

Michael stood there, slowly turning in a circle, the moving lights trapped in his eyes, the haunting refrain of *Amazing Grace*, echoing in his mind. He sat down, watching the fireflies pirouette through the night, rising and falling in some kind of nocturnal dance, their lights causing the tall spruce trees to be illuminated at one moment, dark the next. He was alone and yet surrounded by tiny guides carrying lights as if they were gatekeepers with mobile lanterns to show the way. The fireflies rose higher in the night sky, the twinkling stars in the heavens as a backdrop, white clouds swirling in front of a buttery moon, the fireflies lighting their own small universe in the spruce trees.

Michael sat in awe. He thought about Van Gogh's painting, *Starry Night*, remembering what Kelsey had said one night when they were first dating. They stood on an outdoor deck in Colorado at night, the mountains in the background, the sky ablaze. She'd looked at the stars high above the mountains over the sleepy resort town and said, *"This night is special. It reminds me of Van Gogh's painting ... Starry Night. This night is dreamlike, ethereal. It's nights like this that remind us of how small, yet still significant we are in the universe. It's nights like this that remind us to never stop dreaming ... and to remember to share those dreams with those we love."*

THIRTY

A small, scarlet red leaf fell from the sky, landing in the center of Michael's wet painting. He stood in front of the easel and considered allowing the leaf to remain there. *Nature's helping hand*, he thought, smiling. Mixing the colors of the fall in the mountains of Tennessee was similar to mixing the colors of the wind. He used the tip of a palette knife to remove the leaf, the honking of geese flying south high above him.

As the weather grew cooler, Michael had been painting the change of seasons from the Nantahala National Forest in North Carolina to the Great Smoky Mountains National Park in Tennessee. A chilly breeze blew through the town below him and up the face of the mountains, red and yellow leaves swirling in a potpourri of hues mixed by the wind. The air carried the scent of woodsmoke and pine needles.

Michael was putting the finishing details on a painting of a log cabin built in the late 1800s. The cabin, with its aged timbers, rock fireplace, and wooden porch propped up by hardwood posts, looked like it was hibernating, tucked in the center of a meadow dotted with maple and apple trees. The leaves were their own palette of colors, cherry reds and yellows with the glimmer gold against a cloudless blue sky. It would be his last painting in the area—soon the leaves would turn brown and winter would set in, covering the mountaintops in white.

Michael was intrigued with the old split-rail, wooden fence that zigzagged around the two-acre property, amazed that a fence built with no nails and no posts embedded in the ground could withstand the weather and tests of time. What intrigued him even more were the people who'd built the fence so long ago. Who were they? What were their hopes and dreams? How'd they survive in a hardscrabble land when the snows came with their bone-chilling days and icy winds? How'd they find enough food for a large family? He thought about the pioneers who'd originally cut the trees from the mountains, split the rails and erected the fence. Michael used his palette knife to paint the look and feel of antiquity in the aged wood.

When finished he packed his supplies in his van and then walked to the far left of the cabin, to a small cemetery beneath the sugar maples. The wind rustled from an upwind draft, causing the vivid red and yellow leaves to swirl in miniature eddies, some falling on the worn shoulders of blackened headstones that dated back before the Civil War. Michael looked at the headstones, read some of the inscriptions, and thought about those who'd carved a life from the mountains. One inscription read:

Margaret McBride
1870 -1876
Our Daughter – Our Angel

Michael lifted his eyes, looking across the meadow, thinking about the little girl whose grave was in front of him. He could almost see her playing on the steps of the cabin's front porch on a day like this in late October, leaves falling from the maple trees, white smoke trailing out of the top of the rock chimney. Then he pictured his daughter Mandy playing in this same yard, frolicking in the leaves. He smiled, walking back to his van, the call of a hawk in the woods, nature's confetti falling all around him, his thoughts as tranquil as the autumn day.

* * *

Michael drove his van along winding roads that hugged the sides of the Smoky Mountains. He was soon driving through Pigeon Forge, stopping at an antique store on the southern edge of town. The store was a two-story building, hard pinewood planks whitewashed, green shutters with peeling paint. Four wooden rocking chairs were on the roughhewn front porch.

To the left of the store, an Esso sign hung from rusted chains on a metal pole. A hand-crank gasoline pump, painted the red color of a vintage fire engine, was near the sign.

He parked and got out of his van, stretching his body, his back sore. A breeze caused the Esso sign to squeak. Michael entered the store, the smells of American history greeting him. Solid wood furniture—mirrors and intricate carvings, was packed across a large room. He walked over a scuffed wood floor that groaned under his weight, following a maze through the walls of antiques.

A white-haired man in his seventies, in a faded navy T-shirt and wide-legged blue jeans held up by red suspenders, sat behind a desk older than himself. A pouch of Red Man chewing tobacco was open on the desk. The cash register was the kind that required two fingers to press down keys marked in monetary denominations up to fifty dollars. "Good afternoon," he said though a rasping voice. "Huntin' for anything in particular?"

"I'm looking for something to help me better organize and carry tubes of oil paints and brushes."

"You an artist?"

"Well, I paint. Not sure if I qualify as an artist." Michael smiled.

The old man nodded. He got up from behind the table like a man getting out of a hospital bed, as if everything hurt. "Follow me." He led Michael through a trail that snaked around the American past toward the back of the store. "How 'bout something like this? What do you think?" He pointed to a black suitcase, his fingers bent from arthritis. "It was made in the early 1900s. A famous magician … think it was Houdini, owned this suitcase at one time. Not sure if he carried his clothes or his magic in here." He chuckled, his eyes bright under the dim lights.

Michael took the suitcase off the table, opening it, the neglected smell of aged fabric, trapped air, and time greeting him. The suitcase was solid and in excellent condition. "How much are you asking for it?"

"Ninety-five dollars, and that's a good deal."

"I'll take it."

The old man smiled, his teeth stained from tobacco and crooked as a sawblade. "Yes, sir. Let's take it to the register. Maybe the old suitcase will work magic with your painting. Finding treasures from the past and repurposing them, creates a whole new future for it. I like that. It's the same with old, negative patterns and lost people. You can pull 'em from the dust and make 'em new if you want to. That's my philosophy, anyway." He snorted and laughed at the same time.

THIRTY-ONE

Michael was hungry for diversion. Both in food for his body and for his mind. Oxford, Mississippi, had been on his bucket list for years. The arts, culture, and history all appealed to him. And now he'd take the time to spend the time, allowing it to soak into his pores. If he saw something to paint, he'd capture a slice of Oxford on canvas. Maybe the downtown Square, with its history and architecture, would offer inspiration. If not, perhaps there was something reminiscent from the Civil War that would whisper to him—the backdrop to the nation's greatest historical division. Oxford played a major role on that stage.

His first stop would be to visit at least one of the two independent bookstores—a place where he could leisurely browse through walls of bookshelves, each book with stories to share. In the first one he came upon, a rambling bookstore with century-year-old oak floors and thousands of books, he was met with the musty scent of aged paper, cardboard, and fresh ground coffee beans. He let his eyes adjust to the dim light, walking among the shelves of books—among history and great literature.

He stopped at the section on the history of Mississippi, running his finger down the spines of hard-cover books. He found a book labeled *Hoka and the Birth of Oxford,* removed it from the shelf, and strolled over to a section marked Literary Fiction. He found a novel he'd always wanted to read, but never took the time to do so. The book was by William Faulkner, *The Sound and the Fury.* Michael took both books up to an older woman in a red and blue floral dress standing at the cash register. She was using a small pitcher to water a white orchid in a tall, slim pot, her hair in a bun reflecting a slight blue tint under the florescent lighting. "Find ever'thing all right today?"

"Yes, ma'am. I did." He bought the books and walked toward the door, stopping to read a poster in the store window. It depicted a painting of a Mississippi beach scene with sand-dollars and sailboats. The poster was promoting an art show at a local gallery. Michael went there, spending more than an hour slowly viewing the art—paintings and sculptures, before choosing a farm-to-table restaurant in the Square for a late lunch.

During his stay, he spent his nights out of his van and the cold, allowing himself the luxury of a quaint inn, waking early on his final morning to enjoy a hearty southern breakfast before heading off to New Orleans. With his stomach full and mood upbeat, Michael was looking forward to another adventure somewhere around the bend. If there was ever a city that was moving art, it was New Orleans.

He traveled along a quiet country road, listening to songs on the radio, and changing stations each time the signal went out of range. As he flipped channels, a song he had never heard before, *When We Fall Apart* by Ryan Stevenson, came on the radio. He listened to the words, each one speaking personally to him, each note striking a chord within his heart.

… All I can think about is knowing I have to move on without you somehow … It's ok to cry, it's ok to fall apart. You don't have to try, to be strong when you are not. And it may take some time to make sense of all your thoughts. But don't ever fight your tears, 'cause there is freedom in every drop. Sometimes the only way to heal a broken heart is when we fall apart …

As the song progressed, Michael slowed down—his van going under twenty miles an hour. No other cars were on the road. Just him in a van, the scent of oil paint in the back, and the memories of his life with Kelsey and Mandy before him. He could see them walking through the surf, laughing, sea gulls joining from above. As the song continued, Michael could barely drive and had to pull off the road.

The lyrics of the song spoke deeply to Michael in a way he didn't expect, like a rogue wave of grief washing over him. The final few words of the chorus made him catch his breath.

Sometimes the only way to heal a broken heart is when we fall apart.

Michael sat behind the wheel, turned the motor off, and wept.

THIRTY-TWO

Michael traveled like a migrant, continuing to follow the changing seasons and backroads throughout the South. He stopped to paint and experience Deep South events and traditions, hoping to capture a fluidity and vibrancy that others could feel and think about. And each day, he painted a little more of himself into the world around him, adding color, awakening, healing—forgiving himself. Weeks turned into months ... and months into almost a year. He'd carry his easel and canvas on his right shoulder, grip the old suitcase filled with paints and brushes in his left hand, and walk deep into the outback searching for people and places to paint. Sometimes, however, he would just sit, thinking and reflecting—taking the time to listen and observe the beauty around him.

Every week he called to check in with Derek. His old teacher was becoming less communicative. As Michael drove into Alabama, he called and spoke with one of Derek's three caregivers, a compassionate, middle-aged woman name Joline. "Mr. Mack is doing better than expected," she said, her voice low as she spoke from Derek's kitchen, watching him sit in a recliner staring at blue jays in a backyard feeder. "But it's just a matter of time before he'll need to be in elder care as the disease takes a greater toll."

"Can I speak with him today?"

"Of course. Just like the last time you called, he may feel like talking, or he might not even want to hold the phone."

"If he doesn't want to hold the phone, place it to his ear, okay?"

"Okay."

Michael could hear her walk across the hardwood floor, her voice gentle. "Mr. Mack you have a phone call. It's Michael Vargas."

Silence.

"Derek, it's me … Michael." He waited a few seconds. Nothing. "I just wanted to see how you're doing."

"I'm doin' all right," finally came a weak voice.

"Good. I've met a lot of interesting people in my traveling. This was a great opportunity. I'll always be grateful to you for suggesting it. I've done a lot of paintings, and I look forward to sharing them with you when I get back. I just came from Biloxi, Mississippi, where I painted the Blessing of the Fleet. The priest was tossing holy water across the bows as someone tolled the town bell for all the known fishermen and sailors lost at sea from the area. But it was a festive occasion, too. Before Biloxi I had been painting deep in Southern Louisiana. One area that had a lot of color and life was the Crawfish Festival at a place called Breaux Bridge, in St. Martin Parish. It was a great way to really experience Cajun culture, zydeco music, and unbelievable food that'll challenge some of our best in the Lowcountry. I went frog gigging with two guys who are legendary at the art. I watched them hunt gators the next day. I'm not sure what I like the best … deep fried frog legs or boiled crawfish."

No response.

"Can you hear me, Derek?"

"Yes … I was just tryin' to remember what a crawfish looks like. I can't visualize it anymore. Oh, wait … maybe like a small lobster."

"They could be second cousins." Michael pulled into the parking lot of a Dollar General store, watching a woman push a grocery cart along the sidewalk, the cart filled with plastic bags, clothing sticking out from rips in the bags, a tattered brown suitcase toward the back of the cart. He closed his eyes, listening to Derek breathing, short and raspy breaths. "I look forward to showing my paintings to you. I've done almost a hundred from five states so far—South Carolina, North Carolina, Southern Tennessee, Mississippi, and Louisiana. I just crossed the border into the lower part of Alabama, and from there I'll probably venture into Florida's Panhandle, then up through Georgia."

Silence.

Michael waited and then said, "When I get back, we'll fix some oyster stew, followed with shrimp and grits. After we eat, I'll show you the paintings. It'll be a unique travelogue, hopefully better than looking at pictures of what I'll have completed on this year-long vacation or sabbatical. "Stay well, Professor. See you soon."

Silence.

THIRTY-THREE

The first thing Michael saw was a clock tower. He had left before sunrise, driving eastward, looking forward to the folksy charm that Alabama offered. Michael entered the city limits of Foley. The clock tower was the highest structure in the small town. The clock, with its large, gold-colored hands, blue face, and white numbers, was perched high atop a brick archway. The clock was the focal point of Foley's Centennial Park, a garden spot in the heart of the downtown area.

Michael stopped his van near the park entrance, got out and walked toward a rose garden as clarion bells beneath the clock began to play. The song was from the mid 1930s, *Summertime,* by George Gershwin. Michael listened to the clarity of the ringing bells, the music seeming to harmonize with the buzzing of bees in the flowers and birdsong coming from the pink dogwood trees, oaks, and crape myrtles.

Michael sat on a park bench, remembering the blooming flowers in New York City's Carl Schurz Park. *So long ago*, he thought. *A lifetime ago.* The clarion music changed from *Summertime* to *Somewhere Over the Rainbow.* An older couple, a man and a woman in their seventies, walked hand-in-hand down the center pathway, stopping to watch two squirrels play tag, running around the base of a large oak tree. The woman smiled. "They remind me of the grandkids."

Her husband nodded. "The squirrels don't have as much energy. Sometimes you feel like a nut … sometimes you don't." They both laughed, the early morning light against their jovial faces. Michael watched them enjoying themselves, nature and music—the sweetness of each other's company on a fine morning. He stood to leave.

"How are you?" the woman asked him, smiling.

"Better," Michael said. "Great weather. A lovely park here in the downtown. What could be better?"

There was a loud noise above them, as if a fire breathing dragon roared. Michael looked up as a blue-and-yellow hot air balloon floated a few hundred feet above them.

"How about a hot air balloon festival?" said the elder man. "I don't know if it's better, but it only happens one weekend a year in Foley."

"Where is the balloon festival?"

"Just a few miles from here, off Highway 98. You're not from around here?"

"No … but I've been traveling the South for a while now."

"Where are you going?" asked the woman.

"I'm not sure. Just traveling and painting."

"You paint houses?"

"No ma'am." Michael smiled. "I work in oil paints."

Her husband grinned. "An artist. By golly, that's just great. Well, you might want to visit the balloon festival. Lots of color over there. Could make a good painting."

"Thank you. I just might do that."

Michael drove his van to a large field on the edge of town. He parked, walked to the back of his van, the scent of sawdust, candied apples, and grilled onions in the breeze. Dozens of massive hot air balloons were being rolled out, crew members putting together their rigging. Around the perimeter was a carnival-like setting. Kiddie rides. Pony rides. Corn dog stands. Cotton candy. Simulated rock-climbing walls.

A country band was playing *Sweet Home Alabama* from a small, wooden stage under a big oak. Michael estimated that at least two hundred people strolled the grounds as the balloonists prepped the slumbering, deflated giants lying flat on the grass before them.

Michael took his easel and paints from the van and moved toward the heart of the activity. Within a few minutes, he was set up and mixing paints. He watched crew members assembling the cabling to the burners and the balloons. "Let's go," shouted a bearded man in a T-shirt and shorts to three members of his crew. He grinned. "If Billy hadn't overslept, we'd be in the clouds."

A tall, lanky man laughed. "That's 'cause Billy's got his head in the clouds."

The man named Billy, early twenties, wearing a *Crimson Tide* ballcap on his head, grinned. "Y'all gimme a break. We're all volunteers. It's not like we gotta punch a timeclock."

Michael guessed that there were at least sixty balloons in various stages of prep and early flight. He quickly painted the background, the distant tree line, the soft blue sky, and the clouds. He decided he'd paint six to ten balloons across the canvas.

As the crew of the closest balloon shot a long, horizontal blast of heated air into the mouth of a deflated balloon, the nylon fabric trembled as if it were the colorful skin of an animated, sleeping dragon quivering in the morning sunshine. Within a few minutes, the balloon began puffing up, rising to a vertical angle, as the hot air continued to inflate its upside-down belly.

Michael painted the balloon as it stood proud in its multicolored coat of pink, green, yellow, and red—all designed in a zigzag pattern, like a quilt ready to soar high above the earth. He used brushes to rough out the general shapes of the balloons, quickly converting to a palette knife, layering the colors onto the canvas.

"Mind if I take a picture of you painting a picture?" asked a middle-aged man, in a nylon flight jacket and khaki pants. He wore a wide-brimmed Panama hat and a white handlebar mustache on his brown face, lined and craggy. Eyes like a butane flame.

"Help yourself," Michael said. "It won't bother me."

"Thanks." The man snapped a half-dozen photos. Within a few minutes, other people came up, forming a semi-circle, watching Michael paint.

A little girl, no older than five, shoulder-length hair, stood next to a woman and pointed. "Mama, he paints really fast."

"Yes, he does. You love to paint. Watch the man and see how he does it."

The small crowd observed in silence as Michael used his brushes to paint the balloon pilots and members of the prep and flight crews. The man in the Panama hat said, "That's remarkable. You ever fly in a balloon?"

Michael glanced over at him and continued painting. "No. Always wanted to. Just never seemed to find the time."

"With balloons, time seems to stand still up there. You're using something very primitive to defy gravity. In a balloon, you don't need wings to fly."

"Are you a balloonist?"

"Goin' on thirty years now. We'll be flying this afternoon. I like the flights at dusk because the sky and the earth seem calmer. A good sunset is even more addictive from up there." He paused, watching Michael use a palette knife. "You paint the canvas … we paint the sky."

Michael laughed. "That's a good way to look at it." He watched two balloons lift off, the roar of the burners lifting them into the air. He painted the balloon's ascent into the sky, capturing the awe on the faces of spectators. The pointing. The hands clapping. The high-fives. He glanced at the man. "Are you a pilot?"

"Sort of, I'd say. I operate the balloon. The wind is the real pilot. It carries the balloon wherever it wants to. The pilot can control the vertical rise and descent. The horizontal flight, not so much. That pilot's the wind. After thirty years, I believe God's been my copilot, too. What ballooning boils down to is finding joy in the journey. Letting go, and literally going wherever the wind blows." He smiled, deep creases at the corners of his eyes. "With ballooning, love is in the air."

Michael smiled, pouring his concentration into the painting as the scene changed by the second. More people took pictures while he worked. "This will make a really cool YouTube video," said a teenage boy, shooting video on his phone as Michael painted.

He continued painting until the last balloon rose into the sky, the sounds of the county music band seemed louder as the roar of the burners subsided. Some of the original throng of people stayed, watching Michael put finishing details into the painting. Others drifted away, and new people came, most all taking pictures.

The man in the Panama hat returned. A younger man who resembled him was there, too. The older man said, "It's amazing how it all came together. I thought the colors of our balloons were vivid. The colors on your canvas reflect the energy of the event."

"Thanks." Michael used a thin brush to write his name in the lower right-side corner: *Vargas*

"What's your name?" asked the man.

"Michael Vargas."

"I'm Hank Foster. This is one of my sons, Eric."

"Nice to meet you guys," Michael said. "I'd shake your hands, but you'd leave with a lot of paint in your palms." Michael began packing up his paints.

"No problem," said Hank. "If you'd like to go up in a balloon, be back here at four-thirty. We got room for one more. If you think all these balloons look good from ground level, you ought to see them from the heavens."

* * *

Hours later, it was just before five in the afternoon when Michael stood in the wicker basket with Hank Foster, his son Eric, and Eric's fiancée, a pretty girl with wide hazel eyes and black hair in a ponytail. Hank pulled the lever and the burner fired again, the long, yellow flame belching into the center of the inflated balloon. The ground crew waved an "all clear" check, the balloon drifting above the trees, two dozen more balloons rising in the air at about the same time.

In less than five minutes, the balloon rose to more than five hundred feet above the earth. The evening air was cool against Michael's face. The nomadic, late afternoon clouds were wandering toward the horizon, the big cumulus clouds backlit in soft pastel colors of yellow and orange as the sun crept further west.

"Michael, welcome to our place of adventure—the sweet spot between earth and heaven. What do you think?" Hank asked, a grin on his face, the wind teasing his handlebar moustache.

"It's amazing. I wish I hadn't waited all these years to experience this."

"Good that you're doing it now. No better time than the present … and to be up here. Stress doesn't live up here. You ever see a stressed-out cloud?"

"No, not really. Well, maybe … in a storm."

"Storms pass. And the clouds just paint themselves white again. I like the way you did the clouds in your painting."

"Thanks, but now that I'm up here, just about face-to-face with them, I'll have a better perspective next time."

Hank laughed. "That's what ballooning is all about. Finding a better perspective." He winked at the girl and draped his arm over his son's shoulder. "Right, Eric?"

"That's right. I never get tired of it. Leslie and I might get married in a hot air balloon."

"That'll be a small wedding party." Hank snorted. "Don't tell your mama … and certainly not Leslie's!"

Michael laughed, deeply breathing in the fresh air that felt sweeter as they ascended upward. It was as if the balloon was following the trade winds and the floral scents only found at a higher elevation. He looked at the tapestry of the earth far below, shades of avocado and olive green, the farmland laid out in squares and massive rectangles, bordered by fences. Turning and facing south, he could see the Gulf of Mexico in the distance.

The forests and rolling meadows were not confined to grids, growing without restraint. And then he lifted his eyes to the horizon, the clouds soaking in the western sun, changing their afternoon attire from white to pink, scarlet, and crimson. Michael spotted an eagle at their same altitude, the bird soaring toward the sunset. At that moment, Michael felt like he was soaring. He thought about what Hank said that morning. *In a balloon, you don't need wings to fly.*

* * *

Over the next few months, while painting in and around the Gulf Shore area of Alabama and a swath of the Florida Panhandle, Michael felt that he had come into a peaceful place within himself. In addition to painting the shoreline with its handful of beachgoers, he spent time walking, reading, and thinking. During his last few days in the Panhandle, Michael found and walked areas of a desolate beach, watching and painting the seafaring birds as they casually waded in shallow waters along the shoreline, stalked the reeds looking for culinary delights or soared with majestic tranquility overhead.

Michael knew it was time to leave the Gulf coast states, with its gift of solitude, and move forward on his journey.

THIRTY-FOUR

Michael headed north, driving into the foothills of North Georgia along the Chattahoochee River. Looking out his van window, he could see the river, its water moving fast after recent hard rains, the current crashing over rocks and large boulders, an angry white froth churning into the air above the river.

He drove on, following the backroads and the history of the area, the mountain air cool, the scent of honeysuckle coming in the van's open windows. He had read that the headwaters of the river, at one time, was the site of dozens of Indian mounds, many dating back more than two-thousand years. The Chattahoochee, at almost 450 miles long, was used for years to transport goods into Atlanta and many harbors downriver.

Michael came to a bend in the highway, spotting a sign with directions to an old grist mill dating back to 1866. He turned off the highway onto a country road, driving three miles, the narrow road playing tag with a wide creek that meandered through the woods, eventually flowing into the river.

And there it was.

Almost like an illusion or a slice of Americana that time made a decision, long ago, to ignore.

Michael stopped to look at a grist mill on the banks of a wide, fast-flowing creek, which fed a large pond as it traveled through. The mill resembled a weathered barn on the edge of the stream, the exterior wood faded to a slate gray over time. Water was diverted from the current near the banks, routed through a wooden chute, the torrent falling onto the blades of a paddlewheel the color of a ripe tomato. Near the mill was a covered bridge that spanned the width of the creek.

Michael parked his van close to the shore. The old mill was across the pond on the opposite side. He watched a family—a father, mother, and young boy, feeding mallard ducks and white swans in the millpond. A black man sat on an upside-down bucket, near a large weeping willow tree, holding a cane pole, fishing. The man kept his eyes on the red-and-white bobber floating between the lily pads. After a few minutes, the fisherman lifted the pole, the hook and baited worm coming straight out of the water to be dropped in another spot with a *plop*, the ripple of water breaking the reflection off the surface for a moment.

Michael took out his easel, paints, and canvas and started a new painting. He began with the cobalt blue sky, and colossal white clouds floating in the hemisphere, high above the timeworn mill. He used his palette knife to block out the structure, adding the shadow, texture and look of aged wood. Then he painted the mammoth wheel, using the palette knife and brushes to get the effect of falling water, choosing a fan brush to paint a mist rising directly above the areas where the water spilled from the paddle blades, jostling down the open chute and back into the stream, which poured into the millpond. He painted the pond, capturing the reflection of the mill, sky and trees across the water's still surface.

And then he painted the people enjoying the moment as the water flowed, the big wheel turning, the grist mill operating like it had for generations. At that instant, the black man stood from the plastic bucket, the bobber vanishing, the tip of the cane pole bending. He used both hands to pull a fat bream from the water.

"Look!" shouted the boy feeding the swans. "He caught a fish! Let's go see!"

Michael painted the family standing next to the elder fisherman as he smiled and showed them the bream, the little boy using one finger to touch the fish behind its blue-green head. After a minute, the fisherman bent down next to the pond and lifted a stringer with a least a half-dozen fish attached to it. Michael painted as the proud man displayed his catch, the sound of people laughing and ducks quacking from across the pond.

Michael grinned, watching the chickens scurrying and a rooster strutting in the yard near old stones that served as the ground-level foundation for the mill. He painted the chickens and a large black Lab sleeping near the opened door to the mill, the wheel turning, corn husk dust coming out of one rusted pipe protruding from the tin roof.

After another hour, Michael finished, the setting sun reflecting like crushed rubies off the surface of the millpond. He cleaned his brushes and sipped from a bottle of water. He was tired, having stood in the sun for a few hours of non-stop painting, swatting at gnats, mosquitoes, and not going to the restroom. He had to pee, his lower back in the kidney area beginning to throb. He drove over a covered bridge, the old boards moaning, a rushing creek under the span. He parked in the mill's dirt and gravel lot. There was a Harley-Davidson motorcycle and a black, late model pickup truck out front.

Michael went inside and felt he'd stepped back into the era of the Civil War. "C'mon in," came a shrill voice from somewhere in the mill, the man's voice just heard above the sound of the water pushing the big wheel. "Be right with you," he said. "I'm tryin' to open some windows to air out the ghosts."

THIRTY-FIVE

Michael walked further back into the abyss of the mill. He admired the architecture and the structure—the wood and stone building still standing long after generations of people who operated it were gone. He figured it probably hadn't changed much in more than 150 years, the sound of leather belts and gears groaning with a constant thumping like wooden mallets smacking boards. "Be right there," came the man's voice from somewhere in the mill.

"No hurry."

Michael watched the waterwheel axel turning, the iron shaft connected to a series of wide leather belts. Millstones churned as corn kernels were delivered through a wooden chute and ground between the large revolving stones. The ground meal came through another opening, fed by gravity, and filled cloth bags marked: *Cider Creek Stoneground Mill.*

A man with a flowing white beard, sweat-stained 'Bama football cap, bib overalls, and a white T-shirt, came out of the shadows, tying one of the bags of grits. Fine dust from the ground corn clinging to his bifocals like road grime. "Sorry about the wait. Can I help you?" His southern accent thick as the air.

"How much for a bag?"

"Three dollars."

"Great. I'll take two."

"All right." The man stood straighter, as if his back hurt. He pulled a lever, stopping the fall of grain and pulled another lever disengaging the millstones from belts turned by the axel wheel. The only remaining sound was that of the water flowing through the flume and over the big wheel. He hitched his overalls up, stepping across discarded bags of meal. "Let's go to the cash register."

Michael followed him through the maze of machinery, the smell of grain and corn chaff dust heavy in air that appeared trapped in time. The miller walked behind a timeworn, wooden counter near the entrance, late afternoon sunlight coming through a dirty window in diffused shafts. He set two bags of corn meal on the counter. "Be six even. Tax is built in the price."

Michael pulled the money from his wallet. "Thanks. You said you were opening windows to air out the ghosts. Is the old mill haunted?"

"I wouldn't use the word … haunted. To me, that kinda means naughty ghosts are here, and they don't take a liken' to people. Although, with some people, I cain't say I'd blame them." He chuckled, a wheezing sound coming from his chest. "Let's just say that, from time to time, I see stuff in here I can't explain."

"Such as?"

"My tools get moved. It's like some ghost is playin' hide 'n seek with my stuff. Same thing with my helper, Kyle. He's a young fella. A big boy. Drives the Harley out front. Doesn't scare easy. He says he's seen orbs, shadows, and whatnot move around, especially if we're doin' a special run on a Sunday."

"Are you the owner?"

He grinned, the white beard parting. "Naw, I just run it part-time for the owner. I enjoy it. I figure if a man really enjoys what he's doin' in his life to earn a livin', work will never be a job. That's the way I look at it. The mill doesn't use any power from man. No electricity. Pure waterpower generates about fifteen to twenty horsepower, depending on whether heavy rains got the creek flowin' real fast. The mill creates no pollution, just fine flour and grits." He smiled, used two fingers to press the keys on a century-old cash register, the till opening with a ring.

"How old is this mill?"

The man looked up as if he had to consider a few historical dates. "George Banks built it in 1866 … right after the war. He ran it 'til 1899 when he retired. His kinfolks didn't want it. So, the mill sat idle for a few years. Then it was sold, and three generations of one family ran it for years, up 'til 1999. One of the great grandkids got high as a kite on somethin' they call angel dust. Boy thought he could fly like an angel.

He jumped off the roof one Sunday mornin' … landed at the base of the big wheel. He didn't live long." The man exhaled, looking away. "A businessman down in Roswell, a fella fascinated with old mills, bought it a couple of years ago. He hired Kyle and I to run it part-time."

"Do I have to go all the way to Helen to find a motel room?"

"Yep, pretty much so. You won't find a motel here for fifty miles. Not enough traffic or tourists."

"I'm driving an old van. I can sleep in it. You mind if I park in your lot next to the pond and get a little rest before I hit the road again?"

"Help yourself. I'm lockin' up. Stay as long as you want. I've seen too many people die in car accidents from bein' too tired to drive."

"I know this building is old, but does it have a men's room?"

"It's got one room—a bathroom. Men and women both can use it. It was added in 1932. Before that, folks used an outhouse on the property up near the old cabin." He pointed, a Band-Aid on the back of his hand. "Down the hall, first door on the left. Overlooks the pond, so you can pee with a view."

* * *

It was close to ten p.m. when Michael thought about food. He hadn't eaten since early in the morning, buying a stale bagel at a gas station that sold food sealed in plastic wrap. He reached into a bag of potato chips, sat on the floorboard of his van, both doors wide open, eating chips, and sipping warm bottled water.

He looked out at a full moon rising in the star-filled sky above the millpond, the creamy moonlight spilling over the surface, across the flowering lily pads, casting the cattails along the water's edge in silhouette. Bullfrogs serenaded each other in the honeyed air, the shimmering yellow light urging shadows to come out of hiding and dance.

In the moonlight, Michael could see water bugs spinning in elliptical orbits on the surface of the millpond. He watched the profile of a bullfrog's head as it rose among the duckweed, opening its mouth and hollering at the moon. A breeze blew, rippling the surface, blowing through the weeping willow trees, cattails, reeds, and oaks, carrying a night song of creaks and rustles, delivering the scent of clover and pond water. Fish broke water in silvery trails on the surface as crickets, cicadas and frogs chanted. The millpond, with its teeming, nocturnal cycle of life, was a watering hole for Michael's soul.

He stood on the dirt parking lot at the back of his van, deeply inhaling the night air. He looked up at the mill, the moonlight reflecting from some of the windows. Michael thought about what the miller had said, *"I'm tryin' to open some windows to air out the ghosts … I figure if a man really enjoys what he's doin' in his life to earn a livin', work will never be a job. That's the way I look at it.*

Michael pulled a canvas from the van, set it on the easel, duct taped a small flashlight to the edge of the van door and aimed it on the canvas. He then began painting the millpond at night under the full moon, the lofty oaks draped in hanging moss, the evening dew laced like moonlit pearls on a spider's web among the cattails. He stood there, painting, then pausing to feel what he couldn't see beyond the buttery light falling around him.

After he added detail to the canvas, he looked to the sky. It was cloudless. The moon, with its smiling face, was Michael's sole companion. He turned his attention to the northern section of the sky, into what appeared to be the darkest part of the universe.

He spotted two stars near each other, one slightly larger than the other. Both just as bright and seemingly in their own hidden patch of the cosmos. He stared at the stars, unable to look away, his thoughts racing. Time and place no longer a visible barrier. Suddenly, it was as if the past and the present merged together in a guiding light from the heavens. He pictured Kelsey and Mandy, their smiles … their presence with him, standing somewhere at the edge of his vision.

The breeze across the pond stopped … the stars twinkling with a near hypnotic iridescence, a deep awareness from the heavens entering his pores. His spirit felt drenched in the soft light. Michael took a deep breath, lowering his eyes back to the canvas. He mixed white and silver paint on his palette, in a combination that looked like stardust. And then he added the final touches to the painting—the two brightest stars in the sky, symbolic of a butterfly kiss to his daughter, Mandy, and as a special tribute to his wife, Kelsey. "You were my everything," he whispered.

It would be his last painting on the road.

When the sun rose above the millpond in the morning, Michael was going home.

THIRTY-SIX

He didn't want to call. Michael knew that phone conversations with Derek were becoming too difficult for him. The long pauses. The awkward repeating of questions. Michael wondered if Derek's sense of hearing was somehow being affected as the atrophy of his brain increased. He thought about that as he pulled his van onto Derek's property, parking in the shade cast by the largest oak.

Something was different.

It was as if Michael could feel it in the morning breeze. Walking up to the front porch, he got the sense that no one was home. Even without Derek's old Subaru in his driveway, Michael could tell that he wasn't home. The house simply had the look of emptiness—almost a look of sorrow, not that brick and mortar have a nervous system. But the interior, just like the human body, was somehow permanently changed, causing the exterior of the home to take on the appearance of a certain unkept hollowness.

It was the little things that spoke volumes. Curtains closed. Derek mostly kept them open. Mail sticking out of the box near the door. The empty birdfeeder in the corner of the front porch. Even the silence of the perennial songbirds had its own somber void. Michael rang the doorbell, the ringing no more than a mournful summons that wouldn't be answered. He stood there and thought about some of the last conversations they'd had. Derek always trying to make the conversation about Michael and what he was doing in his travels, while Michael simply wanting to hear from Derek—to get a feel for his condition and, in some small way, help his old mentor with his memory, trying to salvage pieces of his personality along with it.

* * *

The Memory Care Center of Charleston looked more like a sprawling English manor than an assisted living facility. It was a large, one-story complex of aged brick, river stone, and wood built with lots of gables and archways that appeared to cover at least two of the five acres it encompassed. Michael parked in the lot and stood near the front lawn, in awe of the landscaping. He held his last painting in one hand—the painting of the millpond in the moonlight.

The expansive grounds and landscaping resembled something found on the estates of well-manicured English gardens, red maple and oak trees casting deep shade over lush grass, powder blue hydrangeas blooming, red and white azaleas planted in circles under the trees, irises popping in purple, cream, and mauve. The crimson bougainvillea flowers hung from arched, white-washed terraces, giving the appearance of bridges of flowers over trimmed hedges leading to a gazebo under the trees. The meandering stone and grass pathways leading in and out of the labyrinth and the deep shadow had a mysterious feel, like entering a secret garden.

But it was the roses that caught Michael's eye the most. The rose garden was more than one hundred feet in diameter. Fist-sized roses in shades of red, white, pink and yellow dipped their floral heads in the breeze. The rose garden surrounded a cascading black, cast-iron water fountain, the top forged to look like a morning glory flower in bloom, water bubbling from the center and cascading down five tiers until it splashed into a wide pool filled with koi. The fish swam just below the surface in tawny circles of orange, black and white.

A woman came from the shadows of the stone and grass path leading to the gazebo. She held a rose in one hand, walked up to the koi pond and stood there, watching the fish, the breeze filled with the perfume of roses and lilac. Even from the distance, Michael could tell the woman was striking. She appeared tall and had long chestnut brown hair. She wore a blue and white sundress that was as colorful as any of the flowers in the garden. Michael watched her speak to the koi, the fish coming to the surface, bobbing, fins wagging like a dog's tail. He could hear her laughter, her posture animated, using her hands to speak to the fish.

Michael wanted to get closer to her, to hear what she was saying. But more than that, he had a sudden and powerful urge to paint her. The morning light across the splendor of the garden and the beauty of the woman in the center of the landscaping was compelling and tugged upon his artist instincts. He knew she'd be walking away soon, and she'd walk out of the image in his mind. He thought about using his phone to take a picture, but he'd never painted from photographs—only from the moment or his memory of the moment.

He looked back at his van, debating whether to set up his easel. His desire to paint was growing stronger each moment he watched her. She reached down with one hand and lightly moved the tips of her fingers across the water. As Michael observed the woman, he wondered why she was here in this place surrounded by beauty on the exterior, and yet it housed the ugliness of Alzheimer's disease and dementia beyond its walls. Maybe she had a relative inside, or maybe she was a patient, perhaps an early onset of the disease. But she appeared too young, although she was talking to the fish. He smiled, captivated.

Michael wanted to meet her—to see if she'd be there long enough for him to paint her. He didn't want to infringe on her privacy, but he didn't want her to walk away either. He could simply paint the scene as he saw it, relying on his memory. However, there was something about this lone woman in an immense garden bursting with color, light, and moving water that was striking. And it was only striking with her presence in the center point and not literally out of the picture.

Most of the time, he could catch people in action, in the candid moments of life and paint them, as he last did when the old black man caught the bream from the millpond and the young family, especially the little boy, got to experience that.

But, with the woman in the garden, it was somehow different. There was an aura of mystery about her as if she'd come from the deep shadows cast by the red maples across the entry to the secret garden and the path leading to the solitary gazebo. Her presence was crucial to create a painting he would call the woman in the garden. He needed to speak to her. He had nothing to lose.

He picked up his painting of the millpond and walked through the garden toward the enigmatic woman. He thought about the approach he'd take when he got to her. *Hi, I'm an impressionist painter … do you mind standing here for a while? I'd like to paint you in this garden. Should take only two to three hours.*

He had nothing to lose except the opportunity to create his first painting since returning to Charleston. And he felt this one might be his best yet—the mystery of an unknown woman in a garden reminiscent of what some of his favorite impressionist painters would choose to paint. He would take the chance and speak to her. He had to. *Don't walk away,* he thought. *Please, at least not for a while.*

THIRTY-SEVEN

She didn't look up, although Michael felt she sensed his presence in the garden. As he came closer, he watched her walk around the koi pond, still chatting with the fish. She paused, took a coin from her purse, and tossed it into the largest cast-iron tier in the fountain, just above the koi pond, the water cascading over the sides and falling down into the large pool.

When Michael came nearer, the fragrance of the roses was intoxicating. He could hear the hum of insects, the pulsating lavender flowers teeming with bees. And he could hear the water splashing into the fountain and see the koi following her just at the surface.

The woman looked up and smiled. Michael thought her smile was even more compelling than any flower around her. It was as if she was amused, her face filled with bright highlights that began in her eyes. Mahogany eyes gleaming and playful, seizing the morning light with no apologies. Her mouth and full lips had a haughty sensuality as natural as the red rose that she held in one hand. The sundress did little to hide the woman's shapely body.

Michael stopped next to the koi pond, the mist from the fountain splattering across his bare, left arm. He smiled. "Hi … this may sound a little odd … but I was wondering if I could paint you here in the garden?"

"With my clothes on or off?"

"Pardon me?"

She smiled, looking at the painting he held in his hand. "I must admit, that was one of the best lines I've ever heard. I was just kidding about the clothes optional part. We haven't formally met, not that I'm a very formal person. I'm Catherine Kincaid."

"I'm Michael Vargas."

"It's nice to meet you, Michael Vargas. Is that canvas in your hand a really big business card, or do you carry a painting to prove you're an artist?" She smiled wider, pulling a strand of brown hair behind one ear.

"I brought it for a friend."

"Is your friend here?"

"Yes, he is."

"My mother is here, too." Catherine inhaled deeply through her nostrils, pursing her lips and looking at the painting. "Did you buy it for your friend."

"No, I painted it."

"Really?"

"Really."

"It's beautiful. Where was it done?"

"The pond is next to an old grist mill in the Georgia foothills. I painted it one night when I was passing through the area. Started around midnight and finished before sunrise. And then I headed back to South Carolina, my home—or my home again."

"May I have a better look?"

"Sure." Michael walked closer, propping the canvas up at the stone ledge of the fountain. "The day before I did this, I painted the old mill from across the pond."

Catherine said nothing, her eyes taking in the entire canvas. A bumble bee alighted on purple wisteria near the roses. She looked up from the painting to Michael, her voice suddenly softer. "This is exquisite. I love the way you painted the dew in the spider's web, like strings of opaque pearls in the moonlight. And I love how the moon and stars are reflecting off the calm water. I can almost hear the frogs throbbing on the lily pads."

"Throbbing. The word certainly describes the night sounds. There were a lot of frogs that night. So many, in fact, I couldn't sleep … so I thought I'd paint instead."

"That was a good decision. The world is a little brighter because of it. Were you camping out?"

"Sort of. I often slept in my van when I was on location painting."

Catherine angled her head, her eyes meeting his and then lowering them to the painting, like she was looking to discover a four-leaf clover in the grass next to the water. Michael licked his lips and said, "I'm glad you like it."

"I don't like it … I love it. And I'd love to see the other painting of the pond, too. The one that includes the mill."

"It's in my van with a lot more." He gestured toward the parking lot.

She grinned. "Do you travel the country painting and selling out of your van. Are you a gypsy painter, Michael?"

He laughed. "I was more of a drifter I suppose. Sort of following the wind. When it changed directions, I'd do the same. Makes for a rather zig-zag journey."

"No one should live life in a straight line anyway. Boring."

"I decided to take a year to travel around the South and paint some of the things I saw and the people I met."

"How romantic. Was this millpond the final one before you came home?"

"Yes."

"And now you want to paint me in this lovely garden? Does that mean your journey continues or is it the next chapter?"

Michael thought about her question before answering. "Both. I've turned the page where I'm entering the next chapter. And my journey in life hasn't ended, but that specific trip has."

Catherine smiled, glancing down at the koi in the water, their mouths breaking the surface in small O shapes. "I read that the Japanese like the koi because the fish symbolize a destiny fulfilled. The koi are known for their perseverance. According to Japanese myth, a school of koi came to a waterfall on their journey upriver. All tried to climb the waterfall, but only one fearless little fish did. He made it to the top, to calm waters. In recognition for his bravery and tenacity, the Japanese gods turned the little fish into an orange dragon." She looked up from the water, a coy smile forming. "Did you climb waterfalls? Are you going to turn into a fire-breathing dragon and fly away?"

"I went white water rafting, if that qualifies. And I'd rather be a dragonfly than a dragon. All dragonflies have wings, but not all dragons do."

Catherine paused for a second, delight building in her face, and then she burst into laughter, her eyes gleaming, touching her hand to her lips. "You're funny. Aren't painters supposed to be somewhat sullen, maybe slice off part of their ear?" She grinned, adjusting her purse strap across her right shoulder.

"Vincent Van Gogh was one of the best. Torn in different directions about life … maybe a little bi-polar, but a genius. Unfortunately, his genius wasn't recognized in his lifetime. That was a tragedy."

"Tragedy? Maybe. In a Greek tragedy—in theater, the main character falls on his or her sword due to their personal failure and circumstance, often interchangeable, one causing the other. Sometimes heartbreak is not getting what you deserve or conversely getting what you deserve. Maybe Van Gogh knew his own genius, even when others didn't. The fame and fortune can be part of the reward, but maybe the ultimate gift is what he discovered unwrapping his own talents … one painting at a time … sharing them with one person at a time." She glanced down at the painting and then looked up at Michael, her eyes probing.

"Following that theory," he said choosing his words carefully, "what will I discover when I paint you in the garden?"

"Whether or not you have allergies." She laughed. "I didn't commit yet. If I do, maybe you'll discover more about how to paint flowers." She held up the rose. "Could you ever paint something as beautiful as this?"

He looked at the rose in her left hand and was surprised to see no wedding ring. "I wouldn't try. I couldn't improve upon its beauty … its perfection. So, I wouldn't try. But what I could do is to paint my impression of the rose, the way I see it in the garden … or in your hand."

"Okay … I'll buy that Mr. Impressionism. How would you paint me?" She tried to hide her smile, sitting down on the edge of the stone wall surrounding the koi pond and setting the rose next to her.

"Just like the rose."

"Really? But I'm not a rose"

"No, but like the rose, I can't improve upon your beauty … the natural perfection I see. So, again, I wouldn't try. But I will paint my impression of you … at least in an artistic sense."

"Of course. What is your impression of me … in an artistic sense?"

"Highly intelligent. Someone filled with life. Or at least the way life should be lived. You're approachable. You have a beautiful smile. You have a keen sense of humor …"

"Don't stop now. You're on a roll. I haven't heard this since my mother consoled me after my first boyfriend walked out of my young life."

"His loss."

"In hindsight I was not his type. I just didn't know it at the time."

"What type are you?"

"I suppose you can find that out when you paint your impression of me."

Michael smiled. "So, you'll do it, right?"

"I'll consider it. If I do, there will be one condition."

"Okay. What is that?"

"When you finish, you promise to loan or give the painting to this center. There's a great hall in there where many of the residents congregate. Some, of course, have advanced stages of dementia and Alzheimer's. But some residents, like my mother, aren't fully there yet. Some can come out here, supervised, in this magnificent garden and smell the roses." Catherine picked up the rose and stood. "When you're done, I want you to hang the painting in there so everyone can see it. If we can't bring them to the flowers and this garden, we can take the garden inside. It'll make many of the patients smile. Deal?" She smiled and put the rose stem between her teeth.

"Deal."

"Good. Oh, how long do you think it'll take?"

"Well, since I'm going to be painting a larger canvas so it'll display well in the great room, it'll take a little longer than usual."

"What's usual … a few days."

Michael looked around the garden as if he was assessing its scope. "It depends on how much time we have each day."

"I'll only have maybe two hours a day. We can do it the same time, late in the afternoon. Will that work?"

"We'll make it work."

She stepped closer to the painting, staring at his signature in the lower right corner. "Vargas … Michael Vargas. Your name rings some distant bell. Are you famous? Sounds odd that I'd have to ask, but I don't keep up with mainstream media."

TOM LOWE

He nodded. "I'm not part of any stream of media. I just travel off the beaten path to paint."

Catherine looked from his face back to the painting. "Okay … I'm trying to picture your face clean-shaven, maybe with a haircut. I won't pry and ask what you did before you took a year to go off and paint, but one thing that I'm sure of is I've seen that signature before today."

"Where would that be?"

"Oh, I remember … on a painting that's hanging on the wall in a patient's room. He's across the hall two doors up from my mother's room. The painting is of the South Carolina Lowcountry. My mother loves it. At least I think she does because she'll stand and stare at it."

"That's a good thing."

"She was born and raised here. It's odd and cruel how Alzheimer's can strike different parts of the brain … the memory. Sometimes her memory of her childhood is clear, yet she's not always sure I'm her daughter." She paused and looked away, the breeze changing. "The man who owns the painting is so sweet. He allows Mom to come into his room anytime to look at it. In all the times I've been here, though, I haven't seen anyone visit him. It's such a shame, too, because I can tell he's lonely. With your name on the painting in his room, and on that painting you're carrying, it's pretty easy to make the connection. What I don't know is how you're connected. Your last name is Vargas. His is Mack … Derek Mack. Is he the friend you're here to see?"

"Yes."

"I'd love to take you to him … just to see the expression on his face, if that's okay?"

"That's okay."

She smiled, then glanced at his left hand. "When you were gone on your sabbatical year, did your wife join you? I'm not prying, just curious."

"My wife and daughter died. That's one of the reasons I came back to painting, one of the reasons I traveled in a van painting wherever I went."

"I am so very sorry. I feel horrible for your loss. I shouldn't have asked … I just saw your wedding ring … and … sorry … forget it."

"It's okay. Fair question."

"Look," she said softly, pointing to a hedge of summer lilac filled with lavender blooms. "It's a hummingbird."

Michael watched the tiny hummingbird, with its ruby throat, dart among the lilacs. Derek's words in his mind were as soft as the fragrant breeze. He watched the little bird feeding and said, "The man I'm going in there to see once told me that hummingbirds remind us to seek the magic in life. He said, when you see one, he called them the little angels of the birds … Derek said they've been perceived in many cultures, especially among Native Americans, as a sign of good luck and coming joy."

THIRTY-EIGHT

Michael borrowed a dolly—a flat-bed cart, to load more than two-dozen paintings and wheel them through the Memory Care Center of Charleston building. Catherine met him at the entrance to the great room, which appeared to be the community center. It was filled with comfortable couches, chairs, tables, flat-screen TVs, lots of green plants in the corners, and a large river-stone fireplace. There was staff assisting patients in playing board games and with art projects. A half-dozen patients sat at a long table, some using crayons to draw and others using scissors with rounded tips to cut shapes from yellow and blue construction paper. A yoga class was being held in one corner.

Catherine looked at the stack of paintings on the dolly. "That's impressive. Did you get them all?"

"No, there are a lot more in my van. Not enough room on the dolly, and it would be difficult to push. I'll get them later."

She stared at the painting that included the grist mill with the waterwheel, the elder fisherman and the family. "Oh … wow … that is so beautiful. Having seen the millpond in the moonlight, this gives it a great and added perspective. I can almost hear that little boy shouting for joy as he looks at the fish."

"I got lucky. Right place at the right time."

"Maybe. But you knew what to paint … what to squeeze out of that scene, that moment with the nostalgia of an antique working grist mill—the expression on the face of the elderly fisherman and the boy. It's priceless."

"I'm glad you like it. These will be enough to show Derek, at least for now." He looked around the room. "I don't see him in here. Do you know where he is?"

"I spoke with one of his caregivers, not that he needs a lot of caregiving … he's still here in terms of his cognitive powers. It's just that he fades in and out and has difficulty finding his way around, especially outdoors. He's in his room. I'll take you there. But, before I do, I want you to meet my mother. Maybe by showing her a couple of your paintings, it'll stimulate some sensory areas in her brain."

"I'd like to meet her. Where is she?"

Catherine motioned to a group of patients sitting at a long table near the dormant fireplace. "She's over there. They're coloring. Some use coloring books. Staying in the lines can be quite a challenge. Others just like to do free-form, sketching shapes on paper."

"How long has your mother been here?"

"More than a year. I truly believe that Alzheimer's is the cruelest disease. The most heartless. That doesn't mean that cancer, heart disease and all the other horrible maladies mankind suffers from are lessoned. Those awful diseases steal your life. Alzheimer's tries to steal your soul. Imagine the woman who gave you your life—the woman who birthed and raised you … imagine her not recognizing you at times and fearing the time when she won't recognize you at all. This horrible disease knows no boundaries. It tears the heart out of families as much as it rips the dignity and the essence of the person's spirit out of the patient. They become a shell of their former selves. And they don't know how to break out of that shell because they're trapped in there. It is not a normal progression of age. It's an insidious, slow death that kills the mind first before taking the spirit." Catherine bit her lower lip, her eyes welling. "I'm sorry. It's just that I look at all these lovely people and know that their very essence is steadily and cruelly being ravaged and discarded … and they don't even know it."

A tall man in a dark suit approached. He wore black-framed glasses on a slender nose. Pale face. A wide smile forming. He extended his hand to Michael. "Hi, I'm Clarence Moore, the director here."

"Michael Vargas. Good to meet you."

Moore glanced down at the paintings on the cart. "That's a great painting. Is the old mill in South Carolina?"

"No, Georgia."

"You do excellent work. Mrs. Kincaid told me about your generous offer to paint the gardens and loan or donate the painting to us for display here in the community center. Thank you so much."

Michael didn't respond immediately, the word *Mrs.* echoing in his mind. He smiled. "Glad to help in some way, if I can." He glanced over at Catherine who did not look his way.

"That's kind of you. I'm told you're a close friend of Derek Mack."

"Yes, we go back to when I was a teenager. He was my art teacher at one time."

"He's definitely well known in the Charleston area. I understand he was a good artist in his day."

"One of the very best."

Moore nodded, looked across the large room. "When was the last time you saw Mr. Mack?"

"About a year ago. But we've talked on the phone—been noticing the decline."

"He won't, of course, be the same from when you saw him. Dementia is basically a medical term that describes memory loss. With cognitive diminishing, it can affect a patient's ability to carry out normal, everyday functioning. Alzheimer's is a disease within the parameters of dementia. But Alzheimer's is the most devastating. It always will get worse. That's a sad but true prognosis. We have medications to slow the progression, but that's all. There's no known cure."

"What's the cause?" Michael asked.

"It's caused by the deterioration of brain cells. The disease does this by creating a buildup of abnormal substances referred to as amyloid plaques or harmful protein deposits. This wreaks havoc on the neuron fibers inside the brain, inhibiting their normal functions. In the United States alone, a new case is diagnosed about every sixty seconds. And that's expected to get even worse, more frequent. In the meantime, we do all we can to provide excellent and supervised care to patients, diets rich in antioxidants, medication and exercise. And, we're always seeking ways to engage them in mental stimulation on a daily basis."

Michael nodded. "I want to show these paintings to Derek. Maybe that'll be some sort of mental stimulation."

"Art is a great visual stimulus. You should see a positive response. Well, enjoy your time with Derek, and I'll head on my way to a meeting. Thanks, again, for offering to paint the garden for us. We take pride in it. It requires a lot of work to keep the garden in pristine condition. When will you get started?"

Michael shifted his eyes to Catherine then back to Moore. "Very soon. It shouldn't take long to finish, providing the model is available and the weather remains as beautiful as today."

"Excellent," he said, turning to walk away.

After he'd left, Catherine said, "I want you to meet my mother." She grinned. "It's not every guy that I take to meet Mom."

"I assume your husband has met her … Mrs. Kincaid."

Catherine paused, glancing at the center of the room where her mother sat with the other residents. "He did, but that was a while ago. Maybe it's good Mom can't remember him. I wish I couldn't. My life, like many people, is complicated. I don't want to talk about that here … maybe ever. Please, wheel your art cart to center stage, and let's see what responses we can get. You told me what Derek Mack said about the myth of hummingbirds … how they remind us to seek the magic in life. I believe there's magic in your paintings. Let's see if they have some miraculous, restorative properties that can beat back the dragons of Alzheimer's."

THIRTY-NINE

Some of the elderly people at the table looked up from their work. Others didn't. They continued coloring as Michael pulled his cart loaded with paintings near the table. A staff member, a woman in her mid-thirties, hair in a ponytail, smiled. "Look at what we have here, everyone. This gentleman has some paintings to show us."

Perplexed faces filled with wrinkles and hints of curiosity looked up. Gnarled and bent hands holding crayons stopped for a moment. Michael lifted the painting of the old mill, held it for everyone to see. "I painted this in Georgia. The grist mill was built at the time of the Civil War. After all these years, it still grinds corn and wheat."

There were smiles. One white-haired woman pointed to the painting. "That boy looks like Robert."

"Mom, who's Robert?" Catherine asked. "Was Robert a friend of yours?"

There was a blank response, the old woman's face impassive. Catherine managed a smile and said, "That's okay." She pointed to a rope swing hanging from the limb of an oak tree next to the pond. The rope was connected to a tire. "Did you play on a swing like this one when you were a little girl?"

A blank look.

A man with hunched shoulders, a whisper of white hair on his mostly bald head, dime-sized, bronze age spots branded into his scalp, said, "I did." He grinned. "I loved that old swing." He pointed his crooked index finger at the painting. "That's my house. I used to live in that house."

"You did?" Catherine asked.

"Yep. Those chickens were ours. The rooster was a mean son-of-a-gun, too."

168

Some of the people nodded in agreement. The caregiver smiled. Catherine said, "Mom and everyone here … I want you to meet Michael Vargas. He's an artist. He's going to show you some more of his work."

One elderly man reached for a crayon and drew the shape of a chicken on the paper in front of him. Catherine smiled. "Mom, that painting you love in Derek Mack's room … the one of the oaks and the mother and daughter on bicycles … Michael painted that, too."

The old woman smiled, nodding her head. "I used to ride my bike there. I would ride by the marshes with the wind in my face." She looked up at Catherine and asked, "Aren't you Lloyd's daughter … Cynthia?"

"No, Mom … I'm your daughter … Catherine." Her mother seemed to drift away, thoughts lost and buried, eyes lowering to the next painting Michael picked up from the cart. It was the one of Grandfather Mountain and the Highland Games.

"Oh," said one woman, touching her fingers to her lips, big smile. "It's the mountain in the Smokies … I can't recall the name."

"Grandfather Mountain," Michael said.

She smiled. "My parents took us there summers." She stared at the painting, her eyes welling. "Is Mama here today? Is she taking me home?"

"No, Mrs. Reynolds," said the staff member. "Your mother isn't here today."

Michael looked at the older woman and said, "There are a lot of family traditions made on and around Grandfather Mountain." He pointed to the painting. "When I was there last summer, lots of people were dressed in Scottish kilts, and they played ancient games born in the Highlands of Scotland. This tug-of-war took more than an hour to come to an end." He took his phone out of his pocket. "Anyone like bagpipe music?"

No responses.

"I recorded this one evening as the sun set over Grandfather Mountain." He punched a button and the bagpipe music of *Amazing Grace* began playing. Four of the six people at the table stared, slow smiles, one man moving his index finger to the sway of music. Catherine smiled and folded her arms across her breasts, intrigued as she watched Michael using the music and his art to paint even more vivid pictures in the minds of the people at the table.

Michael showed them a few more paintings, telling them about the locations he chose, why he picked the places and how he created the paintings. He wasn't sure how much, if any, they truly understood, but he kept talking—animated, using his hands to help illustrate the stories. When he was done, he walked around the table to where Catherine's mother sat. He said, "You mentioned how you rode your bike as a girl in the Lowcountry marshes."

She stared up at him, nodding.

He looked at the blank sheet of paper in front of her. He gently placed a crayon in her small, trembling hand and said, "Let's ride that bike again." He wrapped his hand around hers and guided it, drawing the shape of a bicycle and a child on the bike, the old woman's eyes wide. Then he steered her hand to draw arched oak trees on both sides of the path. When they finished, she looked at the drawing, a smile spreading over her face, misty-eyed. She lifted the paper, showing it to her friends.

"That's so pretty," said a woman across the table, her white hair pinned up.

Catherine's eyes welled as she watched her mother holding the drawing like a child would proudly display her artwork before it was posted on the kitchen refrigerator. "It's beautiful, Mom," she managed to say after clearing her throat and wiping away a tear.

Michael said, "We just drew what was in her heart. That's where the best pictures are stored."

"I agree," came a voice from behind Michael. It was a weaker version, but still the same voice. "A painter must dip his brush into his heart first."

Michael turned around, Derek dressed in pajamas and a tattered robe, barefoot, standing in front of him. "Forgive me if I can't remember your name … but I haven't forgotten your work. It has a style all its own. One is in my room." His hair was whiter, a strand falling over his tousled left eyebrow. Body much thinner. He held a cane with one hand. "The prodigal painter returns … and from here I can see some of your bounty. I would like to see more."

FORTY

Michael had thought about this moment for a long time. But in the dress rehearsals of his mind, the stage that Alzheimer's set was never in the spotlight. Today it was. Center stage. He was shocked by Derek's appearance, the weight he'd lost, how his old teacher's cheeks were now sunken, ashen stubble on his face, dark circles under his eyes. Yet, even holding a cane, he somehow managed to stand tall, almost defiant.

Michael walked around the table and approached Derek. "It's okay if you can't remember my name. I'm just glad you recognize my work because your influence is in every brushstroke. Many years ago, you encouraged me to go back to a mural I was painting, to add life to it … and then, after I was done, if I was satisfied, I could feel good about signing my work. I never forgot that. And the signature I leave in the lower right corner today is the same as it was back then … Vargas … Michael Vargas."

Derek said nothing, looking from Michael to the cart load of paintings and back. After a few more seconds, as he searched for the right words, he said, "The mural … I remember it. Sometimes I see that ship in my dreams, just at the cusp of the horizon … and in the next moment, my hopes carry me aboard." He paused, licked his dry lips. "I don't want to wake up … because when I do … I know the schooner will sail on without me."

Michael reached out and embraced Derek, the old man's body felt breakable, bones too close to loose skin, shoulder blades angular, arms frail. "It's so good to see you. I painted more than a hundred canvases from North Carolina to Louisiana and from Mississippi to Georgia—eight southern states if I include my starting point, South Carolina. Did a huge loop in seasonal chunks and learned a lot about the Deep

South far beyond the Lowcountry. I learned about the people and culture in the various regions and a lot about myself. I was a vagabond, Derek, and it was good. During that time, I think I became a better painter, painting as true as I can."

Derek nodded. "We all were amateurs at one time."

"Yeah … we were. But I still have things to learn."

Catherine stood to one side, listening to the elder mentor and his former student reunite, Alzheimer's in the shadows but not yet driving a silent wedge between them. She looked over to her mother and the others at the table, most returning to their crayons, markers and paper in front of them, the caregiver starting a new project. "Let's color balloons," she said, holding up a picture of a hot-air balloon.

Michael stepped back from Derek and gestured to the paintings on the cart. "I brought these to show you. There are more in my van outside. Eventually, I'd like for you to see all of them."

"Can you show those to my friends, too?" Derek looked across the room at the residents.

"Absolutely."

* * *

The staff arranged a semi-circle of chairs in the great room, Derek sitting in the center. More than three-dozen residents of the facility and four caregivers watched Michael give his presentation. Catherine sat beside her mother, observing as Michael picked up each painting, standing in the center of the group, explaining where the painting was done and why he chose to do it. And then he'd walk about ten feet in front of each person, so everyone could get a good look.

"This painting is the annual blessing of the fleet before shrimping season begins in Biloxi, Mississippi. I stood on one of the docks and painted as the boats made their parade from the river into the bay. The priest, he's the fella right here …" Michael used one finger to point out specifics. "He performed the ceremonies, splashing holy water over the bows of the shrimp boats. And this older gentleman wearing the captain's hat and standing at the edge of the dock watching, he'd lost one of his grandsons at sea in a hurricane two years earlier. When the final boat entered the channel, the older man …. a navy veteran who fought in Vietnam, saluted the American flag on the boat's stern as sea gulls hovered and fireworks were launched."

Although every patient in the audience was suffering from some form of dementia, Michael managed to hold their attention with the colorful paintings and his stories. Derek watched with subtle pride, his thoughts occasionally misfiring but retaining enough memory to put some of the pieces together. He'd shift his gaze to the other residents to see the joy in their eyes each time Michael held up a new painting.

After the presentation, after the patients returned to other extracurricular activities, Michael took Derek outside into the garden. They walked slowly down the meandering paths, Derek with his cane, Michael putting his hand under Derek's elbow to help steady him as they strolled slowly through the garden. They stopped next to a wrought iron bench. "Do you want to sit … maybe rest a bit?" Michael asked.

The old man nodded his head, slowly sitting and propping his cane up against the edge of the bench. He inhaled deeply through his nostrils. "The air's sweet. They won't let me stroll out here by myself anymore because they think I won't come back. They mean well but, as a painter, I never wore a leash." He looked over at Michael and smiled. "Why am I here? Maybe because it's getting hard to button my shirt. I'm glad you've returned."

"It feels good to be back."

"What are you going to do next?"

"I don't know."

"Your work is even better … at least I think it's better. Sometimes I can't remember. That painting you did of the millpond … it reminds me of Monet's Japanese water garden. The willows and lilies." He scanned the grounds, shook his head. "You know, I can't tell you where I used to live before I came here … but I remember going to where Monet lived in his final years of life. When I was a young man, I visited his house and gardens somewhere north of Paris. Before his death, Monet said he did his best work painting the flowers in the gardens. I believe that to be true."

"I plan to paint this garden."

"Good. Was Monet your inspiration?"

"Maybe … in some veiled way. I've always admired his work. But, what intrigued me was, when I came to see you, I spotted Catherine Kincaid in there picking a rose to take to her mother. The light and color spoke to me like few places ever … maybe never, at least to that extent."

Derek nodded. "Maybe it all spoke to you … the light, the colors of the flowers, and the color in the woman's cheeks and even her lips. She's a striking woman. I miss my wife … but her image is growing thin … and her name left me a while ago."

"Her name was Jewell. When you were in your studio teaching, she'd bring your students sandwiches and lemonade. You used to tell us that Jewell was more beautiful than any diamond."

"I said that?"

"Yes, you said it. Many times. You loved her, and she loved you."

Derek was silent. He looked at the water cascading down the fountain, a blackbird in one tier, using it as a birdbath, frocking like a duck. "It's not fair to live a full life … to look forward to memories and be robbed of them. It's as if I'm trying to search a dark closet … I know the things are in there … somewhere. I just can't find the light."

* * *

Catherine stood at one of the bay windows in the great room, looking outside while the two men talked. She watched as Michael listened closely while Derek pointed to flowers in the garden, commenting. She thought about how Michael had taken her mother's trembling hand and gently drew the picture with her, guiding her along, never forcing the drawing, leading her like he might lead his dance partner. It was bittersweet, and it made a difference. Her mother was more animated than she'd seen her in weeks. Proud of the finished picture, telling Catherine that she wanted to hang it in her room next to her dressing mirror.

Catherine shifted her eyes to the half-dozen paintings Michael had propped up against one of the walls, allowing the residents free range to look at them and to even touch the thick paint on each canvas. And they did. One man standing in front of the painting of a Louisiana crawfish festival stared at the musicians. Then he looked at the people dancing, a black cauldron of water boiling, a mound of pink crawfish on one rustic table, the bayou in the background, and a mauve sky filled with birds. The patient began humming zydeco music. After a few seconds, his head bobbing, he began to sing in a raspy voice. "Sittin' here in la la … waitin' for my ya ya … uh huh … sittin' here in la la waitin' for my ya ya … uh huh …"

Catherine looked back outside, watching Michael reconnect with Derek. She saw a hummingbird feeding in petunias near them, and she remembered what Michael had said about Derek. *The man I'm going in there to see once told me that hummingbirds remind us to seek the magic in life.*

She thought about what she told Michael after she saw his work. *I believe there's magic in your paintings. Let's see if they have some miraculous, restorative properties that can beat back the dragons of Alzheimer's.*

* * *

Derek stared at the hummingbird, a smile working in one corner of his mouth. He looked over at Michael on the bench next to him. "Can you describe my wife's face for me?"

"Okay." Michael took a deep breath, going back decades. "She had a natural smile, and she smiled often at your jokes. She was so easy going. Green eyes like polished jade. Pretty skin with rosy cheeks. Jewell's hair was light brown, and she wore it long, to the center of her back. She was a good listener. And she seemed to have a lot of patience. All of the students coming and going in your studio, none of that ever seemed to faze or overwhelm her. She took everything in stride, and she was a great graphic artist. Her work was on hundreds of greeting cards."

As Michael spoke, Derek closed his eyes and listened, folding his hands in his lap against the tattered robe. "For a brief moment, I saw her again. Like a bit of a dream … but it was the smile that was so real. Just the way you described it … described her. My precious Jewell." He looked at Michael. "Are you married? Do I know your wife? Will she come to visit me, too?"

"No, my wife can't come. She died in a plane crash. My daughter, too. It's just me."

Derek nodded. "All right. I understand." He looked at the roses, the breeze changing and bringing their fragrance to them. "It's so lovely here. Everything's in order. Monet's garden had flowers bursting out everywhere. It was a natural, unrefined, tangled beauty … like his art. His flowers in paint, and in his garden, seemed to beg for your attention, in a good way." He paused. "How can I remember that and not my wife's face or even her name?"

"I don't know. The disease has no sense of fairness."

"Before it consumes me … I want to see the rest of your paintings, and I want to see the one you do here in the gardens. If your passion is as inspired as Monet … maybe it will be your best work to date. I believe something else, too."

"What's that?"

"Although I'm not the man I once was, as a painter … I have always been an observer of people. The woman inside there … the younger woman … what's her name again?"

"You mean Catherine?"

"Yes, I observed her watching you as you drew with her mother. It was a sweet sight to behold. Catherine will be more than a model here in this garden. She will be central to the story you paint with all this color and light. Monet said he did some of his most challenging work in his gardens. I think that might be the case for you, too."

FORTY-ONE

A week later, they met in the gazebo. Catherine was already there when Michael arrived five minutes late. She was dressed in the same blue and white sundress he'd asked her to wear. She wore her hair over one bare shoulder, skin tanned, spotted sunlight breaking through nooks in the gazebo and falling on her face. She looked up and smiled. "I know you wanted me to wear the same dress as you start and finish the painting. What if I were to wear a sundress one day, my favorite faded jeans and T-shirt the next day, and then wear a 1920's Victorian dress the following day? Maybe I'd wear a red raincoat the next time. How would you paint me?"

Michael laughed as he sat down across a small wicker table opposite Catherine. He looked out into the garden and then back at her playful eyes. "I'd begin with your face … the beauty and mystery of a woman alone with her thoughts in a secluded garden. If I can paint that, it doesn't matter what you wear … because that's the most important thing to me as a painter. After that, it'll all become part of a coat of many colors. When I combine that with the acres of flowers, the water and sky … I'll need a large canvas."

She laughed. "You want to paint the mystery of a woman alone with her thoughts. If I tell you too much about me then, the mystery will be gone, and maybe part of your incentive for doing the painting as well."

"Never. It will become even more intriguing. At that point, I'll have to choose how much to reveal, and that will be an artistic and personal challenge."

She hung her purse strap on the back of a wrought iron chair next to her. "It sounds like you're a movie director deciding how much of the character's personality you'll reveal."

Michael smiled. "There are comparisons. When Derek was teaching, he used to talk about how well impressionist painters, like Renoir, could reveal personality traits in the faces of ordinary people doing ordinary things but with remarkable expressions. It was the faces, the appearances of the people in his paintings, that caught your eye and demanded that you take a closer look and peer deeper into those faces. That's what I try hard to do."

"And, you do it well. But I feel there's an incongruity in what you leave on canvas and what you leave with people."

"What do you mean?"

"Your paintings are shimmering with stuff of life, the human existence. But, after spending time with you, watching you with others … you seem very reserved. Are you an introvert? I believe I am. However, I'm not sure an introvert is the real you. I figured if I was going to be spending time with a man trying to capture me in paint, I'd like to know more about him. So, I did what any curious woman might do … I googled you." She leaned forward, wide smile spreading. "I don't use the OMG letters often, but you justify it. Oh my God. I almost didn't recognize you with the three-piece suits on, the short hair—the whole Wall Street look. But the penetrating blue eyes were there. Your picture was on no less than a dozen magazine covers, including TIME. After designing some of the world's most recognizable buildings, and on the verge of building the highest tower in the known world, Michael Vargas walks away from it all. And no one knows why … or if they do, they're not saying. So, if you don't mind … can I ask why you walked away from a renowned career?"

Michael said nothing. He inhaled a deep breath, staring at the fountain and the koi pond across the garden. He looked at Catherine and leaned forward. "I didn't walk away from it all … I walked toward something completely different. It was time. After Kelsey and Mandy, my wife and daughter, were killed, I took a long, hard look at who I was and who I really wanted to be. Continuing as an architect wasn't it. Never was, really."

"You don't have to go there if you don't want to. I shouldn't have asked."

"No, it's okay. I felt guilty because Kelsey wanted me to fly with them to spend some time with her sick mother. But I was too busy, too deep into work and perpetual client presentations. I told her to go on without me. She would have waited, but I couldn't commit to a schedule. So, she left. The plane went down near LaGuardia … I could see the fireball from the office tower where I'd just finished a client presentation."

Catherine was quiet, letting Michael finish. A mourning dove cooed somewhere in the garden. After a moment, she said, "I'm so sorry to hear that. I can't imagine the pain and grief you suffered that day. But I can imagine you still agonize from it. Has painting been cathartic, maybe a way to immerse yourself into work that's more creative on a personal level … been a way to help you heal?"

"It's helped put some bandages over it. There is no healing in the real sense of the word. There's just some kind of empty survival and moving forward. One thing I have come to realize through all of this is …the thing we want the most … time … is the thing we most abuse. That's why I believe the greatest gift you can give someone is your time. And it's reciprocal—a two-way portal, or at least it should be."

Catherine looked at Michael's wedding band and then up at him. "When I was just a girl, living in Columbia, we had a housekeeper, her name was Zelda. She was wise, very kind, and sort of took life as it came, warts and all. I never saw her get flustered, angry, or be negative toward others. If eyes could smile, hers sure did. Zelda used to say, when you learn what is really beautiful in life, you stop becoming a slave to things that are not. I never forgot that … or her. Speaking of beauty, don't we have a painting to get to? Those brushes won't move by themselves." She laughed.

"Absolutely. But, before we get started, you googled my name to learn more about me. I'd rather ask you about yourself. Who is Catherine Kincaid?"

"You can google me, but I may not exist in cyberspace." She smiled.

"But you exist in this space … and that's what's important. So, tell me … who is Catherine Kincaid, and what makes her tick?"

"Well, I like dogs—big dogs, little dogs, it doesn't matter. Because all dogs wag their tails with their heart muscles. I like walks by the sea, and piña coladas. Wait a sec … this sounds so much like a scripted façade on some online dating app bio."

"How would you know? Do you use online dating sites?"

"No, never. But I've seen the commercials. I do love the sea, but I can skip the piña coladas. I'm not complicated. I enjoy the outdoors and being with people who are real and not toxic. I've spent too much time with the energy vampires, people who'll bite your neck and suck your soul out if you let them. I learned to listen to wise people, those who have your best interest at heart … and I finally learned to listen to that tiny, inner voice somewhere deep inside me. I don't know if it's God or just my conscience tugging at my sleeve, but I don't ignore it anymore. It's helped me understand how to sidestep toxic situations … places and people that don't cannibalize my time, energy … and frankly … my spirit."

"Maybe that's a good definition of wisdom."

"Or age."

"Do you live in Charleston?"

"No, Columbia. I drive down once a week to spend time with Mom. I'll usually stay the night. There's a Comfort Inn not far."

"I've seen it. When you introduced your mother, you said her name is Susan Waterman. The facility director called you Mrs. Kincaid. Are you married?"

She paused before answering. "If we talk more about it, two things will happen. One is that you'll have a model in your painting with a frown on her face, and the other is you'll no longer have a mystery woman in the garden. After all, this is a secret garden, right?" She couldn't contain her laughter.

Michael smiled and said, "Touché."

"How do we get started?" There was a buzzing sound in her purse. She opened the flap and pulled out her phone, staring at the caller ID, her expression going from one of happiness to one of distress. "Excuse me. I have to take this. I'm sorry." She got up and left the gazebo, walking away quickly and answering the call, heading toward the splashing water in the fountain and fish that looked up at her with interest.

Michael didn't know who she was speaking with, but whomever was on the line caused a physical change in Catherine, her eyes narrowing, exposing a drastic transformation. And, as a painter, it was a look he didn't want to paint because it was out of harmony with everything here. He looked at a blooming, dark red rose and thought about something she'd just shared with him. *Zelda used to say, when you learn what is really beautiful in life, you stop becoming a slave to things that are not.*

Michael hoped when and if Catherine returned, the woman he first saw in the garden would return with her.

FORTY-TWO

Derek Mack sat in a wooden, high-back chair in his room and stared into the past. It was framed, painted more than a year ago in oil, and given to him as a gift. He just couldn't remember who gave it to him. At least at the moment, that name and face were gone. Another slice of memory's picture puzzle fallen off the table never to be picked up and snapped back in place.

He sat in his pajamas and robe, staring at the painting of the Lowcountry, the swayback oaks, the soft sunlight seeming as if it was pouring through the leafy branches, some of their limbs reaching for the heavens. The others, the heavy old limbs splattered in moss and green lichen, were curved in steepled arches, obeying more than a century of gravity pulling at their arms.

He sat less than ten feet away from the painting, his eyes wandering through the colors and the locale, a place he'd been before, he just couldn't remember when or even where. But he could recall the buzzing of the cicadas in the trees, the smell of wet mud and marsh grasses. He looked at the two people riding bicycles, a pretty woman wearing a yellow shirt and white shorts, and a long-haired little girl in pink, both blondes. He studied the mother's expression—the pride on her face as she watched her daughter peddle the small bike next to her.

Derek could feel the emotion from the people in the painting. And, although he had no idea where the art came from, or where it was done, he knew that the people in the painting were real. More real than anyone he could remember. Because they never left him. Each morning when the sun climbed through his window, they were there, smiling and riding their bikes. And, each night before the nurses helped him with his pajamas and turned off the lights in his room—the woman and little girl were there. He knew when he drifted off to sleep, they'd be there in the morning to ride into his thoughts.

Someone touched his shoulder. He looked up to his right. A woman stood there. He knew her face, at least he thought he did, but he couldn't remember her name. She smiled and looked away from him to the painting. Catherine's mother, Susan, slowly stepped up to the painting. She stood less than three feet from it—her eyes tracing the colors and falling upon the people riding bicycles down the long dirt road.

She reached out, staring at the woman and little girl captured in paint. She used the tips of two trembling fingers to touch the girl's face as if she was a blind woman feeling the contours of the child's face. She traced her smile. A smiled formed in the corner of Susan's tight mouth, her lips trembling, eyes welling. "Catherine …" she whispered. "My Catherine … we ride bikes. She rides with the wind in her hair."

Susan turned around and looked at Derek. He smiled and nodded. "Yes … this painting reminds you of your time with your little girl on bicycles. That's a good memory, Susan."

* * *

Catherine returned to the gazebo, no hint of any form of anxiety. She smiled. Michael asked, "Is everything okay?"

"My mother is across the garden in that sprawling English manor-like building, room twenty-seven, with Alzheimer's … so in that regard, life's a challenge. Everything else is fine and pales in comparison. Now, where were we? I've got on my blue and white dress, and I'm ready to make my debut amongst the flora and fauna, not to mention the birds and the bees, and our koi fish are as colorful as a herd of calico cats." She laughed.

Michael watched her closely, looking for any traces of angst. His talent for observing the subtle nuances, the sharp eye that gave him an artist's perspective of light, composition and character, could only see a beautiful woman with an unbridled sense of energy. "I like the dress you're wearing. It initially caught my attention as you moved through the garden. The red rose in your hand was a nice contrast against the blue and white of the dress. We'll reenact that scene."

"This does sound like a movie, Mr. Director. Should I be heading to hair and makeup?"

"You don't need it."

She smiled. "We'll hold that judgement until after the painting is finished."

"I'd like to have you where I first saw you in the garden … picking a long-stemmed rose. And then I'll position you near the fountain and fishpond. I want to mix the sunlight, the color from the flowers, the shadows, birds in the air, the light off your hair, face and shoulders. I'm trying to borrow the very best from nature and paint it with quick brushstrokes. It's sort of like capturing lightning in a jar."

"Sounds like it'll be your version of The Garden of Earthly Delights. I forget who did that painting … but I never forgot the title of the work."

"It was done by Hieronymus Bosch. The painting is in the Prado in Madrid, Spain."

"Not only do you paint, you've got a good art history background."

"It all began with the man inside that memory care building, Derek Mack. He'd weave art history into his painting lessons, so his students never felt like they were learning history per se, but rather the reasons various painters did what they did."

"How did he do it?"

"Derek would stand in front of the class, sometimes munching a chicken drumstick in one hand and using a paintbrush in the other, jazz music playing from vinyl records. He'd stand next to his canvas in the studio, wearing plaid shorts, T-shirt and no shoes, putting paint on a canvas. He'd be teaching, talking, chicken grease on his lips, oil paint on his fingers … and he'd start to tell us stories of the masters. He'd tell us what drove them, and how they persevered, often in spite of great odds against them. It really stuck with me, and I think with the other students, too."

Catherine looked across the garden to the building. "All that information he's learned throughout his life, his talents as a teacher, the many beautiful paintings he's done—all of that is being destroyed by a disease with no known cure. It's devious, stealthy, and almost patently

184

evil in how it tries to prey on the spirit of a person. Sort of like those energy vampires I mentioned. But, in a bizarre way, I think the soul is untouchable by the disease."

"Maybe the brain and the soul aren't stamped on both sides of the same coin."

"I think that's right. My mother often asks me why she's here. Says she wants to go home, but yet has no memory of home … of my dad who died five years ago, or my sister. She'll pull a vivid memory out of the past somewhere, and a few minutes later, can't recall any of it. If I had a choice, I'd much rather see her dying of almost any other disease than Alzheimer's. With cancer, doctors have morphine and other drugs to give for pain, but for the collective pain caused when a family member's brain is dying, when they become so frightened, angry, incontinent, feeble—a shadow and a true bi-polar image of who they once were … it's heartbreaking. But I believe the soul is intact, just hidden away until … until it's released."

"When I drew that picture with your mom, I could feel her spirit in her small hand. I think the human soul is bigger than brain cognition. Maybe it's just trapped in there and freed at death."

Catherine looked down at her fingernails and lifted her eyes back up to Michael. "When Mom first came here, when I was speaking with one of the senior caregivers, she told me that often dementia patients, people who don't recognize family members, can remember Bible verses or beloved hymns from their youth. She said there are times, especially closer to death when these patients will have great lucidity, able to speak well, as if they're chatting with their mother or father about something from the past."

Michael leaned forward. "And that speaks volumes about the human spirit."

"I don't believe the brain creates consciousness, but rather acts as a filter. For Mom, and others in there, I think we speak to their souls by reaching out to their emotions and senses. And, you did that when you showed your paintings and when you played the hymn, *Amazing Grace.* It went around the sick brains and directly into the warm hearts. I saw lips moving, patients singing and somehow recalling whatever emotional cord that's been with them since their youth. Although a baby can't speak, it doesn't mean that he or she is without a soul. Alzheimer's patients just can't communicate on a cognitive level." She paused, birdsong coming from a nearby sycamore tree. "Your art, too, speaks volumes. Although I can't paint, in a way I feel that I'm contributing something to your garden painting. So, partner, are you ready to get started. We don't want to lose our light, do we?"

"No, we don't. I'll unload my easel and paints, and then I'll meet you in the garden of earthly delights."

She stood and smiled, lifting her purse strap to her shoulder. "What if this is our Garden of Eden. What will you do if evil comes calling? Will you paint the serpent in the picture, or keep it blissfully innocent?" Catherine put her phone back inside her purse.

FORTY-THREE

The canvas required two easels. Michael secured a seven-by-four-foot canvas to the easels and stood on the perimeter of the garden with his paints, brushes and palette knives. He watched as Catherine picked a long stem rose and walked through the garden to the koi pond. "That's great," he said. "Stand right there and simply enjoy your surroundings."

"I'm supposed to be standing still, sort of posing?"

"No ... no posing. Just stand in that position for a few minutes as I work on the background. You'll be able to move around in a little while."

"So, this impressionism you do doesn't require me to be a statue in the garden, right?"

"Correct. The last thing I want to paint is a statue. I want the subtle energy of the woman in nature ... in a garden that touches the senses. It becomes sensual in sight, sound and feel."

She smiled. "I think you might make a good film director if your career as a painter takes a dive." She laughed, smelling the rose in her hand.

Michael used a wide brush to spread a thin coat of white paint across the canvas. "It's not a career. It's more of a driving force."

"Why don't you sell your paintings?"

"Because I'd rather give them away. I don't do it for the money. Never have. And I'm fortunate now that I don't have to. That, of course, like anything in life ... could change." He began painting the sky in graduating shades of blue, lighter at the horizon, darker toward the top, moving a smaller brush in fast crisscross strokes. He switched brushes, painting white clouds against the sky. Moving brushes and palette knives in a wet-on-wet layering of paint.

Michael paused, looking around at the vast potpourri of flowers, shrubs, and bougainvillea hanging from the long terrace. He glanced at the gazebo perched like a sanctuary among the shady trees, and then he watched Catherine in the light and shadows. He set a brush down on one of the easels, picked up a sketch book and charcoal pencil, and walked up to her. "I just need a closer look," he said, studying her face.

She turned to him, smiling. "Does this mean you're invading my personal space?"

"No need to. I don't need to see the pores on your skin to paint you. There … that's the light." He paused, using his left hand to direct her. "Just look toward the sycamore tree over my shoulder."

"How's this? Is that where you want me to look?"

"Yes … and then look at me."

She shifted her gaze from the tree to Michael. At that moment, her beauty was stunning, eyes filled with light and great depth. He quickly sketched her face, moving the pencil with near blinding speed. He added subtle shading, studying her exquisite mouth, drawing her full lips in a striking, feminine appearance. Then he drew the necklace around her long neck, the jade cross pendant hanging from a silver chain close to her breasts.

Catherine smiled. "My mother gave the necklace to me. She bought it in Spain. I love jade. It's supposed to symbolize purity or maybe a pure heart. It's the one stone that's supposed to protect and support loving energy from inside you. Sort of a heart stone."

Michael continued sketching. "Do you wear it to ward off the energy vampires you mentioned?"

"Absolutely. Works better than a garlic necklace." She laughed. "Jade is a preventative medicine from energy vamps. Keeps me from having to drive a wooden stake through their chests. I would say hearts, but vampires don't have hearts, at least not the kind that house the soul." She smiled and looked at the rose in her hand. "When we finish today, I think I'll take this rose to Mom. Its beauty can speak more directly to her than I can with words." She paused, watching him sketch with the passion of a sculptor using a hammer, chiseling away, stone dust billowing in the air. "Why do you sketch and paint?"

"I don't always do it. But I loved the way the light was falling against your face. I'll use my sketch as reference when filling in the finer details. In a few minutes, though, I'll be tackling the flowers, and that will be quite a challenge. Even though it's called impressionism, the painter must convey a strong sense of light and color in the composition."

"I wonder how the word impressionism really came into the art vernacular?"

"Derek told me it came from an original negative comment."

"Negative?"

"Yes. And the comment was directed toward the one man who made impressionist painting of gardens his life's work during the last few years of his time on earth."

"So, Mr. Vargas, as you stand there drawing my face, tell me the story of how the word worked its way into the art world."

"If I remember the date correctly … it was around 1872. A re-nowned French art critic was reviewing an exhibition that included a painting Monet did of a beautiful sunrise. This critic, I forget his name, didn't like any part of Monet's work. He said the painting was unfinished. And, he said it looked more like an *impression* of art than real art. The term, of course, was meant to be disparaging. But the exact opposite happened. So many people liked Monet's style and that of the other painters breaking away from realism to quickly paint, capturing changing light, expressions, and motion, the term impressionism stuck to this very day."

"That's a great story."

"And it's true. The critic, unknowingly, hung a prestigious label of a style of art that, beyond Monet, would include Renoir, Degas, Pizzaro, Gauguin, Picasso, Mary Cassatt, Vincent Van Gogh, and many others."

"Let us not forget Vargas … Michael Vargas, whose work stands with the masters."

Michael laughed. "Hardly. I do a fair impression of the impression-ists, but I can't compare my work to any of the people I just mentioned."

Catherine crossed her arms, a slight pout on her lips. "Since we're talking about some of the French impressionists, I'll use a French term—au contraire, because I saw what your work did in front of a room of

Alzheimer's patients. Your paintings enthralled them. The beautiful colors, the settings, the way you capture real life in an impressionist style, it connected with people whose brains have atrophy."

"Maybe it's the compositions."

"It's much more than that. I saw one man in the community center—his name is unique, Baptiste Boudreaux, whom I have never heard speak before. And, yet, he's standing there looking at your painting of the Louisiana crawfish festival and just starts singing. Maybe it was some zydeco song, but the point is that he sang it perfectly, and in a Cajun accent. Michael, if your work can bond with their emotions … emotions buried beneath dying brains, that says a lot. So, please don't let me ever hear you say you aren't in the same league as all those impressionist artists you mentioned."

Michael watched her nostrils slightly flare, the look of absolute conviction in her eyes. He said, "Thank you. That's kind of you, and it's good to hear."

"That's because it's true. So, don't be so reticent, or are you just being shy?" she lifted her right eyebrow and smiled. "You paint all this fabulous stuff of life, but do you ever paint yourself in the picture?"

He grinned. "Maybe, and maybe like Waldo, you'll have to hunt to find me."

"I'll look behind every tree." She laughed.

"When I finish this … maybe I'll paint myself in the painting."

"Will you be the constant gardener?"

Michael plucked his pocketknife from among his palette knives and stepped a few feet over to one of the rose bushes. He cut through the stem of a deep red rose and came back to Catherine, handing her the fresh rose. "No, I'll be your secret admirer in the secret garden."

She took the rose, wide smile forming. "Thank you. I don't think I've ever had a secret admirer."

"Well, after I finish this painting, if it comes out like I hope, you'll have lots of them."

"I suppose a girl can use a few secret admirers as long as they don't become not-so-secret stalkers." She brought the rose to her nostrils and smelled the scent.

Michael picked up one of his palette knives. "I'll defend you with my sword."

"Ah, such a knight, and in a world where I thought chivalry went away with rusted out armor." Catherine laughed. "When can I see the painting?"

"When it's done."

"You mean I can't see it as a work in progress?"

"That's exactly what I mean. No sneak peeks. No previews. You'll see nothing until I'm ready to show you."

"No exceptions … even for the woman who's agreed to do this out of the goodness of her heart?"

"Nope. You're the one who cut the hard bargain—the deal for me to loan or donate it to the Memory Care Center of Charleston. A condition of that agreement, as stipulated by the painter, is no peeking at the work in progress."

She grinned. "For just a brief moment, I could picture Michael Vargas as the superstar architect, the guy on the magazine covers, wearing an expensive suit, presenting in some New York City high-rise conference room, talking about his newest architectural megastar project."

"Those days are long gone."

The phone in her purse buzzed again. Catherine made a dry swallow and took the phone from her purse, looking at the caller ID. Her eyes unreadable. She set the phone back inside, making a hard zip of her purse. "I have about an hour left. What can you do in that time?"

"A lot."

She nodded her head. "Good, but I know you can't show me. I'm okay with that." She looked toward the west. "You wanted the afternoon light. It's prime time."

FORTY-FOUR

Michael approached the two easels as if he was a composer of music, and his canvas, held up by the easels, was his keyboard. He stood in the center of the canvas staring at the paint he'd already applied while looking at the pencil sketch of Catherine he'd taped to one easel. He lifted his eyes over the canvas to the woman in the garden. Catherine stood by the koi pond, red rose in her hand, the afternoon light soft on her face. He could hear the water splashing in the fountain, the singing of a wood thrush in the trees, and the throbbing pulse of bees in the purple lilac. He watched the pendulum sway of the weeping willow limbs in the gentle breeze.

Michael picked up a wide palette knife, mixed three colors of paint, cut the knife through the blend and attacked the canvas with passionate, bold strokes. He moved quickly, painting trees, blocking out the gazebo, adding more background, applying layers of color, alternating from palette knives to brushes. He worked non-stop, caught up in the swirl of paint, light and imagery until the sound of Catherine's voice broke into his reverie.

"I'd like to see Mom before I go, so I need to wrap in a few minutes."

"Okay, just let me finish something." Ten minutes later, he set his brush down on the tray built into one of the easels, stepping back from the painting and looking at what he'd accomplished and what needed to be done. Although the muscles in center of his back hurt from the tension he applied while painting, he was satisfied with his work so far. He picked up a clean, white rag and used it to wipe as much of the paint from his hands as possible. He left the painting on the easels and walked through the garden to Catherine. "You can relax now. I did all I could in the time you had, but I did reach a good stopping point."

She looked at him and smiled. "Good. And, if I get any more relaxed, I'll turn to butter. It's so beautiful here. And, when you stand quietly in a garden like this, it speaks to you. I've seen more in one spot standing than I would have imagined. It's as if mother nature forgets you're here and comes to you, or at least lets you become a greater part of her. Did you get a lot done?"

"Yes, and I agree about nature sort of letting her hair down. That's one of the reasons I so love painting on location. You become one with the environment."

She smiled. "It's as if you can become part of the natural world and all the critters are cheering you on to illustrate what they already know … their little secret."

"And what's that?"

"They know we're all connected in this world, the universe for that matter. We're all riding together on this ship called earth. We just need to share the window seat with them like they're sharing this space with us today."

"Well, I'm immensely grateful that I get to stand out here, quietly painting, and see nature unfold all around me. There's a real intimacy to it."

"Even from the distance, across the garden, I could see that in the way you work. What I saw was a man in the moment—an artist so laser focused on light and composition, it was as if you were trying to capture lightning in a jar." Catherine paused and reached for the white towel in his hand. "May I see that?" He handed it to her. She laughed softly. "You wear your paint well. There's some yellow on your cheek, red on your chin, and some blue above your blue eyes." She used the towel to gently wipe off the wet paint. "There … now I can see the man when I peel back the layers of paint."

"Thank you. I hope you like what you see."

"I do."

"I can clean up well … well enough to take you to dinner. Do you like seafood?"

"Yes, I love seafood."

"I know a little restaurant overlooking Shem Creek that's one of the best. Their menu is on a blackboard and changes daily, depending on what the local fisherman caught."

"That sounds like a place I'd love to experience, but I can't tonight." She glanced at the watch on her wrist. "I need to be going. I hope you got what you wanted for today. Do you want to meet again the same time next week?"

"Do I have to wait that long to—?"

"I have to be going. I barely have time to give these two roses to Mom. She'll think they're from dad, if she remembers him, and then I'll have to remind her he died five years ago."

"Maybe you just let her live with her memories … at least what's left of them."

She smiled, looked at the roses, bringing both buds to her nose for a moment. "Thank you for the memories I made here today. I really appreciate you asking me to be part of your painting. I can't wait for you to finish so we can hang it up in the community center for all the residents and staff to see every day." She handed Michael the towel, reached for her purse and turned to leave.

"Wait … just a second. Are you Cinderella and have to rush off before the midnight hour?" he said with a grin. "If you can't stay for dinner … how about a glass of wine nearby?"

"I'm sorry, I can't. I have a long drive ahead. But I look forward to next time."

"Before you go … may I have your number? If either one of us might be running late for the next session, it'd be good to communicate."

They exchanged phone numbers, and Catherine said, "Please, don't call me. I'll call you if need be. It's just the way it is."

Michael watched Catherine walk away, the sound of her shoes soft against the paver stones leading from the garden to the memory care building. He went back to his canvas, removing it from the easels and carefully placing it on the floor of his van. In the dome light, he looked at a few of the paintings he hadn't shared with Derek. One in particular spoke to him. It was a painting he'd done of the tall ships regatta that was held in New Orleans.

He removed the painting from the rack, looked at it under the dome light—at the images of the tall ships at sail over blue water, school-aged children aboard for an educational experience, their eyes wide and bright, hands on the ropes, the whitewater spray of the sea in the air. Michael thought about what Derek had told him when he remembered the schooner he had painted on the mural so long ago. *Sometimes I see that ship in my dreams, just at the cusp of the horizon ... and in the next moment, my hopes carry me aboard. I don't want to wake up ... because when I do ... I know the schooner will sail on without me.*

Michael took the painting from his van, locked the doors and strolled through the garden. He walked beneath tree limbs, toward a building where memories were as fractured as the splintered light through the branches of a tall sycamore tree in front of him.

FORTY-FIVE

Michael checked with a head nurse and was told that Derek had finished dinner and was in his room. "Probably reading," she said, looking over the tops of her glasses as she reviewed a chart. "I don't think I've ever seen him without a magazine or something else to read." Michael carried the unframed painting of the tall ships in one hand, and a small hammer and nail in the other. He walked down a wide hall, the sound of the TV game show, *Family Feud,* coming from one of the rooms, the flicker of blue light off the cream-colored walls.

He stopped at room 29, the door partially open. He knocked. There was no immediate response. Michael knocked again. This time slightly louder. He edged around the door and saw Derek sitting in an armchair reading a hardcover book, a novel by Pat Conroy, *South of Broad.* Michael smiled. "May I come in?"

Derek nodded. He remained sitting, the book in his lap. Michael pulled up a chair beside him and sat, he had the back of the painting toward them. "Are you enjoying the book?"

"Oh, yes. I have no idea if I've ever read it. I like the story. But I forget what I read too soon."

"What's it about?"

"It has a lot of the history of Charleston ... the good and bad. It's about the importance of friends and family. That, I think, is what it boils down to."

"I wanted to show you another painting. I know you've seen many of them recently. I was thinking about what you told me when you first saw the mural that I painted on the building near the Charleston Harbor."

"Yes. What was it that I told you?"

"You said sometimes you see that ship in your dreams, and you see yourself aboard her. You mentioned that you don't want to wake up to realize you'd been dreaming, and you're really on land, not at sea."

"Yes."

Michael turned the canvas around to face them. "I thought about that when I was going through some of the other paintings I did while I was on the road. This one is of the tall ships in the harbor at New Orleans during a regatta."

Derek stared at the painting, his eyes slowly taking in every image, as if he was analyzing each brushstroke and trail left by a palette knife. "It moves. It's powerful."

"Most of those ships are two-hundred feet in length. It was a beautiful sight to paint. Lots of people, and some lucky school children got a chance to help set sail for a short trip."

Derek nodded. "The closest ship to us is sailing like she is one with the sea. There's a nautical heartbeat to that kind of sailing. From the wind in her sails and the water beneath her, a ship like that breathes and lives. Look at that one." He pointed to another tall ship. "Look at the people aboard, especially the young folks. Watch their faces as they pull the ropes to hoist the sails. And you can see the delight on the captain's face as he teaches them the sailing techniques and probably the history of the ship. This painting has its own sense of energy. I can almost taste the salt in the air."

"I'm glad you like it."

"It's stunning."

"I want you to keep it here in your room. That way the ship won't sail on without you. You can be part of the sail every day."

Derek said nothing, his eyes lifting from the painting of the tall ships to the one of the Lowcountry oaks hanging on his wall. He looked back down at the name scrawled in the lower right corner. "Vargas … he's an excellent painter."

Michael smiled. "I was hoping you'd like it. I've strung a wire on the back of the frame, and I brought a hammer and nail. Where would you like for me to hang it?"

"On the wall over there … that'd be fine, yes."

Michael tapped the nail into the left, perpendicular wall and hung the painting at the same height as the other one. "How's that?"

"Very nice." Derek stood, holding the book in one hand. He set it on a nightstand next to his bed. "I'm a little tired. If you don't mind, I think I'll lie down. It's easy to see the paintings from my bed."

"Do you need some help?"

"Could you pull the covers down for me? The ladies make the bed so well it's hard for me sometimes to grip the covers."

"Sure." Michael pulled the blankets down, Derek slowly getting into his bed, as if his body might break. He lay down on his right side, head on the pillow. Michael pulled the blankets over the old man's boney shoulders. "Goodnight, my friend."

"Goodnight … thank you. Is my wife here yet?"

"Not yet. But Jewell's not far away … she thinks about you every day." He started to turn off the light.

"You can leave the light on … it's okay. I just want to lie here and look at the paintings. I want to feel the spray of the sea mist across my brow. It's so cooling."

Michael nodded. He stood at the door, looking back at his old teacher, Derek lying in the fetal position, his eyes unblinking, staring at the newest painting like a man standing on the wharf at dawn, watching the ships enter the harbor.

FORTY-SIX

It was close to midnight by the time Michael got to his rented house on Pawley's Island. He pulled his van into the driveway, past bent cabbage palms casting dark shadows in the strong moonlight. He parked and unloaded the wet painting and sketch of Catherine. He could hear the sound of the breakers rolling on the beach, the full moon creating a high tide.

Michael unlocked the door, entering the beach house and walking across the hardwood floor toward the screened-in porch facing the ocean. He opened the sliding glass doors and propped the partially finished painting up against one of the porch walls, setting the sketch of Catherine on a wicker table. The breeze across the rolling surf brought the scent of salt and gardenia flowers blooming in the night.

He poured a glass of red wine and sat at the table on the porch, the full moon casting light across the surface of the Atlantic Ocean, the breakers churning and effervescent in frothy white waves under the moonlight. He sipped the wine and picked up the sketch of Catherine that he'd done. *Just look toward the sycamore tree over my shoulder.*

How's this? Is that where you want me to look?

Yes … and then look at me.

Michael stared intently at the drawing—into Catherine's eyes. He looked at the necklace around her neck, the jade cross resting near her breasts. *My mother gave the necklace to me. I love jade. It's the one stone that's supposed to protect and support loving energy from inside you. Sort of a heart stone.*

He had the sudden urge to pick up the phone and call her, just to hear her voice with the soft roll of the waves in the background. He inhaled the night air, something moving in his heart that he hadn't felt in a long time. Loneliness. He'd felt grief and utter isolation after the deaths of Kelsey and Mandy. He longed for them and felt alone. Traveling the southern backroads in a van, meeting other people, hearing their stories, painting snapshots of their worlds and lives—it had all done what Derek suggested it would. It had helped Michael take steps forward from the dark void he felt after losing his beloved family into building the will to live with a deeper purpose. To do what Kelsey knew he should have done a long time ago.

He had grown weary and tired of the road. The elliptical journey through the Deep South had eventually led him back to South Carolina and the Lowcountry he loved. This was where three generations of his DNA was built from a hardscrabble life, where he found a quiet sense of place. The roots he grew here in the sandy soil—the culture, also grew in his heart. They had given him the wings to travel the world, but like a migratory bird, this was where he needed to return to when the dark clouds of tragedy blew in like a winter's storm—the place where he could heal.

Michael set the sketch of Catherine on the table and stood, walking over to the door leading to the patio, watching the surf. He could see the steady lights of a large freighter on the ocean, the ship moving northeast, heading toward the horizon. He assumed it had left from Charleston Harbor, the crew loading or unloading cargo before they headed back to sea and another transatlantic destination. He thought about Derek—the look in his eyes when he first saw the painting of the tall ships. *There's a nautical heartbeat to that kind of sailing. From the wind in her sails and the water beneath her, a ship like that breathes and lives.*

He unlocked the screened door and put his hand on the handle to open it when his phone rang. He stared at it on the wicker table. The ringing seemed out of place—a sound he hadn't heard in a while. It was as if he was looking at an alien object. He couldn't remember the last time he'd received a call. A few months after the deaths of Kelsey and Mandy, the calls became infrequent at best. He'd changed his number, giving it out to members of Kelsey's family and a few friends. *Maybe the last call was when Kelsey's mother died,* he thought.

He set the glass of wine down and picked up his phone. The caller ID read: RESTRICTED. He thought about not answering it. Maybe a wrong number, someone misdialing in the middle of the night. He could let it go to voicemail. After a half-dozen rings, he pressed the button and answered. "Hello?"

"Michael … it's Catherine. Did I wake you?" She spoke in a voice just above a whisper.

"No, I wasn't asleep."

"I wanted to call and apologize for being so abrupt when I left the garden."

"It's okay. No big deal."

"No, it's not okay. You deserved a better explanation. I couldn't give you one at the moment. I was in a hurry and ran off like it was a fire drill. It wasn't. I just wanted to call and say I'm sorry."

"Thank you for calling. It wasn't expected, but I'm glad you did." He looked at her sketch. "I was just thinking about you."

"I hope they were good thoughts." Catherine was standing in subdued light in her house next to a bay window with open curtains.

"Of course, they were good thoughts."

"Where are you?"

"At the beach house I rent. The full moon is quite spectacular off the ocean. When you called, I was just unlocking the door to the screened porch to go for a walk on the beach."

"Great—I'll go with you."

"But you're not here."

Catherine laughed. "Yes, I am, in my mind. You walk, we'll talk. I want to hear the waves. Take me along for your stroll and, maybe, you can run through the surf so I can hear a bit of splashing, too. I love the ocean—it's so peaceful."

"I can do that." He kicked his shoes off, opened the screened door and walked down a short, wooden boardwalk to the beach. Within seconds he was near the surf. "Hold on a second, Catherine. I'm putting the phone in my shirt pocket as I roll up my pants. The tide is pretty high tonight."

"I can hear the waves crashing."

He rolled his pants up, took the phone from his pocket and walked into the water and stood still, the sound of the crashing surf all around him. "Can you hear that?"

"Yes, it's almost as if I'm there. Describe what you see."

"Okay … under the moonlight, I can't see anyone else on the beach. It feels very primal. The sea looks alive in the moon and bright starlight. It's as if the surface of the ocean is gobbling up the light in the pitch and rolling of waves approaching the beach. I can see minnows or small fish breaking the surface. The horizon is distinct, even at midnight. The line between the sea and the sky is thin, giving the illusion that the sea and the universe are the same. The only difference is the stars are in the sky—as if the constellation was sprinkling stardust across the ocean. And the moon is creating a long silvery path from the horizon to where I'm standing."

"It sounds beautiful."

"It is."

"It sounds like something that you should paint."

"Maybe I will. The moonlight is so bright I could paint someone in the picture, someone walking in the surf and gazing at the moon and stars in the distance. The palm trees would be in silhouette, but everything else would be softly lit."

"Who would you paint in that scene?"

"Maybe, you."

"You're painting me alone in the garden. Will I still be alone on the beach at midnight?"

"No, I might be there with you. Someone will have to protect you from the sea serpents."

Catherine laughed then became very quiet. She listened to the sound of the surf, looked out the bay window to the moon rising above the tree line, her eyes expectant as if something was coming over the horizon. "Although I'm not there to share a walk in the surf, I can share the same moonlight. And, if I close my eyes, I can see everything you're describing and even see you on the beach."

Michael could feel a loneliness in her voice. "Close your eyes, and I'll walk so you can hear the waves crashing."

After a long moment, Catherine took a deep breath, stared at the night sky and said, "I have to go. Thank you for taking me along for a midnight walk on the beach. I'm looking up at a night sky so full of stars ... and I see the absolute brightest. I think it's Sirius. I'll wish upon that star, and maybe tonight in my dreams that wish will come true. Goodnight, Michael."

"Goodnight." He heard her disconnect. He slowly lowered the phone from his ear, looking up at the stars, remembering what Kelsey had said that night in Colorado when the stars were so low and pulsating with light. *It reminds me of Van Gogh's painting ... Starry Night ... it's nights like this that remind us to never stop dreaming ... and to remember to share those dreams with those we love.*

Michael watched the heavens, a meteor blazing a trail over the smiling moon. He stared at the brightest star ... wondering what Catherine had wished. And then he took in the enormity of the constellations, no longer looking at one star but, yet, seeing them all for the very first time as one magnificent universe. After a minute, he turned around, picked up his shoes, and walked toward the house, the sound of the surf following him up the beach.

FORTY-SEVEN

Michael arrived at the memory care garden an hour early. It had been a week since he last saw Catherine, and he wanted to have his canvas and easels set up and ready to go so he could spend more time with her. He'd been a little confused after she had called him at midnight. If Catherine had wanted to apologize, she easily could have waited until they met again.

Today, Michael wore faded jeans, ripped at one knee, and a black T-shirt as he secured the canvas between the two easels. He unscrewed caps from tubes of oil paint and squirted rows of paint on a large plastic palette. He looked at the canvas, studying what he'd done thus far, knowing what he needed to accomplish to finish the painting.

A motion in the garden caught his eye. He watched a caregiver in her early twenties walking with two elderly patients, a man and a woman. The man walked with a cane, and the woman took slow steps, gripping a walker on wheels. The caregiver stopped to point out the newest blooming flowers and the birds that were alighting on one of the three birdfeeders. From a distance of fifty feet, Michael could see the old man and woman smiling as they watched bluebirds and Carolina Wrens sitting side-by-side, sharing the seeds and nuts in the feeders.

"We need to fill up the hummingbird feeders, too," the caregiver said, pointing to a dark red feeder hanging from a short chain on the limb of a maple tree. After a few minutes, the three of them sat on a park bench near the koi pond. The caregiver spoke a little louder, possibly because the elderly couple, or one of them, had difficulty hearing. "I have some breadcrumbs in here," she said, holding up a Ziploc bag with pieces of bread in it. "We can feed the fish before we go back inside to use the bathroom."

"Okay," said the woman, nodding her white head. "Can I take a flower back to my room?'

"Of course. Which one?"

"Oh my … they're all so lovely. I've always been partial to sunflowers."

"Then I'll try to get one for you … the stems can be a bit prickly, though." The caregiver walked to a row of blooming sunflowers and stood there for a few seconds trying to figure out how to collect one. Noticing her predicament, Michael grabbed a napkin and his pocketknife from among his art supplies, walked over to her side, cut the sunflower stem and wrapped it, then turned to hand it to the caregiver. Thanking Michael, she returned to the woman and gave it to her. "Here you go, Mrs. Wright."

"Thank you." She reached out and took the bright yellow flower, holding it in one twisted hand, her face beaming.

Watching the old man and woman, Michael thought about how much time he had wasted in his life. How it took him so long to carve away at the clutter to learn to do more with less. To break the chains to the world wide web of excess. Less involvement with cool apps that led to places that were thieves of time. Less online buying. Less TV. Less social media that had little to do with being social but everything to do with creating lives of fractured time. Fewer followers. Fewer "friends" he had never met and never would meet. The result was that now he had more time, energy and resources to find and experience what is real in people and places that are important to him. He thought about the story of the *Velveteen Rabbit*—a favorite book of his daughter, Mandy—of loving deep enough until you become real. He loved the sweet, animated look on her face every time he or Kelsey read her that story.

Maybe that was the allure Catherine brought to him. She was rare in her talent and resolve to live life with a lighthearted attitude, to laugh at herself, to be pragmatic when necessary, and to give to others unconditionally as she did in volunteering some of her time at the memory care center. But there was also a mystery to her as a woman. This, too, spoke to Michael in subtle notes that piqued his curiosity and intrigued him to discover more about her.

This is what he wanted to paint.

He could feel it coming from inside her. But could he paint it? Would that be revealed in the painting? He thought about that as he walked into the garden and picked a rose he'd give to Catherine when she arrived.

Perhaps two more sessions, and he'd be done, the painting completed. Two more sessions to give him time to spend with this woman. After that, maybe he'd run into her when she visited her mom. But only if she was there when he was visiting Derek. He stared at the unfinished painting and remembered what the forgotten art critic had said about Monet's painting of a sunrise … *the painting is unfinished, and it looks more like an impression than real art.*

Michael half smiled. He thought about why he painted … of which he never had an answer. Perhaps, there would never be one answer— only one reason. What was the hunger inside that commanded him to pick up brushes and paints and move them around a canvas until the colors, now in a new form, spoke back to him? They spoke to his core in images that never existed precisely like that in the history of art.

No two snowflakes are the same. No two fingerprints are exactly alike. The same for art, all different and, yet, all speaking the same language of emotion without the use of words. Mankind had done it since cave art, before written languages were created. Perhaps on a canvas was where his subconscious appeared in visual form. If an artist dips his brush into his soul … does he try to reveal the model's soul on the canvas and then touch the soul of the person looking at the painting? Is it a shared, three-way search for meaning—the human experience?

He looked at the sketch he drew of Catherine. What was it about this woman that so captivated him? Beyond her innate beauty, there was something else. Something with a powerful pull on him that demanded he attempt to replicate it in paint. What was hidden within her that he wanted to paint—had to paint? And, when he finished, would that image, that subject, reveal itself? And would he recognize it?

At that moment, Catherine walked into the garden like she did the first time he saw her, coming from the area of the gazebo, along the winding labyrinth of thick shrubs, trees, and hedges. She moved through the rows of flowers in her blue and white sundress with an elegant rhythm that seemed fitting in a world of flowers, new buds opening, others with aged blossoms, bowing their heads. She stopped and looked toward Michael, a wide smile spreading across her face.

He left the easel and walked to her. "I'm sorry I'm a little late," Catherine said.

"You're fine. Thanks for coming." He handed her a long-stemmed rose.

"You have my prop all ready?"

"It's more than a prop for a painting … it's something I want to give to you."

"That's sweet. Thank you. Where on earth did you ever find such a perfect rose?" She laughed.

"In a secret garden."

"This has always been one of my favorite places. After we're done today, I want to bring Mom outside, maybe before she has her dinner." Catherine glanced up at the back of the canvas. "When will I be able to see it?"

"When it's done."

Catherine tilted her head and smiled. "You already told me that. I mean, when will that be?"

"Art defies a timetable or even a schedule."

She chuckled, pursing her lips, eyebrows rising. "Unfortunately, I'm on a schedule. Not that I want to be, but sometimes life dictates the what, where and when … the latter being when I can get here to visit Mom."

Michael smiled. "It'll be done soon. Probably one more session after this one."

"I'm so looking forward to unveiling it to the residents here. We'll do a special presentation, maybe have it covered in some kind of curtain, and after everyone gathers in the community center, we can do the big reveal."

Michael smiled. "That sounds like a plan."

"I'll pick roses and have them placed in vases throughout the room so everyone can smell the sweet fragrance from the garden for the full affect." She brought the rose bud to her nostrils and looked up at Michael. "Thank you for taking me along for a midnight stroll on the beach. With your description of the beach at midnight and the sound of the crashing waves, I felt as if I was there."

"Maybe one day you can visit."

Catherine said nothing, looking away toward the building beyond the garden.

"Why did you call me?"

"I told you … to apologize for being abrupt. That was rude of me."

"You could have done that the next time we met in the garden. You didn't have to call."

"But I did. Was that okay?"

"Yes. I'm glad you did."

"If something is bothering me, I like to resolve it as soon as I can. And then I don't have to think about it. It seemed like a perfect time to say I was sorry."

"Midnight is a good time for many things, especially a walk on the beach."

"And now it's time we get started on the painting. My dress is laundered and pressed. We're ready to go. How about you, Michael the painter, are you ready?"

"Yes."

"I wonder if Michael is really short for Michelangelo, an artist who was both a fabulous sculptor and a painter. One of the reasons I traveled to Italy was to see his work. The man could take a twenty-foot slab of marble and sculpt the statue of David, among others, and then he could lie on his back and paint heavenly figures on the ceiling of the Sistine Chapel. He's quoted as saying that every block of stone has a statue inside it, and it is the task of the sculptor to discover it."

Michael smiled. "And he's quoted as having said he saw an angel in the marble and carved until he could set him free."

Catherine smiled, looked at the canvas and back at Michael. "There's a difference between the sculptor and the painter. The sculptor, with chisel and hammer, chips away, removing the excess of clutter, revealing the truth within."

"They both seek the truth. The painter takes a blank canvas, nothing but air touching it, and then he adds paint until the image emerges from the brushstrokes, the light against the shadows, the outcome not always planned, but rather discovered."

"Well said."

"What will I discover about you, Catherine?"

"You're the artist … I'm just the subject."

"When the painting is finished … will the subject reveal herself?"

Catherine laughed. "I suppose you'll have to tell me … or show me. Maybe you'll also discover something about yourself."

FORTY-EIGHT

Michael returned to his two easels, standing dead center in front of the wide canvas. He simply stood there for a half-minute, looking from the canvas to the garden and at Catherine near the koi pond. He mixed three paints into a blend, filled a narrow brush with paint and looked intently at the partial painting. The only movement came from the maple tree near him when, suddenly, a breeze blew in causing the leaves to fidget. It was as if nature itself was anxious for him to paint the colors of the garden and the woman before the setting sunlight called it a day. Michael stared at a jacaranda tree, its twisted limbs filled with lavender blooms. He was ready.

* * *

Catherine watched the koi fish and then looked up at where Michael stood on the edge of the garden. To her, at that moment, he appeared to embody everything that personified an artist. The stance he took in front of his work. Posture and shoulders back. The look of pure concentration on his chiseled face. He held the paintbrush like an orchestra leader might hold a baton seconds before tapping his music stand and beginning to conduct a full symphony.

Once Michael started, he began without the slightest hesitation. Quickly applying paint with a feverish pace, alternating between brushes and palette knives. He constantly looked from the canvas to the garden. Catherine could see his eyes following her as she glanced from the rose in her hand to the feeding birds, to the fish swimming near the surface, and to the rows of flowers almost surrounding her.

She was fascinated with the way he painted, a certain element of artistic madness to his frenetic movements, not unlike a sleight-of-hand magician performing on stage. His facial expressions alternated from intense concentration to slight amusement, as if the secret garden he painted was revealing its secrets only to him, some surprises, no doubt, were humorous. And then he would stop, almost becoming a statue in the garden as he looked at what he'd done and then considered what he needed to do. There was definitely a magic to his art. The essence of the man—the artist, seemed to somehow be transferred from his heart, down his arm, through his hand and the brush, mixing with the paints, leaving a form of blood art across the canvas.

* * *

Michael painted nonstop until the light began to change so much that the look and even the perspective started to shift with it. When he put his brush down, his hand was cramping, eyes burning from the concentration and lack of actual, natural blinking. He closed his eyes for a few seconds before using a white towel to wipe the excess paint from his hands. He looked over the top of the canvas and waved to Catherine, a sign that he was finished for the day. The session done. One more time before he would show his work to her or anyone else.

He left the painting and walked up to her. "I'm almost done. It's getting there. Because the canvas is so large, it takes a lot of paint to cover it. Another get-together, and we're done."

"Do you want to finish tomorrow?"

"I thought you only could spare a little time one day a week."

"Let's call the extra time a vacation. I'm not going back to Columbia until the end of the week—on Friday. So, if you want to finish it tomorrow, your model is available." She did a slight curtsy, bending at the knees, smiling.

"Let's seize the time while we can. The weather forecast has tomorrow a lot like today. Our light should be the same."

"Can we start earlier?"

"No, we need to be consistent. That means we need to start about the same time, maybe a few minutes earlier. Okay?"

"Okay."

Michael looked up at the jacaranda tree, studying the blooms and the limbs. Catherine followed his gaze. "The blooms are beautiful," she said. "Do you see a bird's nest in that tree?"

"No, I see a contrast … something I hope to capture in paint."

"What kind of contrast?"

"The gnarled and twisted limbs holding the flowers. It reminds me of something I saw in the garden before you arrived."

"What was that?"

"Two of the residents here … and man and woman walking slowly with a caregiver. They stopped and sat on one of the benches. The elderly woman was awed by the sunflowers, and the caregiver gave one to her."

"That was sweet."

"I could see this bright, colorful flower in the old woman's hand— a hand that was bent from arthritis. She was smiling, holding the flower. Content. And, as I look at the way the bowed and twisted limbs of the jacaranda tree hold the flowers, it reminds me of a painting Van Gogh did, one of the last before he died."

"Was it the one with the sunflowers in a vase?"

"No. It was called Almond Blossoms. It was simply a painting of an almond tree in bloom. But rather than letting the viewer see the whole tree, Van Gogh chose to paint only a few limbs, as if he were lying on his back under the tree and looking up. You can see a sapphire sky behind the branches and white almond blossoms. But, more importantly, at least in my mind, is how well he painted the twisted and gnarly limbs giving birth to these blossoms in the spring of a new season." He paused, looking from the jacaranda tree to Catherine. "Therefore, when I saw the old woman holding the sunflower … because of the contrast, I didn't think of Van Gogh's sunflower paintings, I thought of the one he called Almond Blossoms … a gift he painted for his young nephew."

"I wish I could see it."

Michael smiled. "And you shall. Your wish is my command." He took his phone out, hitting keys to download the painting. Catherine watched him, smudges of green and red paint still on two of his fingers. "Here," he said, handing the phone to her. "This is it."

She looked at the screen, smiling. "It's beautiful. Who would think a painting of just a few limbs, sky, and blossoms could be so striking?"

"Vincent would."

"You really admire his work, don't you?"

"I like the dreamy feel he'd bring into many of his paintings. It was his unique style at that time, something he pretty much had all to his own. The other great impressionists were excellent, but Vincent managed to work in a dreamlike quality that gave his paintings a surreal feel, something even beyond impressionism."

Catherine looked again at the image of the painting on the phone screen. "From what I remember reading, his life wasn't a happy one, suffering from what some believe was manic depression. But, when I look at this painting, I see renewal of life. A sense of springtime joy … and, yet, he eventually committed suicide."

Michael was quiet, thinking. A Carolina Wren sang from the top of the weeping willow tree. "In studying art, I remember some of the things Vincent wrote in letters to his brother. I read one that stuck with me. He wrote: '*I experience a period of frightening clarity in those moments when nature is so beautiful. I am no longer sure of myself, and the paintings appear as in a dream.*' He had his demons. But I suppose we all do."

"Maybe, for artists like Van Gogh, the creative comes with a price, or a compromise. The gift that flows from the end of the painter's brush or in the case of the sculptor with a hammer and chisel releasing the angel from a tomb of stone, the gift can come with conditions. For some it's a concession that can create personal demons."

"Maybe, but not always."

"And, maybe for Van Gogh, as we talked about … the ultimate gift was seeing what the paints would reveal to him and in him … a place of sudden clarity. A place of personal happiness while he was standing in front of the easel." She handed Michael his phone, looked at the rose in her hand, glancing back up to the canvas on the easels. "What are your demons? Do you keep them in a harness, or let them run amuck?"

He smiled. "You mentioned conditions … if you want to know about my alleged demons, you'll have to hear it over a glass of wine and dinner later tonight."

"After I spend some time with Mom, I might be able to do that."

"Does that mean … yes I can, or there's a possibility I can't?"

"Are you asking me out on a date?" She smiled.

"I hadn't thought of it that way. I was thinking more about us starving artists—the painter and the model should be pretty hungry by then." He grinned.

"Okay, since we're doing this project for the memory care center, it would be more of a business dinner."

"If you want to define it, I guess that'll work."

She laughed. "Then I guess I can be there."

"All right. There's a caveat … a stipulation, though."

"Oh, are there conditions? What's that?"

"I want to hear about your demons, too."

"That's assuming I have some." She grinned. "Where do you want to meet?"

"There's a restaurant I think you'll like. It's named for a woman who probably had a lot of demons … Anne Bonny. She was one of the few female pirates during the early1700s. Charleston was her hometown. It's called *Anne's Place*. I'll text you the address. Will eight o'clock work?"

"Yes, but don't text the address to me. I can find it."

Michael watched bees hover around the sunflowers, some alighting in the centers, picking up dark orange pollen on their legs. He pointed to them. "Do bees have secrets? The setting in the novel, *The Secret Lives of Bees*, was here in South Carolina. What is your secret life, Catherine? Anne Bonny, the pirate had a secret. At dinner, I'll tell you what it was. And I hope you can tell me more about the secret you carry like the bees carry pollen on their legs. See you tonight." He smiled, turned and walked back to the easels, removing the painting, placing everything in his van.

Catherine watched him as he drove away, the van turning left, down the long drive, lost in a sea of pine trees. She looked up at the jacaranda tree, her eyes moving from the lavender blossoms to the limbs, thinking about what Michael had said. *More importantly, at least in my mind, is how well he painted the twisting and gnarly limbs giving birth to these blossoms in the spring of a new season.*

FORTY-NINE

Catherine looked for her mother in the community center. She wasn't there, only a few patients playing cards or board games, and some staring at a wide-screen TV, watching a BBC program about penguins. Catherine walked down one of the hallways, stopping at the door to her mother's room, knocking and waiting a few seconds before entering. The bed was made. Crayon drawings were pinned to a corkboard on the wall next to a small refrigerator. Two long-stemmed roses sat in a clear vase partially filled with cloudy water. The bathroom door was closed. "Mom," Catherine said, knocking.

No answer.

She looked at the watch on her wrist, glanced at a dressing table with two framed photographs on top of it. One was a picture of Catherine's mother and father. They were just married, her mom in a white wedding dress, wide smile, and her dad in a black suit. Dark hair combed straight back. Handsome smile. Movie star good looks. In the other photo, Catherine was with her family at her college graduation. Cap and gown. Mom to the left. Dad to her right. Younger sister on the other side of Mom.

She opened the door to the bathroom. Her mother was not there. Catherine left, almost running into a caregiver in the hall. The woman held a patient chart in one hand, a prescription bottle in the other. Catherine asked, "Have you seen my mother?"

"Yes. Just saw her in Mr. Mack's room."

"Great." She smiled. "Are they watching TV?"

"No, they were admiring the art on the walls and drawing on papers. I believe he was giving your mother some art lessons."

"Oh … okay. Thanks." She left and approached the open door of Derek Mack's room. She could hear her mother's laughter. Catherine stopped at the door and watched. Her mom sat at the table next to Derek. He was showing her how to draw a castle. There were turrets, spires with flags on them, and a sweeping vista in the background that led to the coastline and a ship at sea. "Does the princess live there?" her mom asked.

"Of course. She rides her horse every day, too. Can you draw a horse?"

"I don't know … maybe."

"That's okay … I can teach you how to draw one."

"I can draw trees." She raised her trembling hand, pointing to one of the two oil paintings on the wall—the one with the mother and child on bikes beneath the long canopies of live oaks.

Derek nodded. "That painting really makes you smile. It captures the soul of South Carolina, and it makes you think of something happy."

Susan said nothing. She looked at the table and the crayon drawing of the castle in front of Derek. She started her own drawing, glancing up at the painting, then beginning with a blue sky before adding trees. Derek lifted the sketch he did, moving it closer to her. He pointed to the ship in the background and said, "That came from the other painting. I like looking at it. My son painted it and put it up there for me to see each day."

Susan tilted her head and looked at the painting of the tall ships off the coast of Louisiana. "I like boats. What's your son's name?"

"I can't remember. He comes here a lot. We walk in the garden and have some ice cream. He likes chocolate. I like the white stuff." He paused and stared at the paintings. After a moment, he slowly got up and walked over to them, looking through his bifocals at the signature in red on both paintings. He spelled. "V … a …r …g… a … s. His name is Vargas." He stood next to the painting of the tall ships, pointing to the largest. "This is my boat. I'm gonna go sailing again. My son is taking me. You wanna come, too?"

"Yes," Susan said, her voice soft.

Derek turned back to Susan and saw Catherine standing at the door. He smiled. "We're going for a little sail."

"I think that's a great idea," Catherine said. "That's a beautiful painting. I love the children on deck. What a great experience for them."

"They gotta watch out for pirates," Derek said. "They're everywhere off the coast."

Susan nodded.

"Is it time for dinner?" Derek asked.

"Soon it will be. I could smell chicken-pot-pie coming from the dining room. Smells really good." She stepped inside the room and kissed her mother on the cheek. "Hi, Mom. I love the drawings you two are doing. They're very good."

Her mother nodded, a far-away look in her tired eyes. Catherine said, "I have an idea. Before dinner, would you both like to come with me for a walk in the garden? We can feed the fish and the birds at the same time."

Her mother smiled. "I can draw birds." She motioned toward Derek. "He showed me how."

"Let's go see if we can find some birds before it gets dark. Maybe the hummingbirds are out before they fly off to roost."

Derek grinned. "Hummingbirds are lovely. They can fly backwards. The hummingbirds are like little winged angels. They fly with magic in their wings, and they're a sign of good luck and joy." He looked at Catherine. "Did you ever hear that?"

She smiled, moistened her lips and said, "Yes … yes I have."

"Let's go feed the fish," Derek said, walking over to Susan to help her out of the chair. When she stood, he looked at Catherine, gesturing to the painting of the tall ships. "Those ships will keep the pirates away from us."

"Yes, they will," Catherine said, releasing a deep breath, leading her mother and Derek out the door and down the hall to the garden outside. The director was walking in the opposite direction toward them. He gestured and stopped. "Hello, everyone." He looked over at Catherine. "Mrs. Kincaid, how is the painting coming along? Is it done?"

"No, not yet. It's large. Michael thinks he'll finish it in one more session—I think tomorrow."

"Great. Then we can schedule a time to hang it in the community center and invite all our residents. How's the painting looking? I'm assuming he's down to the finishing touches, some tweaking here and there, since he only has one more session to go."

"I don't know how it looks. Michael won't show a work in progress. I'm hoping to see it tomorrow.

"Well, I suppose we shall find out soon enough. Maybe we can unveil it at the end of the week. Friday would be a good day for the residents and staff." He nodded and walked down the hall.

FIFTY

Michael sat alone at a corner table in the restaurant, wondering if Catherine was on her way. It was a few minutes past eight. He thought about calling, but since she didn't want him to send a text to her, maybe the same reasoning would apply to a phone call. *Why?* Because they were both traceable. And, if she was married, maybe she didn't want it discovered. *Then why call at midnight and go for a virtual walk on the beach?*

He tried to push those thoughts from his mind, watching people, mostly couples, arrive to dine in what appeared to be one of Charleston's most popular restaurants. *Anne's Place* was rustic and, yet, had an imbued, upscale feel with its decor and menu selections. The restaurant was decorated with a whimsical sense of the golden age of piracy in the early 1700s. The cypress walls were adorned with replicas of old swords, black powder pistols, tricorne hats, black eye patches, hooks, fake parrots, skull-and-crossbones flags, sashes and bandanas.

There were framed drawings and caricatures—a rogue's gallery of famous and infamous pirates. *Scalawags*, the sign read above the pictures. Blackbeard. Calico Jack. Black Bart. Captain Kidd. Henry Morgan and many others. There were short, biographical sketches beneath each illustration. In the center of the wall of fame, was the largest of the drawings. This one was a black-and-white, hand-drawn image of Anne Bonny standing on a pirate ship and pointing a flintlock pistol at another ship. Directly below the sketch was a plaque with information about Anne's criminal profession as a pirate, one of the few women pirates during the heyday of high-seas piracy.

Michael watched customers enter the restaurant, walking by the gallery without the slightest glimpse. No one stopping to read the historical information. *Maybe they were repeat customers*, he thought. And now blasé to the theme of the restaurant and showcased pirate history. But there was no ignoring the scent of roasted garlic, basil, Cajun shrimp on the grill and bread just out of the oven. He glanced at his watch: 8:15. Michael looked at his phone screen. No calls or messages. He thought about his last conversation with Catherine before he put the painting and easels back in the van.

If you want to define it, I guess that'll work.

Then I guess I can be there.

He stared at the candle in the center of the table, the yellow flame almost motionless in the still air. "Are you meditating?"

Michael looked up. Catherine was standing next to the table. "You were staring so intently at the candle I wasn't sure if I should interrupt. I thought you might be having some interpersonal thing with fire. You know … the artist gene in you, maybe thinking about how to paint fire. It took mankind centuries to figure out how to start it. But I'm not sure I've ever seen a painting that really does fire justice."

Michael smiled. "An impressionist painter strives to capture the way moving light strikes a subject. Fire is light. The sun is fire. Let there be light." He lifted the candle vase, the flickering firelight moving across his face. "And there was light. Please, sit. I'm glad you made it."

She smiled and sat opposite him. "It smells great in here. I'm sorry I'm late. Mom was having a small meltdown of sorts. Her anxiety gets up sometimes. I talked her off the ledge before getting her to sleep."

"I'm sorry to hear that."

"It's getting worse. On a brighter note, I was watching Mom with Derek Mack. He's been giving her art lessons, at least he's showing her how to work with colored pencils, crayons and watercolors. She loves it. And I think he does, too. They've sort of become pals, bonding. I believe it's good for both of them. They're not as lonely."

"That's excellent. I hope it continues."

"An interesting thing happened tonight. I overheard Derek tell mom that his son, Vargas, comes to visit him often. He really feels close to you."

"That's sweet. I wonder if he thinks of me as his son because we have a special bond, or if he's remembering he had a son a long time ago. Derek told me just last year he had a son that died as an infant. Apparently of SIDS. Until then, I had no idea that he and Jewell had a child."

"That's sad. I'm glad he has you." Catherine looked around the restaurant, taking in the decorations. "I love the pirate theme and motif. I stopped for a moment to read the short bio of Anne Bonny. It said she was actually born in Ireland, grew up here in Charleston before running away to become a pirate down in the Caribbean. So, I suppose she was one of the original pirates of the Caribbean. I wonder if she ran with Captain Jack Sparrow?" Catherine laughed, the candlelight dancing in her eyes.

"No, but she did run with a guy nicknamed Calico Jack. His real name was Captain Jack Rackham."

"How'd he get the name, Calico Jack?"

"Because he liked to wear calico clothes. I don't know why. But I do know why he got the girl, so to speak."

"The girl being Anne Bonny, right?"

"Yes. She was the only daughter of a wealthy plantation owner who owned land outside of Charleston. In those days, it was called Charles Town. Anne apparently had a strong lust for life and an Irish temper to fuel that lust. Against her father's wishes, she married a poor sailor who was a part-time pirate by the name of James Bonny. Anne's father was so distraught, he disowned her. Anne and her husband left or fled to Nassau in the Bahamas. Her husband took a job as basically a guy who reported the presence of pirates or suspected pirates to the governor."

"What did Anne do?"

"She took a job serving rum and whiskey in a tavern. It was there she met the dashing John Rackham, not yet known as Captain Calico Jack. That would come later in his criminal career. They fell madly in love and eventually became the Bonnie and Clyde of the Caribbean."

"Oh no … a tragic love story on the high seas?"

"Exactly."

"What happened to them?"

"Calico Jack wanted to marry Anne. He offered to pay her husband money if he'd grant her a divorce. Anne's husband refused. So, Captain Jack and Anne stole a ship and set sail. They convinced other pirates to join them. And, for the next couple of years, they roamed the Caribbean doing what pirates do … plundering other ships. Anne was apparently very good, more than able to keep up with the men. She became pregnant with Captain Jack's child. She gave birth in Cuba. Eventually, Captain Jack and Anne were caught, their ship impounded. Both, along with members of their crew, were found guilty of piracy. Anne told the judge she was pregnant again, asked for time to have the baby before she was hanged."

"Was the judge lenient?"

"He granted Anne the request, put her in jail. The fate of Captain Jack wasn't so good, though. They did hang him."

"What happened to Anne? Did she have her baby?"

"No one knows. She didn't spend that much time in jail, somehow escaping. And, from there, she simply vanished. She was so secretive, there's no historical record of where she went or what happened to her. But she did manage to escape the gallows."

Catherine leaned back in her chair. "Well, let's hope she and her child had a good life in the islands. I wonder if she managed to slip back into America and live the rest of her days here in Charleston?"

"That would be a tender ending wouldn't it?"

"Maybe even a romantic ending."

Michael was quiet. The server, a young, college-aged woman, approached the table. She smiled and said, "Welcome to Anne's Place. I'm Katie, and I'll be your server tonight. Can I get you started with something to drink?"

Catherine glanced at the wine list. "I'd love a glass of chardonnay. Thanks."

Michael said, "I'd like a cabernet … the Black Stallion. Thanks."

"My pleasure." The server turned and walked away.

Catherine stared at the flickering candle for a moment, lifting her eyes to Michael. "I'm looking forward to tomorrow."

"Why?"

"Because that's when you finish the painting, and I'll finally get to look at it. I've been so anxious to see it … to be part of the big reveal."

"You will be the first person to see it. I hope you like what I've done. Speaking of reveal … I want to know more about you. I told you the story of Anne Bonny. I want to hear the story of Catherine Kincaid. You've been a mystery woman … an enigma in the garden. What can you tell me about you?"

"What do you want to know?"

"Let's start with one question … are you married?"

FIFTY-ONE

The server brought the glasses of wine to the table and asked, "Are y'all ready to order? Any questions?"

Catherine looked up from the menu. "How's the halibut with the crab topping?"

"Excellent. Folks love it."

"Great. I'd like to try that."

"Yes, ma'am. And for you, sir?"

Michael closed the menu. "I haven't had shrimp 'n grits in a long time. Let's go with that, thanks."

"Sounds good." The server took the menus and left.

Michael lifted his glass of wine. Catherine did the same. She said, "Let's toast to the memory of Anne Bonny. A woman who left Charleston in search of new horizons and found it. To her swashbuckling sense of adventure … wherever it may have led her."

They touched glasses and sipped the wine. Catherine set her glass on the table. "You asked me if I'm married. The short answer is yes."

Michael said nothing for a moment. He sipped his wine again. "Is there a long answer?"

"There's an explanation. But, before I offer it …" She glanced at his left hand. "You wear a wedding ring, but your wife passed away. I'm not wearing a wedding ring—" Catherine paused, took a deep breath and slowly let it out, then added, "my marriage is dead."

"Then why are you still married?"

"My mother."

"Your mother … what do you mean?"

"Her healthcare. Mom has been suffering from dementia and now the ravages of Alzheimer's for more than six years. For some reason, it began when she was relatively young—early onset in her late fifties.

Because of her age, we didn't know what it was at first. Never suspected Alzheimer's. Her medical care is extremely expensive. Those costs are picked up through the company my husband's family owns and operates. Jerry comes from the wealthy Kincaid family of four sons—no daughters. The patriarch, Ralph Kincaid the third, inherited a lot of money and made a fortune with their businesses, mostly in land acquisition, lumber and construction. They're a family of handed down entitlements, and they have myriad preconceived expectations and conditions after you become one of them. Jerry is the youngest son. I thought he was different from the rest of the pack. We met when the public relations firm I worked for at the time was hired by their company. I was the account manager. Jerry was, I thought, a Southern gentleman. Genteel without being patronizing. Self-assured. Witty. Fun. He was that way for the first couple of years, or at least I thought he was." She took a deep breath again, then sipped her wine.

"What happened?"

"He has a very dark side. It's almost as if there are two different people living inside him … a charming person and an extremely evil one. The only way I can tell which one is in there is by the look he gets in his eyes."

"What do you mean?"

"They're the only thing he can't control. A distant look and an actual change of eye color. His evil, internal twin is a man who's frequently with high-end prostitutes, gambles with reckless impunity and drinks. The demons, which you and I joked about, are very much real with Jerry. They come flying out of the genie's bottle when he hits the whiskey bottle. After that … he wants to hit me. Between the alcohol and the mood alternating meds he's on, I never know who or what personality Jerry will show up as … and that's when he's home. Luckily, he travels a lot."

"Is he physically abusive to you?"

"Yes. Physically and verbally. He's a control freak, and the thought of compromise or relinquishing a smidgeon of control is not in his DNA any more than it is with his father. After Jerry's done his damage, when he sobers up, he begs me for forgiveness. Promises he'll never do it again. Showers me with flowers and gifts."

"Sounds like a vicious cycle."

"He had a mistress …."

"What do you mean … had? Did he end the relationship?"

"She called me one day. Told me her name was Jessica Lasalle, and that she was pregnant with my husband's child. Becoming hysterical on the phone, she demanded that Jerry and I divorce, saying he never loved me. When I confronted him later that night, he denied it all, of course. She lived south of Columbia in Pine Ridge. A month later, she disappeared. A body was never found. There was apparently no forensic evidence. No witnesses. Nothing."

"Do you think your husband killed her?"

"Jerry would never do his own dirty work. But I think he hired someone to do it. He's that diabolical. His flip side is the public persona of Jerry Kincaid—the affable, articulate man concerned with the direction of South Carolina … so concerned he's seriously thinking about running for governor."

"Why don't you file for divorce?"

"Because I can't risk my mother's healthcare being severed. And that's exactly what would happen. He's threatened it. And he'll do it in a heartbeat."

"Do you have children?"

"No. I'd always wanted a child. Jerry didn't. After a couple of years, I didn't either … at least not with him. Cohabitation is difficult enough. I can't imagine what co-parenting would be like with that man."

"Where is he now?"

"Who knows? On yet another of his many business trips or meeting with political cronies. He doesn't tell me anymore. I do know that he's out of the country through next Friday."

"Sounds like an extremely toxic relationship."

"It is, and I'm saddened by it … by what it has become."

"Even more than that, it doesn't sound like you."

"What do you mean?"

"You have an unbridled zest for life. How have you managed to maintain, or rather sustain it, considering the abuse and control?"

She smiled. "I was a theater major in college. I did summer stock. Had some challenging roles. I've had to act around Jerry and others in the Kincaid clan. Not that I wanted to, but I just slip into the survival mode of an actor playing a part. I wasn't and will never be a Stepford wife. I've learned to exist until I don't have to live in that existence anymore."

"I don't want you to think I'm judging you, Catherine, because I'm not. It's your life, and you have to decide how to live it. I made a decision in my life not to live it like a stranger anymore. Unfortunately, it took the tragic deaths of my wife and daughter to shock me back into reality. And that truth came at me like a freight train. I wasn't living, at least by my original definition. I was role-playing. Amassing money. Power. Fame. Becoming the king of the hill, but it was a position I never really wanted. I just became sucked into the torrent because I started to believe a lot of the things the reporters wrote and said about me and the career I was fast-tracking to build. And the compromise came from neglecting the needs of my wife and child … and, unknowingly, my own needs as well."

She sipped her wine. "I understand. It took personal tragedy for you to make the needed changes. My situation is different. I owe my mom, literally, my life. She became pregnant with me when she was young … nineteen. She doesn't talk much about it. Her boyfriend at the time, Collin, stuck with family tradition and enlisted in the Army. He was sent overseas, where he was killed."

"I'm sorry to hear that."

"Mom refused to have an abortion and gave birth to me in the indigent ward at a county hospital. Her parents turned their backs on her, especially her father, until I was about four. My mother was a single parent until she married my stepfather when I was ten. He was older than she was, but it was a good match. Up until that time, she was all I had … and I was all she had. Mom never made me feel that she needed anything more. She always was resolute, always loved me and believed in my potential. When she was under a lot of pressure to abort me, she stuck by her heart and her faith, refusing to do it. And now I refuse to see her waste away from Alzheimer's disease in her small house or some state institution without the care she needs."

The server brought the food, setting the dishes down on the table. "Can I bring you anything else?" she asked.

Catherine said, "Another glass of wine would be nice."

"And you sir?"

Michael glanced at his wine. "I'm fine, thanks." The server nodded and left. Michael looked at Catherine. "Thank you for sharing your story."

She released a deep breath. "It's something I just don't discuss with anyone. I'm not sure why I opened up to you. But I'm glad I did."

"Me, too."

"When Mom passes, I'll file for divorce. If Jerry runs for the governor's job, he'll want a South Carolina-bred wife by his side as a prop. He won't get it from me." She took a bite of her food. "This is delicious. I think Anne Bonny would be proud."

"I'm not sure if her fame included cooking, but she was apparently quite a pirate, primarily because she fell in love with Captain Calico Jack and decided to sail the high seas with him."

"Yo-ho-ho, it's a pirate's life for me, too. When it comes to Anne's decision to have left her controlling husband on the shore, I can relate and, even posthumously, I cheer her memory on and want to believe her swashbuckling days at sea were some of her best." She sipped her wine. "Okay, you know my story. I want to hear yours, too. You still wear your wedding ring. I suppose it causes you to think about your wife often."

Michael started to answer when he noticed someone walking across the dining room heading toward them. A tall man was approaching. He wore a dark blazer sports coat, black T-shirt, and designer jeans with boat shoes. No socks. Michael didn't know what Catherine's husband looked like. But he wondered if the man coming toward their table was married to the woman who sat across from him.

FIFTY-TWO

Even before he got to their table, Michael could tell the man had been drinking. There was a sway to his walk, a pausing between tables, somewhat tilting as he waited for a server to finish taking an order. Catherine followed Michael's gaze, watching the man approach. He was wide-shouldered, flushed face and nose, inquisitive narrow eyes. His lips had the shine of butter on them. "Excuse me, I don't mean to intrude." He shifted his eyes to Catherine, nodding his head, "Evening ma'am." Then he looked back at Michael. "My wife and I are dining across the room, right under that big ol' sailfish on the wall. When I was eating my oyster soup, I looked up and thought I recognized you, sir. So, as I headed to the men's room, thought I'd stop by your table for a quick sec and ask … are you Michael Vargas, the architect?"

Michael smiled. "Yes, and I used to be an architect. Not anymore."

"I read something about that." The man grinned. "I'm Bud Gardner. I'm a partner in the largest architectural firm in Charleston. Maybe you've heard of us … Lewis, Gardner, Durden and Associates."

"Yes, I have heard of you."

"That's good thing, considering the money we pay in PR and advertising." He chuckled, holding the chairback for balance. "Anyway, I don't want to bother y'all. I just wanted to say that your work ranks up there with Lloyd Wright, Frank Gehry, Ming Pei and the other greats."

Michael nodded. "Thank you."

"Can I ask you why you walked away from it all? You were lead dog in the pack."

"It was a personal decision."

"Well, I hope you don't regret the decision. It was architecture's big loss. When they build that tower you designed for Hong Kong, it'll be on my bucket list to see. Y'all have a good dinner." He smiled and walked away, heading toward the restrooms and trying to walk in a straight line.

Catherine turned to Michael. "You made his night. Does that happen often?"

"Inebriated people approaching me at dinner … no."

She smiled. "I meant the part of being recognized, the fame thing."

"Not since I left New York, bought an old van and became a vagabond." He laughed. "But it used to happen more when I was in the city and in the thick of things. I never really enjoyed the fame. The only perk was that it helped to get a table at restaurants where you had to make reservations weeks in advance. Beyond that, I always preferred anonymity."

"Was your wife, Kelsey, comfortable with your fame?"

"It wasn't intrusive. We didn't have paparazzi following us around and snapping pictures from the bushes. She was comfortable in her own skin—meaning she went with the flow, not walking in my shadow. She knew the price of fame and how it came with the career in that highly specialized world of architectural design."

"Please tell me more about Kelsey and Mandy."

Michael smiled. "I was so blessed to have had them in my life." He picked up his phone and flipped through the screen until a picture of Kelsey and Mandy appeared. "Here they are … I'd taken this about two months before they were killed."

Catherine took the phone and looked at the screen. "They're both beautiful." Her voice was soft.

"I'm now a much better man for having had them in my life. Kelsey was smart and a true free spirit. I met her in college. She was deep into the arts. She loved my paintings and encouraged me to have a career in the arts, if that was what I really wanted. She earned a law degree and had a successful practice. Like you, she'd studied acting. Did some plays in school and a couple performances in New York, off Broadway. She loved to work with clay and make beautiful bowls and vases. I have some in my beach house. She was spiritual … and she had a deep belief in God." He sipped his wine. "Mandy was only four when she died, but she had an old soul … a loving soul. She was thoughtful and creative—a happy child. Full of kisses." He was quiet for a few seconds. "I have a troll in my house. She takes care of the home."

"A troll … a female troll?"

"Yes. Her name's Poppy. She was Mandy's pretend best friend. Watching Mandy play with her troll dolls, especially Poppy, was like watching a movie that was half animated and the other half live-action and full of narration. She would do the voices for her entire troll family. And she'd sing her favorite song with Poppy. Mandy said it was the *Get Back Up Again* song. And she sang it on key." He paused, a slight smile forming in one corner of his mouth. "Mandy once told me that she and Poppy both loved the sound of a cowbell. When I asked her why, she told me it was because of the lovely music that came from the bell … music to sing along to and music that you played when you hugged your friends, something that Poppy did often. That's one of the things Mandy loved." Michael looked across the table at Catherine. Her eyes were moist. She sipped her wine. He said, "I miss them and always will."

"Thank you for sharing with me."

"You asked me about my wedding ring. I never took the ring off. Not because I was no longer married to her, but because I felt like I never had a chance to tell Kelsey or Mandy goodbye. And I felt guilty. I couldn't fly with them that day … so I told them to go on without me. Kelsey would have waited a day or two, but I didn't know if I could schedule the time to go to her mother's home." He paused, leaning back in his chair. "The sight of the plane wreckage that night from the balcony of where I stayed to do a presentation will be with me until the day I die." He looked at the candle and then up at Catherine. "More than two hundred people died in that crash. For most, their bodies couldn't be recovered because there was nothing left to recover. Fire is a thing I will never have in one of my paintings … even something as small and innocuous as a campfire. I can paint just about anything but flames."

"I understand." She reached across the table and touched his right hand. "It wasn't your fault, Michael. You are a good man … a compassionate man. You suffered horribly when that plane crashed.

Many people died that night. The innocent families of those victims are no more responsible than you are because there is no liability when you are a casualty, too. That kind of tragedy kills something inside your heart. Bad things, horrific things, happen … and they happen to good and kind people. All we can do is be so thankful for the time we had together, to cherish the memories made with loved ones, and to live in honor and reverence to those we lost."

"I try to do that. But sometimes I have to close my eyes and replay the events I shared with Kelsey and Mandy, to almost go into a form of self-hypnosis to see what I didn't see the first time around, to recreate the sights, sounds and the experience of what we did as a family." He stared at their pictures on his phone screen. "I used to almost live on my phone. But now, if I didn't need it for GPS navigation or use it to look at pictures of my family, I'd probably toss it in Charleston Harbor close to where the first shots of the Civil War where fired." He looked at Catherine. "I can't use it to call you because … you don't want me to call."

"It's not that I don't want you to call me, it's just that I have to be very careful. Even when I leave this restaurant tonight, I don't know if Jerry has hired a private investigator to hide in the shrubs and take pictures. Regardless, you don't need to call me. I'm right here with you, and I'd like to spend more time with you until I have to go. Okay?"

"Okay."

She looked at a one-inch scar on the back of his hand. "When you decided to make that change in your life, Michael, to spend a year traveling and painting, you weren't running away from the tragedy. You were following a new path. You said how Kelsey always encouraged you to pursue your art. Every painting you do is a homage to her and her support of you. She recognized your immense talents as an artist. And guess what?"

"What?"

"Tomorrow, when you finish the painting in the garden, when we unveil it to more than one hundred patients suffering from some form of dementia, they, too, will see and feel how you tell a story with a paintbrush."

FIFTY-THREE

For the first time, Michael moved his easels and canvas closer to the heart of the garden. He chose to use brushes to begin and finish the final part of the painting. The palette knives had given much of the look he wanted—the feel of a garden in motion with the breeze blowing, flowers thick with the vibration of bees, birds feeding, koi swimming, light moving across everything. And a beautiful woman experiencing the natural surroundings. The last component of the painting was to put Catherine amongst the beauty, to let the viewers see and feel the symbiosis—the relationship between the woman and her environment.

Michael's emotions were like the paints on his palette. Mixed. Blended into a hybrid of feelings. Not only did he want to paint Catherine but also to explore a future with her. But at what costs? She was married or in a loveless relationship and would be until her mother's death. He thought about the horrible paradox—the death of the mother to free her daughter's soul from some kind of forced bondage.

It didn't have to be that way. It shouldn't have to be that way.

Was there somehow … someway he could help her break free?

He looked to the right of the easel on the left side of the canvas, studying Catherine's face in the soft light. He'd used the sketch he did for reference, alternating between it taped to the easel and Catherine standing near the koi pond with the long-stemmed red rose in her hand. He stepped around the canvas, a paint-filled brush in one hand. "Catherine … if you could hold it right there for a moment. Look in the direction of the red maple." He used the paintbrush to point.

She smiled, doing as instructed. "How's this?"

"Beautiful. Give me about five minutes like that and then you can move around some."

"Okay."

For the first time since he started the canvas, he painted slower, taking his time to let the colors help him get it right. Even after painting hundreds of canvases, he was still amazed at how a fluke brushstroke, something rather done by chance, could give the painting more depth and take it in directions he hadn't seen before making the mark. This happened as he painted her hair. He paused, looking intently at one of her bare shoulders in the sundress. "Can you move your hair to your left shoulder? Just let it fall naturally, okay?"

"I can do that." She used two hands to reposition her hair, the tresses falling down to her left breast. "Is this what you had in mind?"

"Perfect." Michael watched the diffused sunlight fall against her face and hair. The supple light radiating around her shoulders and head, giving a near halo effect. He mixed paints quickly, using a one-inch fan brush to apply the paint, capturing the light against her body and dress. He stepped back three feet, studying what he'd done and what he needed to do. He changed brushes, mixed paints, and returned to the canvas. He painted the blue and white sundress with quicker brushstrokes, almost as if he was weaving and stitching light itself into the seams.

And then he used a small brush to paint her arms and her hand holding the rose, the red petals took on a dreamlike flare with his impressionist's strokes. Michael painted some details of her face, mixing a touch of realism with his impressionist's skills. The combination was striking, making the painting come even more alive. It was as if the woman in the center had an illusory quality of mystery within the focal point of the garden, commanding the eye to follow her for a fleeting moment in time, light and space.

Michael used a palette knife to paint the path that she walked on—the marbled effect of his mixed paints giving the path a look of shade combined with white paver stones and green grass filled with light and shadows. He quickly painted the fountain, infusing sunlight with the moving water spilling over the multiple tiers, streaming down into silvery splashes in the koi pond. He used a small palette knife to give the illusion of orange and black speckled fish just below the surface dimpled with water droplets.

The final application of layered paints went into the weeping willow tree on the left side of the canvas. He applied fast brushstrokes to give a sense of movement—that the dangling green, whip-like branches were swaying in the breeze. Michael took three steps back and studied what he'd done. Once he finished a painting, once he signed his name and put the brushes down, he never went back to it. He couldn't. It would be like going back in time to lasso light and shadows that had long ago left the field. He smiled, his body drained. It was done, and he was pleased.

He picked up a small, tapered brush, swirled it in a little bit of paint thinner and some red paint. Then he stood in front of the right side of the canvas. Below one of the flowerbeds, he signed his name:

Vargas

He stood back and looked over at Catherine. "Are you ready to see it?"

"That's a silly question. Is it finished?"

"Yes. It's done."

"I can't believe you're asking me if I want to see it … I've been waiting for days and days to see it." She walked quickly toward the painting, the back side of the canvas still in her direction.

Michael used a white towel to clean his hands, especially his right hand where there was some paint. "Before you see it, I need to cover your eyes."

"With what? I don't see a blindfold here."

"We'll have to improvise."

"I can walk past it, keep my back to it until you tell me to turn around. Will that work?"

"Part of your suggestion will work. But I have a flare for the more dramatic. So, if you will, walk by the easels, keeping your back to the painting … I'll guide you."

"Guide me … how?"

"I'll cover your eyes with my hands. Don't worry, I got most of the paint off of them."

"Okay." She walked around the painting, keeping her back toward it.

Michael motioned with one hand. "Come a little further. Maybe ten feet." He nodded. "Good. That's the spot." He walked up behind her, placed the palms of his hands over her eyes. "Okay, we'll turn around, and I'll lift my hands."

She smiled. "Are you sure you wiped off the paint? I can smell paints."

"Maybe what you smell is coming from the canvas."

"No, it's coming from the hands of the artist."

"Consider it my cologne." He laughed.

"I can play along, but I'm glad we're outside and not in a studio. There's less ventilation inside."

"I don't paint in a studio. Okay, let's slowly turn to face the canvas, kind of like we're doing the painter's dance." He gently turned her. "Are you ready?"

"If you ask me that again, I might be forced to strike you with one of your wet brushes. Yes, I'm ready. I shall not wait any longer."

"And you don't have to."

Michael lifted his hands from her eyes.

FIFTY-FOUR

Catherine stood in front of the wet painting and said nothing. She didn't have to. The expression on her face said it all. Michael waited for her to speak. To make some kind of sound—to breathe. She appeared to hold her breath, her eyes roaming across every part of the painting, stopping to intently explore the thousands of flowers he'd painted. She looked at the birds in flight, a chipmunk gnawing an acorn, the water gurgling down the sides to the fountain and splashing onto the surface of the koi pond. She could see the tawny and orange backs of the fish.

She looked at how the light seemed to move across everything that Michael's paintbrush had touched. The slender highlights bouncing off the swaying weeping willow branches, the infusing of light and water in the fountain, giving the water a strong sense of movement, the deep pockets of shade and shadows. She stared at the gazebo, the pink and lavender bougainvillea hanging from the white-washed terrace. Her eyes followed the passageways through the shrubs leading to the gazebo in the shade of colossal oaks draped with moss. The painting evoked a feeling of an English garden on the grounds of a manor laced in Old World antiquity and mystery.

And then she looked at her own image.

She gently bit her bottom lip, her eyes welling. She touched her hand to her lips. "I have no words, Michael."

"Does that mean you like it?"

"The reason I have no words is because what I see here is beyond my power to describe it … it's beyond my ability to express how much this painting moves me. It gives my soul a hug and a chill at the same time, like holding and sipping a cup of tea on a cold December morning. The warmth I feel comes from how much the painting invites me to explore these grounds. It beckons me to come play—to discover the secrets I might stumble upon in the garden. The chill that I feel in my bones is because of what you've done. Even in South Carolina's humidity, it gives me goosebumps because of how well you painted it … how you decided what to paint … what to include and what to leave out."

"There's only so much I can get on a canvas and still replicate what I see, what I feel."

"What you chose to paint is the heartbeat of the garden. Some people might call it composition, but it's more like what Michelangelo did by cutting and shaping the stone until the angel is revealed. You painted a Garden of Eden and bared the raw soul of nature herself."

"And I painted an angel in the garden."

Catherine was quiet. She glanced down at the rose in her hand and then looked at the way Michael had painted it on the canvas. She observed how he'd painted her, the semi-profile of her face, her hair, although brushed, had the healthy look of time spent outdoors, the way it cascaded over her shoulder to her breasts. The way he spun golden sunlight into the locks. She looked at how he'd painted her bare shoulders and arms, how the shadow from the rose fell across her sundress. "Michael, I've had lots of people take my picture, had people do sketches of me … but I've never been featured in a painting. What you did, how fast you did it … it takes my breath way. This is the sweetest, kindest, most profound compliment I've ever had. I don't deserve this." Pointing to the painting, Catherine said, "She looks secretive, mysterious, kind, vulnerable, and content … all at the same time. I can't possibly measure up to the woman you painted in the garden."

"The woman I painted in the garden is you, Catherine. It's the way I see you. It's no one else … no other woman. This isn't my artistic impression of you. It's the essence of you. I may have mixed the paints, held the brushes in my hands, but I took the painting lead from someone else. In looking at you … in watching you interact—talking to the squirrels, birds, butterflies, the scampering chipmunks in the center of the garden, you were like a bright star in the center of their universe. I painted what I saw … and I painted what I felt."

"I've had my guard up for so long—yet she looks raw and real—alive." Catherine's eyes misted. She had to look away from him. Had to look away from the painting. The flood of emotions in the late afternoon sunset was overwhelming. After a half a minute, after wiping tears from below her eyes, she smiled. "Thank you. I know those two words sound so simple ... so shallow when I stand in front of this magnificent painting, but it's all I have right now."

"That's more than enough. You don't have to say anything else. It's in your eyes and your smile. That's all I need."

"Thank you."

"You're welcome." He smiled. "Oh, I almost forgot—there is one thing that I need."

"What?"

"A kiss. It's part of our original bargain." He smiled.

"Oh, really? I don't recall that part. I do remember that you're supposed to hang it in the community center."

"We are, after all, in a memory care facility, where we kindly have to help each other remember things. I seem to recall a kiss being on the list." Michael laughed. "This may not be The Garden of Earthly Delights, but it does have a primal, almost Edenic feel. And we know there was romance in Eden." Michael stepped closer to her. He looked directly at Catherine, his eyes compassionate, probing, and then beckoning. He leaned in, touched her face and gently kissed her.

Catherine closed her eyes, his lips soft against hers. He lingered in the kiss for a long moment, the sound of birdsong in the trees, a breeze moving through the branches, the erotic scent of flowering plants in the warm air, the pulsating movement of bees drawn to the lush odors and invisible commands of nectar and pollen.

Michael straightened up, looking at her. He smiled. "You are the woman in the painting." He motioned toward the canvas. "And to me, you always will be."

"You make me feel like I am that woman in the painting. I see the beauty in the garden and in her ... and I can feel it deep inside me. I also feel the long-suppressed emotions and the need to release them. For my protection, I've learned to be guarded. When I'm in the garden, I feel freer. I appreciate that you recognized the beauty and the complexity and wanted to share it with the world when you captured it in paint. I feel utterly vulnerable."

"You wanted to bring the beauty of the garden inside to the residents who can no longer come outside to experience it. Part of that beauty is in showing the pure enjoyment of it. I hope we accomplished that."

"I know we did. When can we show it to everyone? I can't wait for Mom to see this, and I have to see the expression on Derek Mack's face when we unveil it."

"It needs to dry first. After that, I'll frame it."

"How long will it take it to dry?"

"That depends."

"Depends on what?"

"On which way the wind blows."

Catherine smiled. "Now, you're talking in riddles. What do you mean?"

"That's exactly what I mean. I'm going to take it back to my beach house and put it in the screened back porch facing the ocean and the offshore breezes. The more the breezes come through the screen and across the surface of the painting, the quicker it'll dry. I think it'll be ready in three days."

"I miss the ocean breezes."

"You're more than welcome to come. I don't think it'll be as mundane as watching paint dry."

Catherine laughed. "The beach is never boring, at least not to me. I'm just not sure if I'm ready to spend time there."

"You mean spend time there with me, right?"

"No, it's not that. It's not you … it's me. I'm still an old-fashioned girl at heart, maybe it's the southern in me, I don't know."

"Then think about it. You decide. To help you decide, look at it this way … I can cook a mean steak. Come join me at least for dinner. You gotta eat. If you decide you want to stay longer, there's a spare bedroom that overlooks the beach."

She smiled. "I like my steak medium, a touch of pink in the center. Maybe the color of a late sunset over the ocean—the one with the pink that's promising a good tomorrow."

* * *

From near the gazebo, a long, black camera lens poked through the shrubbery, like the snout of a stalking creature—one glass eye unblinking. There were the quick sounds of the shutter opening and closing, the images of Catherine Kincaid and Michael Vargas standing in the garden, their lips touching, a painting next to them, the woman in the painting wearing the same blue and white sundress.

FIFTY-FIVE

Catherine looked in her car's rearview mirror often as she drove from the motel to Michael's beach house. She didn't think she was being followed, but she was still anxious. The moon rising over the Atlantic Ocean cast the beach house in silhouette. She pulled in the driveway and parked behind his van.

Michael heard Catherine arrive, so he walked around the house from the back patio to the front to greet her. When he spotted her suitcase, his face lit into a wide grin. "Hi there … let me carry your suitcase for you."

"This is so beautiful out here. Lead the way."

"We'll go in through the front door to give you sort of a quick tour. That way you'll have your bearings in case you need to make a fast get-away from too much tranquility and fresh air. It does take a little getting used to." Michael smiled.

She followed him in the door and through the home, which was partially adorned in a nautical motif. "I like the way you decorated the house. It really has a seafaring feel."

"I can't take any credit. It came furnished, down to the cutlery in the kitchen drawers." When they entered the wide, screened-in back porch, Catherine spotted the garden canvas Michael had leaned against a cypress wall next to a cast net hanging on a wooden peg.

Catherine stepped back from the painting. "I love how skillfully you captured the garden scene and the light. It is so beautiful I could stare at it all day … making it a very good thing it's not in my house, or I would get absolutely nothing done." She turned and faced the ocean. "I can feel the sea breeze on my face. It's as if the wind traveled from Africa across the ocean to caress our South Carolina beach. And, I love this beach house. It's relatively secluded and private. How did you ever find it?"

Michael smiled, poured two glasses of red wine, handing one to Catherine. "The house kind of found me, really. I remembered it from the time I was a kid walking the beaches, learning how to body surf and how to toss a cast net. The house changed ownership a couple of times. The last owners … they used it as a summer retreat for extended family. When the elderly parents died, the house was in the center of a contentious estate settlement. Some of the adult children wanted to keep it in the family. Other siblings wanted to sell it. They apparently came to a compromise and decided to put it on the market, but they priced the house too high for the area. After more than a year on the market, they were in agreement to rent it. I made an offer to lease the place with an option to buy. They accepted. And here we are."

"And here we are." Catherine raised her glass. "Let's toast to the winds of change … may they bring warm greetings and new opportunities." They touched glasses.

"I'll drink to that." He sipped his wine. "Are you hungry?"

"Starving. Something about standing in a garden all day doing nothing but watching the birds in the feeder, the koi fish gobbling up bits of bread, bees making honey—all that tends to build an appetite."

"Sounds like toiling work. Well, the barbecue grill is right outside the porch on the patio, ready to go. I'll throw the French bread in the oven to bake, then grab the steaks off the counter and get them on the fire. The salad is tossed and waiting for you to choose a dressing … vinaigrette or olive oil and lemon?"

"Vinaigrette. I'm not used to being around a man who can cook."

"Well, I don't have an extensive repertoire. But, I learned more about it during the past year or so. I met a lot of people along the way who taught me how to make some of my Southern favorites … jambalaya, shrimp and okra gumbo, buttermilk fried chicken … and I can make a mean pot of Brunswick stew."

"As in Brunswick, Georgia?"

"Close. Legend has it that the first iron kettle of Brunswick stew was cooked on St. Simons Island." He pointed toward the south. "That's about 250 miles from where we stand."

"If you want to escape the cooking and clean-up, we can always order pizza to be delivered."

"Not a chance. I offered. All you have to do is hang out around the grill with me and keep an eye out for turtles."

"Turtles?"

"Sea turtles. It's the season."

"Don't tell me you hunt turtles and make them into some kind of turtle stew, maybe a dish you learned to make in Louisiana?" She laughed and sipped her wine.

"Hardly. But I am intrigued by them. Under a moon like we have tonight, we might spot a sea turtle or two crawling out of the ocean to dig holes and lay a lot of eggs. They cover them with sand, and then they crawl back to the water."

Catherine looked down the beach, her eyes scanning the surf. "Tonight, I will try my best to be an official turtle spotter."

"Good, and I'll try to imitate a real chef."

"Let me help you. I'll get the salad and tableware. I can find the fridge for the salad, but just point me to the right cupboard and drawer for the rest."

* * *

In just under fifteen minutes, Michael was taking the T-bone steaks off the grill. He used a combination of charcoal, hickory and mesquite wood to cook the meat, the smoke drifting toward the south in the night breeze. They dined by candlelight on a sturdy oak table inside the screened porch. Catherine sliced through the tender beef and ate slowly. She sipped her wine and closed her eyes for a moment. "This is delicious. I was amazed at how fast they cooked on the grill. You paint fast, and you cook fast."

"When the hickory and mesquite get white hot, it's quick and simple to cook the steaks. Because their thick, it's about five to seven minutes on each side, and they're done. That's it."

Catherine gently swirled the wine in her glass. "Did you have much of an opportunity to cook for Kelsey and Mandy?"

"Not nearly as much as I would have liked. I'd make a pot of chili a couple of times a year, usually in the winter. Kelsey was an excellent cook, though. She took lessons, online and in person, and became very good. Unfortunately, I was late for a lot of the meals she made. Too many times, when I finally got home, I had to get mine out of the refrigerator to reheat it."

"That's sad."

Michael said nothing.

Catherine leaned closer, the candlelight in her eyes. "But look at you now. You're cooking on a grill, and you've gathered recipes and how-to lessons from people all over the South from your time on the road. I look forward to trying your Brunswick stew."

"And I look forward to making it for you. The question is … will you have time?"

Catherine looked at the beach, the moon now higher in the night sky, its light reflecting off the rolling breakers. "I want to make time. It's just … it's difficult right now. But what I do have with you is a few days to play—to be beach bums, to explore the area, and do whatever we want to do."

Michael was quiet. The crashing of waves the only sound in the night air. "What is it you want to do?"

"To finish this excellent meal that a wonderful man made for me. To see the artist in you even closer than I did from the garden while watching you paint like a man possessed. That kind of passion to your art, that kind of dedication to your craft, fascinates me." She sipped her wine then glanced over at the painting. "The painting is beautiful in the light of the full moon. It gives the images an even more dreamlike quality."

"Maybe it's a case of the model being infatuated with the mad artist who is painting her. Not unlike how a patient might become enamored with the doctor because he offers a cure or the hope of a cure." Michael leaned in and placed the palm of his hand on her forehead. "I detect a slight fever. And I think I know the cure."

"Really? What might that be?"

"A walk on the beach."

"Doctor's orders?"

"Absolutely!" He smiled. "If we're lucky, at this time of the night, we might be the only two people on the beach. Let's go find out."

FIFTY-SIX

Michael opened the screened door and stepped outside with Catherine, the night sky filled with stars, the sea breeze jostling palm fronds in the trees. They followed the boardwalk through the long backyard, sea oats on both sides and lined down to the beach. Catherine stopped, staring at the rolling surf. "It's even better than how you described it that night on the phone."

"Nothing beats being here." Michael led her farther down to the breakers. In seconds the gentle surf was rolling over their bare feet. They stood there, watching the moonlight across the surface of the ocean, the breeze cool as it came over the water. "Let's walk north," he said, taking her hand in his and strolling through the small breakers.

After a minute, Catherine stopped and gazed up at the night sky. "The stars look so close. It's as if the Milky Way was putting on a brilliant show just for us." She pointed. "There's the brightest star, Sirius. Maybe I followed it here, or perhaps it followed me."

"The other night when we were on the phone, when you spotted Sirius in the sky ... you said you were going to wish upon a star. Did you?"

"Yes."

"Maybe your wish will come true."

"It has ... I'm here tonight."

Michael leaned in and kissed her, the sea breeze in her hair, warm surf around her ankles.

After they kissed, something in the water caught Michael's eye. "Look over there." He pointed to an object in the surf. "A turtle's coming ashore."

"What a magnificent sight to witness under a full moon. I heard the turtles return to the beach where they were hatched and first crawled to the sea."

"That's true. This could be the first time she's laid eggs, meaning she could have been gone from here for years … swimming in the oceans of the world. And yet, somehow, she has this internal compass that leads her back to the very beach where she crawled out of the sand and scampered to the sea. She's a loggerhead turtle."

"I wonder where she'll lay her eggs?"

"Somewhere above the mean high tide areas on the beach. You want to watch and find out?"

"Yes, but I don't want to invade her privacy."

"We can keep our distance."

Michael led Catherine to a sand dune close to where the turtle was crawling up the beach. They sat in the sand, watching her approach. When the turtle was close to the sea oats, she stopped crawling and began using her back flippers to dig a hole. Catherine looked from the turtle to Michael. She whispered, "This is so splendid. I wish we had a hand shovel. I'd like to help her dig the hole, but I know we can't interfere."

"She's got to dig her own nest. Once she's done and lays her eggs, she'll crawl back into the ocean and never see her young. And she won't return to this beach unless she becomes pregnant again."

They watched until the big turtle scraped the last bit of sand out of the hole. She slowly moved to place the back end of her shell over the rim. Within seconds, she started dropping white, ping-pong-sized eggs onto the soft, damp sand.

Catherine raised higher on her knees. "This is such a powerful scene to watch. Michael, look at the turtle's face in the moonlight. It seems like she's crying as she lays her eggs. Poor thing. I want to use a tissue to wipe away her tears."

Michael smiled. "I think the wet look in her eyes has more to do with the fact that, when she was using her flippers to dig the hole, some of the sand landed in her eyes. As soon as she gets back in the water, she'll be fine."

"That sounds like an answer a marine biologist might say." She grinned. "Where's the dreamy answer an artist would give … you know, something about the circle of life, a mother's sacrifice … crawling out of the sea and venturing onto potential hostile land to give birth?"

"She's laying eggs, not giving live birth."

"It doesn't make it less romantic or sacrificial."

Michael chuckled. "Okay, how about this … maybe for the turtle, or for any mother … the greatest display of caring isn't always about the number of hugs … it's about the number of sacrifices."

Catherine smiled. "I like that."

"She is making a self-sacrifice, daring to come out of her element, the sea, to lay her eggs. She's taking chances, dragging herself beyond the high tide level, risking predators, digging a home for her young. She'll tuck them in before lugging herself—drained, on aching flippers, back to the ocean."

"Look at her now. She's using her flippers to cover up the eggs." They watched in silence and awe as the loggerhead finished her task, covering the nest with sand. After a moment, the turtle, exhausted, tilted her head, looking skyward for a second before slowly following her original tracks back to the surf. Catherine stood to watch her. "It's as if she's following the light from the stars to guide her back to the sea. I wonder if she can hear the surf crashing. I know turtles don't have ears, but can they hear?"

"We might have to ask a marine biologist that question. It's beyond my artist's sphere." He laughed. "But I do have a question for you."

"Okay … what is it?"

"If a turtle loses its shell, is it naked or homeless?"

Catherine burst out laughing. "Both, and that's quite an odd visual—a naked, homeless turtle."

They walked alone up the desolate, moonlit beach, talking and spending time together, chasing the breakers, laughing, watching ships in the distance. Michael chose not to ask her anything further about her fractured marriage. He hoped that, if she wanted to talk more about it, she'd volunteer the information and begin the discussion. And he didn't want to talk more about his marriage, his wife and daughter—the devastating loss. He was trying hard to simply be in the moment with a beautiful woman who, he felt, had an equally beautiful soul. He was just happy she was here with him. He was glad that she wished upon a star and was now walking on a moonlit, South Carolina beach with him.

After a while, they turned back and returned to the shoreline in front of his beach house. He looked at her, light from the cosmos falling on her shoulders. "I don't think I've ever seen you in anything but that dress."

She smiled. "I thought you liked my sundress."

"I do. That's why I captured it in my painting … it's just it's the only thing I've ever seen you wear."

"Well, I did bring a suitcase with a few changes of clothes. Let's go for a midnight swim."

"But did you bring a swimsuit?"

She looked at the flat surface of the ocean, the gentle undulation of waves coming ashore. "No, maybe next time, but not tonight. She pulled the straps off her shoulders and reached behind her back to unzip her dress. In seconds she was out of the dress and standing in her bra and panties. "Last one in is a rotten egg!" She turned and ran toward the breakers, laughing.

Michael stared at her a moment, looked around the beach, undressed down to his boxers and chased Catherine into the breakers and a moonlit ocean painted in shades of silver.

FIFTY-SEVEN

Under the moon and starlight, the moving surface of the ocean had its own celestial look and feel, the reflection of the cosmos was surfing with the ripples. There was no wind and the waves were gently rolling, long silvery furrows that stretched along the coastline. Catherine barely broke water as she swam on her back, looking up at the night sky. Michael ducked underwater and swam up beneath Catherine, touching her back. He popped to the surface beside her. She laughed and used the palm of her hand to splash him. "For a second, I thought you might be a porpoise nudging my back."

"I got your back."

She smiled and began treading water alongside him. "So, you'll keep away sharks and other predators?"

"Absolutely."

"Ahh—you can use your paintbrushes to poke them in the eye."

"Well, I don't have any in here, but I'll use whatever it takes."

She smiled, closed her mouth, and disappeared beneath the water. Michael waited for her to come to the surface. He looked around, the sea barely swelling. In less than half a minute, Catherine surfaced more than thirty feet from him. Michael grinned. "Are you part mermaid?"

"I'll never tell. After spending all that time with the koi fish, maybe they taught me a thing or two about swimming. I used to swim competitively in college. Catch me if you can." She used both hands to splash water at Michael, and then she swam parallel to the shore in quick and precise arm stokes and feet movement.

He shook his head, smiling and followed her. Within twenty seconds, he'd caught up to Catherine. "Gotcha," he said, tapping her on the arm.

She stopped swimming, treading water and catching her breath. After a moment, she leaned her head backwards in the water, pulling her hair from her face. She smiled. "Let's swim a little closer to shore. I want to feel the sand between my toes when it happens." She swam another fifty feet toward the beach, stopping. "The water's so warm and the sandy bottom feels great. Where'd you, mister painter, learn to swim like Tarzan?"

"I grew up on these beaches. And this whole time you thought all I could do was paint, right?"

"Maybe. What else can you do?"

"I have to hold on to some surprises. What would you like me to do?"

"To stand next to me."

He swam up to her. "What did you mean when you said you wanted to feel the sand between your toes when it happens? When what happens?"

"When you kiss me under the stars." She looked at the sky. "I can't remember seeing the stars so bright. It's as if you can see every constellation known to man … and some that are unknown."

Michael reached out, touching her face with the tips of his fingers. "It's the unknown part that intrigues me."

"Is that the artist in you? Freeing the angel? A man who loves the mysterious?"

"The discovery process is what I love. It doesn't make the mysterious less enigmatic … it just makes the discovery more rewarding." He cupped her face in his hands, leaning in to tenderly kiss her. Her lips were soft and sensuous, responsive to him. After a long moment, they broke from the kiss, pulling slightly back, searching each other's eyes. Michael didn't avert his gaze from her face as he reached under the water, finding her hand, lifting it and kissing inside her wrist. Then he took Catherine into his arms and kissed her again, their lips meeting in fiery passion. He leaned her slightly back in the sea, his fingers in her wet hair and holding her head.

After the kiss, Michael held her hand and led Catherine through the water, walking up and onto the beach. The breakers rolling over the tops of their feet, he held Catherine again and kissed her sensuously.

He lowered her to the hard-packed sand, the warm surf barely caressing them. She looked into his eyes. "No, not here. Let's go inside."

"Okay." He helped her up. They gathered their clothes and walked hand-in-hand under the moonlight to the beach house. No one seemed to be around for miles.

* * *

From behind a grove of mango and cabbage palm trees, on a vacant lot near the beach house, the long lens of a camera slid out of the foliage. The lens followed the couple from the beach to the house, the soft click of the camera trapping the images of Michael and Catherine like a spider's web might catch moths in the night. The photographer quickly shot more than a dozen pictures before the screen door to the house closed.

* * *

Michael dropped his clothes onto the tile floor and took Catherine's dress from her, setting it on the back of a chair. He took her into his arms and kissed her, his desire for her uninhibited. With one hand, he removed her bra and panties while tracing her back with his other hand. He stepped from his boxers, taking her by the hand and leading her to the master bedroom. He picked Catherine up, kissing her and laying her across his bed. Catherine looked into Michael's eyes, her body meeting his. The salty breeze from the ocean blew through the opened window screen and across them. She closed her eyes and took a deep breath. A whippoorwill called out from the trees.

Michael was gentle and powerful at the same time. He reached out, caressing Catherine's face, tracing his thumb over her cheekbone, looking deep into her eyes, as if he could see what he felt—her very soul. He grasped her left hand, intertwining his fingers through hers, feeling Catherine's pulse—her heart beating faster. As he gazed into her eyes, he could see her in the garden as he painted her. She was more beautiful than all the flowers. More mysterious than any secret garden. And, yet, trusting. Somehow, at this time, in this moment, not afraid to be vulnerable.

Michael could feel her fingers laced in his, her small hand tightening. But what he couldn't feel was the ring on his finger. It was now all Catherine. Her heartbeat in his hand. Her warm breath on his neck. Her believing eyes looking into his. Tonight, he was with her and she was with him. He felt a stream of emotions sweep through his mind like he was standing under a clear mountain waterfall with this woman, the water and her presence washing away reticence and bringing out long buried feelings. His eyes misted as she looked at him and pulled his head down to her warm lips.

* * *

Catherine kissed Michael with more passion than she ever could remember having. She looked deep into his eyes and smiled. From her position on the bed, through the window, she could see the twinkling stars, Sirius glowing like a night light in the heavens. She closed her eyes for a few seconds, her passion mounting. She could hear the pounding and rhythm of the waves as the tide rose. She heard the rustle of the sea breeze in the palm fronds right outside the bedroom. She watched a meteor fly through the cosmos, its blazing rooster tail creating a fiery wake as it cut a path across the dark purple sky.

A few minutes later, when it was over, she had a spent feeling of bliss and joy. Exhausted but renewed.

She looked at Michael, smiled, thinking about how he had so considerately set her blue and white sundress neatly on the back of a chair. Then she thought about the painting in the moonlight. Closing her eyes, she could see herself in the dress there … in the center of the garden. And now, suddenly for the first time in memory, she could see herself in a new light.

FIFTY-EIGHT

Michael had a surreal awakening at sunrise. The sun rose over the Atlantic and crept like a quiet visitor into his bedroom, nudging the sleep from his eyes. He turned his head and watched Catherine sleeping next to him, the sheet falling from her tanned shoulders to her exposed thigh, dark hair cascading over the pillow. For more than a year and a half, Michael had slept by himself, often on a mattress in his van, and now the sight of this beautiful woman next to him was unexpected, almost an illusion. For the next minute, he simply lay there next to Catherine, listening to her steady breathing, his thoughts replaying their time together last night.

He leaned over and kissed her briefly on the lips. She smiled, keeping her eyes closed, her voice barely a mumble. "I need a date with a cup of coffee."

"I'll put on a pot."

"That would be great."

"Are you hungry?"

"At the crack of dawn, I'm only capable of partial functioning. I have to make one decision at a time." She opened her eyes, slowly sat up in bed, finger-combing the hair from her face, and looked out the bedroom window to the sun rising over the dark blue ocean. "Wow … what a gorgeous view."

Michael stared her. "I agree. Absolutely gorgeous."

She looked up at him and smiled. "You're sweet, Michael Vargas. But I'm talking about the sunrise."

"And I'm talking about you."

She repositioned her pillow against the headboard behind her. "Thank you." She looked back toward the beach at a dozen sandpipers playing tag with the surf. "Let's walk on the beach at dawn with our coffee, maybe have breakfast after that. I'd love to explore some of the area with you. If you can give me a few minutes, I'd like to take a shower."

He picked up a pillow and playfully tossed it toward her. "For a woman who only partially functions at the crack of dawn in terms of decision-making … you just fired off a to-do list."

She smiled. "I'm perfectly happy to hang out here all day and do absolutely nothing or do whatever *we* want to do … whatever inspires *us*." She threw the pillow back at him.

"I like the we-us option."

"On that theme … what do you think about this option? We shower together."

"I think that's the best of all."

"I thought you might."

* * *

A half-hour later, Michael and Catherine were dressed in casual clothes, the coffeepot in the kitchen finishing the last few drops with a hiss. He grabbed two thick mugs from a cupboard. "How do you like your coffee? Cream or sugar?"

Catherine stood next to sliding glass doors overlooking the beach. She turned toward him. "Black would be great, thanks."

"Black it is. I drink mine the same way."

"See how much we have in common as we go through the discovery process?"

"That almost sounds like a legal term." He handed her a mug of coffee.

"Now wait a sec … that's a term you used. You were talking about how much you loved the discovery process when peeling back the layers of the mysterious … or maybe a mysterious person." She sipped the coffee, her eyes playful.

He lifted his mug in a mock toast. "You're right. I did say that, and I like to do it. Maybe there is something parallel with a blank, white canvas. Rather than peel back to reveal, I layer on paint to see what it can become."

"Speaking of white … is white a color or something devoid of color?" She held her mug in two hands, glancing down at the steaming black coffee. "Is black a color or is it the dumping ground of all colors, making it empty of true color … black as my coffee? The coffee, by the way, is delicious. Since you work in colors, thought I'd ask."

"Glad you like the coffee. You won't find black or white in a rainbow. Doesn't mean they don't look great on a zebra or piano keys. Physicists say black and white aren't colors because they don't have visible color wavelengths. But in art, at least for me as a painter, black and white represent the subtle soul of a painting. So, in my book, not only are they colors … they make the other colors the best they can be."

She laughed. "Well, there are no gray areas in your answer. I'll go to the screened porch and check to see how much drier the painting is now. After that, let's do what people who frequent online dating sites say they like to do … let' kick off our shoes and walk along the beach, providing you want to."

Michael smiled and sipped his coffee. "Are you sure you don't dabble in the online thing?"

"Positive. I don't date. I just got smitten with a handsome artist who forced me to model for his garden painting."

"I don't remember twisting your arm."

"You didn't twist my arm … you started by flattering me into accepting your invitation, and then, rather than pull my arm, you gently tugged at my emotions. I think it started when you gently held my mother's hand and helped her draw." Catherine turned and walked down a short hallway to the back porch. She knelt down next to the canvas, looking at the painting. The odd sound of a car got her attention. She stood and looked toward the road. A dark Ford—an SUV, came from the wooded lot next door. The vehicle slowed as the driver came by Michael's driveway. The SUV stopped.

Catherine stood behind the screen, in the deep shadows of the porch, and watched as the driver parked at the end of the driveway for no more than ten seconds and then slowly drove away. She inhaled through her nostrils, her pulse now faster. "Maybe it's the caffeine," she whispered turning to walk back to the kitchen.

FIFTY-NINE

Derek Mack watched the morning sun come through the cracks in the drapes over his window. He got out of bed and rummaged for a T-shirt from one of his drawers. He preferred to wear T-shirts. That way he didn't have to fuss with all the buttons down the center and on the sleeves of his dress shirts. He wore a pair of red flannel pajama bottoms, putting on a white T-shirt, letting it hang over the pajamas. He stepped to his window and looked at the garden, the white gazebo just barely visible below the canopy of trees.

Then he slowly backed away from the window and sat in a hard-back chair in front of the two paintings on his wall. He glanced at the chair next to his, the one where the woman sat when she visited. *What was her name? Sandra … no … maybe Susan … that's it … Susan.* He put his hand on the empty seat, looking up at the paintings. He stared at the one with the mother and child under the oaks. And remembered something the woman said, *… my Catherine … she rides with the wind in her hair.*

Yes … this painting reminds you of your time with your little girl. That's a good memory, Susan.

Derek turned his head a little to the left, his eyes roaming the painting of the tall ships. He remembered the man's voice, but not his name. He was a kind man who had a soft voice. *I want you to keep it here in your room. That way the ship won't sail on without you …*

Derek gazed at the tall sailing ships in the painting, at the smiling faces of the children, the captain and crew. He stared at the ship's masthead, the wood carved into the shape of a beautiful woman, the wind in her dark hair. He looked at the blue water and billowing clouds, a smile at the corner of his mouth, his eyes as wet as the sea spray over the figure in the masthead.

* * *

From the beach, Michael and Catherine watched a sixty-foot sailboat cut through the waves just offshore, the spray coming across the bow. He took her hand in his and stopped walking, looking at the boat, the captain at the wheel in shorts and a red T-shirt. A woman in shorts and a lime green and navy bikini top, sitting on the port side of the cockpit. Michael said, "I used to love to sail. Now I seem to do more painting of boats than sailing them."

"Well, let's change that."

"Would you like to go for a sail?"

"It's always been on my bucket list."

"I can rent a sailboat out of Hilton Head. We could day-sail or even go for an overnight."

"As long as I'm back for the unveiling of the painting on Friday. Then I have to head home."

"At the stroke of midnight Friday, do you turn into Cinderella?"

"I just have to be in Columbia." She stared out at sea, watching the sailboat growing smaller in the distance.

"Hold it right there."

"What? Why?"

"Just bear with me for a second. Look at the sailboat." He picked up a seashell and began sketching Catherine's profile in the sand. His strokes were bold, using the edge of the shell like a palette knife and carving her likeness into the damp sand. He looked up at her. "That's perfect. Just as you are … gazing at the horizon."

Gulls darted in the hard-blue sky, delivering their squawking commentaries as they circled overhead. Catherine said, "It looks like the seagulls are fascinated with your drawing. You've got them squealing. Are they protesting or cheering you?"

Michael chuckled. "Everyone's an art critic. Maybe they didn't like the way I drew them in one of my paintings." He finished with the drawing and stood. "Okay, you can take a look at it now."

Catherine stepped around the portrayal of her in the sand. "That's amazing. How you did that with a seashell is so cool. I love it! Not that I have a best side in the early morning, but I think you captured my better side."

"You don't have a bad side."

"We all do … maybe not a bad side, but a dark side. I just try to minimize it."

"I haven't seen it. I think you've been put in a position to have a defensive side, but that's part of survival."

"I don't want to talk about that. Not now. Not here on this glorious morning, on a beautiful beach with you. All I want is to jump on the crazy rollercoaster ride called life and see what amazing places it'll take us together for the time we have."

Michael smiled. "A rollercoaster, although a fun ride, can only follow the tracks it rides. What if our ride wasn't hooked to rails, and what if we could set our own course and make our own tracks … just for the adventure of it?" He looked at the boat near the horizon.

"One of the good things about sailboats is they don't leave tracks." Michael reached out and took her hand in his. "Let's walk."

"Oh, before we leave this spot … you forgot something."

"What?"

"You forgot to sign your name to the sketch in the sand."

He smiled. "It's low tide right now. In a few hours the tide will come, and the waves will wash this away."

"I know. But, right now, it exists. The gulls can see it from the air. The sandpipers will see it from ground-level. And, if another beachcomber strolls by here, he or she will see it, too."

"Okay." Michael knelt down in the sand. He picked up the shell and wrote his last name under the drawing of Catherine. *Vargas*

* * *

After an hour of exploring the beach, they headed back toward the house, walking in the light breakers as the tide began to come in a little higher with every other wave. They walked up the path to the screened porch. Catherine stopped and motioned toward the adjacent lot. "Do you know who owns the vacant lot beside you?"

"Yes. The same people who own this beach house. They bought three lots back in the day when it was much easier to afford. They chose to build their home on the center lot. The two others are mostly palm and mango trees."

"Do you know if the owner drives a black SUV ... I think it's a Ford Expedition?"

"None of the family members live in South Carolina. The closest one, a daughter, lives in Atlanta. If I recall correctly, she drives a white BMW sedan. Why?"

"When I went out on the porch to see if the painting was still wet, I heard a car engine start from that lot. A few seconds later, a black SUV drove away from it. The driver stopped at the end of your driveway, like he'd forgotten to buckle his seatbelt ... the Expedition just sat there before slowly driving off."

"Because this is such a remote section of the island, we don't get a lot of traffic here. Mostly homeowners, and about half those people don't live here year around. For them, their beach house is a second home where they come for summer vacations. Many are gone by Labor Day. Should the mysterious black car be of concern? Do you think you're being followed?"

She smiled. "I was just curious. That's all."

SIXTY

Michael didn't believe in whirlwind romances, but what he did believe in was Catherine. He could see the toll that her mother's illness was taking on her. He saw how strong she tried to appear, regardless of her mother's health and its rapid deterioration. That, combined with a toxic marriage that steeped in its own emotional illness—a gut rot of the soul, added to the heavy load. Maybe, just for a few days, he could lighten it some for her. He wouldn't try to fix it. He could do nothing to help her mother, beyond reteaching her how to draw. He could do nothing to fix Catherine's marriage except listen when she felt like talking about it.

While Catherine put on a touch of makeup, Michael sat at the wooden table on the screened, back porch. He looked at his painting, now almost dry. He stared at the image of Catherine in the center. For the next few days, if he could do nothing else, he wanted to just spend time with her. He wanted to show her places she hadn't been and to do things she'd never done. To immerse her into a Lowcountry world of nature, history, good food, favorite wines, people and places that were in his blood. As a painter, when Michael first saw her alone in the garden, he recognized her spirit as bright as any of the flowers … and possibly, as perishable. He wanted to give her heart time to recharge, to restore what was already there, a passionate woman with an uninhibited passion for living in the moment.

That was what he sought in his art—in the subjects he chose to paint. And, now, in her presence, he felt he was doing some of his best work. He thought about what Catherine said when she first saw the painting of the garden. *It's beyond my ability to express how much this painting moves me. It gives my soul a hug and a chill at the same time.*

* * *

Michael took Catherine to new places to enjoy along South Carolina's Lowcountry. They took a horse-drawn carriage ride through Charleston's historic district followed by a boat ride for a scenic tour of the harbor. "And that's where the first shots were fired in the Civil War," he said, standing on the stern of the sightseeing boat, pointing toward Fort Sumter. The daunting brick fort was built on a spit of an island leading into Charleston Harbor.

Catherine pulled back her hair in the wind. "Didn't the Confederates fire the first shots?"

"Yes, right over Fort Sumter. Less than a hundred years earlier, some of the nation's fiercest battles of the American Revolutionary War were fought in this harbor."

Catherine was quiet, her eyes taking in Fort Sumter, the harbor, a shrimp boat coming up the channel from the Atlantic. She turned to Michael and hugged her bare arms. "And in the animal kingdom, we're supposed to be the civilized ones. You can actually feel Charleston's history here like the humidity off the water—the pain, the sorrow, the victories. I wish freedom didn't charge such a human toll." She paused and looked toward the sea. "Let's go play somewhere."

"I know where to find more play areas. Some are hard to get to, but that's what makes the journey more rewarding."

Over the next two days, they paddled kayaks through tidal marshes and saltwater estuaries, the snowy white egrets and blue herons eyeing them from shallow oyster bars. They visited Hunting Island Lighthouse and climbed 130 feet to the top, taking in a breathtaking view of the barrier islands and the Atlantic Ocean, how South Carolina's Lowcountry looked when the first Europeans sailed along the coast.

Michael took Catherine to see the oldest living tree in the Southeast—the Angel Oak on John's Island. She stood beneath its heavy limbs and looked at the huge canopy. "Think about what this old tree has seen—the history."

"That's one of the first things Derek Mack said when he brought me here to paint it."

"What a great art teacher he must have been. You were so fortunate that he came into your life when he did."

"He was a huge influence. He made me much better. He took the time and had the patience to teach. And, on top of that, he's a great painter. To see him like he is now … it's hard."

"And now you're giving back to the old master. He loves the two paintings in his room. Mom strolls in there every day and sits next to him … like an old married couple. It's as if they're watching TV, but they're experiencing the stories in your paintings."

"I'm glad. It goes back to the time when I first came out here with Derek, it was early morning. He challenged me to paint fast, to seize the light when it was there. And he told me never try to copy nature, but to be influenced by it and to grasp the scene in front of you—the light, the life. He said that, if I wanted my audience to see that … to feel that, then I had to feel it first … but even deeper."

Catherine touched the tree's gnarled bark with the palm of her hand and looked over at Michael. "You did that when you painted the garden. I can almost smell the scent of the roses just by standing in front of it." She laughed. "And I can almost feel the pulse of this old tree."

"It might be a little weak after five hundred years."

"No, on the contrary. There's a power under this ancient bark. Even after five hundred years, the sap flows. I can't feel its heart, but I can feel its core … its character. When I was a little girl, I used to climb an old oak tree in our backyard. I could tell that tree all my secret dreams. It would always listen, never interrupting." She looked over at Michael. "Do you know what the greatest lesson was that tree taught me?"

"What was it?"

"Patience. Nothing is more patient than a tree." She looked up in the canopy. "Imagine the tolerance this fella had over the last five-hundred years. Even in bad times, when hurricanes like Hugo, tried to tear Angel down, the tree stood its ground. Maybe suffered some bruises but, in the end, this old guy is still here … growing new leaves every year." Catherine walked around the base of the tree, stopping to pick up something. She closed her fingers and then held out her arm toward Michael. She opened her hand, revealing a shiny acorn in her palm. "With patience and the right conditions, even a little nut can grow into a marvelous tree like the Angel Oak." She laughed. A mockingbird in the tree seemed to join in with her.

"Maybe you should take the acorn with you as a souvenir."

She looked at it in her hand, shook her head, and set the acorn gently back on the ground. "No, it belongs here. This is home. I don't have the right to uproot the acorn because it needs the chance to grow roots." She smiled and pulled a strand of her hair behind one ear. "Since we're under this oak tree, I'd like to see the place where you created the painting of all those oaks covering the old country road like a tunnel of trees. My mother couldn't stop staring at it. I think I know one of the reasons. Can you take me there, Michael?"

"I can do that. It's on Edisto Island."

"And, when we're there, maybe we can rent bikes and ride along the road like the people did in your painting. There's something I want to search for."

"We won't have to search for lunch. Are you hungry?"

"Starving."

"When we're near there, I want to take you to one of my favorite backwater places. We might have to wear bug-spray, but it'll be worth it."

"Sounds delightful."

SIXTY-ONE

An hour later, they rented bicycles, put them in Michael's van, and drove toward a remote section of Edisto Island, down a winding, hard-packed sand road. Catherine looked at Michael behind the wheel and said, "Maybe it'd be easier to go there by boat."

He laughed. "Matter of fact, it is. The fish camp, called *Over Yonder*, is on a deep-water tidal creek, a creek big enough for shrimp boats to bring catches to the restaurant's dock. We're almost there. Trust me, it'll be worth the journey."

"Lowcountry is God's country. I'm enjoying the scenery."

Around the next bend, the road splintered off to a crushed oyster shell parking lot with a dozen cars and pickup trucks in it. Tall cabbage palms, lower fronds limp, dry and dark as roasted coffee beans, stood in parts of the lot. The restaurant, made of railroad timbers, driftwood, and a long tin roof, was a ramshackle hodgepodge that looked to have been built in sections—at different points in time. Some of the wood was aged more than other segments.

Over Yonder was built next to marshes and a blackwater creek. Michael parked near three Harley's and a rusted pickup truck with a Gamecocks' bumper sticker on the rear. He led Catherine through the screened front doors to the dark interior, the rich smells of a Lowcountry seafood boil greeting them—crab, shrimp, corn, sausage, onions and red potatoes.

They walked across the scuffed, wooden floor, past a bar where three shrimp boat crew members, one wearing a red bandana, sipped beer from cans, three empty shot glasses next to the cans. The bartender, a brunette in a lowcut shirt, pushup bra, red rose tattoo between her breasts, popped the top off a beer and set it in front of a sunburned man who stared at the white foam oozing from the glass lips of the bottle.

A slender woman, tousled dirty blonde hair, met Michael and Catherine with two laminated menus in her hands. "Welcome to *Over Yonder.* Y'all here for lunch or do you want to sit at the bar?"

"Lunch." Michael said. "Can we sit outside on the deck?"

"You sure can. I call it a porch, but deck works real good, too. Y'all follow me." She led them by an adjacent room where two bearded bikers, lots of fur and ink, shot a game of eight-ball on one of two pool tables. From a jukebox in the corner, came a Darius Rucker song, *Homegrown Honey.*

There were less than a half-dozen customers sitting outside on the large, wooden deck under green and yellow umbrellas positioned in the centers of round picnic tables. From the deck, diners could see miles of salt marshes, green spartina grass and black needle-rush laced with winding, flat water reflecting the sapphire blue sky. To the right, a wooden dock stretched from the kitchen side of the restaurant down to a wide creek. A faded, blue-and-white crab boat was tied to a dock piling, a pelican sitting at the top of the post.

Michael and Catherine sat at a table close to the water, giving them a long view of the marshes. She looked out across the wetlands and took a deep breath. "This is spectacular. If the food is even a touch as nice as this view, it'll be great."

"Trust me ... the food will be as good."

"When was the last time you were here?"

"Last month. I used to think about this place when I lived in New York. You can find so much great food in New York, but you can't duplicate this. You can't really copy the food or the atmosphere of the Lowcountry."

"You really love it here, don't you?"

"Yeah ... I do."

"Why do you think you're so drawn to it?"

He smiled and leaned back in his chair, gesturing to the view. "Just look out there. These salt marshes are the birthplace of life ... at least a lot of life. I've heard people refer to the marshes as nature's kidneys because of their filtration, the ebb and flow of fresh, brackish and saltwater. I prefer to think of them, not so much as kidneys, but rather as a vast womb. These tidal marshes are the transitional habitat between the ocean and the land. What you see before you is one of the most productive ecosystems on earth. The whole cycle of life happens in the seasons and the push and pull of the tides, giving birth to oysters, fiddler crabs, blue crabs, and all kinds of fish, birds and wildlife." He paused and took a deep breath. "Sort of like the scent of rain, you can smell new life out there … and you can hear it. Listen … hear that bird?"

"Yes, what is it?"

"A marsh wren. It sings a great tune, and it makes its nest there, weaving the spartina grasses into a home for its young." Michael motioned toward the expanse of the marshlands. "I wanted to share this with you. Most of what's on the menu came from out there or close by on any of the Lowcountry islands and marshes. Let's eat."

Catherine looked at the menu. "What do you recommend?"

"It's all good. All fresh caught."

"What's the shrimp perloo?"

"It's kind of like Louisiana jambalaya, but with a West African kick to it. The shrimp and crab boil is hard to beat."

"Sounds good."

* * *

Ten minutes later they were eating steaming shrimp, crab, corn, potatoes and sweet onion from paper plates on a table now covered in newspaper. The hot food smelled of garlic, bay leaves, cayenne pepper, lemon, Old Bay seasoning, butter and a touch of beer. They sipped sweet tea out of canning jars and ate with their fingers. Michael looked over at Catherine as she peeled a shrimp and ate. "Do you like it?"

"Love it."

"You'll smell shrimp on your fingers for a day or so."

She laughed. "But it's so worth it."

"It is." He smiled, the breeze across the marsh delivered the scent of black mud and oysters bars.

"How far is Botany Bay and the tunnel of trees from here?"

"As the old crow flies … about a ten-minute drive. We'll go there, unload the bikes and explore."

Catherine was silent as she ate. Michael watched her a moment and said, "You mentioned that there is something in the area you wanted to search for. What is it?"

"I think one of the reasons my mother likes your painting of the area is because she spent some time there as a girl, up until the family moved to Greenville. Mom told me that one time she got permission to bring her boyfriend camping with them to the Edisto Beach State Park. She told me they'd carved their names into the bark of an oak tree near there."

"Is that what you hope to find?"

"One of the things, yes."

Michael smiled. "There are only a few thousand oaks there. Where would you even begin to look?"

"Near a field of sunflowers. She said they used to grow wild there. Fields of them. I'm not sure how or why. She said the old oak is in the field. Close to the road."

"Those fields of sunflowers are still there, leftover from the days of the two plantations that were on the island."

"Really? I just got a chill in this warm weather."

"I'll take you there. The sunflowers are close to the oaks and dirt road I painted. Maybe we can find one old oak by itself with a story to tell."

SIXTY-TWO

Catherine stood next to her rented bicycle at the entrance to the long country road, a tunnel of trees far as she could see, sunlight breaking through the bowed limbs of the moss-draped oaks, the awakening scent of honeysuckles in the warm air. She looked over at Michael. "It's so beautiful and quiet. This place touches all five senses. It's visually overwhelming. I bet I know where you set up your easel when you painted this."

"We're close to the spot."

"I think I can find it." She got on her bike and peddled about a hundred feet closer, stopping to study the perspective. "Here … right in this area. I believe this is where you stood." She looked back over her shoulder to Michael.

"You're right." He pulled his bike up next to her.

She stared at the long steeple of oaks. "And, if I look close enough, I can see the mother and daughter on their bikes, riding … their cares to the wind. Laughing. This is the painting that has captivated my mother—seems to have evoked memories for her." Catherine was silent, the crooning of wrens in the marshes. She turned to Michael. "I can imagine your wife and daughter here … just like you did when you painted them." Catherine peddled her bike. "Come on! I want to feel the wind in my face."

Michael started riding behind her, the wind blowing Catherine's hair as she peddled fast, standing up for a few seconds to gain momentum. And then she sat on the bike's seat and coasted down the road, quickly lifting her hands off the handlebars, laughing, Michael riding next to her, the flecked sunlight falling across them. They rode in partial shade under the long cathedral of trees—just the two of them immersed in the essence of the Lowcountry, the briny wind across tidal marshes, the wading birds stalking the shallows, the mossy oaks—their limbs intertwined and knitted with leafy portholes opening to shafts of light so white and pure the beams seemed to originate from a heavenly source.

A half-mile later, Michael spotted something hiding in the deep shadows beneath the trees to the right of the road. "Let's slow down and stop."

Catherine stopped beside him, glancing in the direction he looked. "What do you see?"

He lowered his voice, smiling. "I don't think this is a designated deer crossing, but there's a deer—a mother doe and her fawn poking their heads from the edge of those trees." He pointed. "Let's see what they do."

In less than ten seconds, the doe stepped from the foliage and onto the dirt roadway, her tail swishing. She looked behind her. The fawn, just losing most of its spots, playfully followed her. They both stopped in the center of the road and looked toward Catherine and Michael. Catherine whispered, "They're so beautiful. And they don't seem to be afraid of us. I love it here."

The doe held her head up, leading the way to the other side, the fawn kicking up his heels and giving chase. Michael said, "The deer are a little smaller in the Lowcountry."

"I was in the Florida Keys years ago, as a teenager, and we saw some deer. They were smaller than the average golden retriever. There isn't a lot of foliage for them to take cover down there. I suppose their size has something to do with the terrain."

"Speaking of terrain … we're close to the fields of sunflowers. They're literally the light at the end of the tunnel of trees." He got back on his bicycle, Catherine following and then riding next to him as they peddled down the winding road. A mile later, they came out of the trees, marshes on one side of the road, fields of blooming sunflowers on the other side. Catherine stopped her bike and stood, taking in the colors. "It's still hard to believe these sunflowers are growing wild out here in this remote land."

"A few generations ago, this was where one of the plantations was built. They grew crops—a lot of corn and some sunflowers. The corn's gone but the sunflowers remain and thrive. They have longevity in their roots."

"And sunshine in their petals. Michael, can you imagine if Vincent Van Gogh could have seen this … rolling fields of his favorite flowers, the sunflowers? He'd have a lot of inspiration for more paintings. I always looked at them as happy flowers, like a glorious sunrise. Maybe that's why Van Gogh liked to paint them … they brought him happiness, at least while he painted them."

Michael pointed to a large oak tree surrounded by sunflowers. It was the only tree in the immediate area, wide canopy, gray moss hanging from some of the lower limbs. "Maybe that's the tree your mother told you about."

"Let's go see." Catherine pushed down her bike's kickstand. "Come on! Let's walk."

Michael followed her through the field of sunflowers, chest high, some blossoms the size of small dinner plates. The flowers had an earthy smell of fresh-turned soil. Catherine approached the oak like someone exploring a cemetery for an inscription on a headstone. She and Michael stood under the shade, Catherine slowly walking around the wide trunk, her eyes searching from ground level to the lower limbs. "Oh my God … Michael, you gotta see this."

He walked around the trunk and looked to a spot on the tree just above their heads. "You think that's it?"

Catherine stared at a large heart carved into the trunk. "You have to be looking to find it … but it's there. It's a heart with their names inside it."

"I imagine when they carved it, the tree was smaller, of course, and the heart they etched at the time was probably chest-level."

Catherine smiled. "But, through the years, the tree has been lifting the heart up toward the sky. I can just barely read the words carved into the center of the heart … it says Collin plus Susan equals love. Long before Mom started to show signs of dementia, she told me about her boyfriend Collin and this place—this tree. She said Collin joined the service to do his patriotic duty and to earn benefits to cover a college education. Unfortunately, he was part of a special forces team that was ambushed, and he never came back … at least not alive. I think she thought about him often … thought about the what ifs that are part of life and death." She pulled a phone from her back pocket and held her arms up to take a picture. "Maybe I can show this to Mom. Even now, it's weird how she can remember things deep from her past but can't remember how to get toothpaste out of the tube."

"We're lucky to have found it after all these years."

"I think it's romantic … my mother and her boyfriend—a teenage love here and leaving their mark on the world. The remains of the heart are subtle, but so are a lot of the good things in life. And I'm amazed the old tree is surrounded by thousands of blooming sunflowers—the flowers with their own smiling personality, the happy flowers."

Michael turned to his right and used his pocketknife to cut a large sunflower, giving it to Catherine. "Here's your happy flower. Now you can hold some sunshine in the palm of your hand, at least for a little while."

She looked down at the flower and raised her eyes up to Michael. "Thank you." Then she looked at the heart carved into the tree. "Sometimes, a little while is all that we can hope for."

SIXTY-THREE

Derek Mack had a plan. He sat at a table in the Memory Care Center's restaurant, finishing his lunch. Susan Waterman sat across from him. Derek placed his spoon in a bowl of she-crab soup, sipped, and looked around the dining area. He lowered his voice. "I want to take you home."

Susan stared at him, her face blank. After a moment, she nodded. "That's near where I went to school."

"I know. That's why I want to take you back to visit."

She smiled and used her fork to break apart a piece of sweet potato. "My daughters live there. I want to go see them."

"I know the way." Derek looked across the large room, more than twenty patients finishing their meals, a nurse helping a man using a walker on wheels to leave a table. "Come with me."

Susan got up from the table and followed him across the dining area to an exit door that led to the main hallway. They walked down the long corridor until they came to an alcove that led to a service entrance, a place that vendors delivered food and supplies. They stood in the hallway. Derek motioned to a small sofa under a framed painting of hot-air balloons. "Let's sit here for a little spell."

"Okay." Susan smoothed her dress and sat.

"When we hear the bell, that means someone is at the side door. It's usually those fellas in the big brown delivery trucks. The nurses let 'em in here with boxes. I noticed that sometimes they'll leave the door unlocked while they show the man where to take the boxes."

Susan said nothing, her thoughts distant, muddled.

They sat there for more than ten minutes when they heard a soft bong.

"That's it," Derek said, his white eyebrows rising, hope showing through eyes slightly clouded from cataracts.

They watched a caregiver, a portly man in his forties, key ring bouncing on his hip, enter the vendor reception area. After a half-minute, he came back into the hallway with a delivery man in a brown uniform behind him, wheeling a dolly with three boxes on it. The caregiver said, "These boxes look to have cleaning supplies in them. They can go into the janitorial area right past the kitchen. But I know Cecil, the custodian, is off today. Poor man's mother passed away. The funeral is today." He glanced at his watch. "The door might be locked. I can open it for you."

"I'd appreciate that."

Derek watched them walk down the hallway, turning left, out of sight. "Come on!" He grabbed Susan's hand. "Let's go. Maybe they left the door unlocked." He led her through the delivery and supply area. When they got to the only door, an exit, he put his hand on the handle and turned. The door opened. Derek and Susan stepped out into the warm sunshine, smiling. She stopped and looked toward the cloudless sky, the sunlight on her face.

Derek gently tugged at her hand. "Let's see if the keys are in the truck."

* * *

Michael rented a forty-foot Beneteau sailboat, *Poseidon,* from a marina at Harbour Town on Hilton Head Island and sailed with Catherine through the channel and out into the Atlantic Ocean. The sea was emerald green near the shore and dark blue at the horizon. They sailed past Daufuskie, turning north and heading toward Pritchard's Island. Michael stood at the helm and sailed with one hand, steering the sailboat in a northwest direction. They both wore shorts and T-shirts, Catherine barefoot, the wind in her hair, smiling. She sipped a rumrunner and pointed to the starboard side of the boat. "Look!"

Less than fifty feet away, four dolphins broke from the surface, jumping through the swells, easily keeping pace with the sailboat. Catherine stood next to Michael, the wind popping in the sails, sea spray coming across the bow. She said, "They're so fast, and they make it seem like they're hardly swimming. More like playing than anything. Maybe they want to race us."

"They'll win. We're in no hurry anyway."

"This is truly liberating, to be out here on the water, to see the Lowcountry from how the dolphins see it … from how the waves approach it."

"It's the best way to travel—to really see the world."

"Where'd you learn to sail?"

"Right here, off the barrier islands, as a kid. I had a very old sunfish sailboat, about twelve feet long. I'd sail in and out of the harbors and up the coast for a few miles at a time. It was a great way to learn to sail. The same principles I learned there, I'm doing right here with a boat that's more than forty feet in length."

"Can you teach me to sail?"

"Sure. Put both hands on the wheel." He stepped to one side as she took the helm, and then he stood behind her, placing his left hand on the top of her left hand, helping her steer. "Okay, first we're dealing with the two W's in sailing—wind and water. The wind is blowing from the northwest, exactly the place we're going. We can't sail directly into the wind, but by working the rudder, you're controlling with the wheel and steering the boat at an angle, using the wind, we can tack in the general direction."

"Aye-aye, captain." Catherine laughed and followed his guidance. "C'mon, dolphins. Let the games begin! *Poseidon* may be slower, but she won't get tired."

Michael chuckled. "No, but we could head into dead calm and lose our wind."

"The words dead and calm seem like a contradiction of terms. What happens in the dead, calm zone? Is it like a twilight zone? I know we're not sailing into the Bermuda Triangle, although Bermuda sounds like a nice destination."

"We only rented *Poseidon* for a few hours, and that includes time for a sunset sail."

"What if we go anyway … just like the pirate, Anne Bonny?"

"We'd go to jail."

She playfully rolled her eyes. "They'd have to catch us first. And, with me at the helm, the smiling dolphins as our security patrol, we might slip away over the horizon and be in the islands before they realize we're gone." She sipped her drink and laughed.

"We'd never make it to the islands. With all we've done these last couple of days, we'd fall asleep at the helm and drift off somewhere. But I'm now convinced you have pirate blood running through your veins."

"I do, definitely. But I was born three hundred years too late. There are no cannons to thunder, no ships to plunder. No wonder I'm out of sync with the times. If I'd been runnin' rum in Annie's day, I think she and I would have been BFF's."

"Two female pirates on the high seas … shiver me timbers. Take no prisoners."

"Unless they're parrots. I'd take them and then set the birds free." She smiled and looked at Michael's hand on hers, a pale ring mark on his skin where he'd worn his wedding band. She was silent, using her right hand to touch his finger where the ring had been.

He turned her around to face him. He said nothing. His eyes conveyed what needed to be felt. He touched her face, looking deep into her eyes, leaning in to kiss her. After a long kiss, Michael looked at the sails. "We're going a little off course."

"I'd say we're right on course."

"We're definitely heading in the right direction. I just need to trim the jib and then the main sail. That'll make for smoother sailing." He moved across the boat, tightening and adjusting ropes, maneuvering the sails for optimum position in the wind.

When he returned to the helm, Catherine took her hands off the wheel. "The pirate in me relinquishes control of the ship to Sir Michael Vargas." She raised her paper cup and looked at the coast a mile to the west. "South Carolina is so beautiful, and our barrier islands, marshes and beaches—they're so worth protecting and never taking for granted that they'll be here without us shielding them."

"I agree. I've come to the point in my life where I take nothing for granted, and I'm grateful for the good things. I include you in there … and right now, you're at the very top of the list." He leaned in and softly kissed her.

Catherine returned the kiss and then smiled. "Am I on your bucket list … or some other list? Somewhere in there with the milk, bread, cheese and—"

"No ... no bucket list. No grocery list. You're separate from any category ... except a category called the most special. And you're the only person, place, or thing there."

Catherine looked at the horizon, shifting her eyes back to him. "I haven't heard words like that in so long, my soul deep down knows how to feel, but my mind isn't sure how to respond."

"A kiss is a good response."

Catherine's phone buzzed on the console near the helm. "It looks like we're close enough to shore to get a cell signal. He lifted her phone, looked at the caller ID. "I recognize this number. It's the Memory Care Center." She answered and listened. After a few seconds, she looked over at Michael, panic in her eyes. "Where is my mom now?" She ran her fingers through her hair, turning out of the wind. "I'll be there as soon as I can." She disconnected and looked over at Michael. "We have to go back. Derek Mack and Mom somehow managed to steal a truck when the driver was making deliveries to the center. Police are looking for them now."

SIXTY-FOUR

The sun was setting by the time Michael and Catherine entered the Memory Care Center. A police car and a TV news truck were parked in the circular drive leading to the main entrance. A blonde reporter and her cameraman were standing near the truck. He was handing her a microphone. When Michael and Catherine walked inside, two police officers were finishing reports and a discussion with Director Clarence Moore and a balding assistant director with a turned-down mouth, tuffs of hair protruding from his wide nose.

Director Moore looked up as Michael and Catherine arrived. "Mrs. Kincaid ... Mr. Vargas ... thank you so much for coming. First of all, no one was injured. There was minimal damage to the delivery truck. A passerby found your mother and Mr. Mack standing by the truck, confused. The truck's engine was running but stuck in a drainage ditch. Considering the circumstances, the delivery company isn't filing theft charges."

Catherine folded her arms. "What are the circumstances? How in the world could Derek and my mother just walk out of here and take a delivery truck for a joyride like a couple of teenagers?"

"That's a good question. It has never happened before now. They apparently walked out a door as one of our staff members was helping the driver with a delivery, showing him where to take the boxes. The door was left unlocked for less than two minutes."

"It should never have been left unlocked."

"There's no debating that. And please be assured we've addressed that with all staff members, in particular the one who made the mistake. Mrs. Kincaid, Mr. Vargas, please accept our deepest apologies for what happened. It won't be repeated."

"Where's my mother?"

The assistant director cleared his throat, his Adam's apple protruding. "She's resting in her room. Mr. Mack is resting in his room, too. As you can imagine, they're both quite confused. Mr. Mack told us he was trying to take your mother back to her hometown … to visit you and your sister."

"I'll go see Mom in her room. Is she sedated?"

The assistant director said, "No, we haven't given her anything but a lot of hugs and some warm tea."

Catherine nodded. "Thank you."

Michael asked, "How about Derek?"

"Same thing," said the assistant director. "When I last checked in with him, he was putting together a picture puzzle on the table in his room."

Director Moore said, "Again, please accept our deepest apologies. We're grateful no one was injured in any capacity. On a brighter subject, if I may ask … Mr. Vargas, we're all so very excited to see your painting. Is it dry yet?"

"It's almost dry. We're still aiming for Friday, tomorrow—how about in the afternoon?"

"That's marvelous. We'll make arrangements to have a nice unveiling presentation for our residents and staff."

The TV news reporter and her cameraman entered the building, walking up to them, the reporter smiling. "Excuse me." She looked at the director. "Mr. Moore, we're going live soon. We'll need to feed your interview back to the control room in the station. Can we do the interview with you now?"

"Of course. Like I said earlier, this is the first time we've ever had any of our residents walk out of the facility. Measures are in place to make sure it doesn't happen again."

"That's great. Just tell us that on camera." She looked at Catherine and Michael, smiled and asked, "Are you related to the man or woman who walked out of the facility and drove off in the delivery truck?"

"The woman you referred to is my mother."

Michael said, "I'm Derek Mack's friend."

"Good. After we speak with Director Moore, can we get quick interviews with either or both of you?"

Catherine shook her said. "I don't have a comment. Director Moore and his staff have assured us it'll never happen again."

The reporter smiled and shifted her eyes to Michael. "Can we get a quick comment from you, sir?"

"I'm glad everyone is okay and they're back here safe."

"Would you be willing to speak on camera?"

He cut his eyes to Catherine and then to Moore. "Thanks for the invitation, but I'll pass."

The reporter cocked her head, studying Michael's face. "I think we've met … I'm not sure where, though. I'm Denise Oliver." She extended her right hand.

"Michael Vargas." He shook her hand.

"Vargas … Michael Vargas. I've heard the name, too. I just don't know where. May I ask how you know Mr. Mack? We've checked, and apparently he has no living family members."

"We met years ago when I took art classes from him. If you'll excuse us." He gestured to Catherine to follow him.

As they walked down the hall, Michael overheard the reporter saying, "Now, I remember … he was an architect, originally from Charleston, who made the news by designing some of the world's most recognized buildings."

* * *

Michael knocked on the door to Derek's room. He could hear jazz music softly playing. There was no response as he opened the partially closed door. Derek was sitting at the table, a picture puzzle in front of him. Less than half of the puzzle was completed. Michael said, "Looks like that puzzle is going to be of some beautiful, snow-covered mountains when you're done with it."

Derek looked up and smiled, white whiskers on his chin. "It's hard to do." He motioned to the scattered pieces to one side, his hand trembling. "They all look the same to me, Doctor."

"Derek … I'm not the doctor. I'm Michael."

"Oh, okay … I thought you were the new doctor."

"I hear that you and Susan went on a little trip today. Was it fun?"

Derek nodded. "Oh yes. I was taking her home. She wants to go home. Do you know where she lives?"

"Yes, I do. Right now, she lives here. Susan's just across the hall from you."

"She is? Where?"

"Two doors down on your left."

Derek looked at his hands, putting both on the table next to the puzzle. He raised his left with a thin gold band on one finger. "On my left," he mumbled.

"Let me help you with the puzzle." Michael studied the images, looking for matching pieces, finding one and setting it in place.

Derek looked up, amazed. "That's a good one." He surveyed the snow-capped mountains, and the dozens of blue, green and white puzzle pieces scattered on the table, exhaling a deep sigh.

Michael picked up a piece, holding it close to Derek. "Okay, let's take a look at this one. See the blue sky on this edge?"

Derek nodded.

"Good, now look over here to the left of the picture. See the spot near here where these colors might match?"

Derek glanced up, his mouth open, his breathing slightly labored. He nodded.

"Okay." Michael placed the puzzle piece in the old man's hand, gesturing to the open spot. "Let's try here."

Derek slowly moved the piece into place, pressing down, locking it. He grinned, a string of saliva in one corner of his mouth. He looked down at his lap, a urine stain growing, his eyes frightened.

Michael touched him on the shoulder. "Don't worry about it. We'll get you cleaned up, and then we'll sit down and work on the puzzle together."

* * *

"Forty minutes later, Michael stood at the door to Susan's room, watching as Catherine sat in a chair next to her mother, holding her hand. Susan said, "I heard a mockingbird singing today."

"You did? Where, Mom?"

"Outside near the flowers. He was singing a lovely tune. I can't remember what …"

"Did you hear the bird singing when you went outside and on a ride with Derek Mack?"

"Who? Your father's back? Where?"

"No, Mom … Dad's not here." Catherine reached in her purse for her phone. "I want to show you something." On her phone screen, she pulled up the picture of the carving in the oak tree. "Mom, once or twice, especially when I was a teenager with all the raging hormones and the emotions that teenage girls can have … I was trying to understand the difference between real love and infatuation."

Susan stared at Catherine in silence.

"I was moping around, not understanding why Donnie Sanders didn't love me the same way I loved him. You did all the things that a great mother does. You didn't try to dissuade me from caring about a boy who really didn't care for me … at least not as much as I thought. But you knew it. I wasn't sure how, but you did."

Susan listened, slowly blinking, a slight nod.

"You told me there is a certain kind of magic in first love because, unlike a magic trick that piques our curiosity and ends, we believe our first love will never end. And you told me that true love, whether it be the first or last … is never wasted. You said it's bestowed inside our hearts. You called it a love poem that's like graffiti on the wall of the heart. I never forgot that. And I never forgot the story you told me about Collin Tucker."

Susan turned her head toward Catherine. "Collin …"

"Yes, Mom … your first love. And that carved heart you always told me about is still on the old oak tree in the field of sunflowers."

Susan nodded, a smile working.

"Mom, look at this." She held up the phone screen. "See that heart. It's on the tree. It's the same heart you and Collin carved into the tree back in the late sixties when you were a teenage girl. Look, it says Collin plus Susan equals love. That love graffiti was left on the wall of your heart. Then Collin went into the army and was sent overseas. Although the heart has faded on the tree, it's still there. And I believe it's still there somewhere in your heart."

Susan stared at the photo, smiling, automatically touching her stomach. "Collin Tucker. He is such a sweet boy. His smile ... what a great smile he has." Susan looked at her daughter, reaching for her face. "Oh, dear Lord, why are you crying?"

"Because I love you so much."

SIXTY-FIVE

The next day, all of the residents, staff and management of the Memory Care Center of Charleston were there to see the painting. The excitement was as palpable as the fragrance of dozens of vases of roses in the community center. Extra chairs and tables were brought in to accommodate more than 150 people. Susan and Derek sat next to each other at one of the front tables with Michael and Catherine. A small stage was erected near one wall. The painting, mounted on the wall, was covered in a white satin cloth. Two bright lights on portable stands were pointed at the cover over the painting.

Director Moore stood from a chair at an adjacent table and walked to a microphone on the stand, picked it up and smiled. "This is a day we've all been looking forward to the last few weeks. As you know, one of the highlights about your home here is our extensive garden. Everyone seems to love to take strolls in the garden. The koi pond and gazebo are two favorites. However, for some of our residents, the walks in the garden have become increasingly more challenging due to physical complications." He looked at the table where Michael sat. "We're honored that a world-class painter, Michael Vargas, took the time to paint the garden on this large canvas behind me." He smiled, looking at the faces of the residents. "I've had a chance to get a sneak peek at the painting. It's fabulous. Not only did he capture our beautiful garden, Michael painted the daughter of one our residents standing in the garden. She is Catherine Kincaid, the daughter of someone we all know … Susan Waterman. Ladies, please stand."

Catherine stood, smiling. Susan, confused, looked around the room. Catherine leaned down, whispered in her mother's ear, and then helped her stand. There was a light applause, mostly from the staff and a few residents. Director Moore applauded. "So, without further ado, Michael would you step forward, and I'll help you with the unveiling?"

Michael nodded and stood. He approached the right side of the painting. Moore stood at the opposite side, still holding the wireless microphone in one hand. "This is where the drumroll would happen if we had a drum. So, on the count of three, we'll gently pull and have a first look at the magnificent work of art. Okay, here we go. One … two … three."

They pulled the corners of the cloth, the cover falling to the floor. There was a physical gasp as the audience looked at the colors under the lights. A few seconds later, staff and management began to applaud, many of the residents following suit. There were murmurs, one elderly resident standing. "It's so beautiful," he said, walking toward the painting.

Director Moore smiled, speaking into the microphone. "Yes, Mr. Stevens, it is beautiful. Come on up and have a closer look. What we want to do is have everyone who can … come closer for a better look at the painting. We'll do it one table at a time. For those in wheelchairs and others needing assistance, staff will be there to assist you. Before we begin the process, let's hear from the artist, Mr. Michael Vargas."

There was a burst of applause as Michael took the microphone. "Thank you all very much. Although I've painted before, I've never really had a showing … at least one where people attended." There was laughter, and he smiled. "I want to thank Catherine Kincaid for volunteering to model … to be our lady in the garden." He looked at Catherine, smiling. And then he glanced at Derek. "Although the garden is bursting with life, I believe Catherine's presence there, the rose in her hand, helped me find the human story in the scene and paint more with my heart than my hand."

The audience applauded as Michael turned the microphone back over to Director Moore. "Okay, let's begin the viewing, table by table. Let me remind you that Michael has donated the painting to our center. So, you'll be able to see it daily." There was more applause. "Thank, you, Michael. All right, let's begin with the closest table." He pointed to the table occupied by Derek, Susan, Catherine, and three more elderly residents, one in a wheelchair.

As they stood, a caregiver walked up to the woman in the wheel-chair, helping her. Michael, standing next to the painting, saw Derek pick a long-stemmed rose from the vase on the table. Catherine waited as the resident in the wheelchair went first. She smiled at her mother. "Okay, Mom … let's all walk up there for a better look." As they approached the painting, Director Moore grinned, nodding. The six of them stood in a half-circle, ten feet from the painting, observing.

Susan looked at the likeness of Catherine in the garden and then turned her head toward her daughter. "Beautiful …" she whispered.

Michael watched Derek explore the painting. He observed it differently from the others. His head moved slightly as his eyes locked in on sections. He began with the sky, probing the subtle changes in the color of blue, the dimensional texture of the clouds, the birds in flight, the wind in the trees. Then he lowered his eyes to the gazebo. He seemed to study the openings in the shrubs, the pathways, the colorful bougainvillea snaking its way through the white-washed terrace. He lowered his eyes to the thousands of flowers, the mix of colors that went beyond the spectrum—dozens of subtle shades of reds, yellows, greens, pinks, purple lavender and more.

Michael followed Derek's perspective, wondering how good his vision was at the moment with the advancing of cataracts. Derek now stared at the image of Catherine in the center of the garden, lowering his eyes to the rose in her hand while lifting the rose in his trembling hand to his nostrils, smelling. He looked up at Michael, Derek's eyes watering … and then he turned to Susan, giving her the rose.

Catherine faced Michael and smiled, trying hard to blink back the tears now rolling down her cheeks.

SIXTY-SIX

Michael could see a visible change begin to come over Catherine. It was four hours later, back at the beach house, just before sunset. Her eyes were wider, as if she wanted to see something at the edge of the room, nostrils slightly flaring when she heard a car coming down the road in the front of the house. She'd checked her watch twice in the last twenty minutes. Michael poured two glasses of wine for them, handing one to Catherine. "Let's walk on the beach. We can stroll down and check the turtle's nest, make sure all the eggs are resting peacefully."

She shook her head. "I'd love to go there, but I can't … the walk's too far."

"You have strong legs." He smiled.

"But I don't have time. I can go for a short walk, though."

"I'll take whatever time with you that I can have. Let's kick off our shoes, go down to the water, and get our feet wet." Michael led her through the house, the back porch, and out the door to the beach. He held her hand and said nothing as they walked in the warm surf, gulls skimming the water, sandpipers chasing the promise of a meal between the waves. They strolled north, the beach empty of people as far as they could see, a mist blowing in from the ocean a mile down the coast.

Catherine said, "I was so moved at the presentation of the painting. It showed me the power of art—great art, to touch people. Even people suffering from dementia and Alzheimer's. You could feel the emotional connection in the room. God only knows how far back in those faded memories your painting managed to stir, and how the residents wanted to speak."

"I'm humbled that they liked it."

"It's so much more than just liking it. It's feeling it deep inside, Michael. There's a kind of hidden magnetism in your brushstrokes—a power that grabs and pulls people. It's a visual force that locks onto them. Most people can't walk by your paintings without looking … pondering. Something stirring inside. When Derek smelled the fragrance of the rose while staring at the painting … he was transported to the garden. Maybe not physically, but his spirit was there. When he gave the rose to Mom, when I saw the look in his eyes and hers, I lost it. Your talent cut through the cloud of cataracts on his irises, into the moments of presence he still has, and into his memories—and it touched his heart."

"I hope that, for the residents in the center and for so many more that will eventually live there, the painting will continue to add joy to their lives."

"It will. You have succeeded with them, and it will with the others who follow."

"But have I succeeded with you?"

She stopped walking, her hand in his. "What do you mean?"

"You tell me my paintings touch the hearts of people … but have I, as a man, not as a painter, touched your heart?"

Catherine said nothing, looking out at the gentle swells rippling over the sea. "Yes … yes, Michael, you have deeply touched my heart, and my soul."

"Then don't go back there. Don't go back to something you hate and someone who doesn't love you."

"Please, I don't have a choice. You don't know all the circumstances."

"I know what's right and what's wrong. It's not right … no, it's unhealthy that you make the decision to stay in a ruined marriage for as long as your mother lives. Why must her death have to occur to free your soul … the soul that you tell me I've touched … and who has touched me in return?"

"I'm not sure what to say."

"Look, falling for you has come as an unexpected but beautiful surprise. I've been in some really dark places since the deaths of my wife and daughter. I've had to reach deep within, obsessively painting myself back to life, from observing life to living it. From forgiving myself to feeling alive for the first time in a long time. I know what really matters now, and uncomplicating life is part of it. Breathing … sharing … loving …experiencing. They're gifts. I see the same things in you, Catherine. And I see more—I see you at your core. That opens a future for us—for you and me. You don't deserve to be with someone who doesn't value you and tosses you aside like a bruised and battered ragdoll."

Catherine turned to him, her eyes searching, tender. "And I've fallen for you, too. It's an amazing place to be … not just loving someone but loving a man who truly returns it. Now that I've finally found it … found you, I don't want to lose it either. I don't want to lose you."

"You don't have to. All you have to do is say you'll stay. Stay with me. I can take care of your mother's medical expenses, and if you let me … I can take care of you." He leaned down and kissed her lips.

Through the kiss, her eyes welled, warm tears falling into the rising tide, waves thrashing around her feet and over her knees, the shrill of gulls lapping the water, the ocean wind in her hair. She looked at Michael. "I'm afraid … not for myself, but for you. Jerry is vindictive. If he did something to you … if he destroyed the kindness, the genius … the beauty of you … I could never live with myself."

"Don't worry about me. Be concerned about you, what you really want in life and what you deserve. You don't deserve the polar opposite. That's a slow death sentence for you, Catherine. You'll die from the inside and, eventually, you won't recognize the outside, the woman staring back at you in the mirror. If love goes unattended, you will lose the childlike innocence I was still able to capture in the woman gracing the garden painting."

She looked out at the sea, a sailboat on the horizon. "Our sailing trip was cut so short. If I come back, maybe we can extend it."

"Not if you come back, it's when you return. I'll sail with you around the world if you want. We'll take our time. We'll dock in hidden coves of crystal-clear water. Eat fresh, tropical foods. Cleanse our bodies, minds and souls of all the stress-induced toxins … forever."

She smiled. "Now, you're the one sounding more like the pirate. Get the girl and sail away with her."

"Whatever it takes." He grinned.

"That's all it takes."

"Good. Then make it happen."

She watched sea oats bending in the breeze coming off the churning surf. "I want to be here with you to witness the baby turtles hatch and crawl across the shore to the sea. I want to be there as you paint more paintings. And, one day, as a symbol of our love, I want to carve a heart with our initials into the trunk of a tree where it can withstand hurricanes and live into the future. I think a tree with deep roots smiles at storms. I just have to be prudent and go about this the right way. Not only will I be fighting Jerry, but the whole Kincaid family, or maybe clan is a better word."

"I'll get you the best attorneys. We just have to get you out of there … and we need to do it now. To me, you're worth the fight. I'll help you anyway I can."

"You've already helped me more than you'll ever know."

"It's the other way around, Catherine. I was drifting across the South, painting life from the outside, inserting myself into the picture more and more until I could breathe the air and take in life as it was happening all around me. That's when I knew it was time to return to Charleston and settle in. I came searching for the roots you talked about, and I know I found them with you. Or at least you have given me reasons to want to plant them with you. I see hope, and I see a future together."

"Michael, I know I want to be with you. But my fear of the consequences is real."

"Look at the real and potentially dangerous consequences of staying with him. That should make you even more fearful. You told me that Jerry has become physically and verbally abusive, especially when he drinks. You said he has a temper. What happens when he snaps one day? And he will. When he does, you'll be the immediate target. You'll be the victim. I don't care how rich and powerful Jerry and all the Kincaids are … I won't stand for them hurting or treating you any less than you should be treated. You're an exquisite, compassionate, intelligent, and loving woman, and you should be treated as such. If you stay there too long, I'll just have to come up to Columbia to take you from that hostile depravity."

Catherine placed the palm of her right hand on Michael's chest, above his heart. She held his left hand and brought it to her lips for a soft kiss. "I'll leave him. It won't be easy, but I'll do it. In the meantime, please don't try to reach me, Michael. I'm sure he'll have every electronic device bugged and hacked. Don't try to call me or contact me. It's too risky. I'll find a way to contact you … to tell you when I can leave. All I need to know is that you'll be there to meet me."

"I'll be there. I'll go wherever you need me to be."

She stared down the beach. "Like those tiny turtles, when they dig out of the sand and run for the safety of the sea … I'll be scrambling for my freedom, too."

SIXTY-SEVEN

When Catherine drove her Mercedes up to the wrought iron gates leading to her house, she took a deep breath. Moonlight broke through the moss-draped limbs of the stately oaks on the grounds of the estate. The ornate gates were attached to imposing brick pillars on either side of the driveway. Old World-style coach light lanterns were mounted to the pillars. One was engraved with the address but no name. That was reserved for the center of the closed gates where a large, brass letter *K* was mounted.

Catherine looked at her watch. It was just after ten p.m., about two hours before Jerry was expected to drive in from the airport. She stared at a black, outdoor surveillance camera discreetly mounted to the left side of one brick pillar, the glass eye staring back at her. It was the first of dozens of cameras throughout the grounds and house. Her husband had them installed ostensibly for security, but in reality, it was so he could keep an eye on her. He'd use an app on his phone to access the cameras from anywhere in the world.

Catherine had the urge to turn around and speed away as fast as she could go. But he'd find her. He'd search the ends of the earth with his posse to bring her back as if she was an escaped prisoner. She sat in her car, engine running, looking through the gates at the large Georgian brick mansion like she was looking through prison bars. The house was built in the center of ten manicured acres, at the end of a long driveway, within a three-hundred acre spread of Kincaid land. She was now on the outside. Once she pressed the remote control and the gates slowly opened with the façade of a wide smile, once she drove in, they'd close like a bear trap.

She reached for the visor above her and pressed a button. That began the sound of an electric motor engaging, gears turning, the groan of the gates opening with the subtle guise of a wide yawn. Catherine looked at her watch, a cold chill moving up the back of her neck. She put the car in gear and drove down the driveway. It led to a circular courtyard and a brick porte-cochere where guests often parked their cars when attending dinner parties.

Jerry's car is here.

Catherine felt her breath catch in her throat. Normally, he always parked in the six-car garage built on the right side of the mansion. Not tonight. His black Jaguar sportscar was parked beneath the covered entranceway like it was ready to pounce on prey. *Why was he home early?* Catherine thought. *Maybe he never left. Was he here the whole time I was away?* She parked behind his car, got out—hesitant to lock her car so there wouldn't be the beep noise when it locked. She didn't. It might help in the event she needed to make a quick exit, not having to unlock the car door.

She picked up her purse, entered the house, and immediately knew he was there. Somewhere. Lurking. Like the predator he was. She could sense it. She could feel it as easily as she could notice approaching rain in the distance. The house had a sinister aura every time he was in it, as if the restored, century-old mansion concealed ghosts from the past. But this evil was in the present.

Catherine walked through the main hallway, across the imported Italian tile and into the massive kitchen with custom cherrywood cabinets extending to the beamed ceiling, stainless steel appliances, a peninsula-shaped, marble-top island for dining. On one side of it, next to a wooden stand of steak knives, was a round cutting board. Catherine put her purse down on one of the counters and began looking through the pile of mail left on the island.

She stopped. Listening closely for him.

The house had an eerie silence. She started to open a large, brown envelope addressed to her. It was written in her husband's bold and precise handwriting. Block letters. All capital. Written with a blue fountain pen.

Her heart beat faster.

She smelled the scotch before she saw him.

He came from the dark dining room behind her. She turned around. He held a glass of scotch in one hand. Jerry Kincaid had the face of an amused poker player at a country club. Thick, black hair. Tanned face. A sardonic smile working at the corner of his mouth. Thin, wet lips. Deep-set, gray eyes that were slightly bloodshot and unreadable. A jutting chin with a cleft in the center next to a small scar he got playing polo years earlier. His hands were large, broad fingers. Manicured, clear polished fingernails.

"Welcome home, Catherine. So good to see you."

"How much have you had to drink?" She stood with the kitchen island to her back.

He grinned, looked at the drink in his hand and raised his vacant eyes to her. "That's a fine greeting. I haven't seen you in days, and you greet me with a question? Come on, Cat." He paused, a shark's grin spreading. "But I'll be a good sport and play along. Whatever I've had to drink is not nearly enough to numb me from your despicable behavior."

"You're drunk."

"No, but before the night is over, I will be."

"What are you talking about?"

"Don't play dumb and certainly don't play innocent. Because you're far from innocent … what you did was really dumb." He took a step closer.

"You're crazy! Stay away from me."

"You're stupid! This is my house. I'll do whatever the hell I want. May I remind you, you married *into* the Kincaid family. You were nothing before that. And you will go back to being nothing after that."

"Don't come near me, Jerry."

"Don't flatter yourself. From the dining room, I saw you going through the mail, but you didn't open the letter addressed to you."

"That's because your handwriting is on the envelope. If you have something to say to me, you can say it in person."

He came closer toward the kitchen island. Catherine moved to the other side. Kincaid picked up the envelope and pulled a knife from the wooden stand, quickly slicing through the sealed package. He reached inside and looked up at Catherine. "I don't have to say it to you, my dear wife. I can show it to you."

He pulled more than a dozen, eight-by-ten, color photos from the envelope, scattering them across the marble counter. There were pictures of Catherine and Michael partially nude on the beach, holding hands, and walking to the beach house. And pictures of them spending time together outdoors, including dinners, sailing, bicycling, and the times Michael painted her in the garden. "One picture is worth a thousand words. But, when you have dozens of carnal photos, they show the debauchery of a cheating wife ... not once, but multiple times."

"You've cheated our entire marriage, you hypocrite. You fathered a child with Jessica Lasalle, and then she vanishes. I know you killed her—or had her killed."

"You have no proof. You're laughable."

"You have no idea what I have. If you force my hand, I'll use it."

He held up the long knife. "I could cut off that precious hand."

"If you take one step forward, Jerry, I'll—"

"You'll do what, Catherine? Hit me?" He picked up one of the photographs of Michael and Catherine and set it on the wooden cutting board. He raised the knife high above his head and brought it down hard at the photo, the end of the blade going through the image of Michael, impaling it to the chopping block. He looked up a Catherine and grinned, a sliver of white spittle in one corner of his mouth. "What color shall we paint the painter? How about the color of death?"

"I'm leaving you!"

"No! Not until ... or if I say you can." He rushed her, drawing back a white-knuckled fist.

SIXTY-EIGHT

Michael stood in knee-deep water in the middle of a marsh, staring at the blank canvas and seeing Catherine's face. He shook his head a moment. It was dawn, and he'd come to paint a sunrise over one of the Lowcountry's most picturesque marshes. The sun, like a smoldering match, backlit drifting stratus clouds above cypress trees and tall grass. The surfaces of the meandering creeks reflected the orange and reds in the fiery sky. Michael stood there barefooted in cut-off shorts, T-shirt and a Panama hat. He mixed paints and applied them with a palette knife to build the sky and horizon line.

It had been three weeks since Catherine left, and Michael thought about her many times each day. Also, he thought about what she had said that last time on the beach. *Don't try to call me or contact me. It's too risky. I'll find a way to contact you … to tell you when I can leave. All I need to know is that you'll be there to meet me.*

He had painted almost every day since she left, throwing himself into his work with a furious hunger, painting from sunrise until sunset, sometimes finishing three canvases a day. Each night, when he returned to the empty house, he'd take long walks on the beach. Last night he sat by the turtle's nest, placing his ear on the sand to see if he could hear scratching from any of the eggs. All he could hear was the soft roll of the surf and one of the last things Catherine had said. *Like those tiny turtles when they dig out of the sand and run for the safety of the sea … I'll be scrambling for my freedom, too.*

He tried to focus on the canvas in front of him and the changing light over the marsh. He began to block in the trees closer to him, and then he worked to capture the multiple differences in color over the spartina grass and water. He added pink and scarlet colors to the clouds, working from the farthest point to the closest.

A large dragonfly alighted on one corner of the frame, close to the wet paint on the canvas. The dragonfly's iridescent, four wings of purple and gold were translucent in the morning sun. The insect cocked its head, big eyes looking toward Michael. He smiled. "You hang with me long enough fella, and I'm going to paint you into the picture. I might not do your wings justice, but I hope I can capture your spirit in the scene. What's a Lowcountry marsh without a big ol' dragonfly anyway?" The dragonfly stayed there for another few seconds before darting over the marsh and vanishing in the vista.

Michael painted straight for the next four hours, stopping only to sip from a bottle of water. His brow beaded in sweat as the humidity rose with the temperature. His feet, like the wading birds in the shallows, were submerged in flowing water and dark muck. Among the last things he added to his painting were a half-dozen aquatic birds, five great white egrets stalking the oyster bars and one blue heron, alone, standing motionless on a sandbar flanked by thick spartina grass.

He quickly painted a dragonfly in flight over the water, smiled and signed his name in the lower right-side corner of the painting: *Vargas.*

Michael remembered how much Derek had loved the salt marshes. His home and studio had overlooked the wetlands. Tomorrow he would take this painting to the Memory Care Center and show it to Derek.

* * *

Michael was exhausted. The moon was rising over the Atlantic when he returned from his nightly walk. He opened a window and sat on his couch in the family room overlooking the beach, the sea breeze teasing the curtains. His mind drifted, thinking about the family he'd lost. He glanced at a framed picture of Kelsey and Mandy on an end table. He missed them, and he missed Catherine, too.

He closed his burning eyes, fatigue building, the soothing sound of the surf in the distance, his thoughts wandering, blurring, sleep beckoning. He dreamt that it was the second full moon since he and Catherine had watched the mother loggerhead turtle crawl up on the beach to dig a nest and deposit her eggs. They sat on the two small beach chairs they'd brought, ten feet behind the untouched nest, the full moon coming up over the Atlantic, gentle swells of rollers lapping across the surface and mixing in the white froth of the breakers.

"You really think they'll come to the surface tonight?" Catherine asked.

"I checked with the South Carolina Department of Natural Resources and the biologist I spoke with said the turtles usually hatch and dig out of the sand within sixty days from the time the female lays her eggs."

"Do we have to call her a female ... sounds a bit impersonal, especially after what we saw that night? Let's call her Mama Turtle. Come on, Michael, she was crying that night ... okay?"

He looked over at her, moonlight on her grinning face. "Okay."

Catherine burst out laughing.

"Shh ... you don't want to scare them."

"You think my laughing is going to scare a bunch of baby turtles who've been buried in that hole for two months? No way. As soon as they break out of their shells, they're going to be madly digging to hit fresh air and freedom."

"Let's hope."

"Think about it. When that time comes—say you're a little turtle, you've just spent two months in a shell the size of a ping-pong ball. You burst out of that shell, and you're surrounded by dark sand. How do you know which direction to dig? If you go south, its heading to China. If you go east or west, you basically become a sand gopher forever. So, you have to head north, to the surface. How do they know which direction to dig for the surface?"

"I didn't ask the DNR guy that. Maybe they hear the waves crashing, and somehow dig up and out."

"Very quietly and so very gently, maybe you can put one ear against the sand on top of the nest to see if you can hear some clawing and scratching." Catherine's eyes beamed in the moonlight.

Michael cocked his head and smiled. "You do it—test your hearing."

"Okay, I'll do it. I'm not wearing my good earrings tonight."

"That's funny. All right, I'll spare your not-so-good earrings." Michael stood and walked to the nest. He knelt down and put his ear against the warm, hardpacked sand.

There was a noise.

It didn't sound like turtles crawling. It sounded like someone turning over a trashcan. Michael opened his eyes, mind groggy from coming out of a deep sleep. The dream seemed so real. He wanted to hold Catherine's hand and watch the baby turtles scamper to the sea. He sat up, the sound of breakers coming from the beach. He stood and walked from the family room to the kitchen, twisting the cap from a bottle of water and taking a long gulp.

He went onto the screened, back porch to see if a raccoon had turned over the trash can outside. Michael picked up a flashlight from a desk and put his hand on the door handle.

"Don't move!" A man with a pistol stepped from the shadows, pointing a pistol barrel at Michael's face. There was a tattoo of a barber's straight razor on the back of the man's hand, red drops of blood dripping from the open blade.

Michael stood there, his heart pumping fast. Not sure what to do or even say. "What do you want? If you want money—"

"We don't want your money?" said a second man, coming from the opposite side of the porch. He stepped within four feet of Michael, a hammer in his right hand.

Michael took a half-step backwards. The man's eyes were flat, like dark knotholes on a dead tree. Two black spots empty and long barren of life. His front tooth was chipped. He said, "This hammer can do some serious damage to those hands. After the bones are shattered, they never grow back the same way … sort of all bent up and twisted. For a dude that holds a paintbrush, that might be a real problem."

Michael gripped the steel flashlight in his right hand. He might be fast enough to swing it into the face of the man with the hammer, but he couldn't defend himself against the man with the gun. "What do you want?"

Hammer man chuckled. "Maybe we'll take a knife to all these paintings you got sittin' out here on the porch. Maybe we'll take a knife to your face. Maybe we'll smash your hands and knees. But we're gonna cut you some slack. Consider tonight a warning. If we come callin' again, you won't ever be able to hold a paintbrush. And, with broken and shattered knees, you won't be able to stand in front of an easel to paint."

Michael said nothing, the pounding of the surf was now louder.

The man grunted and grinned. His bottom teeth crooked. "We're giving you a friendly warning to stay away from Catherine Kincaid. This is what we like to call a restraining order. You violate the terms of our agreement, and you'll have mangled hands and spend a long time in a wheelchair. Got it, fella?"

Michael remained silent.

"I asked you a question. "You got it?"

"Yeah … I got it."

The man held up the hammer. "That's a good boy. I can drive the point home if you're confused." He glanced back over his shoulder to the man holding the gun. "C'mon. Let's leave this ol' boy to his finger-paints." He stared at Michael. "You stay between the lines with your paint-by-numbers. You cross the line, and your number's up."

They turned and left, rounded the house, and walked quickly down the drive to the silhouette of a pickup truck. They started the engine and drove without headlights under the moon for almost a hundred yards before turning them on.

SIXTY-NINE

Michael used his flashlight to inspect the damage the two men had done to the lock on the screen door. The handle was broken, screen ripped. He could call the police. *But what would that do? Cause problems for Catherine?* He'd take pictures for evidence and fix the damage to the door. Catherine's husband had no doubt sent them to deliver the warning and threats. *Was she okay? What, if anything, had Jerry Kincaid done to Catherine.* Michael had to know—had to find out.

But how?

He secured all doors and windows, then sat in the dark in the family room, waiting until the sun rose over the Atlantic. Michael felt completely out of his element. He was a painter and a man who previously had a long career as an architect. Outside of randomly having been shot, he'd never personally been threatened with death or having his bones broken. Deliberately being targeted was another matter altogether. However, all he could think about was Catherine, and her safety. For the next two hours, he replayed the conversations he'd had with Catherine the few times she'd spoken of her bullying husband. *A month later, she disappeared. A body was never found. There was apparently no forensic evidence. No witnesses. Nothing.*

Michael thought about the faces of the men who broke into his home, the threats from the thugs, the dull, listless eyes, the smirking grins of hardcore criminals. *We're giving you a friendly warning to stay away from Catherine Kincaid.*

He closed his eyes, remembering Catherine's concern about her own safety and the comments she had made about the missing mistress that night at *Anne's Place*. If Jerry Kincaid had something to hide, maybe Michael could find someone to help uncover it. But, to do so, he would need that aid to come from outside of South Carolina. Whatever it took, Catherine was worth it. He loved her. And there was no way he was going to walk away from the promise of her health and safety … and a second chance at love … her love.

If he couldn't call or text her, perhaps he could send her an unassuming package with a message in it to call him. He'd convince her to get out of whatever fortress Jerry Kincaid tried to hide things, including her. The realities about Jerry Kincaid had to be exposed. It would be truths brought to light, not the death of her mother, that would set Catherine free.

Michael needed to get her address. Her contact information had to be on file at the Memory Care Center. He would go there first—take the painting of the marsh to show Derek and Susan. Had Catherine visited her mother in the last few weeks? And if so, would Susan even know or remember?

* * *

Catherine glanced out the kitchen window in her country estate home, watching Jerry Kincaid pull his Jaguar from their six-car garage and drive from the side of the house toward the long-winding driveway. She released a deep breath, made a cup of tea and walked into the living room. She glanced at her watch, thinking about Michael. She wanted to call him but was hesitant because she didn't know if her husband had listening devices installed and hidden.

Catherine picked up a remote control and turned on a seventy-inch TV mounted to one of the walls. She flipped through the channels, stopping when she saw a local newscast. The middle-aged news anchorman looked into the camera. "We are following up on a story Channel Seven News first brought to you last week. The skeletal remains discovered in the Congaree National Forest now have been identified as the missing woman from the Pine Ridge area. Maria Williams is live on the scene."

The image cut to a reporter with shoulder-length, blonde hair standing in a rural setting with thick pine trees behind her. She held a microphone. "Behind me is the Congaree National Forest. It was less than one hundred feet off County Road 36, when a man using a hand-held metal detector searching for Civil War artifacts, such as Minié balls and medals, found instead a body in a shallow grave."

The video cut to sheriff's deputies and the coroner's office on the scene the previous week, lifting a body bag from a gurney and loading it into a dark blue van. The video switched to a picture of an attractive young woman as the narrative continued.

"Today, Medical Examiner Doctor Robert Gonzales says the remains are that of twenty-five-year-old Jessica Lasalle of Pine Ridge who went missing about nine months ago. An autopsy revealed the woman died from a gunshot wound to the back of the head. Investigators theorize she was killed elsewhere, and her body brought here where someone apparently was in a hurry to bury it and flee the scene. Doctor Gonzales added that the woman didn't die alone."

The video cut to an interview with a white-haired man in his early sixties, pale blue shirt with a bowtie, standing near the Richland County Courthouse. "Ms. Lasalle, as she's now been identified, was in her second trimester of pregnancy. It's a tragedy that someone would do this and take two lives."

The video cut to a man in a sheriff's uniform and the reporter's voice-over continued. "Sheriff's investigators are calling this a double homicide."

The sheriff, narrow face, strong chin, said, "We're told that the unborn child was a baby girl. It appears that the killer made a conscious decision to take two lives—of a mother and child. We'll leave no stone uncovered as we investigate and seek an arrest for two murders."

The video switched back to the reporter. "Police say, although they have no suspects, they do have a person of interest they're investigating. In the meantime, Jessica Lasalle's family is making arrangements for two funerals ... one for their daughter and one for the granddaughter they'd had hoped to meet—the baby Jessica was going name Harper. Live from near the Congaree National Forest, Maria Williams ... News Channel Seven. Now back to you in the studio."

Catherine stared at the television screen, her stomach churning. She touched her throat, the sick feeling of nausea sweeping over her. She muted the sound on the TV, looking around the room, picking up her phone and walking quickly across the hardwood floor to a door. Catherine went outside, taking deep breaths through her nostrils, lightheaded. She looked up at the sapphire blue sky, cotton white clouds drifting as if they were in a hurry and no longer content with their position in the universe.

She lowered her eyes, a blackbird chirping at the top of a magnolia tree, the bird's cry shrill, yelling a warning to whomever would listen. Catherine called Michael. When he answered, she said, "Jerry is a murderer. Not only did he kill his mistress, Jessica Lasalle … he murdered his own daughter." She paused, her eyes welling, before she could continue with a story that was a nightmare coming to a heinous realization.

SEVENTY

Two hours later, Michael drove into the parking lot of the Memory Care Center, stopped and rolled down the driver's side window. He pulled out his phone and scrolled through the handful of numbers he had kept in his contact list but hadn't seen since he left New York. He found the cell number to Roger Garza and made the call. Garza answered and Michael said, "Roger, it's me … Michael Vargas. How are you?"

"How am I? How the hell are you? What's it been, almost a couple years now since you dropped off the face of the earth? We assumed you were still alive somewhere in the Deep South since there were no reports of your body being found." He laughed, pulling his Porsche into a parking garage in New York City. "Where the hell are you?"

"Back home. South Carolina, the Charleston area."

"Are you doing okay? I know you had a lot of stuff to deal with when you quit the firm—the deaths of your family, the guy in the park who tried to kill you—"

"I'm okay, Roger. Doing better now. I need a favor, if possible."

"You name it. Because of the clients you brought in here, I doubled my bonus. We have three in-house attorneys now."

"That's good. I remember you telling me about your two years with the FBI until you were hurt and took an early retirement. Then you worked as a prosecutor for the justice department before moving into corporate law."

"It was a natural segue because I prosecuted white-collar criminals." Garza laughed, parking in his designated space and shutting off the motor. "What's going on, Michael? Are you in some kind of deep shit?"

"I just had two guys break into my house at two in the morning and threaten to cripple or kill me."

"What? Why?"

Michael told him the story, what the intruders said, and why they'd said it. Also, he told Garza about the discovery of Jessica Lasalle's body—the unborn child and the connection to Jerry Kincaid. "News reports indicate there is a person of interest. Maybe you know people who'll tell you if it's Kincaid, and if they've found anything … or who will look into him for the incriminating evidence that directly links him to the deaths."

Garza chose his words carefully, his Porsche engine ticking as it cooled, glancing in the review mirror as another car was parking. "This guy keeps a trophy wife on a short leash, he's doing high-end call girls, and keeps a mistress on the side not too far from his hometown of Columbia for easy access. Then, the mistress gets pregnant with his child and wants to become the next Mrs. Jerry Kincaid. Makes initial accusations to Kincaid and his wife, Catherine, stuff that wouldn't fly in the Deep South race for the governor's job in South Carolina. Does that pretty much sum up the known facts?"

"Yes, but it's the unknown facts, how Kincaid did it—they're what we need to sink his ship."

Gaza pushed back in the driver's seat of his Porsche, eyes scanning the parking garage. "Having worked in the FBI's Charlotte office, I remember some of the Kincaid family history because they had businesses there. The family has deep connections in the state. Years ago, Jerry Kincaid's grandfather, also named Ralph Kincaid like his father, made the family's money in illegal liquor, moonshine primarily. They managed to parlay that into legitimate businesses, and a century later they're still going strong. Old money. Agriculture, lumber, land development, and construction. Aviation is their newest adventure."

"Jerry Kincaid is expected to toss his hat into the race for governor. If the voters knew he was responsible for the murder of his mistress and a baby that was shy of a few months from being born—his baby, Kincaid would be forced to drop out of the race."

"And he'd drop into a prison, assuming he's found guilty."

"Roger, can you alert an agent or agents with the FBI's office outside of the Columbia area, maybe even the state? The mistress, I believe, was from Atlanta. Maybe she had family or friends she was talking to about Kincaid that might shed some light on her pregnancy, disappearance and death. Because of Kincaid's connections, perhaps it would be wise for the FBI to widen its interest and inquiries so the investigation doesn't get stalled with those who might get paid off."

"I can put in a couple of calls for you. I still have some contacts in the FBI and certainly a lot in the department of justice. Unfortunately, Michael, this kind of disgusting crap happens too often with rich guy pricks who think the law doesn't apply to them. The prostitutes and mistresses are nothing more than some kind of toys, to be discarded after using and abusing. Gotta go. I'll call you back as soon as I hear something."

"Thank you, Roger. If there's anything I can do—"

"Yes, you can get your ass back here and design some more of the world's greatest towers. The building you designed for Hong Kong is in phase one of construction. And, keep a low profile until I can get back with you. Last thing you want is Kincaid's enforcers to return and stand over your bed in the middle of the night. See you."

Michael opened the door to his van, the breeze cooling the perspiration on his face.

SEVENTY-ONE

Michael unloaded the painting from his van and entered the facility. After checking in with the receptionist, he headed toward Derek's room, stopping in the community center. At least twenty residents were there, most participating in art and yoga classes with three members of the staff. Michael held the semi-wet painting by the inside of the wooden frame. He spotted Susan Waterman at a table, a red crayon in her bent hand. She looked up, and he said, "Hi, Susan … how are you?"

No response. Face blank.

Michael turned his painting around toward her. Susan's face changed, a slow nod and smile. "My marshes," she said softly.

"Yes, I just finished this yesterday. I started at sunrise and ended around noon. Is Derek in his room?"

"Who?"

"Derek."

There was no connection. Michael smiled. "I'll check. How is Catherine … how is your daughter? Has she visited you recently?"

"Who?"

Michael pointed to the wall where his painting of Catherine in the garden was hanging. "That's her … that's your daughter, Catherine, in that big painting over there. In the blue and white dress. Has she been here to visit with you?"

"I like flowers."

Michael stood straighter. "I like flowers, too. And I like your drawing. Looks like you have drawn some beautiful sunflowers and a majestic tree. I can see the ocean, too. It's great."

She smiled. He turned and walked down the hallway to Derek's room, pausing to knock on the open door. Derek was sitting at the table, a small flat-screen TV on in one corner of the room. An animated program, Scooby Doo, was on the screen, the sound barely audible. Derek held the remote control in his hand, pressing buttons, his face contorted with frustration.

Michael set his painting down near the door. "I always loved Scooby Doo," he said, approaching Derek. "Are you having a little trouble with the remote? Those darn things can confuse a rocket scientist. Let me see if I can help you." He gently took the remote from Derek and looked at the controls. "Here ... the sound button is on the left side. Just like the ring on your left hand. Maybe that will help you remember it. I'll show you." Michael put the remote back into Derek's hand and pressed the volume control, raising and lowering it. "There you go. Just try to remember it's the big button on the left side of the controller, just like your ring is on your left hand. Okay?"

Derek nodded his head. "Okay."

"Hey, I brought something to show you."

Derek said nothing.

Michael walked across the room and picked up the painting. He stood in front of Derek and held it up for him. "This marsh reminded me so much of the one near your old home. One day, years ago, during class at your studio, it was after class actually ... you took Elijah and me—Elijah was the only black kid in the class, and he had enormous talent. Anyway, you took the two of us to the end of your dock overlooking the marsh. We set up easels—three easels. And you stood there between us, painting right along with Eli and me, giving us suggestions and teaching us to paint with what you said was wild abandonment."

The old man's eyes roamed the painting from one side to the next, and then he looked at the sun peeking between the clouds.

Michael said, "I remember one thing you told us that late afternoon. You said that the paints and canvas are all things touched by the artist's hand. And that, when the painter dies, his or her painting will live on in the hearts of those who look at it ... because a part of you—the artist's hand and heart, stays forever in that painting."

He looked up at Michael. "It does … can't be separated." He lowered his gaze back to the painting, looking at the wading birds. "Always loved the birds … the egrets." He tilted his head, eyes narrowing somewhat. He pointed and grinned. "Dragonfly over the marsh. I can see it. Can you leave this one here, too?"

"I finished it yesterday. It's still wet. I don't want the odor of drying paint to be in your room. I'll take it home and bring it back. In the next day or two, I'll come in and hang it near the other paintings."

Derek reached out and wrapped his weak hand around Michael's wrist, his eyes searching. "Death … when it comes … take me back to the marshes. I want my ashes to rise and fall with the tides in the Lowcountry boil of life … the ladle stirred by the very hand of God, the sunsets from his brushstrokes … take me home."

Michael said nothing for a few seconds. "Okay. Before I leave today, would you like to walk in the garden? Maybe the two of us could hang out in the gazebo … you know, we'll keep an eye out for delivery trucks."

Derek tilted his head and nodded.

Michael's phone buzzed in his pocket. He glanced at the screen. It was Roger Garza. Michael looked over at Derek. "Excuse me, I need to take this call."

No response.

He answered his phone and stepped out into the hall. Roger said, "I have some good news for you."

"I could use some."

"I've been speaking with one of my contacts in the FBI's Columbia office. He's smart and a really stand-up guy … not the type who can be bought. They're aware of the Kincaid family's reputation, how they've managed to skirt the laws—local and federal, for decades, building a dynasty with crooked profits. They've been investigating Jerry Kincaid as a possible murder suspect for a couple of months now. They started looking into him a few months after his girlfriend disappeared."

"Really? How'd they get wind of it?"

"The sheriff's department invited them because of what initially appeared to be a crime that crossed state lines. Something to do with the construction business. Jessica Lasalle is from Atlanta. Kincaid apparently met her there when he attended a builder's convention. The tryst became hot and heavy. He brought her into South Carolina and rented a small house for her in Pine Ridge."

"Were they looking into the disappearance of the mistress or a shady deal in Kincaid's construction business?"

"Both. The disappearance triggered a look into some of the construction deals Kincaid had going on. Jessica's best friend since childhood, Susan Johnston from Atlanta, called police in Columbia a week after Jessica's disappearance and said that Jessica told Susan if anything ever happened to her and her unborn baby, it was because of a Jerry Kincaid. She said, when Jessica told Kincaid she was pregnant with his child, he went into a rage, grabbed her by the neck and said she would get an abortion, take money and go away, or the baby would die inside her … the child would die with her. The problem was there wasn't a body. No physical proof that Jessica was dead until recently. Shortly after Susan Johnston reported that information, she spotted someone following her. She's been in hiding, fearful for her own life. The killer is still out there."

"Does Susan think Kincaid killed Jessica?"

"She thinks Kincaid, most likely, had one of his thugs do it because Jessica told her she saw a man watching her house after Kincaid threatened her. She thought she recognized the guy as one of Kincaid's business associates. Jessica was afraid."

"So, they all think Kincaid is responsible but, as of yet, no one can be pin it on him?"

"That might have been the case if it weren't for a jailhouse snitch or, as I like to call them … informants. A guy arrested for DUI became a little talkative when he boasted he'd be bonded out in a couple of hours. Two days later, he's still in there courtesy of an outstanding warrant. So, then this guy starts bragging to his cellmate that if he isn't bonded out soon, he had the goods on, quote, a 'rich dude'."

"What goods?"

"That's where it becomes interesting. Apparently, when police searched Jessica Lasalle's laptop computer and cell phone, information they found prompted an inquiry into a shady construction deal Kincaid had in Atlanta. They were able to link this guy sitting in jail to Kincaid as his front man in the alleged illegal dealings. Jessica also had made a notation in her computer that this guy was lurking around her house—it was dated just before she disappeared. In a plea deal, he's willing to testify against Kincaid for commissioning him as a murder-for-hire to knock off the pregnant girlfriend."

"Looks like they're leaving no stones unturned in catching Kincaid. What's next?"

"A sting and an arrest coordinated by the FBI. I'm not sure when it'll happen, but it will."

"Thank you, Roger. You've been a great help."

"Stay in touch. This thing will, no doubt, blow up and be all over the news. Stay safe down there in God's country. When the chips start falling, make sure you're out of the way. It'll come down hard and fast."

"Okay."

SEVENTY-TWO

An hour later, Michael walked down the hallway toward the main entrance with the marsh painting in hand when he saw the gurney. Two paramedics pushed it through the open front door, a third paramedic in tow, hurrying, the staccato sounds of emergency radios coming through the corridor. Staff rushed past him, running towards the community center. Fear hung in the air. From where he walked, Michael could see caregivers gently moving residents out of the community center into the hallways and alcoves.

He saw Director Clarence Moore and a half-dozen members of the administration walking quickly, some running, toward the center. He moved the painting from his left hand to his right, closer to the wall to make sure that none of the residents accidently scraped against it. As he came closer, the sad reality was unfolding through the arched entranceways to the community center.

Susan Waterman was lying on the floor.

Michael stopped. The paramedics were giving her chest compressions, one bringing an oxygen mask up to her face. Michael wanted to run in and help, to do whatever he could for her. But she was nearly surrounded by equipment as the paramedics fought hard for her life. Even from a distance of fifty feet, Michael could see that Susan's face was already a foreshadowing shade of blue.

He heard them talking in fast bursts, looking for a pulse, for any sign of life. They made the decision to load her on the gurney, into the ambulance—to take her to an ER in a hospital nine miles away. Each second of the trip, would be trying to restart the heart. Within moments she was lifted to the stretcher and wheeled in front of Michael, out the door with the emergency personnel surrounding her, Susan's eyes closed, the look on her face was one of complete peace.

Michael stood there, his pulse racing, his thoughts erratic as he stared at the front entranceway and watched them load Susan Waterman into the back of an ambulance. A firetruck and two police cruisers were in the courtyard. He wanted to call Catherine. To hell with her request that he not contact her because of a dysfunctional and domineering husband. But, was it his place to call her first ... or should that call come from the Memory Care Center? Was Susan alive? He stood there as the ambulance pulled away, its siren sounding and the blue-and-white lights flashing.

Within a minute after she was taken away, everyone had cleared out of the community center. Michael walked in and approached the table where Susan had been sitting, working on her crayon drawing. Her chair was on its side, a half-dozen crayons on the floor, most next to the drawing.

He knelt down and picked up the paper. Before Susan had collapsed, she had almost completed her sketch. It was filled with brightly colored sunflowers. A young woman with a smile on her face, stood in the shadow of a large tree, moss hanging from its lower branches. She seemed to be gazing at the sea in the distance. He looked at the crayon art and thought about his conversation with Derek as he showed him the painting of the marsh. *You said that when the painter dies ... his or her painting will live on in the hearts of those who look at it ... because a part of you—the artist, stays forever in that painting.*

He took Susan's drawing, picked up his painting, and headed toward the administrative offices.

* * *

Michael spoked briefly with Director Clarence Moore before Moore left the building with the Center's public relations manager, Rhonda Hardeman, a brunette in her late twenties with a pixie hairstyle. Director Moore said, "My secretary's trying to reach Mrs. Kincaid to let her know what happened. Rhonda and I are on our way to the hospital for a while to be available for our patient, or the family, should they need us. Unfortunately, this happens far more often than you might think."

Michael nodded. "I'd just spoken with Susan a couple of hours before it happened." He held up the crayon sketch. "She was working on this drawing. I believe, deep down somewhere, she was drawing a scene from her life many years ago. How can she recreate that but not know her own daughter's face?"

"There are seven generally recognized stages of Alzheimer's disease. As you were aware from your conversations with Mrs. Kincaid, Mrs. Waterman was in an upper stage of the disease. At stage seven, when we see the most deaths, it's a rapid physical health decline. The patient loses his or her ability to feed themselves. Many basic functions, such as sitting up in bed and walking, are gone. Mrs. Waterman wasn't there yet. We're hoping the paramedics managed to revive her. Please excuse us. We need to get to the hospital."

"Of course. I would like to send this drawing to Catherine Kincaid. Do you have her mailing address?"

"We are not authorized to give out addresses from a patient's file, however, my assistant, Angela Prater, would be more than happy to send it for you."

The PR director, Rhonda Hardeman, looked down at the oil painting in Michael's hand. "I love that. It really shows the beauty you can find in a Lowcountry salt marsh."

"Thank you."

Director Moore said, "Angela's office is down the hall, through the glass doors."

"From what I saw with the paramedics working on Mrs. Waterman, it didn't look good. Do you think she'll make it?"

Moore paused and took a deep breath. "I know you and Mrs. Kincaid are friends … and I know that her mother is friends with Derek Mack … but I would be remiss to share my opinion since I'm not a doctor. When we get to the hospital, hopefully, we find that Mrs. Waterman is okay. I've been in memory care for more than twenty years, and I can tell you it doesn't get any easier to have to give end of life news to a patient's family. Having said that, though, and considering the ravages of the disease … passing on can free the victim from a physical and mental anguish that is beyond the capabilities of modern medicine. And, for the families … just knowing that their loved one is no longer suffering from this horrible disease can be as freeing as the loss is painful."

SEVENTY-THREE

Michael didn't know if Catherine's mother had survived. He wanted to go to the hospital. Maybe Susan had been resuscitated and was resting. Everyone at the Memory Care Center was hoping that was the case, as was he. But, Director Moore's words were sobering: ... *considering the ravages of the disease ... passing on can free the victim from a physical and mental anguish that is beyond the capabilities of modern medicine.*

Michael knew that the Memory Care Center had reached Catherine, informing her that Susan was in critical condition when she was taken by ambulance to the hospital.

Was Catherine on her way from Columbia to Charleston? Would she be arriving with her husband or coming alone? Michael had her home address from having glanced in Susan's file when Moore's assistant left her desk to get a larger envelope for the drawing. Michael then made the decision he would rather give Catherine the drawing in person. If he didn't see her at the hospital, if for some reason she wasn't there, he could drive the two hours to Columbia, get her, and give her the drawing then.

Michael wasn't sure if Derek would fully understand what happened to Susan and why she was taken to the hospital, but he didn't want to leave without telling Derek that his friend might not be watching TV or doing art lessons with him for the next few days. He knew that Derek was lonely, and that the emotional part of his brain still functioning had, in a cruel irony, lost the ability to recall many names and faces but still held the capacity to feel loneliness. He owed it to him to try to explain what happened, and to give hope. He knew that a man with Derek's talents could become lonely from the lack of company but also from an absence of purpose.

He turned around and walked back down the hall to Derek's room, hoping he could be articulate—that what he said would resonate with him.

And he hoped that Catherine was on her way to the hospital.

* * *

When Michael approached his van with the painting, he could tell something wasn't quite right. The closer he got, the more obvious it was that the van had a flat tire. That was strange because he'd recently replaced all four tires with new ones. He hadn't driven through a construction site where he might have picked up a nail or screw. He walked toward the left front tire, the one that was flat. He knelt down and looked at a knife slash mark on the sidewall. He touched the puncture with the tips of his fingers, the gash at least an inch long.

Michael slowly stood and looked around the parking lot to the adjacent wooded area, the sound of a semi-truck in the distance. He had a good idea who'd slashed his tire. A gloating reminder from Jerry Kincaid's goons. He set the painting down against the side of his van, opened the back doors and found a jack and a lug wrench. He glanced at his watch, hoping that, if Catherine was at the hospital, she would still be there by the time he changed the tire and arrived.

* * *

Director Clarence Moore hadn't left the hospital when Michael finally got there. It appeared that his PR manager had gone. Moore was in conversation with a boney man in a black jacket and pants, a white clerical collar around his neck.

Not a good sign.

They were standing near a wide doorway to the hospital's non-denominational chapel, which had less than a dozen wooden pews inside a sanctuary lit with low-wattage bulbs. The silhouette of one woman sat alone in the center, front pew closest to the altar. The waiting room was less than a hundred feet further down the hospital corridor. Michael, holding a large envelope in his hand, started to walk there when Moore called to him. "Michael, I'm sorry to say that the news isn't good. Susan Waterman never regained consciousness. Despite the best efforts by paramedics and hospital staff, she passed."

"I was hoping for better news. I just told Derek Mack that his friend, Susan, wouldn't be there tonight to watch TV with him. Have you seen Catherine Kincaid?"

"Yes, she got here about twenty minutes ago." He gestured toward the small chapel. "She's in there. I've spoken with her and so has Father Murphy. She's taking it very hard."

Michael said nothing, an operator on the hospital PA system paging a doctor to the nurses' station in the trauma center.

Moore cleared his throat. "Michael, I'd like for you to meet Father Joe Murphy. Father, Michael Vargas is the very talented artist who did the large painting of our gardens and then donated it to us. It's hanging in the community center."

Father Murphy smiled. His perfectly straight, bone-white teeth appeared bleached. "I saw that painting when I was in there last week. It's truly a great work of art."

"Thank you." He cut his eyes between the priest and Moore. "Excuse me. I need to go in there to speak with Catherine."

SEVENTY-FOUR

There was no one else in the small chapel. No sign of her husband. Michael walked down the center aisle toward the front pew, not sure what he could say to Catherine that might comfort her. Three candles in clear glass vases flickered on an altar covered in a blue satin cloth, a gold cross stitched in the center of the cloth. The air-conditioning was cool, almost cold, the faint but woodsy smell of vanilla coming from the scented candles in the sanctuary. Michael stopped at the end of the aisle and looked to his left at Catherine.

She wore a blue suit, her head bowed in silent prayer. She held rosary beads in her hands. He could hear a small sob. And then she looked up, wearing dark glasses. He approached her and said, "I'm so sorry ... I know how much you loved her."

She slowly stood, biting her lower lip, and reached for Michael. "Just hold me."

He set the envelope on the pew and embraced her, his arms wrapping around her back, her face against his chest, crying softly, almost silent. She stood straighter, wiping at tears escaping from behind her dark glasses. "I knew this day was coming ... I just thought I had more time with Mom. A few months ago, before she got worse ... we were talking about life and the way she lived it. She said she had no regrets about anything she did in her past because she learned from the successes and failures. She said her only regrets came from those things she always wanted to do but never made time for."

"It's wonderful that she didn't have many regrets."

"She had a quiet dignity about her. Even when times were tough, and they were more than not, as a single parent for a long time, she was resilient. Never complaining. She made so many sacrifices but never compromises when it came time to do the right thing."

"I like that she used her failures to learn from and to become the remarkable woman she was because of them. You are her greatest success." Michael reached toward her face and gently removed the dark glasses. Even in the subdued light of the candles, he could see the remnants of a black eye. He felt his breath go out of his body, almost as if he'd been punched in the chest. "Did he hit you? Did Jerry do this?"

"I really don't want to talk about it right now."

"That means he did do it."

"Please—"

"Did you call the police?"

"No. It would have become much worse had I gone directly to the police."

"Where is he now?"

"In Atlanta on business."

"When's he coming back?"

"Michael, please. I don't want to talk about him right now."

"He sent two of his goons to my beach house in the middle of the night. They broke into my home, pulled a gun and threatened me. They said, if I ever saw you, they'd make sure that I'd never paint again. Before I drove here to the hospital, they slashed one of my tires."

Catherine held her hand to her mouth. "I'm so sorry this is happening to you. Jerry only wants me around long enough to get through the governor's race. I overheard him telling one of his long-time friends he was going to publicly announce his candidacy in a news conference in three weeks."

"How long will he be in Atlanta?"

"He'll come back here for Mom's funeral, only because it would be bad form if he didn't. Who knows where he'll be after that? He could stay in Columbia, go back to Florida or our apartment in New York, or he might even travel out to the ranch in Montana to host a private, pre-campaign fundraiser where booze and back-door promises flow abundantly."

"If he's at the house in Columbia, you certainly can't stay under the same roof with him. It's too dangerous."

She half smiled. "He won't draw back his fist and hit me again because he doesn't want me looking like this when he announces. A bruised and battered candidate's spouse wouldn't play well on the news. Jerry Kincaid, the youngest son of one South Carolina's most notable and celebrated families, is a wife-beater."

"And, as bad as that is, being a killer—a double murderer, is much worse on the horror scale." He paused and looked deep into her eyes. "The information that's come forth about the death of Jessica Lasalle and her unborn baby is going to connect Kincaid to the murder. Trust me. He's going down, and soon."

Her eyes welled. "Right now, I need to sit … to mourn the loss of my mother." She sat on the pew.

Michael picked up the envelope and sat beside her. "I want to show you something."

"What is it?"

"It's one of the successes your mother created." He opened the envelope and removed the crayon drawing. "This was the last piece of art that your mom drew. She was working on it when I visited Derek. I stopped at her table in the community center. She was almost done with it then. It's a garden or field with a lot of sunflowers. I think the large tree you see there was the tree we found on Edisto Island … the one with the carving on it. And I think the young woman standing there is her … a big smile on her face. She's looking toward the horizon, the sea. I believe she was reliving one of those successes in her life. She would give birth to you a few months later, in spite of doubts, fears and the pressures of society and family not to do so. She is casting her eyes on the ocean, her soul at peace with the blue sea she drew. And she's at peace now."

Tears rolled down Catherine's face. She stared at the sketch, looking at the smile on the girl's face in the picture. "May I have it?"

"Of course. That's why I brought it."

She smiled, wiping away her tears. "As much as I love your paintings … this may be the greatest piece of artwork I've ever seen. I can see my mother in every line she drew."

"Derek once said that when the artist dies … his or her work will live on in the hearts of those who look at it. Your mother is in there."

Catherine held the drawing closer, the light from the burning candles bouncing off of it. "I'm going to frame it. And I'll hang it in my new home." Catherine looked up toward the ceiling of the chapel, smiling and crying at the same time. "Thanks, Mom."

SEVENTY-FIVE

The painting of the salt marsh was dry the day before Susan Waterman's funeral. It had been three days since he had seen Catherine. Michael spent most of those days walking the beach, watching the turtle's nest, and hoping there would be a raid on Jerry Kincaid's mansion, where he would be arrested and thrown into jail. Michael knew police investigations of this stature took time and a lot of manpower because great wealth bought great attorneys who could often plant the seeds of doubt in a jury.

The day of the funeral, Michael planned to take the painting to Derek, set it up in his room and, perhaps, rekindle his old friend's dormant memories. And he wanted to take Derek to the funeral. Susan had been his closest friend at the Memory Care Center. Her death was equivalent to taking away another reason—another purpose for living, not just existing. Michael could easily visit with Derek, get permission to take him out for a while and drive to Columbia in time for the 2:00 p.m. funeral services for Susan. He picked up the painting from the screened porch and left.

* * *

As Michael walked up to Derek's room door, painting in one hand, small hammer and nail in the other, he was thinking about how the order of the paintings should hang on the walls. Although this was the third to be added to Derek's room, to his friend, they tell a story of the heart. *Maybe, from left to right, it should begin with the painting of the tall ships at sea, followed by the oaks along the country road, and then the painting of the salt marsh.* He knocked on the door. No answer as usual. He opened the door and saw Derek sitting in his chair staring at the art on his wall. His back was to Michael. "Derek, just like I promised, I came back with the painting of the salt marsh. It's one of my favorites. I was thinking that we could place them first with the tall ships, followed by the oaks at Botany Bay, and then the last would be the salt marsh. What do you think?"

No response.

Derek didn't even turn his head.

Michael walked around him and looked down. He dropped his painting and hammer on the floor. Derek's face was ashen gray, his eyes open, arms on the chair's armrest, staring at the ocean in the painting with the tall ships. "Derek …" Michael stood there. Numb. His thoughts racing. He knew his old teacher was gone, having died while looking at his favorite painting—the ships at sea. Michael reached out and touched Derek's left hand, a glint of morning light hitting the thin gold ring, the hand cold.

He blinked tears, remembering what Derek had said about the painting. *Sometimes I see that ship in my dreams, just at the cusp of the horizon … and in the next moment, my hopes carry me aboard. I don't want to wake up … because when I do … I know the schooner will sail on without me.*

Through his tears, Michael whispered. "The schooner didn't sail on without you, Derek. I know you're aboard, somewhere out there on the ocean, the wind in your face, the sun just coming up over the horizon, the endless sea to explore." He picked up the marsh painting and his hammer, walked over to the wall on the right and hung it near the other two, creating a narrative view. He turned back and looked into the face of his old mentor. "Thank you. You were my compass so long ago, and you always pointed me in the right direction. It just took me a while to follow it."

SEVENTY-SIX

Michael didn't want to remember the last time he was at a funeral. Now he'd be attending two more—the first for Susan Waterman and then for Derek. He considered that as he drove from Charleston to Columbia. The sad irony was that he never had the chance to arrange a burial for Kelsey and Mandy—only memorials. There was a difference.

Grief, he'd grown to believe, didn't end when the body of a loved one is lowered into a grave and covered with earth, but acceptance begins with a graveside departure point—an emotional farewell, a goodbye. And the grave, or another chosen location, becomes a special place for returning to leave flowers and find comfort.

Michael thought about his own deeply personal experience with the deaths of his wife and daughter. When a loved one is missing, when a body is never found, there is never closure or complete acceptance of dying without seeing the physical result of death.

On a psychological level, he knew that Kelsey and Mandy's bodies were incinerated along with the other victims. But, on an emotional level, there was no special place to say goodbye or a headstone to return to for a greeting. Just to talk. To think. And to remember.

He drove above the speed limit, knowing he wouldn't make it on time to the service at the funeral home. But he could be there in time for the graveside service. He assumed, with the connections the Kincaid family had, there would be a fairly large group of people there to mourn Susan's death and to celebrate her life. Maybe he could just blend in with the others, lots of dark clothing, sorrow and anonymity.

If Jerry Kincaid recognized him, or if his enforcers did, at this point, Michael didn't care. He knew that eventually Kincaid's criminal dealings would come out from under the rotten logs, and it would become too much for his PR handlers, attorneys, and even his thugs to keep at bay. Money can create diversions and illusions, but habitual offenders deal with the law of averages and a gambler's delusion of more wins than losses."

Michael turned off the main highway onto the road leading into the Magnolia Gardens Cemetery. He was immediately plunged in a world of South Carolina history. The cemetery road twisted around pewter gray headstones weathered from time and nature, some shouldering patches of green and brown lichen. There were old family plots encircled with rusting, wrought iron gates. Michael drove through the spotted shade of mossy oaks older than the nation and past dozens of windswept headstones marking the graves of young men who fought and died in the Civil War. He thought about Derek Mack and how much he'd miss him.

Around the next bend in the road, he saw them.

Dozens of cars had parked on both sides of the sun-dappled road. Many were, no doubt, part of the funeral procession to the cemetery. A black hearse was parked under a sprawling oak, a strand of Spanish moss almost touching the vehicle's roof. People, most dressed in black or dark colors, were walking toward a burial plot.

Michael found a place to park that was across the gravel and dirt road from tombstones that had taken on the look of brown rust, some of the inscriptions now difficult to read. One grave marker was shaped like a stone cradle for a baby. He locked his van and followed the mourners through the oaks to a freshly dug gravesite. Next to the open grave was Susan Waterman's casket, dark bronze, a cascade of flowers on top of it.

Dozens of people began taking seats in plastic chairs under a dark blue, sprawling tent-like awning, both sides printed with the words: *Fairchild Funeral Services.* He recognized the priest from the hospital, Father Joe Murphy, who greeted family and friends with words of comfort, nods, hugs and handshakes.

Michael spotted Catherine. She was nearly surrounded by mourners as she slowly made her way to the front row of chairs closest to the casket. He watched her take a seat in the center of the row next to a woman on her left who slightly resembled her. Michael assumed it was

Catherine's younger sister. A man that Michael recognized from internet pictures as Jerry Kincaid, sat on Catherine's right. He wore dark glasses and a suit to match. His mouth was turned down at the corners, a feature that took away from his good looks. He removed his glasses for a few seconds, eyes blinking as if he was allergic to cemetery dirt.

Michael stood in the shade of an oak and surveyed the crowd. Some people were genuinely filled with sorrow, their grief showing in the way they walked, the defeated posture, the wound on their faces, and their tears. Others, it appeared, were there because of some obligations, either personal or professional. Michael watched a small entourage of men in black escort the patriarch of the Kincaid family, Ralph Kincaid, to a seat in the front row next to his son. A man in his mid-eighties, he walked slowly, small steps, his shoulders rounded, perfectly combed white hair, face unreadable.

More than forty people stood on the perimeters of the tent, all the seats taken. After a few more minutes, the funeral director, a perspiring, heavy-set man in a slightly wrinkled suit, gave final instructions to a half-dozen members of his staff before walking to the front row and offering more condolences to family members. Then he turned and nodded to the priest who began the gravesite service. A crow called out from somewhere in the cemetery, and then the priest began. "Dearly beloved … friends and family of our beloved Susan Waterman, this is certainly a time for grief, for sorrow, but it is also a time to celebrate the remarkable woman and the purpose-filled life that Susan led … and she led by example in how to treat others."

Michael watched Catherine use a white tissue to dab beneath her eyes. Jerry Kincaid folded his hands across his waist, feigning concern to mourners who would be potential voters in the governor's race. As the priest continued, Michael scoured the crowd. From the distance, he wasn't sure if he could immediately recognize the men who had broken into his home. But, if he got closer, he would recognize the hand of the man who held the pistol—on the back of his hand would be the tattoo of a barber's straight razor with drops of red blood dripping from the blade.

There was a small cluster of a half-dozen men in black suits and sunglasses standing fifty feet from the main congregation, close enough to hear and see everything, but keeping a short buffer distance, probably because the Kincaid family most likely employed them. The men stood like Secret Service agents, hands clasped in front of their bodies, dark glasses hiding eyes that roamed the crowd and the immediate vicinity.

Michael looked at their hands, trying hard to spot the tattoo. But he was spotted first. He could tell. Even behind the sunglasses, he knew one man recognized him. The man was tall and wide-shouldered, the same physical features of one of the two men who broke into his home. The man motioned to a mercenary standing to his immediate left, both of them looking at Michael and trying to make it look casual. The man on the left scratched near his ear, his hand displaying the tattoo of the straight razor, the drops of red ink like rubies in the sunlight.

SEVENTY-SEVEN

Father Joe Murphy finished his gravesite comments and invited family and friends of Susan to say their final goodbyes. Michael watched as the front row got up and filed through, Jerry Kincaid, stopping to briefly touch the casket with the fingertips of one hand. His father remained seated, the old man staring out into the cemetery.

As they moved on, Catherine stood there as if she couldn't say goodbye. She looked at a poster-sized, black-and-white photograph of her mother on an easel next to a large wreath of flowers. Then she set a single sunflower on the center of the casket, said a prayer, made the sign of the cross, and moved into the shadows of the awning, people consoling her. The other guests followed, touching the coffin or placing flowers on top, paying their last respects before workers would move to lower it into the grave.

Michael remained standing near the rambling oak, Spanish moss barely moving in the breeze that carried the scent of old dirt and fresh-cut grass. The congregation drifted from the awning as the cemetery workers lowered the body of Susan Waterman into the grave, an erratic squeaking sound from the cranks, gears and nylon straps as the casket slowly descended into the hole. There were lots of hugs as guests, family and friends said goodbye, most heading toward their cars. The pretty woman who had sat next to Catherine, turned toward her, and they embraced for a long time. Catherine said something to her, then she bent forward and kissed her cheek. The woman glanced at her watch, turned, and walked to a car where a driver was waiting behind the wheel.

From Michael's perspective, he saw movement at least a hundred yards from the mourners. At first he thought it was someone visiting a grave in the distance or a cemetery worker. He looked in the direction, beyond the weeping willows, beyond the hunchback oaks, and over graves dating back to the mid-1700s.

He saw another man in black. But this one was not wearing a suit. Not wearing a sports jacket. He was dressed in a black polo shirt and dark pants. The letters, FBI on the back of the shirt. They were looking in the direction of the funeral service, one man lifting a small pair of binoculars to his eyes.

As the funeral ended, and the mourners left, the FBI arrived quietly. "Jerry Kincaid," said one agent, a woman, her dark hair pulled back. "I'm Special Agent Paula Beasley with the FBI. These are Special Agents James Porter and Frank Garcia. Mr. Kincaid, we have a federal warrant for your arrest on charges of two counts of first-degree murder for hire. You have the right to remain silent. Anything you say can and will be used against you in a court of law. You have the right to an attorney. Do you understand your rights?"

SEVENTY-EIGHT

Jerry Kincaid's mouth turned down at the corners, his eyes hot, filled with contempt. He turned back to the FBI agents. "Murder? You're crazy. Anything you think you have on me is manufactured. I'll be released in less than an hour. Shall one of my associates follow you so I can save the taxpayers money by not getting a ride back in a government vehicle?" He looked over at Catherine. She held his hard stare. "If I find you're behind this—"

"You'll do what?" She fired back. "Beat me up again? It's over, Jerry. It was over long ago. They got you on this one ... now you'll be going to prison for a long time."

Michael walked closer as the two FBI agents handcuffed Kincaid and started to lead him away. As they took him toward a waiting SUV, Michael followed behind the agents. When they walked close to the men on the ground, Michael got the attention of a wide-shouldered agent who stood next to them, his hand on the grip of his holstered pistol. "Can I speak with you a moment?" Michael asked.

The agent nodded. "Yes. What is it?"

Michael pointed to two of the six men. "Those two. The one with the tattoo of a straight razor on his right hand, and the guy next to him on his left—I bet he has a chipped front tooth."

"What does that mean?"

"It means he and the guy with the tattoo broke into my house recently, held me at gunpoint and threatened my life. They were taking orders from the man you guys just arrested, Jerry Kincaid."

"Really?"

"Yes, sir. They threatened to kill me or cripple me if I had any communication with Catherine Kincaid. The order came directly from Jerry Kincaid. Their threats give me great concern for my welfare today."

The agent looked at Michael. "Beyond your eyewitness identification of these two, do you have anything that can place them at your house?"

"Yes, one of my security cameras caught them entering my home. I'll show you." Michael tapped an app on the screen of his phone, handing it to the agent.

He watched the video for half a minute, handing the phone back. The agent looked at his colleague. "See if they have ID on them. We'll run background reports from the field. I have a feeling we'll get quite the history on these two. Let's read these guys their rights and take them in for more questioning."

Michael thanked the agent and walked back toward Catherine. She was standing in the shade of a tree watching and speaking with Father Murphy. Most of the Kincaid family remained under or near the awning, two of the brothers working phones, calling attorneys and political contacts. The old man sat in one of the plastic chairs, hands clasped tightly around his cane, his clear polished fingernails now white—the only visible evidence of his anger and embarrassment.

Father Murphy recognized Michael and nodded as he approached. "Well, I've officiated hundreds of funerals in my long career. This one will go down by far as the most unusual I've ever seen." He glanced at Catherine. "I'm just glad the service was completed before all of this happened. It's as if the FBI was here the entire time, respectful of the funeral. However, when it was over, they converged out of nowhere. I'm sorry this happened on the day of your mom's funeral. I hope you're okay."

She nodded. "You did a fine job, Father. It was a thoughtful and dignified service, both at the church and here in the cemetery. I'm grateful to you, and I'm thankful the FBI came in when it was over to arrest Jerry Kincaid in front of his entire family."

"Indeed. If those allegations are true, it may be difficult to find an impartial jury anywhere in South Carolina. Well, if you two will excuse me … I need to be getting back to Charleston." Father Murphy held a small, black book in one hand that resembled a Bible, his car keys in the other as he strolled around FBI agents, deputies and news media, heading to his car.

"Let's get out of here," Michael said.

Catherine gave a slight smile. "I'm ready. It'll be a tough next few months, but it'll all be worth it. I hope they don't allow Jerry out on bond. He would retaliate against me for whatever role he manufactures in his head that he thought I played in his arrest. I know him. I know how vengeful he can be, especially when he's drinking."

"I'm sure the federal prosecutors will argue against bond. With his private jets and overseas properties, he's definitely a flight risk."

They walked closer to the cars. Michael turned to Catherine. "I visited Derek this morning. Took him the painting of the salt marsh that he liked. I found him in his chair. It looked like he'd been staring at the painting of the tall ships at sea when he died."

"Oh, dear God … I am so very sorry for you." Catherine reached up and embraced Michael. They hugged in the warm air, the solo melody of a brown thrasher in the top of a cabbage palm tree.

After a moment, Michael's eyes damp, he looked at her. "Maybe your mom's death had something to do with Derek's passing. They were close. He loved giving her art lessons with the crayons."

"And she loved getting them from him."

"He told me that he'd experienced a heart attack in his early sixties, and he had a condition that weakened his heart muscle. I don't think he died of a broken heart. It was just worn down over time and poor health. Derek told me that, when he died, he wanted to have his ashes scattered in the salt marshes."

"When you scatter his ashes, I'd like to be there with you … if that's okay?"

"That's so much more than okay."

SEVENTY-NINE

TV news trucks lined up in front of the federal courthouse three hours before the bond hearing for Jerry Kincaid was scheduled to be held in front of U.S. District Judge Barbara Mazzola. The stately courthouse was packed. The case, generating national interest, drew network and cable news reporters, as well as prominent bloggers with millions of followers on podcasts and video blogs. In the back row, Catherine sat in a dark suit.

Jerry Kincaid wore an orange jumpsuit, shackles around his ankles, sitting at the table with his defense lawyers, three of the best attorneys that money could buy. One was from a prominent New York City firm that specialized in performing criminal defense work for politicians, movie producers, sports figures, celebrities, lobbyists and white-collar criminals.

The other two attorneys, on his left, were with a prominent corporate and criminal defense firm in South Carolina, and they had represented the Kincaid family and some of their business interests for years. Jerry Kincaid leaned left and whispered something to one of them, both men nodding, the attorney jotting a note on a pad on the table in front of him.

The Department of Justice had sent in two of its finest prosecutors. One was from the Atlanta office and the other was a female attorney, known for her impressive track record, from the U.S. attorney's office in Columbia.

U.S. District Judge Mazzola, a recent appointee of the president, entered the courtroom with a large file in her arms, black robe rustling just above her high heel shoes. In her mid-forties, she wore her dark hair up. Very little makeup on an oval face that was all business.

The people stood as she made her way behind the bench, glanced up and leaned toward the microphone. "Please, be seated." She put on her glasses and read silently for a moment before raising her head to look toward the prosecutor's table, then at the defense. "In the case of the United States verses Jerry Kincaid on two charges of murder for hire, causing the death of Jessica Lasalle and her child in utero, the court understands the defense indicates its client is pleading not guilty to both charges, correct?"

The lead defense attorney, a man in his fifties, silver hair, wire-rimmed glasses, and dressed in a dark gray suit, stood. "Yes. That's correct Your Honor—my client enters a plea of not guilty to each of the two murder charges."

She nodded. "The purpose of today's hearing is to decide what bond, if any, to set before trial." She looked over her glasses at the prosecutors. "Let's hear first from the U.S. attorneys."

A slender woman, dressed in a dark blue suit, brown hair worn to her shoulders, stood. "Thank you, Judge Mazzola. Jerry Kincaid is a cold-blooded killer. There's no softer way to state it." She held up a file folder. "In here are police and autopsy photographs of the remains of two bodies: Jessica Lasalle, Mr. Kincaid's mistress … and their unborn child. It is the government's contention that Jerry Kincaid is definitely a flight risk and no amount of bond will guarantee that he'll show up for court. He directly owns a Gulfstream jet, and through his family's multiple business interests, Mr. Kincaid has access to a second jet. In these capital murder charges, we must keep Mr. Kincaid confined through the due process. Additionally, Mr. Kincaid is under investigation for a real estate construction deal with interstate criminal charges to be brought against him any day now."

Judge Mazzola cleared her throat. "Which one of the attorneys on the side of the defense wants to offer a rebuttal?"

"I will, Your Honor," said the lawyer with the thick, silver hair. "First and foremost, these are simply charges, just that—charges. Allegations. Nothing proven beyond a reasonable doubt. Our client is innocent of all charges. Also, any other alleged investigation has no bearing here, and the prosecutor only threw that in to muddy the waters and cause undue influence. Jerry Kincaid is not a flight risk. He has strong ties to his hometown of Columbia, his family going back more than five generations. As we prepare the defense for trial, we submit that our client should be released on a reasonable bail. Thank you, Judge Mazzola." He sat down.

The judge looked at the defense and prosecution tables. "As difficult as these allegations are to hear, at this point, that is what they are ... allegations. That, by no means, undermines or reduces the severity of this case. The suggestion that the defendant be released on his own recognizance isn't going to happen.

"However, if he can secure a ten-million-dollar bond and be confined to inside his Columbia home at all times, wear a GPS monitored tracker connected to the U.S. Marshal's offices in South Carolina, I will allow bail. A date for the first murder trial, in the death of Jessica Lasalle, will be set in approximately one hundred twenty days. And, I do hope, Mr. Kincaid, for your sake, that your attorneys are correct—that you are not a flight risk. Because, just one foot outside your door, your bond will be revoked. Court adjourned." She stood and walked back to her chambers amid the hubbub of the spectators, many now standing, reporters filing out into the hallways to do interviews with attorneys.

Jerry Kincaid stood up behind the defense table with his attorneys, the lawyers discussing their next strategy, making bond arrangements and working with the U.S. Marshal's office to have their client transported to his estate in Columbia. As many of the spectators and most of the news media filed out the wide doors, Catherine stood near the last row. She stared at Kincaid. He glanced over the shoulders of his lead attorney and looked back at Catherine, his face arrogant.

EIGHTY

Michael was alone in Derek's room, the heavy feeling of loss stirring through him like the moving shadows of tree branches across one of the walls. He stood in the center of the room, the bed neatly made, Derek's clothes hanging in the closet, a framed picture of his wife, Jewell, on the dresser, a finished crossword puzzle on the table. Although Derek's things were here, his presence was not. The reminders of his life, one of his paintings over his bed, the photographs of him with Jewell, his watch still ticking on the table next to a box of crayons, were present. But the core of the man was swept away, leaving the room empty and abandoned.

Per Derek's wishes, which were laid out in a one-page will that also included an addendum that had been added just over a year ago, Michael made arrangements with a local funeral home to handle the death certificate records and the cremation. He would box up all of his old friend's personal property and have it removed. In his simple will, Derek requested that his home and property be sold, the money going to three charities for children in the Charleston area, one of which was focused on furthering artistic talents. He promised Derek he would take care of his affairs, and he would. Right after he took Derek's ashes to the marshes.

His phone buzzed in his pocket. He looked at the screen. Catherine calling. He answered, and she said, "What a morning. Have you seen the news?"

"No, I'm in Derek's room, boxing things up. What happened in court?"

She told him and added, "Jerry's attorneys managed to get bail for him. It's very high, ten million. The U.S. Marshals are escorting him to our house in Columbia. I have nowhere to go right now. And I only have the clothes on my back."

"Yes, you do have somewhere to go. You have my house … and you have me. We can get you all new clothes … and we can get you an all new life."

Catherine stood on the steps of the courthouse, the wind blowing her hair. "I could use both. Thank you, Michael. See you soon."

"I'll be at the beach house waiting, bye." Michael walked over to the paintings on the wall. It was now time to take them down. As he reached for the paintings, he remembered what Derek had said when he initially saw each one. The first was the country road and the tunnel of old oaks. *You captured the majesty of light, shadow and composition … but then you added the sweetness of the mother and child enjoying their time together …*

Michael set that painting down, propped it up against the bed railing, and then he removed the painting of the tall ships. *The closest ship to us is sailing like she is one with the sea. There's a nautical heartbeat to that kind of sailing. From the wind in her sails and the water beneath her, a ship like that breathes and lives …*

Michael stared at the painting for a long moment before setting it down, removing the last one, the marsh. *Take me back to the salt marshes. I want my ashes to rise and fall with the tides in the Lowcountry boil of life … the ladle stirred by the very hand of God, the sunsets from his brushstrokes … take me home.*

* * *

When the U.S. Marshals, all armed, large, raw-boned men, escorted Jerry Kincaid up the steps to his South Carolina mansion, Kincaid's long-time attorney was there to greet them. He stood near the wide teak wood and inlaid bronze front doors under the porte-cochere, his face flush in the humidity. "Thank you, gentlemen, for escorting my client back to his home. I can take it from here and get Mr. Kincaid situated."

The tallest of the marshals, a man in a Stetson hat wearing a beige sportscoat over his holstered pistol, shook his head. "We're not here to deliver the prisoner to you. We're here to make sure he goes inside the house. That's the judge's orders. Mr. Kincaid is to be confined inside the home at all times. If he even steps outside to his mailbox, he will go to jail."

The man pursed his lips, looked at the horses in the fenced pasture, then eyed Kincaid. "I'm sure you have people to feed and care for the livestock. Remember this, Mr. Kincaid, the GPS monitor locked to your ankle is so sophisticated and accurate, we'll know when you go to the bathroom. If you leave your house … well, we have a full digital rendering of the house and property. You best stay put. Is that understood?"

"Of course. No offense, but I really don't want to see you boys again." Kincaid grinned.

The marshals did not. "Open the door. We're to escort you inside."

Kincaid used a key to unlock the doors, everyone following him inside the house. The marshals gave the entrance foyer a cursory look. They scanned the imported Italian marble floor, expensive artwork, nodded and left. Kincaid glanced at his lawyer and said, "I need a drink." He walked down the hall to a great room, high beamed ceilings, mammoth stone fireplace, pool table at one end of the big room, western artwork on the walls, a 100-inch wide-screen TV in front of overstuffed couches and chairs.

Kincaid stood at the bar and poured three fingers worth of Stagg bourbon into a heavy crystal glass. "Care for a drink?"

"No thanks. I have to get back to the office. I'll call you in a couple of hours. I'm sure news media will be setting up camp at the electric gate entrance to your property. Just keep a very low profile, all right, Jerry?"

Kincaid didn't answer, his eyes hard. He sipped the bourbon, closing his eyes a moment as he swallowed the straight bourbon. He took a deep breath and looked at a framed photo on the bar of a man wearing a Confederate soldier's uniform and standing next to a live oak, thick moss hanging from the lower branches. "That's my great grandfather. The photo was taken right after the Civil War. That tree still stands on this property. You passed it when you came down the driveway. The Kincaid family goes way back here in South Carolina.

We almost lost this place and other property during and after the war. But the family fought the battles, persevered and won against tough odds." He knocked back his drink and shifted his eyes over to his attorney. "Level with me, Colton. What are my odds now? Can I beat this thing, or am I gonna have to do time in prison?"

"After thirty years as a lawyer, I never try to second guess a jury."

Kincaid slammed his glass down on the bar. "I'm not asking you what a damn jury will or won't do. What am I looking at … how many years? What's the max in prison? And how can you reduce it?"

"I'm not going to sugarcoat it, Jerry. We're not looking at multiple capital charges as in what a serial killer might face. However, there are two deaths—and in the collective eyes of a jury … two murders. This is extremely serious. If things go bad, and they might, you could be looking at forty years to life in prison. But, before we get all worried about the what ifs, let's deal with what we know. We'll come up with a strategy for a reduced charge and—"

"No! What, twenty years? Hell, no! My family has paid your firm millions over the years. And you—with the best defense lawyers we've hired to assist you—are you telling me that I could be lookin' at the rest of my life in prison? That can't happen. Grow some balls. Do what you're paid to do!"

"Jerry, what we have to accomplish first is—"

"Get out! Just go, all right? I need to think this through, and I don't want anyone hanging around here. My wife's gone. My family's embarrassed. My candidacy is over." He reached for the bottle and refilled his glass. "Just go, Colton … I need to be alone."

* * *

It was nearing eleven p.m. when Jerry Kincaid pulled the cork from a second bottle of bourbon, downed a glass and filled it again. He walked through the big, empty house in his socks, cocktail glass in one hand, his eyes red, a fire churning in his gut. He stood in front of the stainless-steel refrigerator door, opened it, and pulled sliced ham from a package. He ate the ham with his fingers, dropping the package to the marble floor, fingertips greasy as he picked up his glass and walked back into the great room, turning on the television.

A middle-aged TV news anchorman looked into the camera. "The double murder case involving billionaire real estate developer and potential candidate for governor here in South Carolina, Jerry Kincaid, made it through the bond hearing today. Kincaid was granted bond, but at a very steep price. News Eight's Michelle Sullivan has the story."

The picture cut to images of attorneys, media and spectators coming into the federal courthouse. The voice-over narration began. "The thousand-dollar suit was gone. Today, Jerry Kincaid, a member of one of the wealthiest families in South Carolina, wore an orange jumpsuit courtesy of the Richland County Jail. Kincaid, charged with hiring a hitman to murder his mistress, Jessica Lasalle, and their unborn child, was stoic as he was led into the courtroom. U.S. District Judge Barbara Mazzola listened to the defense and prosecution present why Kincaid should or should not be released on bond until his trial date.

"Jerry Kincaid's defense lawyers say their client is innocent and will be cleared of what they're calling politically motivated charges. Prosecutors say the alleged hitman, in a plea deal, will testify against Kincaid. After posting a high bond of ten million dollars, Kincaid sits under house arrest, wearing a GPS tracking device, and confined to his estate on three hundred acres in a rural, but wealthy area north of Columbia. The murder trial in the death of Jessica Lasalle is expected to take place in about one hundred twenty days, with the trial of the unborn child following. We'll update you as soon as firm trial dates are filed with the court. If convicted on all charges, Kincaid could face life in prison. From the federal courthouse, this is Michelle Sullivan reporting."

Jerry Kincaid stared at the television, his eyes blurring, thoughts caught in mental quicksand. He felt paralyzed. "Bitch!" he yelled and threw the heavy glass into the center of the screen, creating a large, spider-web crack. After a few seconds, he got up from his chair and stumbled toward the bar. He stood, holding onto the edge of a wooden table to steady himself. Behind the bar, he found a loaded Colt single action revolver. He looked at the framed photo of his great grandfather in the Confederate uniform. "You may have lost the war, but you won a lot of the battles. I lost the war, and I won't win the next battle. See you in Valhalla."

He placed the end of the pistol barrel against his right temple and pulled the trigger. Jerry Kincaid was dead before his body hit the imported marble floor.

EIGHTY-ONE

The following month, Michael and Catherine motored a sixteen-foot, wooden boat into a world where the land and the ocean met twice a day as the tides jostled in and out, baptizing new life and taking old life back out to sea. It was the salt marshes and the Lowcountry islands, strung like jewels in a long necklace, where the rim of South Carolina met the neck of the Atlantic.

They piloted the small boat toward the sunrise, the marshes cast in inky silhouette, tufts of cabbage palms dusted in a halo of crimson. Egrets and blue herons were coming down from their roosts, stalking prey in water reflecting morning light with the shimmering look of ripe cherries. The sea breeze over the wetlands had the briny smell of birth and death—new flowers blooming, old dying off, the musky scent of crabs, oysters and fish propagating in the tidal pulls of life.

Catherine sat on the bench board in the center of the boat. Michael near the stern, his right hand on the throttle of an Evinrude outboard motor, a V-shaped wake trailing behind them in a ribbon of scarlet ripples that tickled the roots of the spartina grasses. Catherine pointed to a large otter that poked its head above the surface near an oyster bar, water droplets falling off the animal's bearded chin.

Derek Mack rode with them.

His ashes were tucked away in a sealed urn surrounded by crumpled newspapers in a cardboard box. He hadn't, of course, been specific in terms of where he wanted his remains spread in the salt marshes. So, Michael picked a pristine area close to where he'd painted the salt marsh and not too far from Derek and Jewell's old homeplace.

He followed the widest of the tidal creeks that twisted through miles of verdant green grass, spartina and needlerush. There were small islands, or palm hammocks, in the stream of wetlands that seemed to march to the curvature of the earth. An osprey dove out of moving clouds tinged in orange and burgundy, pulling a striped mullet from a wide creek that ran its watery fingers for miles through the thick grasses.

As Michael steered the boat around an elbow bend in the creek, the water spread wider, dozens of long-legged egrets and blue herons, standing like silent sentries along the fringes of grass and mud flats. He shut off the motor and looked at Catherine. "I think this is the place."

She smiled. "It's certainly beautiful. The morning colors of the sky and water are breathtaking." She paused. "I can hear the ocean, the waves rolling on the beach. I wonder if Derek ever came to this exact spot. Somehow, I believe he did."

Michael smiled and looked at the urn. "How do you think we found it? Maybe he was our guide. Actually, Derek and Jewell didn't live too far from here. Let's just drift in the tidal current and release Derek back to the place he so loved."

"The tide's incoming."

"He once told me the salt marshes shouldn't be confused with swamps. He said water doesn't flow in swamps like it does in the salt marshes. Out here, he said, is where Mother Nature whispers to you and lets you see her hand gently rock the cradle of life. It's … light from the heavens shining down, the sea pushing its salty influence into the inlets and tidal creeks, and the land pushing back with its fresh water in a spirited tug-of-war that isn't a war but rather the push and pull of the seasons. He called it the pot liquor of life, a unique land simmering in a broth so rich in spirit that you could taste and feel its soul in the wind on your face."

Catherine took a deep breath, the sea breeze in her hair. "I can feel it, and I can taste it."

"One of the last things he told me is that he wanted his ashes to rise and fall with the tides in what he called the Lowcountry boil of life … the ladle stirred by the very hand of God … the sunrises from His brushstrokes … he wanted to go back home … to come here."

Michael lifted the urn and removed the top. He leaned over the side of the boat, looked at the wading birds and the creeks snaking through the tall grasses. "We've brought you back home, Derek." As

Michael emptied the ashes into the water, a stronger breeze from the ocean blew across the grass, carrying Derek's remains with it in a windswept dance over the water. The wind subsided and the ashes fell into the blue surface reflecting the sky, the yellow sun like an orb riding the small ripples into a horizon where the water and sky became one.

Michael's eyes welled as he watched the last bit of ash carried away in the current. "Goodbye, old friend. Thank you for making me go back up the ladder that day and finish the mural. Follow the current to the sea, and board that ship of your dreams. It's waiting at the cusp of the horizon." A tear fell from his chin into the water.

Catherine motioned for him to sit beside her. "Come here." She turned to face him. "I absolutely love how much you loved him. And, I want you to know that I am awed and appreciative of how much you loved your wife and daughter. It's great insight into your depth. Do you think you could ever love me the same way … as much?"

"Not the same way, but as deeply. To quote F. Scott Fitzgerald, he said, 'There are all kinds of love in this world, but never the same love twice.' So, Catherine, my promise is to love you for you."

They sat on the center bench next to each other. She reached out and held his hand, her eyes, too, tearing as the tide changed direction and began to flow back out to sea. The wind followed, a breeze now blowing across the marsh toward the shoreline. "Michael, look at that." Catherine pointed to three dolphins that had entered the creeks from the inlet, coming in with the tide. They turned circles in the wide creek, as if they were playing a game, fins breaking the surface, the playful faces rising above the water. "It always looks like they're smiling. I wonder if it means they're always happy."

Michael watched the dolphins swim, moving farther away. "I think today they're happy because a new friend just joined them."

Catherine squeezed his hand. They sat there in silence for a while longer, a blue heron gliding over the marsh, the dolphins following the tide as it made its journey back to the sea. Michael turned toward Catherine. "You said that you wanted to be with me when the baby turtles hatch. It's about that time … I think it'll be soon, maybe tonight."

"And I said I want to be with you when you paint more paintings … I think that will be for the rest of my life."

* * *

Later that night, after nine p.m., Michael and Catherine held hands, walking the beach toward the turtle's nest under the light of a full moon. She turned to him. "I hope we haven't missed them—do you really believe they could hatch and come out tonight?"

"The time is right. If not tonight, we'll come back every night until they do. But, tonight is a good night—the moon's out to guide them. All they need to do is claw through the sand."

"Sounds daunting for baby turtles not much wider in size than a quarter."

"I had a dream that you and I were at the nest and you asked me how, under all that dark sand, they knew which way to dig to find freedom."

"What did you say in your dream?"

"I didn't have an answer at the time. Now, I believe they dig their way to the surface by instinct. The only compass they have is their heart, and that's what they follow."

"Ahh, I like that—a turtle's intuition." Catherine smiled.

When they got to the nest, Michael knelt beside it. Under the moonlight, he could see the sand was smooth. "It looks like they're still down there. Let's sit on the blanket. Maybe it'll be soon."

They sat on the blanket, the sea oats all around them barely moving in the night breeze the sky filled with twinkling stars. Catherine stared at the rolling breakers. "It is so peaceful here. It's nights like this that I don't want to end."

"They don't have to. I made a purchase offer on the beach house and the adjoining properties. They've accepted. But the only condition is that I don't live alone. You have to move in with me."

She smiled. "So, is that the caveat?"

"Absolutely. The only stipulation."

"The sellers seem very insightful."

"Oh, they are ... almost prophetic."

"Do they tell fortunes?"

"Yes. And they told me what I already know."

"What's that?"

"That I've found the greatest gift … and that is you." He leaned in and kissed her.

Catherine felt her eyes well. "Don't make me cry. I don't know if I have any more tears to shed." She smiled, used her finger to wipe away a tear under one eye. "Michael, I want to do something for you, and for Derek, too."

"What is it?"

"One time you told me you've never done an art show … never had your paintings on display under one roof, like a gallery. I want to arrange that for you. We'll do it in downtown Charleston and invite the whole darn South. You painted the soul of the South. All those paintings, together, tell so many beautiful stories of the South. People need to see them, to stand in front of them, to put themselves in your shoes and experience what you saw and painted. Also, I thought it would be appropriate to include some of Derek's paintings. When he died, he left you at least two-dozen or more paintings that have never been seen by the public. You told me that those paintings are some of his greatest work. It would be so cool for you two—the teacher and his prodigal student, to have your collective work in an art show together."

Michael smiled, the sound of the surf crashing, coming further up the beach. "I'm both surprised and grateful Derek gifted some of his artwork to me. He was very talented. He must have added the addendum to his will right after he gave me his paints and brushes … he has always had faith in me."

"Derek knew you would enjoy them differently than anyone else … and as much as he enjoyed yours."

"A gallery showing is a great offer. Thank you. I just wish Derek was here to see it."

"He'll see it. I know he will. And, more importantly, the public will see him. His work will live on in the hearts of those who look at it … because, as he told you, a part of the artist stays forever in that painting. Derek will be there."

"Okay, let's do it, the three of us."

Catherine glanced over at the nest. "Look!" She rose to her knees. "A baby turtle. They're coming up and out."

THE PAINTER

They watched as turtles popped their small heads above the surface of the sand, little flippers clawing, tossing sand, tiny eyes blinking, searching for light. Within a minute, the first half-dozen turtles were free of the sand and scampering toward the sea, the moonlight over the ocean guiding them, like a lighthouse in the distance.

Michael and Catherine held hands, as if they were proud parents watching their children playing a sport, a steady trek of baby turtles digging out of the sand and escaping into the rolling surf. After a half-hour, there were one or two stragglers still making their way down the beach. Michael chuckled. "I was trying hard to keep a running count as they scampered to the waves. I'd guess between eighty and a hundred baby turtles made it out and into the ocean. Ready to head back to the house?"

"Let's wait a bit longer. Maybe there's another little fella or two who are just running behind. It's amazing they know to head down to the sea."

"They use the moon over the water as a guide. If the houses around here had a lot of floodlights turned on, the turtles might get confused and crawl inland rather than out to sea. The state DNR requires residents to keep outdoor lights off during the turtle hatching season."

Catherine gestured. "There's another one. Maybe he's the last little guy to emerge." A blanket of clouds rolled over the moon, casting the beach into deeper darkness. "Michael, I don't think the last one is going toward the ocean. Can you turn the flashlight on your phone to see which direction the poor thing went?"

Michael hit the light on his phone. They could see the turtle was crawling in the wrong direction, toward the road. Catherine stood. "We need to help him or her." She walked over to the turtle, gently picking it up, cupping the baby in her hands. "I'm going to release the turtle into the ocean." She turned and walked to the breakers, moving deeper as the surf rolled over her knees. Michael followed her.

At that moment, the clouds parted, the moon appearing, laying a buttery trail to the horizon. She lowered her hands into the water. The little turtle scurried away, heading toward the light. Catherine smiled. "Swim for the moon, okay little one? You were in the dark a long time … and now you've found your freedom. Explore the world … because it's here for you."

347

Under the soft moonlight, Michael leaned in and kissed her—two silhouettes coming together, embracing as one with the sea.

The End

To be released soon, MIDNIGHT'S WHISPERER

A new novel by Tom Lowe

Here is an excerpt for you –

ONE

As a kid, Ty McGill always wanted to travel to Mars, and now he felt like he'd landed on a Martian surface. He thought about that as he rode in an Army Jeep west on Highway 10 through the Saudi Arabian desert. To the south were massive tracts of undeveloped land, the sand windswept in rolling furrows, the distant and craggy vistas reddish in the afternoon sun. The terrain reminded Ty of pictures he'd seen taken from ground-level on Mars.

To the north, it was different. The land was dotted with a few commercial properties—gas stations, multi-story apartment buildings, strip shopping centers, and dairy farms. Ty, in his late twenties, strong face with intense eyes that appeared wiser than his years, wore his Army fatigues—riding in the front passenger seat. The arid breeze, moving through the partially opened windows, smelled of dry, baked earth, dust and decay—carrion in the wind.

Ty thought about the comparison between the Saudi Arabian desert and the surface of Mars, the red and coppery sand. He no longer wanted to go to Mars, and he was ready to finally leave the Middle East. *Less than two months, I'm goin' home*, he thought, watching three Bedouin men riding camels over the sandy terrain, coppery dust kicking up around the camel's hooves.

The Jeep's driver, Kenny Gallagher, who had guarded eyes and a small, white scar on the bridge of his slightly crooked nose, was two years younger than Ty. He took one hand off the wheel, pointing to the Bedouins on the camels in the distance. "Looks like the three wise men from the Bible," he said with a Boston accent, his eyes moving back to the road ahead.

Ty watched the men and their animals. "Yep, but over here, the Bible doesn't mean a whole lot." Ty's voice had a slight southern tone. Not a twang, just a soft Texas cadence to it.

Gallagher said nothing for a few seconds. He pulled the sun visor down, glancing into his rearview mirror. "I guess that's why we're here … in the Middle East."

"Because of the Bible?"

"No, because of the differences in religions, the interpretation and the way all that crap is carried out. Man, I'm not looking forward to relocating into Iraq soon. It's been a nice gig the last thirty days kicking back at the base here in Saudi Arabia. I even got a taste for Kibbeh."

Ty laughed. "I wouldn't call additional military tactical training as kickin' back."

"Well, it sure as hell beats combat. You just got to stay safe and bide your time, my man. You made sergeant. Now, you just gotta make it home."

"Paid my dues. This is my fourth and final tour after we're done in Iraq. I wanna say I'll miss you out here, Kenny. But we'll catch up back at stateside." He chuckled.

"You've beaten the odds. Your first tour was in Afghanistan, then Syria. And, in a few days, when we head back to Iraq, you'll be wrapping up your second tour in that country before you know it. You ever think about dying somewhere in the Middle East?"

"No. But it's not dying that scares me. It's making a wrong decision that puts my men in the line of fire. That'd be hard to live with if it all went to hell in a handbasket."

"That handbasket stuff, must be a Texas thing." Gallagher smirked, reaching for a pair of sunglasses from his front pocket, putting on the dark glasses. "We ought to be getting close to the place. The captain said turn right at the water tower, and the stables are supposed to be at the end of the road. I can see the tower up ahead."

"Back in Texas, when I was a kid, you'd see windmills pumping water into open holding tanks for cattle. Out here, I guess it'd evaporate too fast. But there are a lot of cows. Wonder where they get the water."

"I know you come from a long line of cowboys, but do you think you can really help these folks with their horse farm … or the new horse that's supposed to be a real bugger?"

"Never know. Just like people, every horse is different. And like people, every horse has some of the same characteristics. You just gotta quickly figure that out when you're in the pen with them."

"And you got this oddball assignment because Captain Williams is pals with Saudi General, Ameer Khan, right?"

"Sort of. Captain Williams should be at the ranch already." Ty glanced at the watch on his left wrist. "We're supposed to meet them at 1600 hours. We ought to be right on time. General Khan's been friends with Cap Williams for a few military campaigns. Cap told me that Khan wants to retire from the Saudi Royal Guard in a couple of years, and he's in the process of buying breed horses to build up stock … Arabian horses mostly."

"Guess that makes sense considering we're in the middle of Saudi Arabia."

Gallagher turned near the base of a silver-colored water tower, following a two-lane asphalt road, passing fenced property scattered with mesquite trees and scrub bush. "Unless you're raising camels, there's not a helluva lot of grazing land in this part of the ol' Kingdom, you know."

"There are plenty of cattle and horses in this country. A lot of top racing thoroughbreds back in the states have some Arabian blood in them. The breed goes back thousands of years. Bedouin and other desert tribes bred them for strength and endurance. They carry themselves like no other horse. They're not as large as some horses, but they're intelligent and have incredible stamina. Out in this desert … they need it."

"How'd you learn so much about horses?"

"My grandpa. That old man was so good with horses that just about everyone else in West Texas paled in comparison. Many people knew and respected him for his talent. He taught me a lot. Other stuff I picked up working on ranches and the season I traveled the rodeo circuit."

"So, you *are* a real damn cowboy, eh? Growing up in South Boston, the only cowboys I'd ever seen were on TV and in the movies."

"It's not glamorous, at least not like the stuff on TV. It's hard work."

"Look at this freakin' place." Gallagher turned into a long driveway that led up to a sprawling villa, a three-story mansion with a cream-colored adobe-style exterior, arched windows, and a Mediterranean red clay tile roof. More than a dozen imported canary date palms were planted in landscaped garden areas adjacent to the large home. Soft red dessert rose flowers circled at the base of the palms. A gardener in a long-sleeved, white shirt and jeans pulled weeds from one of the flower beds.

Gallagher parked the Jeep next to a Humvee that was painted in a desert sand, camouflage-color scheme—two shades of brown, beige, and light grays.

Ty looked around. "It appears to me that the Saudi military pays a helluva lot more than what the U.S. Army pays us."

"I heard that General Khan is related to the Saudi royal family, the house of Saud and all the trimmings that go with it. He's one of the most trusted dudes in the Royal Guard, and their job is to protect the king at all times."

A tall man wearing a white robe, or a thobe, and a red-and-white checkered keffiyeh on his head, came from a side entrance to the compound. He smiled approaching the men, his face coffee brown, neatly trimmed black beard. "Gentlemen, I am Jalil, the general's assistant. Welcome."

The men exchanged greetings, shaking hands. Jalil nodded, bowed slightly. He eyed Ty. "I understand that you know the ways of horses like few others."

Ty smiled. "I wouldn't say that. Plenty of folks know a lot more about horses than I do. But I did have some good teachers, and I count horses among them."

"Very good. Come, please. Everyone is in the back, at the stables. You both are our special guests today." He looked at Gallagher. "Are you good with horses as well, Specialist Gallagher?"

"Me? Heck no. To be honest with you, horses scare the shit outta me. I'd rather fly a kite in a storm before getting on the back of a horse."

Jalil's smiled melted. "I see." He turned toward Ty, his black eyes probing. "The horse you are to meet, although he comes from pure Arabian stock, he has a dark side, Sergeant McGill. One of our groomers calls the horse *Al Shaitaan*. In English it means the devil. The animal has killed one man already. I hope today you will not suffer such a fate. Please, let us proceed."

TWO

They walked through a series of high walled passageways, security cameras and locked wrought iron gates along the way. The last gate led into a compound that was one of the largest stables Ty had ever seen. Four-board-high fencing, painted bone white, separated a half-dozen large paddock areas, green pastures, sprinklers pulsating in the warm air. The fencing went as far as the eye could see.

Ty counted fourteen Arabian horses grazing in the immediate compounds. There were three long barns with dozens of stalls and large fans built into the walls for flow-through ventilation. The warm air carried the pungent scent of fresh-cut hay, manure, and sulfur from the water sprinklers.

Groomers washed down and brushed horses as trainers worked with a chestnut brown stallion in a round ring. Standing near the fencing were General Ameer Khan and Captain Joe Williams. Khan wore a flowing white robe, white keffiyeh held in place on his head with a black rope called an agal. His brown face was deeply lined. Dark moustache. Eyes like shiny black marbles. Almost unreadable.

"Welcome!" he shouted over the noise of a tractor heading into the fields.

Ty and Gallagher followed Jalil to the training ring, a large, circular fenced compound. Captain Williams, tall, early fifties, close-cropped gray hair, held a cigar in one hand, white smoke snaking up from the hot ash. He grinned. "Right on time, boys. General Khan, this is Army Specialist Kenny Gallagher. He's with and the fella I told you about, Sergeant Ty McGill … one of the finest horsemen to come out of the great state of Texas." Williams puffed his cigar.

"Welcome, gentlemen," General Khan said, greeting them with firm handshakes.

Captain Williams half smiled, smoke trailing through his wet lips. "I've known McGill for two tours of duty over here. I come from Kentucky. Many of us there know something about horses in the Blue Grass State. But Sergeant McGill is what I'd call a guy who talks to horses, and I don't mean any of that horse whisperer stuff. I watched a YouTube video of him doing his thing … working with a troubled horse, and he doesn't whisper. He more or less talks to the horse, like he's holding a damn real conversation when them. And they listen, or they seem to."

General Khan flashed a wide smile, nodding. "Sergeant McGill. Do you know much about Arabian horses?"

"I've worked with them. Not on a regular basis, but some. They're fine animals."

"Indeed. Some of the best stock on earth is here where the breed originated more than four thousand years ago. No horse carries himself like the Arabian. The way they run. The way they hold up their heads. Royal bloodlines create champions. Also, that can create what some call problem horses. Temperamental. Stubborn. Difficult to break."

Ty smiled. "I've never broken a horse … no more than I'd break a person. I use a different approach to work with horses that some folks say have issues. Most often, it's not the horses with issues."

General Khan folded his arms across his chest, shifting his eyes to the pasture for a second before eyeing Ty. "I can understand that. People and horses … each can be complicated. Please, follow me." He led them to another circular pen and motioned to a bearded groomer. He nodded and opened a stall from one barn leading into the ring.

A powerfully built, white horse, an Arabian stallion, entered the paddock. The horse pranced, muscles rolling, mane flowing in the wind, nostrils flaring—testing the breeze, head and tail held high. Khan gestured to the horse. "In Arabic, his name is Tarek. It means *conqueror*. I'm told the groomers have another name for him. He comes from some of the best bloodlines in the Kingdom."

Ty nodded. "He's a fine-looking horse."

"Yes, however, he seems to have inherited a gene for fury. Before I bought him, he'd kicked and killed his last trainer. You told us that you don't break horses, Sergeant McGill. Are you willing to walk in the ring with that horse, attempt to break him with only words ... and English words at that?"

"Doesn't matter the language. It's how you speak. It's your physical presence. I won't break him. I'll get to know him ... and he'll get to know me. It's my hope we can meet in the middle." He glanced over at Gallagher who shook his head, his eyes filled with anxiety. "And then we'll take it from there. I have one request, though, if you can get it."

"Of course. What is it?"

"Something I can hold in one hand. Like a branch stripped of leaves, three or four feet long with a white rag tied to one end."

A smiled worked at the corner of Khan's mouth. "Do I assume you will need the branch as a whip? We do have horsewhips."

"No whips. Just a stick. Or a trainer's stick if you have one. The white rag is really a white flag of truce. I'll show you what I mean."

THREE

More than a dozen groomers and trainers stood outside the ring, talking in whispers and watching as the American soldier, dressed in uniform, walked into the pen and faced an Arabian horse that paced near the far fence boards. Ty held two ropes and a five-foot long bamboo pole with a white piece of cloth tied to one end. The horse snorted, nostrils testing the arid breeze, eyes wide. Ty stopped in the center of the ring. "It's okay fella. Nobody's gonna hurt you. I just want to get to know you. Maybe we'll hangout ... just the two of us."

He didn't take his eyes off the horse.

Ty held the bamboo pole close to the ground. "What's on your mind, boy? Show me what you're thinking?"

General Khan stood next to the wooden fencing, watching. He swatted at a fly, glancing over at Captain Williams. "I can already tell he's fearless in the ring, but he's not trying to dominate the horse. How many sessions do you think it will take him to succeed, if he can succeed?"

"Don't know how long it takes him. I do know that he's being sent into Iraq in three days. So, let's hope he can somehow do it today in one session."

The horse rose on its hind legs, snorting and punching the air with its front legs, hooves flinging sand and dirt toward Ty. General Khan watched the horse a few seconds before turning to Williams, smiling. "Today … just one session. With all due respect. I think it is impossible."

Kenny Gallagher cleared his throat. "Maybe not, General. Ty told me about a time he was hired to help tame wild mustangs when the federal government was gonna have to relocate some of the herd in Montana due to overcrowding on public lands. Ty said he and five other cowboys caught and *gentled*, that's the word he used … *gentled* more than two hundred wild horses one summer."

Khan nodded. "An American mustang is not an Arabian horse." He turned, nodding at one of his trainers, a lean man in his late thirties.

Ty watched the horse, slowly approaching him. "Man, I don't blame you for being pissed off. Somewhere along the line, you must have had the rough end of a relationship. That's all behind you now." The horse started running around the inside perimeter of the ring. It ran fast in a clockwise position.

Ty turned, staying near the center of the pen, his body rotating to always face the horse. When the animal gyrated and ran in the opposite direction, Ty pivoted, rotating in that position. "Run like the wind, fella. You'll get tired and need to take a breather."

After a few minutes of running, the horse stopped, heavily breathing. "It's okay. Let's meet in the middle." Ty walked closer. The horse's ears dropped back, and it ran toward Ty. He quickly sidestepped, like a matador moving out of the path of a raging bull. The horse ran by him, stopping and kicking up its hind legs, dirt flying. When it turned to face Ty, he tossed a rope, quickly lassoing the horse's neck. It rose on its hind legs, snorting and neighing. "Settle down. Nobody's gonna hurt you."

The horse bolted around the ring. Ty followed, holding one end of the rope in one hand, the bamboo pole with the white rag in the other hand, letting the horse tire and feel less threatened as he ran a half dozen laps. "It's okay … just settle down, and we'll have some oats together." He held the rope loosely, allowing for slack, walking up to the horse. It trotted in a circle, Ty closing the gap with the rope, keeping the bamboo pole and white rag in the air. He moved closer toward the horse, the fence directly on the other side. "That a boy … you're fine. Let's talk a little bit. Tell me, Tarek … what's on your mind?"

The horse's ears stood up, moving to follow Ty's soft voice. Its tail rose in the air, head angled, watching the man approach. "What do you say we trade that lasso for a lead rope, okay?" He stood next to the horse for a minute, simply talking, pausing to gauge the animal's reaction. Holding the rope, he slowly reached out and touched the horse's shoulder, talking, caressing. He could feel the tremble in the animal's muscles. "Let's have some fun … you and me. There's no boss … just the two of us. Remember fella, it takes two to tango. Before we do the tango, let's get to know each other and do a little waltz. Follow me."

He gently led the horse to the opposite side of the ring, the groomers and trainers exchanging glances. General Khan looked over at Captain Williams. "Your man has a way with horses—however, he has yet to put a saddle on him. The last man who tried, I am told, lasted five seconds before being bucked off and landing on the fence. He broke seven ribs."

Williams smiled, pursing his wet lips, spitting a sliver of tobacco from the corner of his mouth, his green eyes bold. "Maybe Ty can go eight seconds." He nodded at Gallagher, grinned and took a puff from his cigar.

Gallagher said, "My money's on Ty from Texas."

Ty led the horse around the ring three times in one direction, turned and led him three more times in the opposite direction. From an adjacent ring, three other Arabian horses stood and watched. The animals seemed as curious as the groomers and trainers who stood or propped up against the fence watching the American work with the horse.

Ty stopped on the opposite side of the ring. "Whoa boy. Let's get that rope off you and try something a little more comfortable." He lifted a halter from one of the fence posts, holding it in his hands for a few seconds, letting the horse see and smell it. Then he rubbed the animal's head, talking softy. "They tell me you come from royal Arabian blood. I get that. I grew up around quarter horses and mustangs. Then I got to know some thoroughbreds. When I look in your eye, I see their eyes, too. We're all connected, pal. All in this together."

With that he slipped the halter over the horse's head, causing the animal to back up a few steps, snorting, shaking its head, thick mane rising. "You're doing great. What I want to ask you is this … how am I doing? Remember, it's gotta be a dance."

After a minute, Ty used the rope to lead the horse back to the fence. He lifted a saddle, again letting the animal see and smell it. "I heard you wore one of these once. Maybe it was too tight. Maybe you didn't like the load. Whatever, let's work together to make this more comfortable for you. Were gonna forget the fight or flight thing for the time being and move on in a different direction."

He caressed the horse's back and then eased the saddle up and on him. The Arabian snorted and trotted sideways in a 180-degree half turn, Ty staying right with him. "It's okay." He tightened the straps. "Not a bad fit. What do you think?" The horse eyed him, ears twitching. "That's what I was thinking, too. "Okay, let's do this dance. He set the bamboo pole against the fence, stood next to the horse for a few seconds, placing his foot in a stirrup, mounting the horse, talking in a low tone all the time."

The horse rose up on its hind legs, whinnying. It came down, bucking twice. Ty staying in the saddle. The groomers sitting on the top of the fence, leaning backwards for a moment. Then the animal took off, running around the perimeter of the ring, bucking twice more and kicking. Ty held on, moving with the horse, not against it, talking in a calm voice. After a minute of this, the horse stopped bucking, Ty gently holding the reins, working in sync with the animal. Less than thirty seconds later, the horse slowed to a prance-like trot, almost as if it were a proud champion entering a competition.

Captain Williams looked at General Khan. "I know that you frown on gambling here in the Kingdom, but if we'd made a bet on whether or not Sergeant McGill would get on that killer horse, I'd wager I'd be taking your money about now."

"Indeed. Although I am not a betting man, had I been one, I would have lost today."

"But you win, General. Your prize new stallion is ready to ride."

Ty rode up to them and said, "General Khan, if you'd have one of your men open the gate, I think Tarek is ready to show you what he can do."

"Absolutely." Khan signaled to one of his groomers. "Open the gate!"

The man nodded, dropping from the fence and running fifty feet to the ring gate. He opened it wide, standing back as Ty and the horse trotted through, turning a half circle in the paddock, tail and head held high. Ty lead him toward a pasture. Within seconds, he had the horse at a full gallop, muscles moving under the gleaming white hide, mane flowing like a flag in the wind, head and tail arched in a gait unique to the breed.

After a hundred-yard run, Ty turned the horse around and came back to the paddock, slowing to a fast trot, the animal snorting and prancing as if it were the lead horse in a parade. When Ty pulled up to the men, he stopped and dismounted. Kenny Gallagher was all grins. "Way to go, bro."

Ty handed the reins to General Khan. "He's a fine horse. His name fits him well."

"Thank you. Please, allow me to compensate you for what you did. It's the least that I can do."

Ty smiled and shook his head. "Happy to do it. You don't owe me anything."

"Surely I can repay you. Just tell me how. What can I do?"

"Well, since you asked … toss out the horsewhips. I know you recently bought him from another owner. I'm sure you treat your horses well and with respect. A horse like Tarek is unique. He's intelligent, intuitive, and expressive. He wants to perform. He just doesn't want to be forced to do it. And you shouldn't have to. He, like a lot of horses, thinks initially in terms of fight or flight. We just got to help them think in terms of being friends."

"Thank you, again, Sergeant."

"No sweat. I'd love to have a dozen horses like him when we go on patrol in Iraq soon. Arabians have been ridden into a lot of crusades. They're probably the original war horse." He gestured to the saddle. "From up there, you can see danger coming. You can run toward it, or if you have to … move away from it. Maybe that's one reason the breed has survived more than four thousand years."

Made in the USA
Middletown, DE
28 September 2020

20439512R00209